THE DARK TEMPEST

BOOK I OF THE
THE DESTROYER'S WRATH

N. P. COOPER

The Dark Tempest
© Nathan Cooper, 2020
All rights reserved.

ISBN - Paperback: 978-0-6488510-1-1
ISBN - ebook: 978-0-6488510-0-4

Cover typography and design by BRoseDesignz.com

This is a work of fiction. Any similarity between the characters and situations within its pages and places or persons, living or dead, is unintentional and co-incidental.

NATIONAL
LIBRARY
OF AUSTRALIA

A catalogue record for this work is available from the National Library of Australia

FOR HEIDI, AUTUMN, AURORA, AND WESLEY.

BULWARK ISLANDS
JERA
GREAT NORTH OCEAN
ASMERE
DARK IRON MOUNTAINS
NORTHWATCH
HARVERNESS CRATER
KARVER
NESTARN
ICE RA
STONEKEEP
MIRALTHRALL
MIRALLYN RIVER
CLEARBROOK
DANAREL
CORDAVA
HILLCREST
RAILAIN
HEARTLAND'S GATE
SEALCOVE
LAKE PRISTINE
GREENTREE LAKE
THE BONE COAST
ROLLING HILLS
CLIFFSIDE
LAKE TOWN
MIDLAN
WESTERN PORT
GULLTOWN
SOUTH
WESTERN WATERS
THREE SEAS
TO AVSAN
SEA

NON
TO JERANAH
N
ANGARA
HENMAR'S POINT
MOUNT WHISPERWIND
TERRALIV HOMELAND
CLAIREMONT
THE JADE CO
GES
CONCLAVE CITY
PERESET
JEPHSTAT
GRANDELL
MIDWAY
THE WRAITH WOODS
MOON RIVER
CARUEL
DAMERETTE
RIVERS BEND
FOX HEAD LAKE
TO SUNSET ISLES
GAMAR RIVER
ARAMAR
SEA
THE EMERALD SEA
ARBORII HOMELAND
EASTERN WATCH
INT
SILVERTOWN
OAKVIEW
AIDEN'S INLET
SEA OF DREAMS
LLAN'S LANDING
F FISHES
MARASDAN

SPRING

PROLOGUE

THE MAGI OF MIRALTHRALL

Heramiir's eyes searched the city far below, measuring, weighing. Miralthrall, ancient even when his ancestors had come to these shores over three millennia ago waited, its architecture superior, and somehow alien to that which the men of Jeranon were capable of constructing. From his vantage at the very precipice of the Cloudburst Cliffs, at the base of which the great city nestled, the landscape stretched before his gaze in every direction. In the distance, farmland and towns spread out before him as if in miniature scale on either side of the rushing Mirallyn River as it cut its way through the city, dividing the farmland beyond as it flowed steadily eastward.

The spray from the majestic waterfall just to his north drifted across Heramiir's face as the wind changed direction. The torrential flow plunging unabated from the cliff as he watched, filling the Star Lake at the centre of Miralthrall and feeding the Mirallyn on its long journey east. Heramiir breathed deeply of its clean, crisp scent.

All appeared peaceful in the city below, the sun was shining, a light breeze blew, and the populace were going about their lives as if this were an ordinary day. That was how it should be; how he needed it to be... for what was to come next.

Despite the tugging of the wind, the thin outcropping of rock on which he perched gave Heramiir no pause. He stood silently, his eyes aflame with anticipation. As he continued his examination of the city below a sudden gust of air caught against him, blowing the hood of his Gift-wrought cloak back against his shoulders. The rest of the garment billowed out behind him, small flashes of lightning in its depths splaying jagged runes across the furious black clouds the thing was made of.

All the years of planning, all the scheming, all the lies and deceptions, all the murders necessary to keeping their activities unknown and unopposed; all of it had been for today.

For a long moment Heramiir savoured the sight before him as he gazed down on Miralthrall's daily bustle one last time, before turning back towards the west.

As he did so his gaze lit upon the seven forms of his most powerful lieutenants, archmagi all, each sat upon a black steed of immense proportions, mutated through the dark enchantments Heramiir himself had placed upon them.

The riders waited in silent anticipation for him to give the order; the silver-lined black cloaks of their rank ruffling gently in the breeze.

It was not the point of no return, for that had long since passed. Now they waited for the order which would announce their intentions to the world, and transform them from servants to outlaws, and very shortly, rulers.

Heramiir stepped forward and approached his own mount. The horse, if it could still justifiably be called so, stood almost thirty hands high and was covered from nose to hoof in a coat so black it shone a deep blue with the reflected light of the sun. Its teeth, no longer shaped for grinding fodder, were now formed into razor sharp tusks which protruded from its jaws. Its tail was different as well; the fine strands of hair it had once sported replaced by a writhing mass of barbs which hung about its upper thighs.

In a single swift movement Heramiir vaulted up onto its back, using only the slightest wisp of the Gift to propel himself the additional distance. He gave each of his lieutenants one final searching gaze before turning to the attractive middle-aged woman seated on the steed beside him, barely concealing her impatience.

Beneath her, the mutated black mare she rode shifted its weight from foot to foot, picking up on its slender rider's mood.

Heramiir took a deep breath, his own stallion beginning to prance with excitement, and then spoke the words he had waited so very long to say.

"If it pleases thee Deshara," he began, his voice low and intent, "Order my general to attack."

The woman shot him a grin a wolf would have shied from and nodded.

"It shall be my pleasure... Sire," she added as she closed her dark brown eyes, the grin becoming somehow more feral as she did.

"Nereth has received his orders, Archmage," She announced as her eyes re-opened and once again sought him out. "The attack commences."

Even as she finished speaking, the giant bell at the city centre peeled sonorously, the sound faintly reaching them even up here, and all throughout Miralthrall people milled in confusion as they wondered why the bell, usually tolled at the marking of the hour, was sounding now.

*　　*　　*

"Where did she go!" Jarl yelled in frustration as they rounded a corner into a busy market square adjacent to the north gate.

Hassan skidded to a halt as he scanned the crowd and shops which lined the square's perimeter, but it was no use, the urchin they'd been pursuing through the crowded streets for the last five blocks was gone for good this time, along with Jarl's coin purse.

"She's a fast one, no doubt about it," Hassan responded, wiping away a bead of sweat and feeling more winded than he was happy with after the short but frantic chase. "Hope you didn't lose too much."

"That's hardly the point," Jarl snarled back as he jumped up on a nearby cart to get a better view of the crowd. "If criminals are now stealing from military officers in full daylight with impunity, we've failed as a city."

"Hard to argue," Hassan responded. He would have said more, but Jarl's yelling was already attracting more attention than was seemly for two officers of their rank.

"Anything? No, then come on down from there and stop making a scene. We can ask the gate guards if they saw her come past."

Jarl just looked at him for a moment in frustration. "Is that an order?"

"Does it need to be?" Hassan replied in mild surprise.

With a low growl Jarl jumped down from the cart and began stalking towards the gatehouse.

"You're pleasant today," Hassan remarked as his usually focused subordinate left him behind. "Something happen at home?" It was a question he would never normally ask one of his men, but he'd served with Jarl on and off for the better part of two decades and something had had the man out of sorts all week.

"Aria's leaving me," Jarl barked without breaking stride. "Says she doesn't know who I am anymore, whatever that means."

Hassan's stride broke momentarily before he recovered and caught up.

"I'm sorry to hear that," he said, struggling to find words. "You two have been together what, fifteen years?"

"Sixteen," Jarl snapped. "Though I've been on campaign with you for most of that time. Things have always been good between us when I was on leave or we rotated back to Miralthrall for some other reason, but since we've been assigned here permanently, it's just not working the way it should. Oh, don't get me wrong, it was great at first. But as it turns out we just don't know how to live together for more than a week without driving each other crazy."

"Sounds like maybe you both just need to take a step back and give it some time to get used to the new situation?" Hassan offered.

"Tell her that, I'm not the one who's leaving! Or better yet have Sumi do it!" Jarl snapped back, before taking a deep breath and attempting to calm himself. "Bah, why am I even telling you this."

"Because it's less embarrassing than talking about getting robbed and outrun by a twelve-year-old girl?" Hassan replied with a raised eyebrow and knowing grin.

Jarl just stopped in his tracks and looked at him for a long moment before barking a terse laugh and shaking his head.

"I suppose it is at that," Jarl replied, the tension on his features visibly melting away.

In the heart of the city the great bell sounded, and the two officers shared a surprised glance at the clearly inaccurate timing.

"Someone's going to lose their job for that," Jarl remarked, slightly amused.

Hassan nodded with a sympathetic grin, but before he had a chance to reply, a young and painfully green officer in charge of the gate post came rushing out of the customs room beside the city exit, his sword out and arms waving for attention.

For a moment he stopped and looked bewildered as he turned about, and it was only then Hassan noticed that the men who should have been guarding the gate were no longer at their posts.

"Hassan, Sir!" the young captain cried out, struggling to don his breastplate as he spotted them in the crowd.

"My men, they're gone. I have orders to close the gates! We're under attack, please Sir, help me close the gates!"

The two veteran soldiers looked at him blankly for half a moment, then around at their unremarkable surroundings. Traffic was moving at a steady pace across the wide, cobbled street, the guild houses and shops built against the outer wall were open for business, and most importantly, no western army was charging at the gates.

"Close them! Close them!" the officer shouted again as he struggled with the armour he should have been wearing all shift.

With a shrug, he shared a meaningful glance with Jarl at the empty guard post, and motioned his officer to follow the captain's lead despite his misgivings. The two men moved into a position that should have been guarded by four others, and set themselves to the giant wheels which controlled the outer gates' movement.

Better to make a mistake than do nothing but argue while an assault is imminent, Hassan reasoned.

All the yelling about an attack however, coupled with the sight of the two officers hauling on the gate apparatus was enough to incite a panic, and those civilians immediately outside the gate rushed to get inside the city before they were locked out, while those already inside began to scatter around corners or into nearby shops.

Heaving on the apparatus, all Hassan could think was that this must be some kind of colossal misunderstanding. There had been no warning from the outer provinces, nor from the College of the Arts, at least according to his briefing from the general this morning.

The young captain, Fisher, Hassan thought his name was, finished with his armour and rushed over. A swing of his well-cared for sword cut a series of knotted ties next to the wheels the two guardsmen were hauling on.

"What are you doing?!" Hassan bellowed as metal screamed. Civilians frantically jumped clear of the gate in both directions as they saw what was happening, even Hassan dived behind the cover of the wheel, pulling Jarl down with him.

With the sound of a rattling chain the portcullis came slamming down far too hard, shaking the ground with a deafening crash as its Gift-wrought metal met the stone paving of the road, sending tiny shards of granite flying in every direction while leaving the metal unharmed.

The captain staggered back a step as one of the shards bounced off his armour hard enough to sound a ring of its own.

Springing back up as soon as it was clear, Hassan was relieved to see that no one had been killed by the young officer's stupidity. One man running into the city at full pace holding his arm seemed to have been the only one injured, but he was gone before Hassan could call him back.

It took a moment, but Fisher regained his balance and shouted a few choice oaths at the contraption before turning toward the wheels where Hassan and Jarl were just returning to the task at hand. The captain added his own strength to the huge device, and eventually the vast wooden gates swung ponderously to a close. The thick steel bands screeched as they came together, allowing only the thinnest streak of dust shrouded sunlight to filter through between.

The three men stood back after locking the mechanism in place, panting as Fisher turned to face the others.

"Let's get inside the customs house and I'll brief you, Sirs. We should not discuss the details in public," the young officer cautioned them, his hands up placatingly as Hassan began to demand an explanation. After another shared glance with Jarl, who shrugged minutely, Hassan led the way.

As they crossed the worn stone paving blocks of the square, Hassan couldn't help shooting glances down the road and up to the top of the wall, trying to spot anything out of place. Everything looked as it should, save the street was now empty of suddenly panicked people.

Reaching the small building first, Hassan put his hand to the heavy door, pushed it open and preceded the others inside. It was far past time for some answers, and Fisher's had better be good.

Even as his eyes adjusted from the sunlight to the dimness of the customs house, he heard a distinct thump behind him accompanied by a low moan, then the sound of a crumpled body hitting the floor. Hassan spun without conscious thought, his right hand automatically unsheathing his sword as he came to rest in a relaxed stance, his blade ready to face whatever creature stood before him, just in case he'd been wrong.

For a veteran such as he, it was a familiar experience, and vaguely comforting that he hadn't lost his edge after these last few years of peace.

He wasn't confronted by some fearsome denizen from beyond the Dark Iron Mountains though, and for just a moment he froze at the sight which greeted him.

"Why?" Hassan demanded of the former officer standing before him, anger and curiosity filling his voice in equal amounts.

Fisher smiled grimly in response.

With the barest flick of his eye, Hassan saw that Jarl appeared to be unharmed save the wound on the back of his scalp where Fisher had struck him with the flat of his blade. There was a disproportionate amount of blood streaming from the small cut, but such was the way with head wounds. It would be easily enough dealt with by the nearest Herbalists and Apothecaries guild house when this was over.

"Because a new day is dawning Colonel, and I for one intend to be a part of it."

"The offer," he continued, "Is open to all. Join us, and I will put up my sword and we can walk out of here in peace. All of us," he added, tilting his head towards the prone form of Jarl lying sprawled near the doorway.

Thinking frantically, Hassan could only conclude that although there were no Imbic or Augrahl warriors throwing themselves at the city gates, they were indeed under attack, only this time it was from within. And whoever was orchestrating this coup thought they had a real chance of taking the city whole. Closing the outer gates would have been worse than useless to them otherwise.

The magi must be involved.

Without the support of either some of the most powerful magi he realised, or most of the lesser-Gifted ones, shutting the gates during an open rebellion would be suicide. Most of the Gift users were trained in battle magic and having fought beside no small number of them in the past, Hassan knew very well they were not to be trifled with.

"Who exactly makes this treasonous offer?" He demanded, his blade unwavering.

A slight grin tugged at the corner of Fisher's mouth.

This one is arrogant.

If it came to a fight, and right now there was little doubt in Hassan's mind that very soon this conversation would be spoken with blades rather than words, he knew he could use the young fool's arrogance against him.

"Why, the Archmage Heramiir himself of course," Fisher replied civilly, though Hassan noted his opponent's blade also remained ready to call into action in the merest instant.

"Join us Hassan," Fisher tried again, "You are a veteran

of much esteem to our forces, as well as a skilled swordsman. We would benefit greatly from your support."

Hassan backed up a step to give himself more room.

"If you know that much about me, you must also know that my loyalties lie firmly with the King of Jeranon and the Duke of Miralthrall," he answered, stalling.

Strangely, his words seemed to make Fisher relax a little, even to the point where he lowered his blade a few inches.

"Come now Hassan, we both know that's not entirely true…"

Hassan's expression grew cold, and Fisher hurried on.

"Hear me!" the younger man hissed, "Even as we speak, every position of any strategic importance has been, or is right now being overrun by small squads of troops loyal to the archmage. Their orders, as mine, are to secure the city and turn the loyalty of as many guardsmen as possible. Failing that, we have orders to take as many prisoners as we can."

He paused for a breath and to give his words a chance to sink in.

"Hassan, we already control nearly half the guard, with the element of surprise the city will be ours within the hour. I implore you to weigh your next action carefully. Even if you kill me, you can't fight the entire guard by yourself."

Fisher motioned at the prone form of Jarl lying crumpled on the dusty floorboards by the door.

"Besides, there will be hundreds, if not thousands of prisoners taken in the coup. They may be offered the chance to re-join the guard, under the archmage, once the city is secure. That part will be up to you."

"What are you talking about?" Hassan demanded, his patience at an end.

When the young traitor answered, his voice was calm, relaxed with the confidence of an authority higher than his own.

"The archmage himself ordered me to pass on a message to you Hassan. He says he desires to meet with you in person, to discuss the disposition of the prisoners' futures."

"Rubbish. There's no way Heramiir could have known that I would be here for you to convince..." Hassan frowned slightly.

Fisher noticed his expression and cocked his head towards a table at the side of the room. "The archmage leaves nothing to chance."

Hassan followed his gaze and saw a small coin purse resting conspicuously on its surface. An irritated groan escaped his lips.

"Why?"

"Because he knows as well as I that the men hold great respect for you, and if you tell those who resisted it is in their best interests to follow the archmage... they may listen. You might well be the only one who can convince them Hassan. The only one who can save their lives."

"And if I tell them otherwise?"

"They will be executed to a man," Fisher told him regretfully. "Right before you are."

He almost sounded genuine, though Hassan had a suspicion it was for the number of soldiers they would lose, rather than any real concern for the men's individual lives.

A thousand lives. Probably more.

He snorted, "They will not listen to treason, no matter whose lips it comes from."

But even as he spoke the words, his blade wavered a fraction of an inch.

Fisher must have noticed the slight movement because he took a risk, sheathing his own blade in a single quick movement.

"I understand if this is all somewhat confusing, but at least meet with the archmage."

He pointed at Jarl again. "It's already too late for you to subvert our attack. Don't condemn your men. Don't condemn your friends, to a pointless death because of nothing more than your own stubborn pride. I leave the choice to you."

So saying, Fisher turned his back on Hassan, opening the door and walking out towards where fifty of the archmage's men were standing in formation, blocking the now secured gates.

The sight of the guard company holding the gate position wasn't lost on Hassan as the 'captain', and he used the term loosely, exited the customs house.

Hassan's mind spun as he sheathed his own blade and moved to Jarl's side. From what Fisher had let slip, the attackers had divided their forces into tiny groups spread throughout Miralthrall to gain the necessary element of surprise for their assault. If that were true, segmenting the population of the city to stop any large-scale resistance forming would have been vital to their plans.

Without question, the inner wall would be their primary goal in subduing and isolating any major pockets of resistance. Fisher's cutting the portcullis ties meant a major delay in reopening the northern gate though. If the other gates had been sabotaged as well, it effectively locked both attackers and defenders within the now segmented city.

The question was why? The outer walls were always manned and could just as effectively shoot flights of arrows at attackers within the city as without… and yet no such defence had materialised.

Exhaling slowly, Hassan realised that if the archmage could spare fifty men to stand guard in the open street here with no opposition in sight, the traitors must already be in control of both walls, or at the very least, be highly confident of success.

Hassan sighed, his shoulders slumping despondently. If the College of the Arts was truly complicit in the assault and the archmage now controlled both walls as well as the exits from the city, the enemy forces along with the magi could sweep the rest of Miralthrall at their leisure. They would easily quell any small pockets of troops which had managed to fend off the masterfully efficient attack.

The battle for the great walled city of Miralthrall, old even when the wars of founding revealed its empty abandoned structures to the men of the fledgling nation of Jeranon some three thousand years before, truly was to all intents and purposes already over.

Pushing the gloomy thoughts to the back of his mind, he knelt by his friend's side. As Hassan sank to his knees to inspect the wound on Jarl's scalp, the fallen man murmured something as he regained consciousness, abruptly flailing about, fumbling for his sword briefly before Hassan had a chance to calm him.

"It's okay Jarl, it's over," Hassan spoke calmingly, trying to reach through the groggy confusion which gripped the other man.

"Over?" Jarl echoed, attempting to sit up.

"What's over?" he asked as he sank back to the polished wooden floor, a sudden wave of dizziness overtaking him.

"My head hurts," Jarl grumbled.

Hassan wasn't sure if the comment was meant for him or whether Jarl was simply speaking to himself, so he let it pass as he finished inspecting the wound.

"What's going on?" Jarl tried again, irritation beginning to show on his face as some of the confusion began to wear off.

"Hold still," Hassan told him, pushing Jarl gently back to the ground as he tried to rise once more.

"You're bleeding, that's what's going on. Now hold still while I bind the wound," he told the other man, more forcefully this time.

Making sure Jarl stayed put, Hassan got to his feet and crossed the room to remove a bandage from a small pile which was kept in one of the customs rooms' cupboards, before snagging the coin purse from the shelf as well.

Hassan made his way back to where Jarl lay and knelt again, helping his friend into a more upright position and handing him the purse before carefully beginning to bind and wrap the wound.

"You found it. How?"

"Turns out the theft was just bait to get us where they wanted us," Hassan replied angrily as he finished with the wound.

"Why were we brought here? Who attacked me?" Jarl asked a little more lucidly.

Hassan surveyed his work with a critical eye. It was nothing more than a battlefield dressing and he knew it, but it would do until the man could be taken to a Herbalists and Apothecaries Guild practitioner to be cared for. Not much chance of finding a sympathetic mage in the city right now he supposed.

"Tell me what is going on!" Jarl demanded, irritably pushing Hassan back to arm's length as he finished inspecting the dressing.

For a moment Hassan was silent as a great weariness descended on him.

He rocked back on his haunches, squatting comfortably as he faced his long-time comrade, and gave him the dire news.

"Archmage Heramiir has taken control of the city," he stated dully, rubbing a hand across his suddenly weary eyes.

"His men control the city, and the walls. Even now fifty of them wait outside this room."

"What?" Jarl exploded, struggling to his feet, only to immediately sink back down as another wave of nausea took hold.

"Easy," Hassan admonished, leaping up to catch Jarl as the man's knees gave out. He lowered his friend back to the ground and returned to his previous position.

"We have to stop them..." Jarl said weakly, abruptly gagging as he tried to repulse an obvious urge to sick up.

"I'm open to any suggestions," Hassan replied, but Jarl was too busy fighting his own rebelling stomach to give any kind of answer.

Hassan's shoulders slumped as he conceded the extent of Jarl's concussion, the man was in no condition for a fight, and he wouldn't be the only one.

He nodded subconsciously as he made his decision. If what Fisher had told him about the attack was true, there would be hundreds of men, at the least, captured throughout the city. Most would probably be wounded, and due to the particular nature of the assault, even the soldiers who weren't would be in groups too small to offer any kind of sustained or meaningful resistance against battle trained magi.

Abruptly, Hassan found himself very much wanting to know exactly who had orchestrated this attack. An attack which had captured the single most fortified city in all of Jeranon so effortlessly. On the other hand, if he found that Sumi or Luthor had been hurt in the archmage's unprovoked rebellion, he would just as happily slide all four and a half feet of the cold steel his broadsword was made from straight through that same general's heart.

He considered his choice for one moment longer before moving to the door. If Fisher was telling the truth, he might be able to save the lives of some of those men. But it would mean supporting the rebellion, at least openly, and committing treason against the king, his king.

Then again, if enough of the men had resisted the attempts at conversion, then been taken prisoner, perhaps it would be possible to turn the enemy's tactics back on himself. He couldn't take the city back from the magi on his own; they were far too powerful for that. But there might well come a time in the future where a battle hung in the balance. Even magi weren't all powerful, and the archmage's forces *could* be overthrown. But Hassan knew he would need a core group of trustworthy men if he were ever to achieve anything of significance.

Turning back to Jarl, who was still retching in the corner, he took a long last look.

"Let the men outside tend you," he said at length, then opened the door.

"Where are you going?" Jarl asked, his voice low and suspicious.

Hassan just shook his head before shrugging faintly.

"To save what I can," he finally replied, before stepping through the doorway and into the bright sunlight outside.

As Hassan left the custom's house, he began walking towards where Fisher was waiting. His pace didn't falter when the fifty guardsmen drew their swords, nor when they moved to surround him. He kept on towards his target, keeping his own sword safely sheathed in the scabbard strapped down the length of his back. Hassan was no fool and knew that to so much as reach for it now would mean his death. He closed the final few paces to stand nose to nose with the traitorous officer, and looking down at the man, spoke in a voice both bitter and commanding.

"Take me to the archmage. Now."

So saying, he turned his back on Fisher and strode without pause through the ring of guards who parted just enough to let him pass, the captain and six of his men hustling to catch up. He began the long walk down the ancient stone-paved street towards the inner gates without waiting for Fisher to show him the way. It was a guard more than an escort; a not-so-subtle reminder that trying to escape now would only condemn others to die in his place.

After a few more steps the traitor caught up, walking silently beside him while making no move to guide him or take the lead.

Just as well, Hassan thought grimly. After all, he knew the way.

His own house stood not three blocks from the college gates.

*   *   *

The order had been given, the bell rung. Now nothing could be allowed interrupt the sequence of events his painstaking preparations had set in motion.

"Come," Heramiir told the others, pulling his mount around to face the cliff edge, "It is time."

With the slightest pressure from his knees the giant steed leapt toward the precipice at a sudden gallop, the seven figures behind him urging their own mounts forward with just as little effort.

In the heartbeat it took him to reach the edge, the view expanded before Heramiir's eyes and as he made the final leap into nothingness, Miralthrall, fed from above by the vast flow of the Mirallyn River cascading into the aptly named Star Lake far below, was revealed in all its shining grandeur.

Without pause or interruption the steed's hooves came thundering down onto the air beyond the cliff, only to be stopped as though they were meeting solid ground below. Heramiir himself had endowed each of the steeds' shoes with the magic as soon as their intended rider had mastered them. It had proved to be a useful, but very taxing bit of arcana to create and was only one of several very useful things he had learned to make recently. It didn't allow the horses to fly, not even the red book could do that. Instead, the spell merely simulated the resistance of their hooves hitting the ground, tricking them somewhat into thinking they were still running on a solid surface.

Coupled with specialised training and firm riders, it was enough that the horses didn't panic as they began the thousand span plunge to the city below.

The others fanned out behind him, their steeds 'running' along an almost vertical line now, straight towards the College of the Arts at the heart of Miralthrall. It should have been a headlong plunge into oblivion, but the steeds ran the course as sure-footed as if crossing one of Miralthrall's stone-paved streets.

Heramiir grinned maliciously, though it was nothing compared to Deshara's own expression of a few minutes before.

The others thought this rebellion was about gaining political and military power, about ending the oppression of the magi, about ending this Maker forsaken war with the western nations. Whilst all of that might be true on some level, none of them, not even Nereth, knew the true reasons behind his actions.

There was something buried beneath the foundations of Miralthrall.

When the voice had first spoken to him in his dreams; *no, not a voice,* he thought grimly, the intensity of the memory momentarily blinding him to the outside world. It had been more an impression of something... vast. He remembered starting awake, confused at the unusually vivid dream. Most of his dreams faded quickly from memory, but over the weeks and phases that followed, the feeling that something was waiting for him had never truly left. It was as though something were prickling at the back of his consciousness, reminding him of some chore left undone.

As his mount continued its plunge, he remembered the

day clearly, several phases after that initial contact, yet still nearly twenty years gone now.

Come! A voice had screamed in his mind, driving the much younger version of himself to the hard bluestone floor.

Heramiir clutched at his head, shaking uncontrollably. The torch which had fallen from his hand guttered and died as it rolled across the rough stone floor, sending a cockroach scuttling for the cover offered by a thin crack in the stonework.

For a minute he just knelt there on grazed knees, trying to focus on something other than the pain.

Slowly, his vision cleared enough for a few glowing embers left over from the torch to resolve themselves into clarity. He climbed to his feet, every muscle protesting as if he'd just run twenty miles. The agony was subsiding, but each word he spoke still felt as though an Imbic brute was using his head for an anvil.

"Who are you?" Heramiir tried to shout, bracing himself against a nearby wall with an out-flung hand.

When the voice returned though, it brought none of the mind-numbing agony of a moment before. Instead it had a soothing, caressing tone, reminding him of the glass chimes hanging outside the window of his tiny dorm room.

Come, it repeated, and on the far wall a section of seamless masonry ever so slowly appeared to peel back on itself, revealing a passageway beyond.

With a start, he realised the only reason he could see at all was that a soft orange glow had filled the room. It was dim enough to leave more shadows than light; just enough to see by, and no more.

"Who are you?" Heramiir whispered again in awe. Any mage at the college could have duplicated the light and voice, although the way the wall truly appeared to be coming apart was a little trickier. Any mage that is, who happened to be within a direct line of sight of the spells they were casting.

One of the archmagi? But even some of them would be hard pressed to set up a ward of this complexity. As the wall segment finished revealing a tunnel entrance beyond, Heramiir peered into its depths. Blackness consumed the interior within a dozen strides, but what he could see was about seven-foot across and overgrown with mould and filth.

Why would anyone bother setting up such a ward in the first place?

The voice had urged him on, so clearly it was not meant as a warning, and if it were someone's cruel idea of a joke, it wouldn't be that painful. Even an archmage would be called to account for inflicting that level of pain without legitimate cause.

When the voice spoke the third time it caught Heramiir off guard. Different again, it had the same musical quality coupled with all the power and authority of its first contact, though thankfully none of the pain.

I am the one you have been searching for, it whispered into his mind. *Come.*

Heramiir inhaled deeply as a realisation struck home. As... whatever it was, had spoken its final word, the feeling of being drawn had been almost overwhelming. It was the same sensation he'd had for what seemed like forever, only here it was a dozen times stronger.

Finally, he understood. Since the day he had woken from that strange, vivid dream, feeling as though he had something to do, something he could not quite put his finger on, he had been driven to this point; compelled to search these abandoned tunnels for... something.

Come, the voice called again, and Heramiir found himself unwittingly moving towards the opening.

Shaking his head as if to clear it, he made himself stop walking, and for the first time in years felt fear grip his soul hard enough to make the simple act of breathing almost beyond him. Whatever this being was, it was utterly alien. He knew that now with absolute certainty. Even the most powerful of archmagi could not control men's minds, nor could any of the other known races for that matter.

Magic comes from within, not without. The mind is the tool which moulds that power. It can access the Gift, but the mind itself cannot be accessed.

It was one of the first things apprentice magi learned when they began their studies.

"Why should I come to you?" Heramiir asked, no longer bothering to raise his voice.

A long time passed in silence and he began wondering whether it was too late to turn around and begin the long climb back up to the populated levels of the college.

The silence stretched; the only sounds in the dank basement the beating of Heramiir's heart and the soft scuttling of an insect as he waited for an answer

After what seemed like hours, his body still aching from that initial contact, Heramiir forced himself to turn his back on the silent opening and head slowly for the stairs.

As he took the first step a strange and overwhelming sensation overtook him, as though he were suddenly weighed down by grief, leaving behind everything he had ever wanted.

He could get it all back, he knew that for a fact. All he had to do was follow that beautiful round hallway...

Before he knew it, he was standing in front of the entrance just short of where the wall had peeled back. With a shudder he threw the sensation aside and planted his feet squarely on the well-cut stone.

"Why should I come?" he repeated, growing angry with the powerful being's continual attempts to manipulate him, as foolish as he knew that was. For a moment there was silence, then the sensation became even more insistent, before cutting off abruptly when it failed to move him even a step.

I wish to show you something! The voice boomed through Heramiir's mind, and only a quick hand clutching at the open wall segment stopped him from being driven to his knees once more. That there were no chimes to soften the voice this time was not lost on Heramiir as he attempted to stand his ground on legs too shaky to hold his own weight.

To show me something? Of all the reasons it had led him this far, guided him towards this moment for so many phases, that was simply not one he had ever considered.

"And what might that be?" he gasped in return, his natural curiosity warring with a strong desire not to offend this powerful creature.

There was a long pause, then the feeling of yearning returned before cutting off abruptly, as if the being below had once again changed its mind.

Power! The voice boomed in his mind.

Heramiir's hands reflexively came up to clutch his head, and without the wall to support him the agony drove him to his knees once more.

I will teach you things you cannot yet even imagine. And when you have performed a small task for me, I will grant you the power to perform them.

The world spun around Heramiir as the voice, and the agony, continued. In a daze, he realised he had curled up on the hard stones of the floor at some point, his knees gripped convulsively to his chest by arms as responsive as the cold stone below.

What did the voice say?

He tried desperately to remember as the pain continued to course through his body.

A task? Yes, that's it, a small task.

"I'll do it," he gasped. He would have shouted, but the molten fire running through his veins made that impossible.

"I'll do whatever you ask!" and right then he knew those were the five truest, most fervent words which had ever passed his lips.

Suddenly the agony ceased, leaving Heramiir curled up on the floor, gasping for breath. Not because he was still in pain though, he wasn't. In fact, he felt fitter than he had in years.

Nothing he knew of could have repaired the amount of physical damage which would have been necessary to cause that much pain in so short a time, and as he uncurled slowly, the expected protest from his overwrought muscles never came.

Eventually he pulled himself to his feet and stood once more before the dimly lit tunnel, only to find he was unharmed. With a start, his eyes jerked towards his legs as he realised the grazes on his knees were still there. A simple thing, but it set his mind spinning.

If those wounds are still there, then the creature hasn't healed me.

But in turn that line of reasoning led to him not actually

having been injured in the first place. All of that he could accept, but it left him only one very disturbing possibility. Somehow the being had made him think the pain was real. He nodded to himself, his mind working furiously.

Yes, that would explain why the pain simply stopped instead of fading away.

The creature had manipulated his mind in a visceral and immediate fashion.

Heramiir grinned then, knowing his course had been set, dangerous though it was. He would keep his promise, even though made under duress. The creature needed something from him, and that gave him leverage. Yet he knew instinctively that to play this being false would be his death.

He took a half step forward before asking one final question.

"Will I be as powerful as you?" he asked, trying not to let his thirst for this creature's arcane knowledge outweigh his caution, and failing badly.

No.

The voice sounded amused, but at least there was no pain this time.

But you will come to wield more power than any other on this world. It is inevitable.

Before Heramiir could ask what that meant, a voice called down the half-forgotten stairwell behind him. He spun at the sound, but even quicker than his startled movement, the dim light faded and the wall closed as seamlessly as if it had never been parted.

Irritation that bordered on fury erupted within Heramiir as he worked a small spell to reproduce the orange glow the newcomer must have seen. No one must know what he had found down here. The feeling was so strong for a moment that Heramiir suspected the creature of planting it in his mind, then dismissed the idea. Whether the creature's or his own, he knew it to be true.

"Who goes there?" the voice called again from the stairwell.

He knew that voice. It was one of his instructors.

Archmage Rellarin, he thought as the heavyset man's distinctive footsteps became clear.

As the portly and mostly bald man emerged from the stairwell, he stopped to study the young man below, and even in the dim light Heramiir could see the sparks of anger deep in the archmage's eyes.

"Do you know how many wards you have tripped boy?!" Rellarin shouted at him.

"Wards, what wards!" Heramiir scoffed, "I tripped no wards on my way down here."

At least that much is true.

"Are you blind and deaf boy? You triggered six separate warnings and then destroyed their constructs. The pattern of their destruction was like a line of beacons which led me straight to you."

Heramiir's mind spun.

Either Rellarin is lying through his teeth, which he found unlikely, *or else the creature cleared my way.*

That, unfortunately, made far more sense.

The archmage must have taken Heramiir's silence for an admission of guilt, because when next he spoke his voice was filled with suspicion.

"Why are you down here Heramiir? Did someone tell you to come to this room?"

"No," Heramiir replied, tensely, "I was just exploring

until you interrupted me, Archmage," he deferred.

"I really didn't trip any wards," he threw in on the end to make the rest sound like truth as well. The look on Rellarin's face said that instead, Heramiir had only succeeded in making the whole statement sound a lie.

"Boy. Coming down here is grounds for execution, the last two wards stated that clearly."

"What! Why?" Heramiir demanded, now far less sure of himself.

The old mage dipped his head without taking his eyes off Heramiir, and when he spoke his voice was hushed.

"There is… something, down here," he whispered.

"For nearly three thousand years the magi of Miralthrall have guarded it well. Not to protect it mind, but to keep it locked down here. We do not know what it is, only that even in its dormant state it exudes a sense of power far surpassing our own."

Rellarin took a deep breath and continued.

"Every few decades it reaches out from its prison, but only the most powerful of us can hear its call. In all that time though, only one mage has been fool enough to allow himself to be beguiled into doing the creature's will. His name was Eldrik, perhaps you are familiar with it?"

Heramiir's stomach did a flip at the name as he nodded. Eldrik the Black was counted the most infamous mage in college history, and the most powerful. He conquered half of Jeranon with his rebel army before the king's forces rallied and drove him and his remaining men across the sea where a final desperate naval battle had been fought just off the southern continent of Avsan.

"The part of Eldrik's story which most people don't

know," Rellarin continued, "Is that after his eventual capture he went mad, raving about a prophecy and the being imprisoned below Miralthrall. He considered it his sacred duty to free the creature and have it rule the world with him as its trusted servant. So I ask you again, were you summoned here?"

Kill him! The creature's voice urged within his mind.

No. I will not!

Prepare yourself.

For what? Heramiir thought back at it, but the only answer he received was silence.

Heramiir thought he did well not to let the unspoken conversation show on his face, but just as Rellarin began to speak again the dim orange glow filling the room transformed itself into a deep blue which leeched all colour from the chamber.

"Is that it boy? Did the creature do that? Speak Heramiir, I would have sensed the Gift if you had caused it."

Any reply Heramiir could have made was cut off by the now familiar scraping sound of the wall peeling back, revealing the unlit passageway beyond.

"Heramiir," a rasping voice whispered, "I had begun to think you were not coming back."

Rellarin stared in horror at the opening for a second, then shook his head as if relieving himself of a great weight.

"It is true then!" he whispered, drawing up to his full height, which almost matched Heramiir's own. When he spoke again, his voice carried all the authority of an Archmage backed by thousands of years of tradition.

"For the crime of conspiring with the power of Miralthrall, I hereby sentence Mage Heramiir of Miralthrall to death to end the corruption. So says Rellarin, Keeper of the Wards for this generation."

When Rellarin finished the intonation, he took a deep breath.

"I understand this will come as small comfort Heramiir, but you are the finest student I have ever taught. I truly regret that things have to end like this."

As Rellarin raised his hand to strike, the voice whispered urgently into Heramiir's mind.

Kill him!

And suddenly it was all so simple.

Even as the beam of fire came arcing in towards him, Heramiir slowed its passage enough with his own gifts to allow it to pass over his head as he dived to the floor. Before he had even stopped falling, he imagined the stone of the floor sweeping up to embrace the archmage's legs, his power in the Gift making it so, and holding Rellarin for a moment as Heramiir sent his own lance of fire blasting from an outstretched hand.

Rellarin threw up some form of shield which deflected the gout of flame, then adapted it to angle the continued stream back towards Heramiir.

For the second time Heramiir was forced to dive away, even as he discontinued the blast.

Taking the moment to regroup, Rellarin kicked the stone away from his legs, having weakened it somehow, and advanced on the sprawled form of Heramiir.

Kill him! The creature's voice insisted.

How?! Heramiir thought back at it. *If you ever want my help, then tell me how!*

Like this, the voice whispered in his mind, and somehow Heramiir found he knew what to do.

As Rellarin raised his hand to finish their duel, Heramiir imagined the air around the archmage transmuting into water and triggered the Gift. Rellarin gagged as he abruptly found himself without air. He tried to reverse the spell, but Heramiir focused and relentlessly held it in place. Once again he brought the stone up from the floor, to the archmage's waist this time, and without pause sent a beam of flame racing in at the besieged archmage.

Rellarin began struggling free from the moulded stone again and desperately threw up a barrier once more. This time Heramiir was ready though. He imagined the continued bar of flame shrinking in width, magnifying its strength as he drew it down to the size of a pin. Rellarin tried to scream as Heramiir's attack broke through, searing a tiny hole right through the archmage's chest and making the water around him boil. The archmage took in a lungful of water and panicked, shrinking his shield down to a size which he imagined was concentrated enough to block the fire eating through him.

Heramiir smiled grimly as he made his move. Without hesitation he brought his other hand up, and with a sweeping motion slashed a second bar of fire as strong as he could form across the archmage's torso, cutting his opponent in half and leaving a blackened scorch line engraved into the bluestone wall behind.

Breathing hard from the effort, not to mention the adrenaline still running through his veins, Heramiir let his focus lapse, causing the various spells he was still imagining to dissipate. He watched in distaste as Rellarin's body slumped to the floor, along with a great gush of bloodied water, and thought about what he'd just done.

Come, the voice urged him without pause, with what almost sounded like satisfaction.

Heramiir turned to view the passageway with open hostility. Whatever this thing was, it had just forced him into killing a man, and if he hadn't known Rellarin as a friend, he had envied the man's vast knowledge. Knowledge he would never possess now.

The voice in his mind laughed. *Come mortal thing, I will show you what knowledge truly is!*

Heramiir looked down the blackened corridor for a long moment in anger, then back at the stairs leading up toward Miralthrall before deciding. He took Rellarin's corpse by the arms and dragged the archmage's remains down the corridor. After a few minutes of pulling the heavy weight though he found himself hoping he wouldn't have to go much further until he found a suitable place to dispose of the man's heavy body.

After all, he still had to go back for the legs.

His mount whinnied, jolting Heramiir back to the present, and he squinted into the rush of oncoming wind. There was but one more thing to do, one more resistance to quell. He nudged the steed's flanks, his cloak trailing behind like an angry thunderhead, runes carved in lightning running all over like jagged ethereal lacework.

He had only deciphered a third of those runes so far, but today their function didn't matter so much as their appearance. Aside from his own well documented powers in the Gift, he would need every bit of authority, every piece of logic, every flair of persuasive ability, and every scrap of mystique he could muster for the next step of the attack. And while all those things were firmly within his control, he also wasn't above exploiting a non-functional piece of arcana to make a suitably impressive entrance.

*   *   *

A sharp rapping on the door startled Derrack from his sleep.

This has to be a nightmare, he thought groggily as he rolled onto his side in the forced darkness of his room and struggled to wake. Again someone pounded on the door, jolting the young mage into a sitting position on the edge of his bed.

Using the Gift, he bathed the room in a dim blue glow, not enough to hurt his eyes, but enough to give form to the featureless grey it had been before. With a glance he checked the elaborate timepiece he'd been ordered to forge and construct with the Gift as his final exam in the construction of arcana only a few weeks before, and groaned.

Two hours.

Since finishing his basic training, the archmagi in charge of his education had decided he was ready to learn the fine art of spirit magic, and of course spirit magic always worked better at night, so that was when the classes were held. Coupled with his other studies it left him only the mid-afternoon to get what little sleep he could manage in the sunlight.

The first afternoon he hadn't slept at all, and by the time he'd arrived for his lessons that night, Derrack had been so tired his teacher had ordered him to board up his windows and get some rest.

After the lesson, of course.

So when the knocking on the door persisted all he could do was stand and shout, "Who is it!"

There was a moment of silence, then a young, frightened voice, called back through the wood-panelled door.

"The Archmage Heramiir requires your presence."

What?!

"I'll be right out!" he shouted back, pausing just long enough to throw on some trousers. He pulled them up past the old burn mark on his left leg, fastening them before throwing on some shoes and a shirt and grabbing his new black cloak. Unlike his old one, which held the white lining of an apprentice, the one he now owned proudly sported a blue lining, signifying his rank as a full Mage at last. It had only taken him twelve years and was still new enough that he couldn't help grinning a little at the fact. Some apprentices took upwards of twenty before they were elevated.

Once he was clothed in something more suitable than his undergarments, he crossed the room to open the door.

The servant, whom Derrack now realised was only a boy, simply stared at him for a moment, taking in his wild bed hair before moving ahead at Derrack's irritable wave.

The boy set a fast pace, but frequently checked over his shoulder to make sure his charge was following behind, and as Derrack finished smoothing his hair down and securing the cloak correctly on his shoulders, the boy sped up to a trot which Derrack was forced to match.

"Where are we going?" he called to the youth, who was hurrying towards the flight of stairs which pierced the centre of the college building. The boy hit them at a run and Derrack was compelled to speed up again to keep the servant in sight. As he climbed, the staircase twisted its way toward the upper floors of the college, passing doorway after doorway until Derrack began to wonder if he hadn't somehow bypassed the boy in his dash up the stairwell.

He paused for a moment to look over the ornately carved red-stone railing which stood on the inner edge of the stone steps and stared down the well at the stairway's heart. He was on the eleventh floor, high in the college's main building, but as far as he could tell the landings below were empty, the light shining through the doorways unbroken by any form but his own, which was unusual in itself.

Where is everyone?

Reaching out with the Gift, he sensed the others' auras somewhere high above, probably at the great circle. Turning his gaze upward, Derrack was just in time to see the boy come to the rail two levels above and beckon him onward. Derrack trotted up the stairs, only slightly out of breath as he completed the two circuits around the central well to bring him face to face with the young servant.

"Where are you taking me?" Derrack asked him again, starting to feel vaguely nervous. There were only two doors they had not yet passed, one led to the archmagi's quarters, the other followed a last staircase up to the roof.

When finally being promoted to the title of Mage a few weeks before, Derrack had been summoned to the roof level for the ceremony. It was the first and only time he'd stood in the great circle.

The builders alone, whoever they had been, knew why they'd constructed the stone amphitheatre on top of the enormous college structure, but then he supposed it hadn't been the College of the Arts at the time the builders constructed it. Now that he thought about it, he never had been told what the massive building's original purpose had been.

Perhaps no one even knows? After all, Miralthrall's mythic builders had disappeared over fifteen thousand years before the wars of founding.

Derrack had always wondered why the dark nations had left Miralthrall untouched for all that time. Perhaps they knew more about the city than anyone gave them credit for.

"The archmage awaits," the boy blurted, breaking Derrack from his thoughts. He waited for more information, but the messenger had said all he was going to.

"Where?" Derrack prompted the lad, a slightly amused smile creeping onto his lips.

Instead of answering the boy just pointed and then ran off, back down the stairs. Derrack watched him leave and then turned toward the indicated doorway. He regarded the carved wooden friezes on either side of the opening for a moment before releasing a breath he hadn't realised he was holding. What could Archmage Heramiir possibly want from him that it required the meeting to be held in the great circle? With more than a little trepidation, Derrack headed through the doorway and up the darkened stairs. This passage was never lit as only formally ranked magi, archmagi and those about to be elevated were allowed past the carvings at the base of the stairs. Derrack motioned to cast a small light out ahead of himself so he wouldn't trip on the worn stone steps, and once he could see properly, began the steep climb.

This final staircase differed from the great spiral which plunged its way through the heart of the college in that it was only wide enough for two people to walk abreast. The stone walls were smooth and straight, and the roof was little more than eight feet high, but the defining feature, Derrack thought, was the rectangular construction. Where the main staircase was a wide spiral, this upper one was designed as a straight flight of stairs with a right-angle turn at each of the three landings. At the top of the fourth flight Derrack paused at an apparent dead end, where the stone ahead of him appeared to be as solid as the walls and the floor he stood on, and unless you had the Gift, it was.

Using that Gift, he reached out with his mind and nudged the latch deep inside the wall with a wisp of power, just enough to make contact. The lock responded and the wall in front of him moved aside to admit the blinding midday sun. Derrack blinked rapidly, squinting against the glare as he stepped out onto the college roof.

To the east, the view was amazing. All Miralthrall spread out below him like something from the old stories, the buildings and streets gleaming like new, even after aeons of weather and use. At the eastern wall the huge river gate was being opened for a ship leaving port and embarking on its journey down the Mirallyn, and it seemed somehow right that the sails on each of its three masts were stiff and straining with a full wind on this fine spring dusk day.

Past the city and the outer wall, green hills dotted with farms and trees dominated the landscape, and in the distance he could make out several villages, even some moderately sized towns.

As he turned toward the great circle, Derrack couldn't help but look up, past the pinnacle of the amphitheatre and beyond to the vastness of the Cloudburst Cliffs and the Mirallyn River pouring out of a deep fissure in the mountainous stone cliff face. Returning his mind to the task at hand, he let the light spell fade as he walked a short distance through the sunlight and crossed under an archway that marked the outer wall of the great circle.

As he did so, a surly mage, not too much older than himself, pointed up to the stands before instructing him to find a seat, saying only that Heramiir would be with them all shortly. Derrack began to object, then thought better of it and shrugged slightly as he let out a small sigh of relief at the other mage's words. It seemed he wasn't the only one the archmage had summoned.

The mage was clearly irritated at being set this menial crowd-control task, and seemed in no mood to give more detailed instructions. Derrack left him and walked the short distance to a ramp which led up to one of the nearby galleries, again wondering what all of this was about. There was plenty of sunlight slanting in through the slated rows of seats above and beside him to see by, and as Derrack came to the top of the ramp he abruptly became aware of a great many other magi seated all around the circle.

That's where you all are.

For a moment he didn't know whether to feel relief or terror, but decided it was far more likely the others had been summoned as he had, rather than the alternative, that they had all been called to witness a meeting between himself and the archmage.

Somewhat relieved, Derrack decided he should just do as instructed for now.

As he looked around though he realised he couldn't see any familiar faces in the nearby rows. It was not unexpected he supposed, since he had only been a full

Mage for such a short time. Most of his close friends were still apprentices, and therefore not allowed up here yet. He walked along the top row of seats until he came to a place where he had a good view of the falls cascading down from above, and sat, looking down on the crowd. There must have been three hundred magi here, nearly every spell caster in Miralthrall's college at present, and others who had to have been summoned from the surrounding countryside as well. He still couldn't see the archmage, but what he did notice was several of the more powerful magi and nearly all of the archmagi showing signs of impatience, as if they had been here for some time.

Keeping a casual eye on the entrance he noticed that each of the magi who entered over the next few minutes was young, inexperienced, or not very powerful, and it set him thinking. Derrack knew he was not yet privy to all the college's customs, but one thing he knew was that you didn't keep an archmage waiting.

The general hubbub of conversation around the great circle ended abruptly as the great bell at the centre of Miralthrall began its resonant tolling, accompanied by a selection of startled or puzzled looks from the assembled magi.

Across the circle one of the elderly archmagi stood from his seat and began walking towards the exit. He didn't hurry as he crossed the floor in his silver-lined cloak, but there was something in his step which spoke of a certain urgency, and it made Derrack nervous all over again.

As the old archmage passed out of sight he couldn't help but notice most of the other magi were suddenly busy conferring with one another.

This might be his first time in the great circle as a full

Mage, but it was obvious something more than just a poorly timed bell ringing was amiss.

A few more idle moments passed and Derrack looked around the great circle itself in wonder. The huge thing would have held five thousand people when full he guessed, but now there were only the magi, most seated in the first few rows, and a great number of empty seats.

It wasn't long before the old archmage came storming back into the circle, and even from where he was seated near the back, Derrack could see his wrinkled face was livid. The archmage strode into the very centre like a man half his age and worked a small air spell to amplify his voice, not that he needed to with the way he was shouting.

"The entrance has been warded closed. I will know who has done this, now!"

The buzz of conversation around the circle became ten times louder at the archmage's proclamation, and Derrack began to run spells through his mind, refreshing their intents and accompanying gestures or words in his memory for quick use. Unlike some of the archmagi he wasn't even close to experienced enough to cast them solely with his mind. Something strange was happening here though, and he had no intention of being caught unprepared by it, whatever 'it' might be.

When no answer was forthcoming from the crowd, the wrinkled archmage scowled and stalked back out of the circle followed by two other magi from the stands.

The sunlight dimmed for a moment as a small wisp of cloud drifted across its path, and as Derrack looked up, he noticed what at first glance resembled a small flock of birds flying down from the Cloudburst Cliffs.

He shielded his eyes from the glare as the cloud moved

on. There was something about the flock which struck him as being out of place. He couldn't make out any details at this distance, but he was sure they were coming closer. For a few moments longer he watched them grow, and despite the warmth of the day, a sudden chill worked its way down Derrack's back as he realised with sudden trepidation that the eight birds he had been watching so avidly, had no wings.

"Look!" another mage called from across the circle, shielding her eyes as she pointed at the sky. The crowd hushed as it took in the sight above. The eight jet-black horses and riders were now close enough to see clearly as they galloped through the air at frightening speed straight towards the college roof, and several magi in the stands began preparing spells.

As the first of the riders levelled out and made a controlled landing on his giant ebony mount, the crowd fell silent. The rider's Gift-wrought cloak swirled around him like a storm as it settled, drawing the eye until a moment later, the other seven silver-cloaked figures, almost forgotten in the spectacle, landed heavily in an outward facing circle around their leader.

Archmage Heramiir had arrived.

*   *   *

"Why have you summoned us Heramiir, and why have you brought these, perversions before us?!" The wrinkled archmage who had been halted at the exit called as he strode up to the central figure and waved an arm at the mutated steeds.

"I hadn't realised we were on a such an informal basis,

Poller," Heramiir replied as he turned his steed to face the archmage addressing him.

"Why are we here?" the old mage repeated.

Around the circle silence reigned, the conversation interrupted only by the wind and stamping of Deshara's mount.

"I have come to offer you a choice," Heramiir called up to the crowd, ignoring Poller completely. His voice was well suited to public oratory and reached the back rows even without the aid of spells to amplify it.

At least three hundred magi and archmagi were seated amongst the stalls of the great circle, but as he began a slow circuit around the stone floor, he briefly met every gaze directed at him as he spoke.

"For so long we have led the life of servants, residing here within the walls of this building we call 'the college'. For so long, we have gone where other men have pointed, fought for other men's causes; died, in other men's battles. We devote ourselves to lives of study and introspection for them, but even that is tainted. Consider the things we are forbidden to learn. Consider the things we are forbidden to do!"

He paused a moment for dramatic effect, then continued with growing passion.

"It was no mage who bound our hands, but a king hundreds of years dead in response to a disaster which was never proven to be our fault. Yet for the stability of the kingdom we have obeyed their strictures, we have always been loyal to the Duke of Miralthrall and the King of Jeranon. For what?" Heramiir shouted to the assembled crowd.

"Riches? Surely not," he called, raising his arms wide.

"For what mage would desire mere gold when he has the power of the Gift?"

Somewhere in the stands, one of the magi laughed humourlessly.

"What about lands?" he asked them, allowing his arms to fall to his sides.

At that there was an angry murmuring in the crowd, one which was not lost on Heramiir.

"We do not even have our own homes anymore because tradition says a mage spends his time studying and wants to be close to his books. So now we have college quarters instead. Another 'tradition' which over centuries has become a rule, and now a law for but one purpose; to control what we learn, where we go, what we do. To keep us dependent upon the king's generosity so we have no choice but to fight against the nations beyond the Dark Iron Mountains."

He paused for a moment to check the mood of the crowd. Most of them looked intrigued by his speech, a smaller number were outright furious, but he judged that none of them were ready for what he planned yet, and so he continued.

"How many of you have wondered just how far your power could go, how it could be developed, or simply what things you could discover on your own if it were not against the king's law to experiment? I put it to you all, here and now that with each passing year we have to look harder and harder to find those with the Gift, not because there are any fewer children born with it though. No, it is because they no longer come forward."

Around the circle the assembled magi were almost silent now, listening, a few of the older ones even nodding their heads in agreement. He knew even those most loyal to the king would have to concede that point.

"Brothers and sisters, magi all. These restrictions we have abided by for far too long have turned our order stale. It has been a full decade since the king has approved a new use for the Gift, but while he sits on his throne in the capital, it is we who bleed and die on the battlefield to hold the nations of the west beyond the mountains."

Again he paused for breath, and while some were clearly angry at his treasonous speech, all was silent now save for Deshara's horse. They were nearly ready, just a little more.

"Since before the great cataclysm forced our people from our ancestral home of Jeranah, all throughout the wars of founding, and for every day since then the magi of Jeranon have held our people together. We have always been the first line of defence against whatever threatened. Whether the danger came from the western nations or the southern island of Avsan, or even from within our own borders. For five thousand years we have been protectors, defenders, and healers. There was a time when being a mage meant having the utmost respect of the people. But sadly, that time has now passed. We have become nothing more than a tool to the nobility, sent into battle and swept out of sight once the danger has passed, into the college walls where they can pretend we no longer exist... until they need us again."

"My friends, it is the magi of Miralthrall's college, as well as our city's soldiers which form the backbone of Jeranon's defence. But even so, the Giftless no longer hold us in awe, some even consider us so without honour that they hide their children from us when it comes time for the testing. All here know how slight our numbers already are. For the sake of our order, and for Jeranon itself, we cannot allow this practice to continue, otherwise the next generation of magi will simply not have the numbers to hold back the western nations."

Before his words had even quieted, an angry mutter ran through the crowd, they knew the truth of that last statement all too well.

His timing perfect as usual, Nereth came striding past Archmage Poller on foot and walked into the circle. A quick meeting of the eyes told Heramiir all he needed to know, so he took a deep, satisfying breath, and began what he'd come here to do.

"I come here to offer you a choice," he called up to the assembled magi.

"Even as we speak, my forces have taken control of Miralthrall. Today has seen the end of the duke's reign."

"This is treason!" Poller hissed.

"Yes, it is. But hear me out!" he called for the rest of the crowd's benefit.

A mage in the stands began a spell that would burn Heramiir alive if he didn't stop it, but before even he could act, a man next to the mage punched him squarely in the jaw, sending him tumbling down several rows of seats. Several members of the crowd rose from their benches and began shouting or hurrying towards the door. Many more looked as if they were ready to fight, though whose side they were all on was difficult to tell.

"Be silent!" Archmage Tavic's vastly amplified voice boomed from the stands, bringing the sudden commotion to all but a halt. "There will be no violence in this circle. We will hear Archmage Heramiir out. Then together we will

46

decide what response his conduct warrants."

The crowd grudgingly accepted the assembly arbiter's order, and Heramiir raised a slight eyebrow at the unexpected support, but thought it best to waste no further time now that he had their undivided attention.

"From now on the college will be the highest authority in this city," he announced simply. There were a lot of shocked looks around the great circle at the pronouncement, but only a few angry murmurs and not a single shout to be heard.

"With you as some kind of emperor I suppose?" Poller spat at him.

"Can you think of someone better?" Heramiir asked just loud enough for the magi in the stands.

"I alone had the will to rebel against the Giftless duke of this place and wrest control of Miralthrall from him. Only I have had the courage to stand up and say, 'I will be used as a weapon and discarded no longer'. With the aid of my most trusted lieutenants, I have regained liberties for us with just a few short years of planning that our order has not been able to convince the Kings of our land to return in the last five hundred years."

"My friends," Heramiir said as he jumped gracefully down from his steed, his cloak swirling around him like a tiny storm as he moved.

"This very moment we stand at a crossroads. You must choose whether you will follow me, one of your own, or whether you truly want to return to the way things were."

There was a strained silence throughout the circle now, and Heramiir knew he had them.

"If you choose to follow me, I will grant you lands and homes of your own. Even the most destitute peasant can work towards this basic right, but not us, and we have been denied it far too long."

There was an intermittent but audible buzz of conversation from parts of the stands at that pronouncement, and Heramiir found himself smiling.

"Furthermore, the ban on experimentation with the Gift will be lifted. However, there will be certain procedures put in place for the safety of all concerned."

An excited murmur ran through the crowd this time, which was more or less what he'd expected. He had just handed them a big carrot to whet their appetite, and now it was time to finish this little speech by showing them the stick.

"Make no mistake though my friends, regardless of how you choose, Miralthrall is now mine and I will tolerate no opposition to my rule. If you join me, together we will advance the learning of our order and in doing so usher in a new era for the college. Through our future actions we will then improve the lot of all within our borders and once again regain the power and respect which was the birthright of our forebearers. I warn you plainly though, although I have no wish to harm any of you, any kind of armed rebellion will be counterproductive to the achievement of these goals. After today I will not allow us to be further weakened with pointless infighting, whatever the cost."

He looked around the stands again as he finished, his cloak billowing as the wind resumed its whistling passage through the circle.

"I may not be a king, but from this day on, I am Miralthrall's ruler."

Heramiir turned to face the furious old archmage

behind him and had to admit, for a man of nearly ninety summers, Poller had quite an intimidating visage.

"I cannot let you do this Heramiir," the old man snapped, "You openly admit to rebelling against your king and taking arms against the populace. How can you expect us to follow someone who so readily betrays those to whom they are supposedly loyal?"

There was a moment of silence in the wake of Poller's accusation, broken only by the constant frisking of Deshara's steed. As the magi around the circle waited impatiently to hear his answer, Heramiir approached Poller, his eyes burning with hatred for the old man. Everything depended on having the support of the magi, without them his power base would be shattered next spring when the king's armies would no doubt march against him, if he even lasted that long.

Once he reached the old archmage, Heramiir confronted him directly, lowering his voice for privacy.

"You will follow me because you know this is the best chance to get what we have sought for nearly half a millennium. You will follow because it is in Jeranon's best interests for our knowledge of battle magic to increase. And Poller," he said, his voice deadly serious, "You will follow me because you have no other choice."

Most other men would have cowered away at that point as the swirling cloak Heramiir wore whipped itself into a frenzy. Not Poller though, he just stood there with all the calm dignity of his years, unflinching before Heramiir's fury, and simply folded his hands behind his back.

"There are always choices," he said before turning his back and walking out of the great circle without another word.

Should I deal with him? Deshara asked silently with the Gift.

No. Right now I still have uses for him, Heramiir replied through the curious link Deshara had formed with his mind. As far as he knew, she was the only mage who had ever developed that particular art. Only his most loyal followers even knew of her newfound ability. It was one of the more interesting skills the master had shown him how to glean from the red book it had led him to in the catacombs beneath the city on that first visit, all those many years ago.

"Is that what you truly want?" Heramiir called up to the crowd. He had to keep his mind on the business at hand.

"Do you really want to return to the way things were? Do you really want to spend another five hundred years in a fruitless pursuit of justice? Or will you join me and make our nation strong once again. Now is the time to choose, but know this before you do. After today there will be no middle ground. Each of you will either be with us, or against us."

There was a profound silence around the circle as Heramiir finished his speech, and a palpable tension hung across the stands like an invisible fog, despite the warmth of this spring dusk day.

"Any who wish to leave this city, announce your intentions honourably before us all. Do so now and there will be no reprisal. Do not make the mistake of staying and opposing me later."

Once again there was silence while Heramiir remounted his steed. Only Nereth remained on foot in his black enamelled, Gift-wrought plate armour and silver-lined Archmage's cloak, which the breeze stirred on occasion as he made up the eighth point in the rough circle around Heramiir.

For a full minute no one moved, and then one of the archmagi in the stands stood to face him.

"If we do this it will be war," she said gravely, "What makes you think we can hold off the king as well as the western nations?"

There was a general murmuring at the question, and Heramiir looked right around the circle before turning back to the young archmage, which was to say she was not all that much older than Heramiir himself.

"You do," was his only reply as he looked around the stands.

The woman who had asked the question stood for a moment longer, and then sat.

"Then I am with you," she said, and a chorus of agreements sounded around the circle as more and more of the magi seated there added their voice to the pledge, along with several angry or disparaging shouts from those more loyal to the king.

"What say you Archmage Tavic?" Heramiir called up to the supposedly unbiased assembly arbiter. "Do my actions warrant an axe, or a crown?"

The older archmage looked around the stands, at the reactions of the gathered magi, then stood.

"Your attack on this city, while it may be of long-term benefit, must have cost the lives of many loyal soldiers whose only crime was doing their duty well. For that alone you deserve the axe." There was a vocal outcry from both sides until Tavic held up his hand for silence.

"However, with this many of our brethren supporting your actions, I see no way of enforcing that decision, or of many of these magi being content to go back to how things were now that you have granted them the real possibility of a different path. The thing that disturbs me most in all of this is that despite your despicable methods… I am not entirely sure you were wrong to do as you have."

There was another uproar from the stands at the normally passionless arbiter's speech, and it surprised even Heramiir to hear that admission, but he regained his composure quickly.

"You do me great honour," Heramiir said once the noise had finally died down.

"You have taken the first step, the hardest step. We will be strong once more, but for now I ask you to be patient. I will hand the details of the new administration down in a few days, but until then know this. Whatever happens now, whether in victory or defeat. Today we are free."

With the slightest nudge of his knees Heramiir's steed broke into a run and dived out the door of the great circle; followed closely by his lieutenants and the sound of excited conversation which had broken out the instant he had left, along with Poller's raised and opposing voice.

Nereth followed at a more sedate pace, and when they were all standing at the edge of the college walls Heramiir turned to face him.

"Bring Hassan to my study, and see to that," he said, pointing to a distant fire which was getting out of hand in an eastern part of Miralthrall.

"I don't want to have to put up with an uprising by the Giftless because of a few burned houses."

"As you command," Nereth replied.

From the corner of his eye, Heramiir saw Deshara grin when Nereth spoke. There was something going on there he decided, filing it away in his mind for future thought.

"See to your duties," he dismissed them. "Make sure that any magi who flee the city are intercepted and brought to the holding facility. We can't allow them to strengthen the king's numbers if the spring campaign is to be a success."

Unfortunately, while the magi appeared to be with him, and the city had fallen to Nereth's assault with almost miraculous ease, mopping up always took an inordinate amount of time. There were many other things which had to be dealt with before he could journey down into the catacombs and at last come face to face with the master, and after a decade of waiting, Heramiir was more than ready to take that step.

Despite guiding him to the red book on that first occasion, the being under Miralthrall had always held off on meeting him in person, telling him he was not yet ready, and would not be until the city was firmly in his control. And now, finally, it was.

He dismounted and opened the door at the top of the stairs, leading the others who had work to do in the college back inside while the remainder leapt off the rooftop on their steeds' backs to attend to their predetermined tasks. Today had been a beginning in so many ways.

In some small measure he even felt sorry for Poller. The old man always had been loyal to the king, and Heramiir was willing to put money on the old fool sticking around to gather a force he could try to strike back with. He would be a major locus for any potential resistance among the magi, and knowing that made Heramiir's job a great deal easier.

He had always admired the man's thirst for knowledge, but Heramiir's warning to the magi had not been an idle one, and Poller would very quickly learn the truth of that if he ever did move against Heramiir's forces.

But that is for later, he thought as he lit the corridor ahead of them with a bright orange light. For right now there was other work to be done.

*   *   *

"Thank you, Captain, you've done well," Nereth said blandly as Fisher escorted Hassan into the archmage's private office.

"Thank you, Sir," the young man replied.

"You are dismissed," Nereth told him when he just stood there.

Fisher turned about quickly, realising his mistake and exiting the room with as much grace as possible under the circumstances, closing the carved wooden door behind him.

As soon as they were alone, Hassan stepped right up to the archmage's wooden desk and looked Nereth over. They weren't friends, but he had fought beside the armoured archmage on enough occasions over the years to know that although Heramiir may be in charge, only the man sitting calmly before him could be the true mastermind behind the assault on his city. Even here in the college's heart he wore the massive black enamelled suit of plate armour which Hassan had never seen him without, as well as the more customary silver-lined Archmage's cloak over his shoulders. When Nereth remained silent throughout his inspection, Hassan eventually leaned over the desk to place his hands on top of its dark, well-polished surface.

"So, the magi now control the military," he stated in disgust.

A slight grin tugged at Nereth's lips as he stood, his height easily matching Hassan's, who straightened unconsciously in response.

"No Hassan," he answered the guardsman. "Not the magi. Me."

Hassan nodded.

"I should have known you were the one behind this attack."

"Yes, you should."

He'd fought beside Nereth twice before in campaigns against the western nations, and both times the archmage had used innovative strategies to send the enemy fleeing home with a minimum of loss to his own forces. Hassan had always felt that if the man had been born without the Gift, he would have long since been placed in charge of the duke's armies.

"Bring me to Heramiir," Hassan told him, in no mood for any further conversation.

"You will refer to the archmage by his proper title," Nereth returned in just as blunt a tone as he began a slow circle of the room.

"If Heramiir truly has committed treason then he is no longer a citizen of Jeranon. He will be declared renegade, hunted, and killed. He is a criminal, and not worthy of one of our titles."

A slight narrowing of the eyes and a sideways look from the archmage told Hassan his remark had exacted the desired effect.

"You presume much Hassan, but that is why I wanted to talk to you first. Although our military has been weakened by the events of the day, I am in full command of what remains, and you know I have both the talent and the will to see this course through to whatever conclusion may eventually play out."

Nereth walked over to the large window which overlooked the north wall of the college building as he spoke.

"What I lack is a field general who will lead the troops and inspire them on the ground. It would have occurred to you by now that a civil war is inevitable as soon as the king learns what has transpired here today, but regardless of that fact, the dark nations still need to be kept contained. If you truly decided to join us, I could give you nearly free rein along the border. For three thousand years the western nations have raided our lands, burning and pillaging since the time of the wars of founding. Together we could put an end to that. I have the skill to arrange battlefields and organise campaigns just as I did here today. You have the valuable skill of being able to pull order from chaos on the field even once the lines have merged and turn it into victory. You and I could bring peace to our nation. Peace like we haven't known since our ancestors were forced to leave Jeranah and settle here over three thousand years ago."

Another step to the side, and sunlight from the window wreathed Nereth, turning his face to shadow as he continued his slow pacing around the large room.

"In a moment I will take you to Heramiir and he will make you an offer, my advice is you take it. Regardless of your personal loyalties, you cannot protect Jeranon if you are dead."

Without further discussion, Nereth walked past Hassan to open the door.

"Follow me," he commanded, and then proceeded down the corridor.

There seemed little point in attempting an escape at this stage, so Hassan followed the armoured archmage through the corridors of the college building until they reached the huge circular staircase which cut through the levels like a village well cuts into the earth. The sloping staircase took them up six more floors to the second tier from the top, where they exited through a doorway which had so little decoration it seemed to be just a natural hole in the stone, albeit a perfectly rectangular one.

A short walk later and the pair arrived at an ornate wooden door gilded in gold and emblazoned with blue enamel work. It was quiet here, and it occurred to Hassan that the black-enamelled, steel plate armour Nereth was wearing hadn't made a single noise during the entire walk through the halls.

"Wait here," the archmage commanded as he knocked on the door and entered without waiting for a response. There were the sounds of a muffled conversation whose words he couldn't make out, and eventually the door swung open without the aid of either of the men inside.

"Come in Hassan," Heramiir told him once the door had opened.

As he entered the private quarters of the most powerful archmage in Jeranon, Hassan noted that Nereth took up a place behind Heramiir on his right side, hands clasped at ease behind his back. Whether any of his previous claims had been true or not was open to debate, but one thing was clear, Nereth stood high in Heramiir's treasonous circle.

There was no seat in front of Hassan, but that suited him just fine. He moved across to a marble pillar and leaned on it as insolently as he could manage.

"What do you want, traitor?" he asked bluntly.

There was a slight indrawn breath from Nereth, and Hassan noticed him begin to watch Heramiir from his place at his back.

Hassan had the sudden uncomfortable feeling no one had insulted the archmage like this before, at least, not since he had declared himself Miralthrall's ruler. There was little else he could think of which would make a man like Nereth take such interest in a casually thrown insult.

"Let us cut to the heart of the matter," Heramiir said as he stood, ignoring the remark as he approached Hassan.

"My forces control Miralthrall. Any opposition you could raise at this point would be nothing more than a token resistance. The city is ours."

The archmage stopped for a moment to see what effect his words would have, but Hassan managed to keep his face satisfyingly impassive, to Heramiir's clear annoyance.

"My people have taken nearly four thousand prisoners, many of whom are wounded. I give you this one chance to join me. You will denounce the king and help me expand my sphere of influence to include all of western Jeranon. Once that task is complete, we will push back the dark nations beyond the mountains and put an end to this insane war which has gone on for countless generations. If you join us you will be an important part of that campaign, and I will order the magi to begin treating the injuries of the prisoners we took in the coup at once. If you decide foolishly, then you will be executed along with the others. Their fates I tie to your own."

By the time Heramiir was finished, Hassan was no longer leaning against the pillar, but standing stiffly in front of the archmage as his odd, rune-splayed cloak swirled around him.

"I do not understand," Hassan bit back. "I am just one man. Why is it so important to you both that I join your rebellion?" He could not betray his king; the man was like a father to him. Yet he also acknowledged privately that he would never condemn four thousand loyal men to death just to keep his own hands clean.

"It is not," Heramiir replied coldly, "But you are an exceedingly efficient front line commander and you have the respect of enough of the men to keep them in line. That is a resource I can use."

"If you truly believe I have that much influence, aren't you concerned I might turn them against you?" Hassan returned glibly, immediately wishing he could take the words back.

Heramiir laughed, and the abrupt sound echoed off the walls of the chamber.

"Not at all," he said seriously.

"If you ever betray me, I will kill your family and the family of any man who joins you. You don't even want to know what your fate will be if you try to oppose me."

Hassan found his hands clenching into fists again and had to force them to stop. Now was not the time for rash action, not with two of the most powerful archmagi alive in the room.

"Good," Heramiir said, noticing the small action.

"I see you are not so careless with the lives of those around you as you are with your own. Do not think to insult me again, or try my patience. Your life is in my hands!" he finished with a shout, green eyes flashing with barely concealed fury. "Your presence would be a boon to us, but I will spend no more time on this. Choose, now."

There was silence in the room as Hassan hastily reviewed his options. Attacking the archmagi was suicide, as was refusing their demands he suspected. They were high up in the college, far above the street, but the window was too small to try and jump through. Not that he had any desire to kill himself, but he wasn't about to be the cause of his own family's execution. That only left one thing, and this time his hands did ball up into fists so tight they took on a white pallor as the blood was squeezed away from the flesh. He would have to give Heramiir the oath of service, even though he was already sworn to his king's cause with the one oath he would never break.

With a sneer on his lips he reluctantly sank to one knee and drew his broadsword from the scabbard on his back. He placed the gleaming metal point down on the stone floor and murmured the words which would make him a traitor to the man who had saved him.

"My sword and my service until death," he spoke the ancient form of the pledge. And as simply as that it was done.

"Now order your magi to heal those men," Hassan demanded as he stood, locking eyes with the most powerful man in the world.

After a long moment Heramiir snorted softly in amusement and motioned to Nereth, who nodded and left to do the archmage's bidding.

"You may go as well," Heramiir told Hassan as he smoothly re-sheathed his sword.

"Nereth will have your orders in the morning."

Hassan nodded fractionally and left the room, not trusting himself to speak as he shut the door behind him.

He had spoken the words of the pledge to Heramiir, but in his heart and in his mind, it was his king to which he had renewed his vows of service. As he re-entered the spiral staircase at the heart of the college building, he wondered briefly if he had done the right thing, then dismissed the thought. In his line of business there was only the present and the near future, and he had plans to make. There was no chance he could overthrow Heramiir by himself, but perhaps an opportunity to take the advantage would present itself over the coming phases. At the very least he had to let the king know what had happened here today. He would bide his time until next spring when the monarch's armies would surely march against them.

Hassan had defeated many enemies for his king, but Nereth was a whole different kettle of fish. There would be spies everywhere he knew, and right now he needed someone he could trust, someone who had been with him through long years of campaigning.

Someone like Jarl.

'When the cataclysm rained around us, we ran. We ran to the east, to the north, to the west and to the south. Everywhere the fires burnt around us, until we had nowhere left to run. Until we had nowhere left but the sea.'
Excerpt from the log of Admiral Chain, commander of the desolate fleet.

CHAPTER I

THE CLIFFS ABOVE GRANDELL

It's too early to be this hot.

Jayden took a short rest, wiping the sweat from his brow and flinging the salty drops into the dense foliage beside the track. Through the forest canopy he could see the mottled iron-grey of the storm clouds which had settled in the day before last, clouds which had yet to produce any substantial downpour.

Just hurry up and rain, he cheerlessly thought as a slight breeze brushed against him, carrying with it the tang of salt from the nearby Sea of Dreams. Jayden sighed as the modest breath of wind faded, replaced once again by the oppressive stillness which had shrouded the seaside town of Grandell all week.

It was still spring dusk, and weather like this was rare on the eastern coast of Jeranon, even in high summer. From the talk around town Jayden knew it was becoming a concern to some of the local farmers, and even his own father had recently become accustomed to wearing a frown while inspecting their holdings.

He pulled the stopper from his water-skin and forced himself to swallow a mouthful of the already tepid liquid.

A small insect fell on him from one of the overhanging branches and he swiped it away. On any normal day, those branches would have provided a welcoming shade. Truth be told they did today as well, unfortunately the heat was not so much coming from the sun this morning as it was just saturating the air and everything in it.

Resealing the skin, he tied it back on to his belt and continued up the track. From a few paces into the trees he noticed one of the skittish shore birds who made their nests in these hills mark his passage with a lethargic turn of its head. It didn't even bother trying to move away.

Jayden smiled to himself and tried to keep a steady pace as he made his way arduously towards the top of the steep incline.

After some time, he came to a place where the trees to either side of the track thinned enough to give him a good look at the overcast sky.

It's too hot not to be able to see the sun.

It took him longer than usual to reach the tip of the path, but as the barely recognisable track emerged from the forest, it revealed the usual stunning vista of the Sea of Dreams beyond.

He paused for a moment to soak in the view, as he always did when he came up here. Something indefinable relaxed and appealed to him about the different shades of blue and green water as the waves lapped against the jutting cliffs and secluded beaches of the eastern coast of Jeranon far below.

For a thousand leagues and more to the west, he

knew from his lessons, the sprawling empire of Jeranon had lain for almost three millennia, since shortly after the cataclysm which forced the desolate fleet to flee the ancestral home of Jeranah for an uncertain future at sea. From the outset it had weathered adversity from what were now the nations beyond the Dark Iron Mountains in the west, and the machinations of the southern continent of Avsan. But here, on the easternmost shore of the isolated Anchorhead Promontory, and on the very tip of the kingdom itself, those concerns belonged to other men.

Far below and to the south, the harbour mouth was visible where the docks and shipyard which serviced the fishing and trading vessels of the region were located.

Even as he watched, one of the great three-masted ships which were the mainstay of Grandell's economy sailed into view. It wasn't Crest, his father's ship, that wouldn't sail until tomorrow.

He observed the sails unfurl but hang almost limp on the distant vessel as they struggled to catch the all but non-existent breeze. At its sides, the crew was working the oars to a measured drumbeat. The rhythm was barely audible, but he listened for a minute as the ship began its long run south around the promontory. After that it would cross an open stretch of the Sea of Dreams before sailing up the Camar River to Aramar, the largest city in Jeranon, and seat of the king.

Even up here in the open there was very little in the way of a breeze, but despite the heat of the day Jayden still felt refreshed by the sight of the great ship and the distant sound of the waves crashing far below. By the time the vessel caught the breeze he thought it must be close to midday, though the sun still elected to absent itself from that assessment.

Taking a last look at the vessel he turned away and headed north up the final stretch of the track, towards where it ended at the very highest point of the rocky cliffs.

After a few minutes of walking along the rough surface of the barely discernible path, Jayden came to a place where a huge boulder had been split apart by lightning at some point in the distant past. Beyond this point the track became a steeply slanted crevice which time and the elements had worn dangerously smooth.

Bracing his hands against the walls of the fissure, he carefully began picking his way upward. He'd fallen down this path once as a child and been forced to make his way back to town with a broken wrist and arm.

Planting his feet, he reached up the last stretch with an effort and pulled himself to a sitting position on top of a smooth granite plateau which overlooked the Sea of Dreams in both directions, and a good stretch of the Jade Coast as well.

He stood up from the familiar climb after taking a moment to catch his breath, then allowed himself a small smile of relief as he spotted Rhianna at the very edge of the plateau closest to the sea. It was over a thousand spans straight down into the rock-strewn water at the base of the cliff, but it seemed not at all to worry the young woman who sat gazing out at the ocean, her legs dangling absently over the edge of the precipice.

"I thought I might find you here," Jayden said carefully as he moved to join the lithe form of the reason he'd hiked all the way up here.

He waited, but the tall blonde girl didn't react, or even seem to have registered his words.

He sighed. He'd been doing a lot of that lately, when he talked to her.

"Rhianna," he tried again, "Your parents are worried. It's been two days."

"They're not my parents," she answered dully.

It wasn't the response he was looking for, but at least she was talking today. It was a start.

"Have you been up here the whole time?" Jayden asked as he looked out over the sea.

More than anything, he wanted to look at her, to understand what was going on behind the expressionless mask she'd adopted of late. But he knew full well how much she hated people staring at her.

Even me, he wearily acknowledged. And so he waited.

She had drowned last autumn's dusk, and as he stood beside her on the cliff top, he couldn't help but recall the day which had changed everything, for both of them.

"Rhianna look out!" he'd shouted as the huge oak she was climbing in cracked with a sound like thunder. She looked up just in time to scream as an age worn limb fell from the ancient tree above her, crashing through the foliage and coming directly toward the branch on which she was balancing. With a cry she flung herself off her branch and into the river below, barely a moment ahead of the falling limb smashing its way through everything in its path. In a flurry of wooden debris, the rotted limb followed Rhianna into the water, settling over her and pinning her under the surface.

"Rhianna!" Jayden bellowed as he rushed into the waist deep water with Genna and Morrec close behind. He pulled at the huge branch, trying to move it off Rhianna's thrashing form.

"Help me!" he panted as the others reached him. His feet began slipping on the muddy riverbed as the three of them desperately tried to slide the branch away, even as her struggles weakened.

"This isn't working!" he shouted. "I'm going to try lifting it from one end. See if you can pull her out from underneath!" He scrambled deeper into the icy river and crouched, putting all but his head under the surface to take hold of the narrower end of the huge branch.

He heaved on the wood, but the only effect was for his feet to sink into the mud at the bottom. He pulled them free and tried again, this time getting a somewhat better response as he set one foot against a rock which it blindly encountered. He put most of his weight on it, and pulling at the branch with all his strength, the enormous limb moved a few inches as he renewed his efforts.

"Get her out," he said hoarsely, his teeth clenched tight from the strain of holding the massive branch and the shock of the river's swift, cold water.

If only I could use the Gift!

Like most children though, the spark which set the magi aside from the wider community was not part of his birthright.

Morrec dived beneath the surface to where Rhianna's struggles had all but stopped, and Jayden felt the rock his foot was braced against slip. He tried to adjust his weight, but the rock continued to slip away even faster as it lost its hold on the muddy silt below.

"Come on Morrec. Hurry!" he howled as the rock moved further away. He would only be able to keep his grip for another few seconds at this rate.

Morrec burst through the surface, taking a gasping breath at the same time Jayden's footing gave way. The branch settled back into the water with hardly a splash and his bad footing sent him sprawling out of the way of the sinking piece of wood.

"Where is she?" he demanded when he saw Morrec resurface alone.

"I, I can't get her out!" he shouted, and Jayden thought some of the wetness on his cheeks might not have been from the river. "I tried, the Maker knows I tried, but I couldn't pull her free."

"No," Jayden found himself saying as he waded desperately back to the branch.

"It's too late," Morrec said as he began to shiver uncontrollably, "She's dead. I was looking right in her eyes when, when she just..."

"No!" Jayden screamed, "NO!"

In a fit of grief, he'd found the strength to lift the log just enough so that Morrec and Genna were able to drag her blue and breathless body from beneath the surface and out onto the riverbank. His shoes ripped free from his feet as he struggled out of the river mud which had claimed him up past the knees, so he ran as best he could manage on legs half numb from the cold to where the others were kneeling, shivering around her lifeless corpse.

Dropping to his knees he shouldered Genna aside without even noticing and tried to feel for a heartbeat. Her skin was cold.

So cold, he thought, even as he bent over, straining to listen for any sign of breath. He pressed his fingers harder into the cold flesh of her throat, but there was nothing to find. The river's water had stolen her breath away forever, and its cold had stopped her heart dead.

Dead.

The word echoed in his mind like a searing coal which had embedded itself in his brain. He longed to fling it far away from him, to rid himself of its infernal influence, but it burned in him, searing away all else until it became his entire world. Time seemed to slow around him, but that scarcely mattered.

He didn't know how long he knelt there in a daze, but it was the physical contact of a hand on his shoulder which snapped him mercilessly back to the even bleaker reality which was now his world. He realised with a start that at some point he had lifted Rhianna's lifeless form into his arms and taken her in a crushing embrace.

Reflexively he loosened his grip so as not to hurt her.

The blasted realisation of what he'd done gripped him, and for a moment it was all he could do to breathe as fresh tears scolded their way down his cheeks. For an instant his grief turned to blinding anger, but just as swiftly transformed itself into defiance, of what he didn't know, or care, as he renewed the embrace with all his ebbing strength.

As he pulled her frozen body closer he saw a mouthful of the river's water flood from her lifeless blue lips. For half a moment it froze him still, and then a feeling began growing in him. Fury, he would have called it, if his mind had been capable of forming a clear thought.

Oh, he had been angry before in his life. But not like this. This feeling was like a fire that burned in his soul until it charred away every coherent thought, every desire. It left him but one purpose.

He loosed his hold again and then gripped her lifeless form as hard as he was able. A torrent of water erupted from her lips. Again he released her, again he squeezed, and again the bitingly cold water was expelled. He had to get it all out he knew. The river had killed her, and he would not abide it to remain with her, inside her very body, any more than he would have allowed her murderer to be buried in the same grave. Again he squeezed, again and again. Abruptly he realised his throat was hoarse from screaming. Funny, how he didn't recall a single word.

To his surprise, the others had backed away and were looking at him with haunted eyes. There was something strange in those looks he realised as he squeezed the last of the water from Rhianna's lifeless body.

Fear, he recognised dimly.

Of me?

He couldn't help but laugh at the thought.

What must I look like though? Some distant part of his mind asked.

His short burst of laughter seemed to break the trance the others were in. Genna flinched, and little Dinah, who had been playing with some younger children a bit further upriver but was now standing ashen faced before him, gave a high-pitched shriek and turned to sprint back towards town. The gazes the others turned on him were far too accusing for his liking, but it all barely registered as he held Rhianna close one last time.

The water was gone, and with it his strength flowed away in an instant. Slowly, ever so slowly, he released her prone form. Perhaps it was some trick of the light, but it appeared that her lips were not as blue as they had been.

With a shudder, his mind seemed to snap back to full

awareness, and he understood the frightened looks on his friend's faces as his memory came flooding back. Tears coursed down his cheeks and his throat was red raw from screaming at the river, "You can't have her! Do you hear me you vermin infested stretch of filth! She is not yours to take! You! Can! Not! Have! Her!"

He looked down into her lifeless eyes once more and then gave her one final, vice-grip embrace before releasing her.

And then the impossible happened.

With a great gasp, a shuddering breath, she convulsed. Her back arched as she seemed to draw in all the air in the world and then coughed it out again. Spluttering and gagging the last of the water from her lungs in a display which was both revolting, and yet somehow the most beautiful thing he ever hoped to see.

She hung there in his arms, as weak as a day-old kitten. She was soaked through, and still her lips and fingers carried more than a tinge of blue.

But she is alive! He thought with an intensity that frightened him for nothing so much as its total lack of direction towards any goal or emotion. It seemed a force unto itself. He couldn't drag his eyes from her face, and yet something made him look up.

He met Genna's gaze with a wild grin which only increased the red-headed girl's agitation. Her expression was one of awe mixed with a large portion of horror as she stared at the two of them. At Jayden holding a girl she had grown up with in his arms, a girl who had just drowned before her eyes, a girl who was quite obviously no longer dead.

Things like this just didn't happen. When someone was

dead, they were dead. They didn't begin breathing again, and they most certainly never, ever, spoke again.

Once, long ago, Jayden and some of the other youths had seen a mage heal a man who had severed his leg at the knee. He'd been lucky enough to have his accident on the day an Archmage had been visiting the old count on some business of the king's. The rooftop on which they'd been playing had made a spectacular vantage point, and the friends had watched on in awe as the mage reattached the limb, leaving the man weak, but whole.

Just as clearly Jayden remembered the mage clapping the man on the shoulder and saying, "You're lucky I was so close. Much longer and I think you would have needed a necromancer more than a healer."

It was a joke, nevertheless the crowd hushed and parted as the mage made his way back to the keep.

Not even an archmage could cure death, everybody knew that. It was said that the most powerful of magi were able to reanimate a body, but the souls which were brought forth to control the flesh were never the same as the ones which had departed. Some said they were not even human, but rather some nightmare creatures from the underworld which clawed their way up from the eternal prison.

Necromancy was outlawed in Jeranon under pain of death, as was aiding a necromancer in any way. It was one of the kingdom's oldest laws, dating back even before there had been a Jeranon, before even the cataclysm which had forced his ancestors to this continent millennia ago.

"Jay…" Rhianna whispered, "C..cold."

The words shattered the silence which had descended around them.

With a horrified expression, Morrec backed away a few

steps mouthing the word 'demon' and then turned and bolted back up the path.

"Genna, run ahead," Jayden told her. It wasn't an order, but his tone said it wasn't open for debate either.

"Tell Rhianna's parents to bank the fire and prepare some blankets."

For a moment Genna just stood there as he lifted Rhianna's prone form from the ground.

"Now!" he shouted, and as Genna fled back up the path to Grandell he called after her, "Tell them to heat some broth too!"

As he began the journey up the river path, he became keenly aware of just how cold Rhianna was. He had to get her to warmth soon or she still might not last the night.

It reminded him of his own soaked clothing, and he realised with dull interest that the toes on his left foot had gone completely numb. He loped on, but it wasn't long before his legs throbbed with the sharp ache of cramping muscles. Still, there was nothing for it but to keep going. Rhianna had already lapsed back into unconsciousness, although the sensation of her shallow breathing on his shoulder was a slight reassurance. The track from the river to Grandell was a short one, although today it seemed an indeterminable length.

As he crested the small rise which revealed the town to his sight, he suddenly felt exhausted beyond all measure. He stopped for just a moment, and that was his mistake. When he attempted to walk again, it was as though his legs didn't remember how to move. He tried again, and this time the lack of response kindled a deep anger inside him.

Come on Jayden, one foot in front of the other, he told his obstinate limbs. He lifted his left leg, moved it forward, and fell to his knees as he discovered the numbness which had claimed his toes was spreading rapidly throughout his foot, which he suddenly noticed was now covered in blood.

Must have cut it in the riverbed somehow.

He'd barely kept his hold on Rhianna as he stumbled. It was a bad sign, some still cogent part of his mind informed him, that she didn't even stir.

He pushed painfully up from his grazed knees, his aching muscles screaming in protest as he struggled to balance on his right foot and what felt like the stump of his left.

"One foot in front of the other," he reminded himself wearily. He moved his left leg forward, balanced, then limped forward a step before doggedly repeating the procedure. He continued that way in a shambolic, half-dazed state for some unknowable amount of time until eventually, with a start, he realised he'd already passed several rows of houses.

"Help," he pleaded to a group of townspeople who were watching his progress fearfully from the door of a local tavern. When none of them moved he twisted painfully on his good foot to face the small crowd.

"What's wrong with you people!" he shouted at them, suddenly furious. He took a lurching step towards the door and several of the onlookers darted inside. He had to find help here. He had to. He didn't think he was capable of making it the rest of the way on his own frozen legs.

As Jayden took another lurching step forward, the portly innkeeper came bustling out of the doorway.

For a moment Jayden thought he was seeing double as two hulking young men, so similar in appearance they must have been brothers, came outside to stand nervously behind their father, truncheons in hand.

"Be gone evil one, you'll find no aid here!" the innkeeper shouted, doing his best to disguise the fear in his voice. "Be gone I say, and take your demon cursed hell spawn with you!"

"What?" Jayden murmured, his dazed mind not understanding what he was hearing.

"Master Orran, I need to get Rhianna near a fire. She needs some blankets and hot broth."

"You can't come in here Jayden," Master Orran told him regretfully. "I don't know where you found the time or the opportunity to corrupt yourself with such a dark art, but Rhianna deserves better than to have her body reanimated by the soul of a demon!"

Jayden took a lurching step forward towards the flickering of the fire still visible through the open doorway.

Morrec was just inside that door. "Help me carry her," Jayden implored his friend.

"Stay where you are son!" Master Orran commanded without looking over his shoulder.

Jayden swung his leg forward in preparation for another agonising step.

"Stop where you are Jayden. I don't want to hurt you, but I can't let you come in here."

To Jayden's dulled mind, Master Orran's words were a distant thing. His only thought at that moment was the flickering warmth of the tavern's hearth.

Down the street he fancied he could hear horses, but as surely as a moth, the tavern's fire lured him closer without any thought of consequence.

As he took another dazed step forward, he heard Master Orran say something which might have been 'I wish you'd changed your mind,' then the men in front of him parted.

Jayden lurched forward and fell abruptly as one man cracked a truncheon down hard on the back of his good leg. As he went down he twisted to the side, losing his grip on Rhianna in the process, and as they both tumbled to the packed clay street Jayden felt another stinging blow brush past his ribs. A moment passed, and then a shock of pain as something in his arm gave way to yet another crushing blow from one of the men.

He wanted to jump up, to fight back, or at least take Rhianna and flee, but in his weakened state he could do little more than curl into a tight ball as the brothers rained blows down upon him.

From where he lay huddled, he could just see Rhianna lying prone where she had fallen. Master Orran watched her as he might have a sleeping lion he'd stumbled upon outside his door.

From his tilted view of the world Jayden felt the stuttered impact of horse's hooves against the street, but couldn't tell where they were or which way they were headed. He tried to cry out, but his brief plea was cut short by a sharp jab to the ribs. Jayden lay there, struggling for a breath which would not come, and then as if from a great distance he heard the horses halt and the sound of men running on foot. As he gasped for breath, black flecks began dancing before his eyes and suddenly a familiar voice was yelling.

"Stop this Orran, or I'll run him through!"

Something came down hard on Jayden's head, and then there had been black.

It hadn't been until much later that he'd found out the man on the horse had been his father. Genna had attempted to get help from Rhianna's foster parents first, but after telling them of the events at the river they had refused to come. Fearing even the possible taint of necromancy, and the criminal repercussions of aiding anyone practising that arcane art, they had physically pushed her away before locking themselves inside the safety of their home, abandoning Rhianna to her fate.

Genna had been forced to run to the other side of Grandell, to the manor house Jayden's parents owned to find help. By the time she'd reached it she was exhausted, the water from her soaked skirts washing away the blood from a cut on her leg where the Ginfrons had thrown her out into the street.

Jayden's father received her immediately, and despite the risk had ridden out just in time to stop tavern master Orran from beating them both to death.

Both Genna and his father had risked their lives to help him and Rhianna that day, and although he and Genna were still friends, it always created a sort of awkwardness between them which had forever changed their relationship.

All that had been nearly a year ago now, and as the two of them recovered over the next few weeks, the villagers had come to see Rhianna was indeed her own self and not some demon he'd called up from the underworld. Or at least, some of them had. To many others, matters were not so clear-cut, and rumours proliferated of a plot to murder the demon's host, banishing it back to whatever bleak realm it had emerged from. In the end it had taken a public edict by Count Dael to quell those rumours, to the effect that she had recovered from her ordeal by entirely natural means. That was supposed to put an end to it, but not everyone was so easily appeased.

Two days later she was attacked. Injured, she had barely held the man at bay until the guard had arrived. The out-of-town sailor wielding the knife had seemed almost confused at the fuss, citing the law against necromancy as a defence for his actions. He had claimed he was acting for the public good, but Dael had been in a foul mood that day and the attacker had hung from a makeshift gallows in the town square not a full hour later. It was lost on no one that the man had only arrived in Grandell after Rhianna's accident, and must have been set on his course by the sly whispers of one of its citizens. Although the wound hadn't been life threatening, it had left yet another scar on Rhianna's side where the blade had been clumsily thrust into her flesh, as well as an abiding mistrust of everyone around her.

So now he was forced to watch the sea instead of the young woman beside him, and hope against hope she could find some way to escape the bleakness which had settled over her these last few phases.

A sudden gust of wind swept up from the sea below, bringing with it the tang of salt and a moment's relief from the oppressive damp heat of the day.

Without so much as turning her head, Rhianna finally spoke, and it was a question that sent a chill all the way up Jayden's spine.

"Have you ever wondered what it would be like to fly?" she asked, staring at the flock of gulls wheeling through the air below them.

"No," Jayden replied, quickly seating himself beside Rhianna, "And neither should you... at least, not while you're sitting on the edge of a cliff," he glanced at her then, only to find her already returning his quick look.

He expected to find sadness or pain reflected in those eyes, but the dead gaze which met his own was far worse. It was as if the vital spark had been extinguished, and Jayden found himself unspeakably saddened by what had become of this young woman he loved. She had always been so spirited, so alive, always the first with a joke or a smile, always the one the other children came to with their problems. She had been like a cherished big sister to the merchant children of Grandell and had rarely had a bad word to say about any subject. Before the accident she had been well liked by the townsfolk, the more so for not taking advantage of their goodwill.

In all his life Jayden had met no one else like her. Although Rhianna may have been like a big sister to the children of the town and a trusted confidante to those her own age, recently Jayden had come to realise when she looked at him with those deep brown eyes of hers, there was nothing of brother in that gaze. At first he had chalked it up to some strange reaction stemming from his saving of her life, but as the phases after the drowning and the attack drew on, he'd started to believe there was more to it than he'd first thought. From there it hadn't been long until he realised his own feelings for her were becoming much more than the simple friendship they'd enjoyed whilst growing up as friends in the same town.

Rhianna leant forward to rest her elbows on her knees so she could look straight down off the cliff, and for just a second Jayden thought she was going to keep on going. He reached out and placed a restraining hand on her shoulder before realising she had already stopped herself. With eyes the colour of the darkest honey, Rhianna turned to regard him, and an awkward silence stretched out as it became painfully clear that she knew exactly what he had been thinking.

After a moment she placed her hand on his and then gripped it hard.

"Not while I have you," she said, her voice taking on the slightest of tremors.

"What's happened Rhianna?" Jayden asked, but the only answer he received was a slight trembling of her lip as her gaze returned to the ocean.

"Rhianna," he tried again, "You know I love you, and you know I will do anything I can to help you, but you have to tell me what's happened."

For a minute or more there was no response at all, but eventually she spoke, her voice barely audible above the crashing of the waves far below.

"Two nights ago I came home at sundown, I stabled Merry and came in the back way," she recited, almost as if she had prepared how she was going to tell him her news.

"I was headed upstairs when I heard voices in the main living room. Two of them belonged to my foster parents and I was sure I recognised the third, so I snuck closer and listened from the hallway."

She stopped to swallow hard before continuing in a choked voice. "Jay, it was Count Dael. He was trying to convince the Ginfron's to allow an arranged marriage between himself, and me."

"What!" Jayden exploded, "He can't do that. By law arranged matches are only for the nobility, not commoners like you and I."

More silence. The gulls below suddenly wheeled away in unison as they spotted a school of shimmering fish just below the surface, and with their departure the wind became the only distraction as it whistled its solitary way up the cliff.

"I recently found out my great auntie has been wed to a minor nobleman from the south."

"But that's not even a blood link!" Jayden declared, confused.

"How can Dael justify an arranged marriage without a blood tie to the nobility?"

Slowly Rhianna reached out to stroke two fingers down the line of his chin.

"It doesn't have to be by blood. Dael brought an old parchment with him to convince my foster parents the law only says that a, 'link of relationship' is required. Apparently the author of the law assumed the words 'blood link' were unnecessary."

"Surely your foster parents wouldn't agree to the match without your consent," he said, a sudden dread taking hold.

"Not at first," she replied bitterly. "Not until Dael handed over a purse full of gems from his mine. That ended their objections almost immediately."

"But..." Jayden floundered, suddenly finding it hard to speak. The words which usually came so readily to mind seemed to have vanished, forcing him to start again.

"What will you do?" he asked. He knew Dael had been fixated on Rhianna for years, even knowing she felt nothing for him, but this was not something Jayden had expected. The young count could be cruel and petty, and often was for no other reason than his own twisted pleasure, but he wasn't usually devious.

"I don't know," she said. "Ever since the accident, it feels as though everything is spinning further and further out of control. Some days it seems my life is barely my own any more."

"It is yours though Rhianna, and only you can decide what to do with it," Jayden told her vehemently.

"Forget about Dael, what do *you* want?"

"What do I want?" she mused as she leant her head against his shoulder.

"I want to go somewhere where people don't watch me with fear or hate. I want to be far away from here, from Dael and from Grandell. I want to live without having to always be looking over my shoulder for the next rock, or rotten lettuce the children throw when I go by. And just for an instant, for one, shining moment I want to take control of my life again and not be afraid of what anyone else will do to me just because I'm alive."

He had no idea what to say to that, everything that came to mind seemed out of place or foolish, so in the end he just held her.

"I love you Jay," she sobbed eventually, "And I will not marry Dael."

Well, that makes life interesting, Jayden thought, careful not to let the concern show in his expression.

With the marriage already arranged, the only way out he could see for Rhianna was to leave Grandell and go somewhere Dael would never find her, and he couldn't let her do that on her own.

It took only a moment for Jayden to make his decision, and despite the fact they had both grown up here, and almost everything they knew and loved was in this small town, he found it wasn't a very difficult decision at that.

"When do you want to leave?" he said as he finally turned to look at her.

Very, very slowly she lifted her head off his shoulder to look into his eyes, and for what seemed like the first time in ages he thought he saw hope in her expression.

"Really?" she asked, her eyes searching hard for any sign of a lie.

"Really," he answered with a small grin as the first fat raindrops began to fall.

"We should wait a few days though. Dael will be watching you closely for the next week or so."

"To make sure I don't run off again," Rhianna finished with a grimace.

"Exactly. When we leave Grandell, we will want as much of a head start as we can get. I'm sure I can get some supplies from my father and we both have good horses..." he faltered.

"But Rhianna, if we do this, you know as well as I do that Dael will come after us," he told her finally, "And he'll bring his guards."

"I will not marry Dael!" she repeated.

"I wouldn't marry him even..." she stopped for a second, as if unsure of herself, before proceeding, "Even if I wasn't in love with you."

It wasn't the first time she had told him, even today, but it was still new enough to send a thrill of delight through him and add a quick smile to his otherwise serious face.

The rain suddenly became persistent, the fat drops replaced by a driving torrent from above as a fresh wind blew in from the sea below. The gulls which had been fishing for their lunch only a few minutes before had all but disappeared ahead of the rain, and although the water coming down from the clouds above was slightly warm, the deluge wouldn't make the trip back to Grandell any easier for them as they descended the steep, slippery path.

"Rhianna, we should probably head back soon," he suggested, not sure how she would react.

For a moment her face fell, but then she stood, letting go of his hand and stepping back from the cliff edge.

Jayden followed almost immediately, but Rhianna stood gazing out at the sea and storm, which was quickly gathering momentum just off the coast.

"I will never stand here again," she said with quiet conviction before meeting his eyes.

He had known Rhianna his whole life, and this was the place she always came when she had a problem she needed to sort through in her mind. Now he thought about it though, he had never actually seen anyone else up here with her, and he wondered whether anyone else in Grandell even remembered the ancient track existed. It began as nothing more than a few fallen trees and a jumble of rocks well back into the forest, a long way from anywhere you would go in your daily routines.

He looked out over the Jade Coast as far as the falling rain would let him see, and then out at the green and azure Sea of Dreams. It was possible no one else had shared this view since the path had been cut untold years ago.

"I think we should live somewhere by the coast, I've always liked the sound of the waves," Rhianna said as she turned her back on the ocean for the final time.

Jayden couldn't help but smile. It was the first time she had said a positive word about the future since the day she had drowned. Even now Jayden still wasn't sure what had happened that day. He had no ability in the Gift, of that he was sure; but dead people didn't spontaneously come back to life either, and she had not been breathing when they'd pulled her from the river. On the other hand, he also found he didn't really care. He never had, not from the moment she'd taken that first gasping breath. Rhianna was alive and well, and that was enough for him.

As he turned to leave, the downpour ceased as abruptly as it had begun, and he cast one last glance out at the ocean before following Rhianna carefully down the cleft in the pitted, stone plateau. Grandell awaited them in the valley below, and he had no idea how to tell his parents he would not be coming back, or even if he should. There were so many things to decide, so many details to prepare. It was a little overwhelming.

Leaving Grandell would be easy, staying ahead of Dael's trackers and guards would not.

As two of the town's wealthiest merchant families, both his own and Rhianna's parents had often sent them to play with Dael when the three of them had been children, and the young noble had always been a bully. Over the last few years though, ever since the old count's death and his ascension to his father's title, Dael had changed. It had already begun before Dael's father had passed away, but the sudden inheritance of power and the realisation the commoners had no choice but to do as he commanded seemed to push Dael over some kind of edge, making him colder, more aloof than before.

There was no doubt in Jayden's mind that Dael would order his guards out to bring them back, or at least to bring Rhianna back as soon as he found out she was missing. It didn't seem likely they would thank him for his efforts and send him on his way either.

As the two of them walked back down the cliff edge trail toward the cover of the forest canopy, it occurred to

Jayden they would have to make a living for themselves if they managed to escape. He knew enough about the running of a ship to find employment as a hand on most vessels, but that would keep him at sea for phases at a time, perhaps entire seasons, and away from Rhianna. He could take up a trade he supposed. He would be old to take an apprenticeship with one of the guild houses, but it wasn't unheard of. Anyway, there was plenty of time to solve that question, and there were many others which demanded much more immediate consideration, like where to go and how to raise the funds to get there without letting anyone know they were going.

When they finally turned away from the cliffs and entered the cover of the forest path, Jayden realised Rhianna was as soaked through as he was from the sudden downpour. There wasn't much to do about it though since it had been far too hot to wear a coat when he had trudged his way up here earlier on in the day. For a while they walked on in silence, eyes downcast as they carefully made their way down the slippery mud track.

"Do you ever think about where your life is headed?" Rhianna asked as they came to a small clearing in the surrounding trees, pierced by a misty stream of sunlight slanting in through the leaves above.

The rain had stopped several minutes before, but Jayden was still catching drips that were making their way through the thick foliage as he slowed to regard his best friend.

"Sometimes," he replied. "Why do you ask?"

Rhianna looked around before moving to sit on a waist high, moss-covered rock which lay beside the path.

"I don't really want to go back there," she said, absently

staring off through the forest in the direction which Grandell lay.

"I know," he acknowledged, once again taking hold of her hands, "But if you want to avoid this arranged marriage to Dael, then we have to get away from Grandell clean. That means not arousing his suspicions while we prepare for the journey. If we leave now, some farmer or townsperson is sure to see us, and if that happens, word will reach Dael before sundown. He will have you back here by dawn and me for lunch for helping you escape."

"You're afraid," Rhianna accused, snatching her hands back and pulling her knees up to her chin.

"Of course I am. Dael has an entire garrison at his command and I'm running off with his future wife. Or at least that is how he will see it," Jayden responded in no uncertain terms.

"I will not marry Dael," Rhianna told him yet again.

"You won't have to," he assured her, "But we can't afford to make any mistakes. You, more than anyone, know just how much he has changed since he took on his father's title. If he finds out what we're up to he will no doubt order the garrison to confine you to the keep until the ceremony. If that happens, the hard truth is that I have no sure method for getting you out," he told her pointedly. "Not to mention he'd kill me if I tried."

The dripping of the rain was the only real sound occupying the next few moments until a brightly coloured bird swooped right between them, giving them both a start. Jayden barked a short laugh, but Rhianna just watched as the bird winged its way up into the canopy of leaves above, sending a flurry of thick raindrops plummeting towards the earth.

"I'm sorry," she said as she slid down off the rock. "I just want this all to be over."

Jayden smiled as she came into his arms.

"In a week or two Grandell will be nothing but a bad memory. We will be far from here and on our way to a whole new life," he told her as convincingly as he could. Privately he was sure of no such thing, but he didn't want to add to her worries right at the moment, so he left that bit out.

"You promise?" she asked as she pulled away from him.

"Of course," Jayden replied, hoping desperately that he wasn't lying through his teeth.

*　　*　　*

Finally believing what she saw in his eyes, Rhianna reached across and took Jayden's hand again before starting slowly back down the track which led to Grandell.

She would go back. Knowing this would be the last time gave her that much strength at least.

"Come on," she told Jayden at length, "The sooner we get back the sooner we can leave."

As soon as the words were out of her mouth, a whole nest of butterflies seemed to rise up in her stomach. She was terrified of leaving the place she had grown up. Unlike Jayden, she had never been further away from Grandell than the edge of the Anchorhead Promontory where it was joined to the mainland. What lay beyond was no more real to her than the tapestries and paintings her real parents had kept as decoration on the walls of their house.

Even so, she had no hesitation about leaving if Jayden was with her. Whatever waited to the west had to be better than marrying that twisted little tyrant who was now Count of Grandell.

She would escape, no matter that the contract had been signed. She had been afraid to tell Jayden that part. Her foster parents had already signed the document which made the marriage legal, but she had overheard them adding a clause which said Dael had to wait an entire season, three whole phases before the ceremony could be held. After all, they wanted nothing about it to seem improper.

She despised the Ginfrons for signing that contract, but it did give her a little breathing room to work with.

But only a breath

She would just have to see how long she could hold it.

The worth of a man can be found by taking his every secret desire, and examining those upon which he acts, and those upon which he does not.
Ancient Jeranonian proverb.

CHAPTER 2

DAEL

The sun had finally emerged from behind iron-grey clouds and was just sinking below the western horizon by the time Rhianna led Jayden out of the canopied forest path. A few birds flew gracefully overhead, casting long shadows in the burnt orange light of dusk as they winged their way back to nesting sites, and the tang of ocean salt in the air was gradually being replaced by the acrid scent of wood-smoke coming from the lit ovens of Grandell's homes.

As they entered the township proper, the sun disappeared behind the mud-brick peasant houses which crowded both sides of the path, and both she and Jayden were grateful to no longer have to squint against its glare.

Most of the rude, one-storey log and mud structures had appeared since Dael's ascension to power, and were populated mainly by the farmers and craftsmen his unjustifiably high taxes had forced off their land.

He brought them here to work off their debts as servants in the keep. Some of the worst constructions were finished with thatch roofs for the Maker's sake, Rhianna noted grimly.

As though clay tiles are hard to come by.

The poor excuse for housing he provided these unfortunates with was nothing more than a show for the city people. 'Demonstrating my generosity and goodwill to all,' Dael had said when opening them at a ceremony last year. She had wondered from time to time whether Dael was actually fooling anyone but himself with the gesture. It was just one more thing to despise him for.

As they continued through the poorest quarter of the otherwise prosperous town, the sound of horses reached her preoccupied mind a moment before a loud voice commanded from behind.

"Halt where you are!"

"Let me handle this," Rhianna whispered, placing a restraining hand on Jayden's arm as he turned.

A pair of guards dismounted, dressed in Dael's grey and maroon livery. The guard on the left passed his horse's reins to his companion before approaching them with a cocky swagger, hand on the hilt of his sword.

"What seems to be the problem?" Rhianna asked before Jayden could act, adopting a tone of arrogant irritation.

I should have told Jayden about this before now, she thought.

She'd been dreading this confrontation. She knew it was inevitable, but she hadn't been expecting the guards to find her so soon.

"Count Dael has ordered that you be brought back to the keep as soon as you were found," the burly guard said as he approached them, before turning to give Jayden a contemptuous stare.

"The count will not be happy to learn you were with her."

The big guard reached out and took hold of Rhianna's arm.

Jayden took a step forward to intervene, but quick as he

was, Rhianna's knee found the guard's groin before he could do more than that, and the big man dropped to his knees, relinquishing his grip as he fell.

"If Dael truly wishes me to be his bride, then you will treat me with all the respect due the future Countess of Grandell," she told him as she backed off a step and waited, prompting the other man to rush over and help his fallen companion, but not to draw his weapon.

After a long moment, the guard painfully regained his footing with the help of his comrade.

"You may be the count's betrothed," he told her spitefully, "But have no illusions Rhianna, you are no lady."

"Never claimed to be," she replied in an offhand manner, "But I have a more favourable position with the count than you."

She locked her dark brown eyes with his. "Don't ever cross me."

Jayden stared at her for a moment in surprise, but she kept her attention on the guard.

"Very well, Rhianna. Play your games," the guard said with an arrogant smirk as he hobbled back to his horse, and with great difficulty remounted the beige mare.

"No games, guardsman. If you handle me again in that manner I will have you hung."

The big man looked at her in disbelief, then had the audacity to laugh.

"You don't have the authority, or the support."

Rhianna smiled as she took a few graceful steps forward.

"Do you truly think I need either when I have the count wrapped around my little finger," she asked sweetly, waving at the guard with that same little finger. "It would be a simple matter for me to tell the count that you handled his future bride… inappropriately. He would have no choice but to make an example of you, even if for no other reason than to quell the rumours which I would no doubt start."

The guard gave her a hard stare, taking her measure, but for the first time since ordering them to halt he seemed to take her seriously.

"I still have to escort you back to the keep," he told her in no uncertain terms.

She continued staring at him for a long moment, her sweet smile turning mischievous as it crept further across her face.

"If those are your orders," she allowed.

"Of course, I can't walk like any ordinary peasant. I am the count's betrothed after all. I know, I'm going to need a horse, and I think yours will do nicely. After all, you know how delicate we noble ladies are, don't you?"

The guard scowled at her for a second, the beginnings of a serious anger building on his face. At least until Rhianna let her head loll to the side, sticking out her tongue and doing a fair mime of someone hanging from a gibbet. The guard scowled again, but dismounted, clearly still in some amount of pain, before handing her the reigns as she walked over to take them.

She swung nimbly up on to the beige's back, her long hair whipping around as she did. As soon as she was settled, she reached down to pinch the guard's cheek like her mother used to do when she was a child.

"Good boy," she told him in her most condescending manner.

The guard growled as he jerked away from the contact, and Rhianna laughed.

"Easy boy, when you make sounds like a dog, it makes me think the count's order to bring me back might have included the word fetch."

She saw Jayden struggling to hide a grin as the big guard curled his hands into fists and went red in the face, but restrained himself from saying anything further.

As Rhianna started the horse walking, Jayden fell in beside her as the two guards followed a few steps behind, one mounted and one on foot.

"You're just going to go with them?"

"Better this than in chains," she whispered, then reached down to touch his shoulder when she saw his shocked expression.

"I know what I have to do," she said loud enough for the guards to hear, "Goodbye Jayden. Thank you for coming to find me. Perhaps I'll return the favour someday."

With that, she prodded the horse to a trot, forcing the burly guardsman whose mount she was riding to jog or be left behind, which he did with yet another pained scowl.

When the guards both followed her and left Jayden without further harassment, she breathed a sigh of relief. She was nearing the centre of town now, and here both people and activity were still plentiful. She had known most of them for years if not her whole life, but as she rounded a corner and came within sight of Grandell's massive, fortified keep, she suddenly felt very much alone.

*   *   *

Jayden continued walking up the stone-paved street by himself as he watched the trio move further and further away, finally disappearing around a corner.

Rhianna's hint had been a little too obvious, and he hoped the guards hadn't picked up on it. It would be more difficult to conceal his preparations for leaving Grandell if he had to keep suitable provisions ready enough to leave at a moment's notice, but it was not impossible. Most of what they would need could be gathered and stowed at the back of his parents' hayloft, and of course Strider, his beige stallion, could be prepared on the instant. He assumed Rhianna would bring her own mount, but it would be better to have another available in case it was needed. That only left the question of where they were to go once they made good their escape from the trackers Dael was sure to send after them.

He kept walking as he thought on the problem, even considering appealing to another noble for protection. Despite his new relationship to Rhianna via her aunt, the Baron down in Damerette was outranked by Dael, and unlikely to have the ability to successfully intercede. Duke Timon was Dael's superior in the duchy of Lansia and had the power, but was also bound to obey the law when called upon for mediation between commoner and nobility. In the end, Jayden decided that his answer might well be not to give them shelter given the law script Dael had produced for the Ginfrons, and any such request would most likely lead to Dael being summoned to Conclave City for the proceedings. It was too big a risk.

As he continued through the town, the windows in the surrounding houses began to glow yellow as candles lit by the people who lived there replaced the fading sunlight. Jayden eventually passed the three-storey mansion which had belonged to Rhianna's parents. It was one of the largest structures in Grandell beside the keep, and definitely the most ornate. They had died last dawn of spring, a few phases before Rhianna's accident, a wild storm sinking the ship they were taking to the capital. Rhianna herself should have been amongst those lost, and Jayden found himself thanking the Maker yet again that she had been too ill at the time to accompany Paiter and Kathrine on the trip.

At the moment though, all but a few of the rooms which could be seen from the street were dark, only those of the servants' quarters and the entryway exuding the soft glow of candlelight as far as he could see. That in itself was strange, Rhianna's foster parents, whom Jayden understood to be some distant relations of hers, had appeared less than a phase after her mother and father had been killed, and were not known for their social fervour. Rather, they were notoriously hard to coax out of the mansion which they had taken custody of until Rhianna reached her twentieth birthday next year and came into her inheritance. Jayden wondered where they were now. It was possible they were out looking for her just as he had been, but he found that notion unlikely as they employed plenty of lackeys who could be commanded to conduct the search for them.

He didn't know much about the Ginfrons, but he got the impression that before they'd come to Grandell they hadn't been very well off.

He'd always found that a little odd, as Rhianna's real parents had always been generous people. It was hard to believe Paiter and Kathrine wouldn't have provided for relatives close enough to be entrusted with Rhianna's guardianship if the worst were to occur.

With only a vague suspicion that something was amiss though, there wasn't much more he could do than take notice of anything out of the ordinary, and hope the sinister notion was nothing more than his imagination getting the better of him.

Rhianna was a joy to be around, or at least she was when it seemed half the world wasn't trying to pull her down, but keeping her safe was becoming a full-time job.

Not that it isn't worth it, he hastily amended, but sometimes he wondered if there would ever come a time when they would just be able to be happy.

Shaking off that frustrating thought he continued the journey along the main street until he arrived at the carriageway which serviced his family's manor house, the structure straddling a shallow hill. The rain had barely loosened the dirt here, where it had been packed hard by years of foot traffic and the horse-drawn carriages which came and went in a constant stream to visit Grandell's most prosperous merchant. His father ran a fleet of small fishing boats along the coast as well as three trading vessels. The largest of them was Crest, a triple-masted giant which David personally captained once or twice a year on a trip to Jeranon's capital of Aramar, where he made a good percentage of their annual income. The other main asset Jayden's family owned were the sprawling vineyards which lay directly to the north of Grandell's main population. Technically they belonged to his father, but for as long as Jayden could remember, his mother had made the final decisions concerning that portion of the family business, and quite a portion it was too. The wines and vinegars which the vast estates produced were exported over half of Jeranon, to say nothing of the small army of labourers it took to work the fields and drive the delivery carts. Lyssa oversaw it all.

He had never quite understood how his mother could keep everything running smoothly with so many things constantly going on around her, but as a person who thrived on details, he had to admit she was perfectly suited to the task.

Once again lost in thought, he noticed far too late there were already two carriages parked outside the entrance to his home. One bore the familiar green and yellow markings of Rhianna's merchant Sigel, the other was painted an ominous black, a red sun rising over a grey ocean embossed on its gilded door.

Dael's emblem.

The count must have decided that Jayden had something to do with Rhianna's disappearance, or at least that he knew where to find her. There was no other reason for both Dael and Rhianna's foster parents to be here at the same time.

Well, Jayden thought ruefully, *he's right on the second count, and he'll soon be right about the other as well.*

He considered trying to sneak in through the back door, but Dael's carriage driver had already noticed him, and would surely tell his liege if Jayden went scampering off into the woods behind the house.

He couldn't help but grin as he pictured how ridiculous he would look scampering past the carriage in full view of the driver, while giving the man a comical wink and a nod to tell him to keep the secret.

Putting the stupid image out of his mind he walked confidently up to the heavy wooden door of the sprawling, single-storey manor house, even giving the driver a nod of greeting on the way before knocking firmly with the brass handle. *What kind of a word was scamper, anyway?*

Within a few seconds an over-tall teenager only a few years younger than himself opened the door, and seeing who was there he moved aside with a quick bow.

"Your parents, Count Dael and the Ginfrons await you in the sitting room," he said in a quiet voice.

"And Miya?" Jayden asked after his little sister, who was still only nine years old, and would not be able to defend herself if this meeting went poorly.

"Safe at Marissa Horgan's birthday celebrations."

"Thanks Jake," Jayden replied as he gave the young man a quick nod. Jake was a hired hand, not a house servant, although he performed some duties such as greeting guests and taking care of the various plants Jayden's mother insisted on scattering around the house.

"Oh, and Jayden," the tall youth added. "The count does not look happy."

"Nonsense," Jayden returned, matching his tone.

"Give him a few minutes, then you'll see just what unhappy really looks like on Dael's face."

At that, Jake's own face broke out in a mischievous grin which he was still trying to suppress as Jayden continued on, down the long corridor towards the large sitting room where Jake had told him the others were waiting.

He could imagine how this would go as he moved through the huge manor in his still drying clothes, barely noticing the mess he left on the carpeted floors or the new painting which now adorned the left side of the entryway. That hadn't been there this morning. Dael would be in a fury as usual, accusations would be made, and eventually it would likely come to blows. If Dael were anyone but the nobility, a magistrate would have sentenced him to military service in the west years ago for displays of public violence. Yet Jayden didn't think Dael was ready to shed blood over this situation with Rhianna quite yet. Soon, if he knew his one-time friend as well as he used to, but not yet.

Of course, if he were wrong, Jayden doubted he would live through the night, but Dael was habitually cruel, and liked to toy with both prey and rivals alike, and in Dael's mind he still held all the power here. Fortunately, that gave him a little time. On the other hand, the count was nobody's fool. If he sensed in any way he was the one being played, Dael would likely take out the needle thin rapier which never left his side anymore, and run it straight through Jayden's heart, right here in his own home. If it came to that, Jayden doubted Dael would feel the slightest twinge of regret, either.

The door to the sitting room was just ahead now, and as Jayden stopped in front of it he took a deep breath, prepared himself, and pushed it open.

"What have you done with Rhianna?!" was the first angry shout that reached his ears as he was revealed to Dael's sight.

As the door finished opening Jayden stepped inside the room, noticing too late that in the corner to his right, hidden behind the inward swinging door, was a pair of Dael's personal guard. They remained still at the moment, but Jayden was under no illusions they were only there for decoration, or that Dael couldn't call upon them at any time if he so chose. For a long second Jayden hoped he hadn't badly miscalculated just how far into the chase they really were.

"I imagine she's reached the keep by now," he told the furious noble as he moved further into the room, taking a seat near the small fire to help dry himself off. Dael clearly wanted to intimidate him with the presence of the guards, so Jayden did his level best to appear more confident than he felt.

"At least, that's where she was headed when we parted ways a little over half an hour ago."

He could feel the seven pairs of eyes which were keenly staring at him as he motioned to a servant who was little more than a child and also Jake's little sister, to pour him a drink. Despite her youth the girl moved efficiently to bring him a glass of the iced tea his mother always kept standing on a table to one side of the room on hot days, the Gift-wrought glass pitcher keeping it refreshingly cold despite the day's abominable heat.

"Thank you, Marion," he told the girl as she handed him the glass with a smile and returned to where she'd been sitting cross-legged near the empty fireplace. It was unusual to have such a young servant, but Jake and Marion's father had been his mother's right hand in the vineyards for over twenty years. When he had died without warning a few years back the children had become orphans. Due to their long friendship, Lyssa hadn't hesitated to take in his children, and while Jake and Marion performed a few basic tasks in return for their keep, they were more like family than employees by now.

"I see," Dael replied flatly.

It was clear the young count wanted to say more, but with his reason for harassing Jayden gone he couldn't very well haul him off to the keep for questioning. Not with so many influential witnesses around anyhow.

Jayden had no illusions that obstacle would hold him for long.

He would have to watch his back for the next few days

and try to stay in public places until Dael's tantrum had passed, again. He was fed up with being made to live like this; always having to look over his shoulder in case Dael had decided today was a good day to put him in his place. He'd done it before, and for that beating alone Jayden counted a score to settle with this man he'd once called a friend. Not that the ledgers were ever likely to be balanced, not with their imminent departure from Grandell and Dael's sphere of influence.

"Yes, it's a pity you didn't know enough about your future bride to guess where she would be," he said, taking a long drink from the chilled glass in his hand. There were shocked looks from both of his parents, and for a second he thought he'd gone too far as Dael shot up from his chair, turning red and taking a threatening step forward.

"I assume you've told my parents, who are so graciously hosting you this fine afternoon that you are forcing Rhianna into a marriage she is completely opposed to."

If anything, Dael became redder as he stared daggers at Jayden, but he stopped his advance.

"Is this true?" David Torell, Jayden's father, angrily demanded; his eyes switching between his son, Dael, and the Ginfrons, who were trying hard not to meet his furious gaze.

No one spoke, but the mood in the room was clear.

"You two told me when you arrived that you had asked the count to help find Rhianna because she had been missing for two days. Is this why?"

Again, there was only a guilty silence from the pair, but it was as good as a confirmation as they continued to avoid his gaze.

"I don't know who you people are," David told the Ginfrons, his dark eyes flashing, "And I don't know where you came from or how you got here so quickly after Paiter and Kathrine's accident, but until Rhianna inherits her parents' estate, you two are supposed to be looking after her best interests."

David fell silent, his arms crossed and waiting for a response which was quite a long time coming.

Jayden could see his father running out of patience. It took a moment, but Gerald Ginfron brought himself to meet David's stare, and although the smaller man flinched away again for a second when he met David's gaze, his eyes eventually held.

"David, how can you say arranging a marriage to the only noble within a hundred miles is not in her best interests?"

David's arms dropped limply to his sides, and his furious eyes became very cold indeed.

"Did you just say this was an arranged marriage?" he asked quietly, "That's not even legal."

"You at least should know that," he told the count flatly as he turned his attention back to Dael.

Far from intimidating the noble though, David's statement triggered a predatory grin which overtook Dael's face as he crossed his arms over his well-muscled torso, rippling the fabric of his black calf length coat and stretching the grey and red emblem across his chest for everyone to see.

"As it happens you are wrong," he replied in his most self-satisfied voice.

"While it is true the law forbids nobles from forcing arranged marriages on commoners, that same law clearly states only that a 'link of relationship' to the nobility is required for an arranged marriage to go ahead."

"But there is none," David shot back. "Both Rhianna and her parents are commoners, they have no relation to Jeranon's nobility."

"Wrong again, David. You must be slipping in your old age," Dael insolently replied.

"I recently became aware the old Earl of Damerette has been wed to a commoner, once quite a beauty by all accounts and Kathrine's auntie no less."

"That is not a blood link," David said, struggling to keep his fury in check.

"Turns out it doesn't have to be," Dael replied cheerfully as he picked at a bit of fluff which had attached itself to his coat.

"So you see, it's all perfectly legal, and there's not a thing you can do about it. I will marry the girl, and you will stand by and do... nothing. Quite frankly, I don't see why you're getting so worked up about all this. After all, it's not like she's your daughter David. She's Paiter and Kathrine's. Or is she?" he asked with a slyly raised eyebrow and a calculatedly condescending grin.

The two guards against the wall glanced at each other and Jayden subtly prepared himself to leap out of his chair and help his father if necessary, even as David balled his powerful hands into fists and took a step towards the young noble.

"You dare to come into my house and insult my honour!" David shouted, "Paiter and Kathrine were our best friends! That girl is like a niece to us both and I know for a fact you are probably her most hated person on this earth. What did you do to make her agree to this? And why choose her in the first place when you know how she feels about you?"

There was a sudden silence after his father had finished, and Jayden became sure Dael was about to order his guards to do something drastic. The air between the two men radiated hostility like heat-waves coming off an iron stove.

"You presume to tell me what I dare!" Dael demanded instead.

"You would do well to remember you are only a merchant David, and a commoner at that. I, on the other hand am your ruler, and what I say is law! It would be a simple matter to have you hanging from a gallows in the town square."

Lyssa gasped, and Jayden stood from his chair while motioning subtly for Marion to move as far back into the corner as she could. The guards by the door had their hands on their sword hilts now, and Jayden was beginning to wonder whether he would in fact leave this room in one piece.

"My ruler! The king is my ruler, Dael. Grandell is too small to need a viscount, and so only the barons stand below you in rank. Do not delude yourself boy, you are the most minor of nobles running a far-flung rural district. Now answer my question!"

"Boy? I'm twice the man you will ever be, David," Dael replied coldly, his voice returning to a more normal level as the self-satisfied smirk returned to his face.

"And as for your question, I didn't have to do anything to make her agree to the marriage. As a nobleman with no older kin it is my right to arrange my marriage with any suitable woman of an appropriate age. So long as there is a… 'link of relationship' to the nobility of course," he added with just the right timing to add insult to injury.

"As for why her… well, Rhianna's a beautiful woman David, and I'm a man of shall we say, appetites. I'm sure you can figure out the rest."

David took a step forward, and although he didn't intend it to be menacing, it certainly looked that way to Jayden, and obviously to the pair of guards still standing near the doorway who loosened the swords in their scabbards in response. His father abruptly turned to face the Ginfrons, who sat, silent and timid, watching the exchange from one of the three expensive cushioned couches which dominated the room.

"You two must have agreed to this!" David shouted, suddenly turning his anger on them.

"Dael might have the right to arrange his own marriage, but he would need your consent as Rhianna's guardians to make it legal. What did you do?" he asked coldly as he turned again to face the still smirking count.

"Nothing really," Dael replied as the smirk became even more pronounced, "Just a small bribe. Quite small actually," he said with a chuckle.

David's eyes blazed as he rounded on the Ginfrons, knuckles stained white from clenching his fists as he stood over the pair.

"You are no longer welcome in this house. Don't ever come here again."

Rhianna's foster parents stood quickly from the couch, and as they moved past David, the big man refused to acknowledge them, his back now facing the mortified pair.

"David," Gerald said nervously as his skinny wife pulled at his arm to keep him moving.

Whatever Gerald had been about to say was lost as David spun, took two quick steps and slammed his fist into Gerald's jaw, lifting the loathsome little man off the floor with a crack as his jawbone gave way under the force of David's blow.

"I said get out!" he bellowed even before Gerald had hit the ground, his fall only slightly cushioned by the thick carpets which lined the sitting room floor.

For an instant there was silence as Gerald landed hard on his back. When he tried to speak, he realised that his jaw was broken, not just hurt, and he cupped both hands over his bloodied mouth. Another tug on the arm from Gerald's wife was enough to break his momentary paralysis and send the slight man scrambling out of the room as soon as he regained his now unsteady feet.

As the pair fled around the corner and out of sight, David turned at the sound of Dael slowly clapping.

"Well done David," the count said glibly.

"One might be tempted to think you were still in the guard with a strike like that. I see you haven't lost your touch."

"Your father would never have approved of this," David told him almost calmly. The fury which had seen him strike out at Gerald a moment before seemed to have fled, and once again David was in control of himself and all that surrounded him, much like how he appeared when he stood bellowing orders from the foredeck of his beloved 'Crest'.

"It matters not at all," Dael returned with a suddenly serious face.

"My father, whom you so eloquently compare me to, is dead. I rule Grandell now and you would do well to remember that necromancy is outlawed in Jeranon."

He turned a quick smirk and a wink at Jayden before returning his attention to the big man in front of him.

"Your son's ghost will not come back from the grave to help you if you cross paths with me."

"It won't need to Dael, your own arrogance will be your undoing."

"You may be right," the count allowed with a laugh.

"After all, who else could get the better of me, than me?" With a small gesture he motioned the guards to wait outside before making his way to the door himself. As he reached it he turned, fixing Jayden with a pointed stare.

"If I see the two of you together again, your mother will be delivering flowers to your grave."

With a mocking bow to Lyssa he left the room and Jayden found himself having to forcibly uncurl his fists and stop his hands from shaking. He couldn't tell whether it was with anger or fear, but hoped it was the former. Dael was certainly capable of carrying out his threats, and now more than ever Jayden wondered what had changed him into such a tyrant. He had always been cruel as a child, but Jayden couldn't help but think there must be more to it than just a cruel child grown abusive of the limited power he had inherited as the new Count of Grandell. To listen to Dael, you would think he controlled half of Jeranon, when in fact his writ ended not even a hundred miles to the north, and not quite half that to the south and west.

The last two years had changed his one-time childhood friend so much it was hard to believe Dael was even the same boy he and Rhianna had grown up with. Still, even with this latest tantrum, everything would turn out all right, somehow. Wishful thinking perhaps, but what else was there? The power of men like Dael lay in intimidation and threats. Unfortunately for Jayden, Dael had Grandell's garrison to back his up.

"I want you to go to Crest," his father told him abruptly.

"There are a few things I need to get from the ship before I sail on the morning tide. I wish the timing weren't so bad, but it can't be helped now. I want you to wait for me in my cabin. I'll join you there in a few minutes."

"What, now?" Jayden asked over his mother exclaiming, "You can't be serious."

"No, tomorrow when Crest is halfway down the peninsula," David replied sarcastically.

"Of course now! Now go."

Jayden retreated from the room with a frown as his father began saying something to his mother which Jayden couldn't quite catch.

David had snapped at him. His father never snapped at anyone. In fact, now that he thought about it, he wasn't sure he'd ever seen his father angrier than just now. David Torell simply didn't lose his temper, he didn't need to. He was just one of those people whom others listened to when he spoke. He said it was something he had picked up since taking command of his first ship, but Jayden had always thought it had more to do with the man than any rank he might have achieved.

As he passed Jake in the corridor, the tall servant handed him the rare, curved Oo'vi blade in its scabbard which was one of Jayden's most prized possessions, and half whispered with a laugh, "I don't know what you said to him, but the count was not happy when he left. Didn't even wait for his guards to mount the coach before driving off. Made the poor brutes walk all the way back to the keep."

"It's a warm night and they're big boys," Jayden answered as he tied the scabbard of the sheathed blade to his belt, but then stopped.

"Go and see if Marion's all right, she was looking a bit shaken when I left. And Jake, thanks," he said, patting the blade which was now secured against his left leg, before turning towards the door.

He opened it a crack, checking to see that Dael and his men had indeed left, then exited the house when he saw they were gone. With another cautious survey of the surrounding trees he headed down the drive, which for once was empty of traffic, and set off purposely towards the docks. He was probably just being silly though, if Dael was going to do something he would have done it back at the house. He wasn't the type to lurk in the bushes.

While he was inside, the sun had finished setting and a gibbous moon had risen beyond the hills to the east, bathing the landscape in a yellow glow that was bright for this time of year. The clouds had finally drifted off towards the Sea of Dreams, but the night was still hot and muggy. Thankfully though it was nothing compared to the oven-like temperatures of earlier in the day.

The walk from his house down to the docks where Crest was tied up took him the better part of an hour, and he suddenly wondered why he hadn't ridden Strider down here instead of making his way on foot. He walked along the waterfront for another few minutes until he reached the longest pier in the harbour, then continued out onto the solid wooden construction which his father had purchased from the previous count several years ago. David's crews had spent a year rebuilding the dilapidated wreck for his own personal use, until now it was the deepest draught mooring in the cove.

To either side of the dock, a single masted fishing boat was tied up for the night with only a skeleton crew aboard, the rest of their sailors no doubt on shore leave after delivering their cargo successfully back to Grandell. The other dozen on this part of the coast would still be out at sea, along with Spray and Fortune, the other two trading ships in his father's fleet. Straight ahead though, weighed down with goods and ready to depart on the morning tide was the hulking form of Crest. Backlit by the enormous moon, the silhouette of the huge ship seemed like something out of a story as it rested, completely still in the sheltered waters of the cove.

All the sails were tied and secured, and as Jayden reached the end of the dock he called out, "Hello the ship!"

For a moment there was no answer, and then Esdern, the ship's boy, poked his head over the rail.

"Is that you Jayden?" he called back, and it was clear he couldn't see who was standing in the shadow of the giant vessel despite his searching gaze.

"Yeah, it's me," Jayden called back.

"I'm coming on board so get someone to help lower the gangway."

"Yes Sir!" Esdern replied before disappearing behind the rail.

Officially Jayden had no actual rank on board Crest. Unofficially however, everyone knew his father was training him to take over as captain when he finally retired. If that did in fact ever happen.

The short wait while Esdern got the night watchmen to swing the thin wooden gangplank out onto the pier was not entirely unpleasant despite the night's earlier activities, and Jayden grew sleepy as he listened to the gentle sloshing of water against the pylons below the dock.

The gangplank eventually hit the pier with a thump and the watchman called out an apology as he saw Jayden start at the noise.

Jayden hated being startled, he always jumped like an idiot when someone managed to sneak up on him, or on occasions like this where a sudden loud noise was involved. Still, he supposed it was no less than he deserved for not paying attention.

As he crossed the thin beam he told the watchman, Nicholas he thought the man's name was, to leave the gangplank down for his father who would arrive shortly. The heavy-set man was new to Crest's crew and Jayden hadn't sailed with him yet, but if his father had hired him then Nicholas knew what he was about. No sailor made it on board Crest without at least a few years' experience, and even then, his father was picky about the people who crewed his flagship. The watchman gave him a quick acknowledgement before returning to his post on the afterdeck where he had a clear view of the whole ship and the pier it was tied up at. Jayden nodded to himself as he saw everything was in order, then walked across the deck and opened the hatch which led to the bowels of the ship. Climbing down the steep ladder he did an about face and headed back towards the prow where the captain's cabin was located. Making sure no one was watching or listening, he whispered a short phrase into the lock and heard the latch open from the inside. His father had done a few favours for various magi over the years, and as a result Crest had a few little oddities that no other ship he was aware of possessed. The locks were one, and could be set to accept whatever pass phrase you desired, or just used as a normal latch if that were preferred.

He pushed open the door and entered the sparse, though well-appointed cabin.

Secured against the left wall was his father's bed, above which was a shelf with a rail six inches above it to keep the books stored there from falling off at every roll of the hull. The opposite wall held a beautifully painted map of the known world. It focused on Jeranon but ranged from the ancestral lands of Jeranah, which his people claimed far to the northeast on the other side of the Sea of Dreams, all the way across the huge sprawling continent which contained Jeranon and the western nations who lived beyond the Dark Iron Mountains. From there the map travelled south, across the Western Waters and down to the southern continent of Avsan. Scattered across the various oceans were dozens of islands, some merely specks on the painting and some larger with names written beside them to mark their importance.

The entire Anchorhead Promontory on which he had spent most of his life was little more than eight inches long on the wall-sized map. Seeing it for the first time as a child was what had opened his eyes and made him dream of adventure in the first place. That and the two giant claws from some horrific sea monster his father had fought off before Jayden had been born, which he knew were mounted behind him on either side of the doorway. He had never seen a sea monster himself, but from the four-foot long claws which adorned the cabin wall, he wasn't sure he wanted to either. In the middle of the room an antique mahogany desk was nailed to the deck. In its locked draws were his father's navigational maps and charts, scrawled with the locations of tiny reefs and treacherous currents which the captain was constantly marking out when he discovered them.

Jayden walked around the desk to the far end of the room before unlocking and opening the small window which opened out just below the swordfish figurehead that stood sentinel on the main deck. The air was still warm, but at least the breeze was stopping him from feeling too sleepy. He stood that way for quite some time and then jumped, feeling stupid as he nearly hit his head on the low ceiling when someone coughed loudly behind him. Spinning, he was relieved to see it was only his father, looking slightly amused at the fright he had caused, but otherwise in a thoughtful mood. David closed the door behind him as he entered the cabin and moved to sit on the edge of the desk.

All sorts of warning bells started going off in Jayden's mind as his father began to speak. He was too serious. David was an easy-going man unless on watch as captain, or when he had some terrible news to impart, and Jayden had the distinct impression this was no exception.

"Son, I have to ask you something. And I need the truth."

In all his life Jayden could never remember his father asking him not to lie, he didn't need to. It was just a given to Jayden that he could discuss anything with his father, for the simple reason that David Torell made it a practice never to make light of what his children had to say.

"Okay," he replied, a little uneasily, "What is it?"

His father gave a great heaving sigh before continuing.

"As soon as you left, I checked my law books for the passage Dael mentioned, and as much as I hate what he's done, he appears to be correct in his interpretation, although I don't imagine this is what the author intended when the law was first drafted."

David paused for a moment while he studied Jayden's face, which was quickly contorting into a mask of rage.

"I've already dispatched a messenger to Damerette to find out if Dael's claims about Katherine's auntie are true, but if they are, then Dael hasn't technically broken any laws. Without that I'm afraid we have no grounds to appeal to Duke Timon for intervention."

For a moment Jayden just stood there, stunned.

"So, you're not going to do anything?" he asked, a little voice in his mind adding in, *just like Dael said.*

"The question I have to ask you is this," David continued, ignoring Jayden's stricken gaze, "Have you two planned anything yet?"

"Not yet," he muttered. On his way back from the cliffs he had been more than half hoping his father would aid them in their escape, but with every passing sentence that seemed more and more unlikely.

"Good," his father responded with obvious relief, "Because now is not the time. Dael will watch both of you closely over the next few weeks. If you are going to try something it will have to wait until we get back from Aramar."

"Aramar!" Jayden shouted as he stood from behind the desk, "I'm not going to Aramar, I can't leave Grandell now."

"So, you *are* planning something," David asserted.

Jayden just looked at him, knowing he'd been caught out.

"I don't want to talk about it," he said, angry with

himself, he hadn't meant to let on to anyone yet that they were leaving.

David stood there for a long time without answering.

"When Crest sails in the morning, I want you on board."

"No," Jayden replied, his voice as hard as stone. "You know I can't do that."

"You have to!" David hissed. "Even on the way here I saw two of his guards keeping an eye on me, and another watching Crest from down under the pier. He's already waiting for you to make a mistake Jayden. Whatever you're thinking of doing, Dael will be all over you before you can even make the attempt."

"Are you telling me not to help her?" Jayden asked, astonished and more than a little disheartened.

"Do you think I want this?!" David exploded as he stood and began to prowl around the cabin.

"What would you have me do? We might be the most prosperous merchants on the promontory, but Dael has the entire garrison at his command, and you know as well as I do he's been itching for an excuse to seize our estates ever since he came into power. Besides, if we tried any kind of direct action against him Grandell's streets would run red with blood, and I think you know the townspeople wouldn't lift a finger to help either you or Rhianna after what happened last summer."

Jayden sat down wearily at his father's desk. He hated every word the man had just said, the more so because he knew they were true. He and Rhianna couldn't fight the entire garrison, but if they couldn't flee either then what did that leave?

Jayden turned the problem over in his mind for some time, but eventually drew a blank.

"So what am I supposed to do?" he demanded as a helpless feeling began to sink in.

"You come to Aramar with me and let things calm down here. Crest will be back a phase before the wedding and Dael will not be watching as closely if he thinks he's already won. Jayden, listen to me. If you go back to town now and pull some stunt to stop the wedding, Dael will kill you this time. For a while there I thought he was going to try it tonight, right there in our own house!"

Jayden's shoulders slumped as he realised with certainty that his father had spoken the truth, and as much as it pained him, he knew deep down that to leave now would give them a better chance to escape when he returned. That was if Rhianna would even forgive him for running off and leaving her here. But what other option had been left to him?

"All right," he finally whispered after what seemed an eternity, and with no small amount of hesitation, "All right, as long as I have your unconditional word we will be back in plenty of time."

"You have it, Son," David told him.

"If you want, I can have one of my contacts in the keep deliver a short letter to Rhianna once we've set sail. I know it's not much, but at least she will know you're coming back."

Jayden grimaced, but nodded as he accepted his father's offer with a deep sense of foreboding.

"Good. My advice is you mention nothing in detail and finish the note by telling her to burn it. It would only aggravate matters if Dael found out."

His father sighed again while he came around the desk and unlocked a draw which held a variety of writing implements and several sheaves of blank paper.

"I'll leave you to write in peace," David said as he walked towards the door, but as he passed the threshold, he turned halfway back to look over his shoulder.

"You've made the smart decision. Everything will work out, you'll see."

David hesitated for a second longer, as though about to say more, but then just nodded and closed the door behind him to give his son some privacy.

Once his father was gone, Jayden slowly took out the paper and fine charcoal pencil used for marking the charts and began to write.

His father had said he was making the smart choice, but as he tried to put into words why he was leaving Rhianna with Dael for the next two phases, the next ten weeks, he couldn't shake off the nagging sensation that on this occasion, the smart choice, might not be the right choice.

SUMMER

One bird, hope. Two birds, trouble. Three birds, disaster.

Common Jeranonian saying when referring to traffic from the Messengers Guild.

CHAPTER 3

THE STREETS OF ARAMAR

"Stay on the ship Jayden, see to the unloading."

The new year had been rung in before they'd even rounded the Anchorhead Promontory and most of dawn of summer was now spent. Crest had tied up at the east docks of Aramar that morning after nearly a phase at sea, and those were the last instructions his father had given before leaving the ship. In addition to the captain's absence, Jarvis, the first mate, had also been gone all morning, out securing supplies for the journey home. That left Jayden in complete charge of Crest while the two senior officers were away, and he was determined that everything should go smoothly during their disembarkment, so the ship would be ready to sail at the earliest opportunity.

A few hours after the officers departed, a runner wearing the yellow waist sash of the Messenger's Guild had arrived on the dock, informing Jayden in a self-important voice that the captain had graciously accepted the hospitality of his host.

His father had sent such messages before. It meant he had sensed some new business opportunity and was attempting to garner a deal with the merchant who brokered their goods throughout the city. If that were true, it was likely he would not return until well after supper.

Jayden was thankful the unloading was going smoothly enough, because truth be told, his mind was elsewhere today. Even so, by mid-afternoon the bulk of the work was done, and Crest was riding high and light in the sheltered waters of the capital's docks.

As he waited for one of the officers to return and relieve him, Jayden eventually watched from the foredeck as the lamps on the waterfront began to glow dimly with a yellowish light far steadier than any candle could maintain, as they always did at this time of day.

What a mundane use for the Gift.

He idly wondered what it would have been like to be born with whatever spark it was that let the magi do what they did. It would have been nice to have the ability to put a bit more wind in Crest's sails at times. He loved the ship like a second home and had since childhood, but since the first day of this journey he had wanted nothing more than to be back in Grandell with Rhianna. There was a tugging in the depths of his mind every morning when he woke, and despite all the good, logical reasons for his leaving, Jayden still couldn't shake the feeling he'd made a terrible mistake by allowing his father to convince him to come.

A heavy footstep sounded on the deck, and Jayden knew without looking that Jarvis had returned, and now stood behind him on the foredeck. No one else on board walked with such a distinctive gait.

"Did you be havin' any problems with the unloading Jay?" Jarvis asked, confirming his identity in the strong accent he carried from his childhood home. The first mate's tales of the Sunset Isles had always made Jayden want to see the tiny independent nation which stood just over two hundred leagues east-southeast from the southern tip of the Anchorhead Promontory, and he promised himself once again that one day he would make that journey. Jarvis' stories of woven grass huts, palm-lined beaches, and coral reefs with schools of fishes every colour imaginable had always made him think it sounded like a grand place to grow up.

"No hitches," Jayden returned.

"We should be gettin' some of those for Grandell," the first officer remarked as he came to stand beside Jayden at the prow, tilting his stubbled chin towards the lights.

"That's probably a good idea. The way things are going back home the streets won't be safe to walk in another few years."

"Hmmf," was all the response he got as Jarvis leaned over to rest his elbows on the railing.

"So you'll be leavin' us soon then lad?" Jarvis asked in a strangely offhand manner.

"What do you mean?" Jayden replied evasively as he turned to face the hulking first mate.

For a moment Jarvis just regarded him thoughtfully.

"Don't be playing coy with me Jay, I've known you far too long I have. Everybody knows that you and Rhianna are in love. Don't even be bothering to deny it, it be all over the both of your faces every time the two of you youngsters be together."

There was a long, awkward silence before Jayden returned to staring at the docks.

"The thing of it be this boy, I used to work for Rhianna's parents sometimes before they be killed in that accident o' theirs. I got to know Rhianna a good bit durin' those years..."

"Whatever you're dancing around Jarvis, just spit it out already," Jayden interrupted, in no mood to be questioned on the subject yet again.

The hulking first mate shrugged and took his weight off the railing to stand at his impressive normal height.

"All right Jay, if you be wantin' it straight up, I'll be givin' it to you that way. I've been knowin' that girl for almost as long as I've been knowin' you, and the truth be told she has more strength in her than most of the men I've known. But lately it be seemin' as though every time I hear her name mentioned, it be because some other terrible thing be happening to her. I saw the two of you coming out of the forest together the night before we shipped out I did, though I don't think either of you two be spottin' me there yourselves. The look I saw in her eyes said pretty clearly that she be reachin' the end of her rope. People can only be takin' so much."

He paused then to take a breath and sigh.

"I've been knowin' you almost all your life I have, Jay. You're a good man you are, and I know you'll be doin' right by Rhianna because you do be in love with her. Right now, that be meanin' that you're planning to get her as far away from our malicious young count as possible. Before the wedding, yes?"

Jayden just stood there staring at the ship's first mate, feeling utterly pole-axed.

"Is it that obvious?" he asked at length.

There didn't seem to be much point denying it now, not to Jarvis anyway. The man had always been a friend, even riding at his father's side last summer when Master

Orran had tried to beat both him and Rhianna to death outside his tavern. Jarvis had risked his own life to protect them and Jayden trusted him implicitly, but it was still a shock to realise the heavily built man could read him so easily.

The townspeople had been in an uproar for weeks after the incident. After the sailor had stabbed her though, Dael had finally been forced to make a public announcement in Grandell's town square stating that Rhianna was not in fact a demon, and no further retaliation would be tolerated. That surprise had come even as the knife man's body swung on the gallows for all to see. Jayden himself was never mentioned in Dael's speech, but by implication if Rhianna wasn't a demon, then by proxy he was no necromancer. He had never been sure why Dael had helped them that day, but in light of the count's recent actions Jayden supposed it made sense. After all, he couldn't very well make a demon the next Countess of Grandell.

"Only because I've been knowin' the both of you for so long," Jarvis replied, breaking his train of thought. "But you should be keepin' in mind that Dael has been knowin' you for almost as long as I have, so be careful Jay. If you be needin' my help when the time comes you have only to be askin'. I be havin' no special love for our new young count, and the truth be that I've managed to save up enough over the years to be buyin' my very own ship I have. Nothing like Crest here you understand, but enough to be being my own master, to travel where I want and be answerin' to no one but the winds. Not that I be dislikin' the captain," he hastily amended.

"But to be captainin' a ship of my own, that's something I've been wanting since I was five years old."

He quickly raised his hand to hide an embarrassed cough.

"But when I do be getting' that vessel, I'm going to be needin' a crew that don't mind leaving Grandell, permanently. Know anyone who might be being interested?" he asked with a raised eyebrow.

With a small smile Jayden looked out at the city.

"That's a very tempting offer," he eventually told the first mate. "But we both know Rhianna deserves better than to live on a ship, and I can't just abandon her for phases on end while we sail off into the horizon looking for adventure, or profit, or… whatever."

Jarvis nodded knowingly as he gave Jayden what he probably considered a friendly pat on the shoulder, which nearly drove him to his knees.

"Good to see you be usin' your head as well as your heart boy, you'll be needin' the strength o' both when you and Rhianna leave Grandell I be thinkin'. But as I said, if you be needin' help, you need only to be askin'."

He gave Jayden's shoulder a last squeeze which left a nagging ache before letting his hand drop.

"Now listen here, your father won't be being back till well after full dark I be guessin', best you get yourself into the city and see if you can't be findin' something to come back to once you leave Grandell. Just make good and sure you is being back before the captain returns, otherwise he'll have me hangin' upside down from the rigging for not keepin' you out of trouble he will. You'd best believe that when he finally lets me down I'll be making sure that you be havin' your turn as well," he said with only a half joking grin.

"Now off with you boy, before I be changin' my mind."

His father hadn't precisely ordered him to stay on board until he returned, but they both knew that was the implication when he'd told Jayden to see to the unloading. Once again Jarvis was sticking his neck out for him.

"Thank you," Jayden told him sincerely as he left the foredeck and hurried back to his cabin to collect his sword. The long Oo'vi blade was sinuously curved back and then forward again to give it a vaguely serpentine look, which was only enhanced by the two fang-like protrusions which formed the pommel. He couldn't help but smile as he slid it soundlessly out of its scabbard, checked the blade quickly and returned it to its sheath, then strapped the ancient weapon to his belt. It had been given to him by his father on his eighteenth birthday, the year before last. Jayden had pressed him on where it had come from, but all David would tell him was that he had acquired it years before from an Arborii trader who seemed quite glad to be rid of it. Since then Jayden had been learning to use it whenever he could find the time, though he knew in a pinch he would still be hard pressed to beat even a mediocre swordsman with proper training. He quickly added a small leather purse full of mainly silver coins to his belt. Not that they were worth much, but they were more than he would need for a few hours in Aramar. As he left his cabin, he took down the grey woollen cloak hanging on a peg by the door. He settled it over his shoulders with the hood hanging loose across his back before stepping through the doorway, securing the room, and returning to the steep ladder which led up to the main hatch.

Coming back on deck he gave the sun a quick glance and headed down the gently rocking gangplank which bridged the three feet of water between Crest and the dock. There would be barely two hours until full dark if you included a long dusk, and he had the uneasy feeling it was nowhere near enough time for this endeavour.

As he looked around at the docks, he immediately dismissed them. If he ended up on a ship, he would choose Jarvis' over a stranger's all six days of the week. Right in front of him though, a broad street headed directly away from the waterfront, and lacking any better destination, he began walking up the gently sloped incline. The road itself was paved in cobblestones worn smooth over the passage of time, and as he moved further away from the docks, the air seemed to become crisper, although he couldn't detect any real difference in its scent.

To either side of him lay the usual assortment of rough taverns and smokehouses which thrived on any waterfront, but soon enough they gave way to different trade-shops like blacksmiths and chandlers, farriers and even the odd weapon smith.

He didn't know much about metal working, although horses were something he did have experience with. He made a mental note to put the farrier on his list and kept walking.

Eventually he came to an intersection. To his right the road bent quickly out of his sight, heading back towards the docks. He decided to take that one on the way back and turned instead to his left.

In the other direction the road was filled with merchandise laden carts being dragged along by horses or sometimes the men themselves, most of them making their way to and from the great markets which stood just outside the inner city's fortified walls.

Entering the city wasn't a problem for travellers or anyone without a cart full of goods, but as soon as a merchant brought their wares through the gate, or their ship to the docks, the customs officers descended like a pack of vultures at high summer. As a result, the markets had grown over the years into a permanent fixture outside the walls and generally sold items which catered to the general public. The overpriced trinkets the nobles of the city valued so highly could be found elsewhere if one had the coin and the inclination to look.

On any other day he would have enjoyed a trip to the markets. There were always interesting items to be discovered there from the far edges of Jeranon, or even across the ocean from Avsan or the Sunset Isles. But with only a short amount of daylight left, it was, unfortunately, out of the question.

Beyond the intersection the road widened considerably, easily giving room enough for a dozen carts to move side by side. Jayden followed the road, dodging traffic as he crossed the busy intersection and kept on going. As he passed a last row of four-storey buildings he was abruptly confronted with half a mile of open grassland dotted only by the occasional flowering tree or the sparkling of a slowly moving brook as it fed into a series of shallow lakes.

The road continued across the grassland, heading straight towards the other side of the idyllic park lands where it was swallowed whole by the main gate of the hulking wall of Aramar. The huge fortifications had been built during the Wars of Founding, and supposedly the kings of Jeranon had never stopped improving them. As he walked toward the implacable, hundred-foot high wall,

Jayden looked in wonder at the massive turrets which protruded out from its length at regular intervals designed to give archers a clear shot at the outside of the wall from the arrow slits which dotted them like honeycomb. Across the top of both wall and turrets, crenulations ran the length of the overhanging parapet and afforded a wealth of murder holes from which boiling pitch and stones of a suitable size could be thrown down on any army which assaulted the fortress-like city.

Aramar was the heart of Jeranon's realm and traditional seat of the royal house, and due of its formidable defences, the military might of the city had never been contested since the Wars of Founding had finished nearly three millennia before. Still, it made quite a sight for someone more used to the simple rural structures of the Anchorhead Promontory. It was true, Dael's keep was an eight-storey stone monstrosity that towered over the region, but aside from that one structure it was uncommon to even find a three-storey building back home.

As beautiful as the park lands were, Jayden knew that they were primarily yet another defence for the inner city, and kept the land near the wall unobstructed by the cover of buildings where an enemy could hide. Jayden remembered walking with his father and mother around the entire inner city through these park lands when he had been a child, taking most of the day to explore the overgrown outer paths and man-made lakes that had been here for untold generations. It was one of his earliest happy memories. Unfortunately, today his route was by necessity far more direct.

After some time, Jayden came to the vast steel gate protecting the city's main entrance and walked without hesitation through the giant portal. Above him on either side of the bailey were ledges, not as high as the top of the wall, but high enough to be very difficult to attack. Jayden made no claims as to being a soldier, but he was positive he would not want to be held up here in what was obviously a killing ground while his army was trying to batter down the second set of steel-worked doors that lay fifty yards beyond the first. As he crossed a line of holes in the ground, he looked up to see a giant portcullis carefully concealed.

Ready to be sent crashing down at a moment's notice, he thought as he hastened through the second set of gates.

As he passed the threshold and entered the city proper, a gust of wind shoved his cloak to the side, and Jayden noticed a suddenly interested guard looking at the Oo'vi blade strapped to his waist. The large man wore the livery of the city watch and began making a note about Jayden on the writing board he was holding. Since weapons weren't banned in the city however, the guard didn't bar his way and Jayden continued, heading towards the boulevard revealed to his sight as he came through the city's main entrance.

The boulevard was really a double street with a wide stretch of grass running down its centre, broken only by the paved crossing of intersections across its path. On the grassed area, a row of giant Oaks lined the way, providing shade both one way and then the other as the sun ran its course through the cloudless sky. Right now, the shadows were stretching thinly to the east as the sun began its downward plunge towards the horizon.

By this time even the spacious boulevard was filling with people leaving their places of work for the day, and customers trying to get to them before they did. Jayden unconsciously walked faster as it became evident his time was growing short. He knew he had yet to accomplish anything significant, and he had a feeling this would be his last chance to scout for a place to settle when he and Rhianna left Grandell.

Along this stretch of the boulevard were the shops belonging to the more successful merchants in the city. Fine tailors could be found in abundance, as could some of Aramar's most expensive inns. To his right, a building stood on the end of a block which could only be described as a glorified barn. If it had been a dwelling, he could conceivably have thought of it as a palace belonging to one of the nobles. The double doors which stood wide open to the street looked into a cavernous area though, and the sound of horses whinnying floated out to him on the late afternoon breeze. Above the door was a newly painted sign with the word 'Jemalar's' overlaid on a picture of galloping horses, and Jayden instinctively knew he'd found what he'd been searching for.

Crossing the wide stretch of grass in the middle of the street, Jayden was intercepted at the entrance by an overly officious man deep into his middle years.

The short man, whose few remaining strands of hair were combed across his large bald spot in a vain attempt to hide the truth was busy dry-washing his hands as he took in the functional, yet well-made cloak which Jayden wore over his ship's uniform.

"Young master, I am terribly sorry but Jemalar's is already closed for the day," he obsequiously apologised. "Perhaps if you come back tomorrow?" he suggested nervously.

"Actually, I'm not here to buy a horse."

"I see," the short man interrupted, his entire demeanour changing.

"Would I be able to see whoever is in charge?" Jayden asked casually, but his question seemed to rub the little man the wrong way.

"Jono, Ralph," he called, and two large stablemen came to the door from where they had been working nearby, "Finish closing up."

The two burly stablemen looked at each other for a moment as if the order were something unusual, but Jayden had to let it pass as the bald fellow turned his attention back to him.

"Master Jemalar is not here at the moment but has left me in charge whilst he is away. So, if you are unwilling to talk to me then you will just have to wait until tomorrow. Good day young master," he said, ducking backwards through the door which Jono and Ralph were quickly securing.

Before Jayden could say a word, he found himself staring at a closed and painted panel of wood which had been an open doorway only a moment before. He knew he shouldn't have expected to find work at the very first place he looked, but as he quickly glanced at the sun, he realised his time was already up. He had only about fifteen minutes before he would have to head back to the dock where Crest was tied up, but with all the shops closing there was little more he could accomplish here.

If only Jarvis had returned an hour earlier.

Suppressing his irritation at missing this opportunity, he decided to start back now and take the longer way around the palace at the heart of Aramar. It was unlikely he would find anything there, but the view of the distant forest known as the Emerald Sea, and the landscape which lay beyond Aramar's walls to the southwest was not one to be missed for someone who came to the capital as infrequently as he. He picked up his pace as he headed towards the polished stone walls of the king's palace and considered his next move. Perhaps living in Aramar wouldn't be the best idea after all. It was possible that if Dael traced them this far, being under the noses of the most powerful nobility in Jeranon might become dangerous in the unlikely event Dael had any friends among them.

At any rate, he was going to enjoy his last hour in Aramar, and the view from the hill which the palace dominated. He had a hunch that when he returned to Grandell things were going to quickly become complicated, and before that happened, he wanted to have a few minutes of peace by himself to sort through his thoughts.

Eventually, he found himself walking along a wide street which was flanked on his left by the thirty-foot high palace wall which kept it separated from the rest of the inner city. He knew the main gates to the palace were around the other side, but the view from here was much better. He found a place to sit in a small, hilly park which afforded a vantage point over the southwest of Aramar and the countryside beyond.

I have to bring Rhianna here once we leave Grandell, he thought. First, they would have to escape Dael's trackers and guards though. Then they would need to find somewhere to live together, somewhere no one judged them by what had happened in the past, even if only because they didn't know about it. It might even come to changing their names if Dael pursued them vigorously enough.

He was worried about all of it, but with no immediate solutions coming to mind, he decided all he could do for right now was take things one step at a time.

The sun soon dropped to the horizon, causing Jayden to jump up from where he'd been sitting, lost once again in his thoughts. He muttered an annoyed curse at himself and began to jog along the palace wall as it curved back towards the docks. If he wasn't back by the time his father returned, Jarvis would be as good as his word. Friend he might be, but Jarvis was also first mate and took his responsibilities seriously. Since Jayden had no real desire to find himself hanging upside down from the rigging either tonight, or any other, as the sun disappeared and revealed in its place the first and brightest stars in the sky, he ran.

*   *   *

"Everybody out!" Archmage Tolmarak boomed as he strode through the carved wooden doors of the King of Jeranon's throne room.

There was a sudden quiet as the musicians halted their song, and the conversation in the room faltered as the assorted nobles and court functionaries turned, one by one, to look down their noses at the intruder who had interrupted their gathering. At least they did for the space of time it took them to notice the black, silver-lined cloak which proclaimed the ageing man a full Archmage.

Some functionaries hastily obeyed his shouted order, but most of the nobles, especially those of middling rank simply stared, their expressions ranging from disbelief to nervousness and on to affront. Highest ranking magi in the country he might be, but this was the king's throne room, and these morons wearing the ridiculous feathered hats that reached up almost half a span which were apparently the fashion of the day considered it their domain, and no place for the college to be exercising its considerable muscle.

"Move!" he shouted again as he passed through the rows of huge columns flanking the red carpet which ran in an unbroken line from the entryway to the raised dais dominating the far end of the hall. The dais held only a pair of banners and a pair of thrones, one of the intricately carved seats slightly larger than the other. It was to the larger of the two, or rather the crowned old man who sat upon it, that Tolmarak had trained his attention.

"I bring urgent news from the west, Sire," he announced as he finally drew near. "It would be wise if you and the council were to hear it alone,"

Almost as an afterthought, he gave a slight bow which tradition said should have been much deeper.

He could feel the eyes of the assorted nobles boring into his back as he straightened, and inwardly winced. Running through the palace halls like a madman was not the best way to maintain respect, nor was bursting into a roomful of snot-nosed courtiers and shouting orders at possibly the most arrogant and stubborn group of people in all of Jeranon.

Erian the Third of the House of Savani inclined his head towards the archmage and gave his old friend and adviser an intense moment of study before levelling his gaze on the assembled court.

"Clear the room. The council and ambassadors will remain," the ageing monarch proclaimed in a deep, resonant voice better suited to a man half his age. The king could have just as easily sequestered them into a private meeting in the council room, but Erian had never gained a taste for pandering to the excesses of his court, and was no doubt just as glad for an excuse to send them all away.

One by one the courtiers bowed their way out of the king's presence, many of them making a pointed show of the correct courtly manners which Tolmarak had neglected with his hasty entry, until finally only the six Dukes who made up the military council remained. Along with them Terall, the Arborii representative from the Emerald Sea and Droik, the Teraliv envoy from Whisperwind Mountain in Jeranon's north, stood patiently, making no move to leave. Though not officially part of Jeranon's military structure, the ambassadors nevertheless held a vote on the council. Terall and Droik spoke for their people, and the longstanding alliance between the three races gave them every right to hear these urgent tidings from the west. As leader of the College of the Arts, Tolmarak himself rounded out the council's final number.

When the room finally cleared and only a pair of royal guards in the all-encompassing red and white armour of Erian's house remained over by the door, Tolmarak took a deep breath, and began.

"Sire, I bring dire news from the west. Miralthrall has fallen to treachery."

"What?!" Erian exploded, almost flying out of his throne despite his advanced years. There were stunned looks and gasps from the others, and Tolmarak even saw Droik fingering the hilt of the large knife he always carried at his belt.

"Have the dark nations invaded? Say on man, and be quick about it," the ageing king commanded.

Tolmarak took another deep breath despite the king's urgency. What he was about to tell Erian could see the dismantling of the College of the Arts permanently if he wasn't careful; an establishment to which he had devoted his entire life, in loyal service to his king.

The magi of Jeranon had fallen into disrepute over the last hundred years, and Tolmarak had recently become aware of a widespread conspiracy which had its roots within the nobility, aimed at undermining the general population's faith in their order. He would have to deal with that eventually he knew. Unfortunately, right now he just didn't have the time, and with Heramiir's open rebellion declared in the west, he was forced to acknowledge the possibility that the two things together could very well bring the college to its knees. So, when he finally spoke it was with a heavy heart, knowing his next words would likely change the magi's place in Jeranon forever, not to mention set the entire country on the road to civil war.

"Erian the Third," Tolmarak intoned formally, "King of Jeranon and Defender of the Realm. It is with much regret I must inform you Archmage Heramiir has by force of arms taken Miralthrall, declaring the College of the Arts now the ruling body in that city."

Tolmarak studied his friend's face intently while he spoke, but the king had gone unusually silent, and remained so as Tolmarak continued.

"In addition, my sources have reported Heramiir is preparing to take other cities in the west with an army already loyal to him, led by Archmage Nereth."

"Maker protect us," Erian whispered.

Tolmarak knew the monarch had met Nereth twice

before. Once to officially reward the archmage for repelling an Augrahl attack. Nereth had been badly outnumbered, but with barely a quarter of the force anyone else would have needed just to hold them off, he had prevailed. Seventy men, just seventy, and for over a day and a half he had held back two entire legions of Nostahl and Augrahl warriors, including a pair of powerful sorcerers, until he had finally routed them. Nereth's forces had left only a single survivor among the enemy once the fighting was done, whom he had promptly interrogated and then escorted back across the border with a cart containing the sum of its companions' heads. Their second interaction had been nowhere near as cordial.

"What else?" Erian demanded quietly, "Danarel? Karver?"

"I don't know," Tolmarak carefully replied, shooting an apologetic glance at the Duke of Keral, whose vast western estates included the city of Karver.

"The information is two weeks old, sent by pigeon on the day of the rebellion by Archmage Poller. I expect by now that Heramiir and Nereth will be finished consolidating their hold on Miralthrall. If they haven't already moved against Karver and Danarel, I would think an attack against those two cities is only a few days away at most."

There was a knowing silence among the council at that piece of information. The Dukes were all veterans of various campaigns either on the border or at sea, and they knew well the strategic importance of those two cities in relation to Miralthrall's defences.

Tolmarak took a step forward to hand two tiny bone message cylinders to the king, who stopped his pacing of the dais long enough to take them and examine the contents.

*   *   *

Without a word Erian hesitantly took the tiny scrolls from the man he had called friend for almost sixty years; a man he was suddenly unsure he could trust.

He unrolled the first of the cylinders carefully to reveal its meagre contents, a necessarily brief missive of seven words.

'Rebellion has been declared in Miralthrall. Poller.'

Erian curled his hand into a fist, crushing the fragile bone cylinder and crumpling the tiny piece of paper before letting the pieces fall to the ground.

Slowly, and with great precision, he took the second message from the case and read.

'Nereth leads the soldiers. Heramiir leads him.'

"Are there any others?" he asked coldly.

"Yes Sire," Tolmarak answered, calmly pulling the final bone cylinder from a pocket and handing it to the king.

"Three birds arrived together, and the third carried this."

Erian unrolled the tiny message, fervently hoping the old saying wasn't true.

'Count on no aid from Miralthrall's college. He owns them.'

Erian, ruler of a suddenly broken nation just stood for a long minute, staring at the tiny piece of parchment which had thrown his entire world into chaos. For Heramiir to take Miralthrall by force he must have needed the support of more than just the magi. While there were certainly enough of them to flatten the city given time, they just didn't have the numbers to spread out and keep every farmer and peasant over an area the size of the west subdued if the commoners decided to force the issue.

Perhaps he had only himself to blame, he hadn't really paid enough attention to the western reaches of Jeranon over the last few years. To the border certainly, but not to the central duchies where little happened except commerce and the usual minor scheming of ambitious courtiers. And now for his carelessness he had a rebellion to put down.

Flicking the message over to the white-haired Duke of Keral, King Erian came to stand face to face with Tolmarak. The two of them had been friends longer than some men lived, and had fought more battles together than he wished to think on. Of the archmage's loyalty he had little doubt, but there was one question that very much needed answering.

"Will the magi in the college of Aramar still follow me, now that one of Heramiir's reputation has placed himself in direct opposition to the crown?"

Tolmarak looked at him directly, and Erian could see there was no uncertainty in his tone.

"For three thousand years since the desolate fleet limped across the Sea of Dreams to claim these shores for their own, the magi of Aramar have served the kings of Jeranon with honour. We will not stray from that path now. Heramiir is a traitor and renegade, he will be dealt with as any other, and just as a mage has smeared our name with this treason, know that a mage will right it again by putting an end to his crimes."

It was cold comfort given the circumstances.

"Then there will be war," the king remarked tiredly.

"Let us retire to the garden to discuss this matter further," he bid the others, who so far had remained silent while the archmage delivered the dire news.

I spend too much of my time indoors these days, Erian thought as he sombrely led the way. He was always rushing from one meeting to another, trying to deal with the commoners, or settle petty disputes among the nobles. It was a constant source of irritation to him that so many of his days were filled with trivia which should not have even been brought to his attention. He would have to do something about that once this current crisis had passed.

He had been King of Jeranon now for forty years. Nearly half of those had been spent at war with the nations of the west, and most of the others were marred by skirmishes and feints if not an organised campaign. Things had settled down considerably during the last decade though, and he had idly been hoping he could live out his few remaining years in some semblance of peace. But now he had another war to wage, this time against his own people, and that worried him deeply. Jeranon had stood for three thousand years against all manner of attack from the dark nations because it had been united. In all that time there had only been one occasion when the Kingdom had nearly faltered. That juncture had been almost two millennia ago when Eldrik the Black had seized control of the west against King Orallan in an unsuccessful attempt to take over the country.

Eldrik had been defeated a great cost, but that victory had left Jeranon weakened to a point where it had almost fallen to a combined force from the dark nations when they attacked the following spring.

As Erian passed by his royal bodyguards at the throne room door, he halted.

"You two are sworn to secrecy about what you heard just now," he said as he made eye contact with each the two men.

He knew they would die before revealing any of the state secrets they routinely overheard, but he suddenly felt the urge to say it anyway.

The two guards dressed in the red and white of House Savani both bowed formally before straightening, the one on the right opening the door for his king. The other guard moved through it first though, and as soon as Erian and the council had exited the throne room the guard pulled the door closed behind them and followed at the back of the procession.

King Erian set a fast pace through the maze of corridors as he led the way across the building. The others knew enough to hold their peace as they moved toward their destination, and finally the king and his inner circle exited the palace through a small entrance to his private garden, near the rear of the giant structure. There was another pair of guards stationed at the garden entrance and Erian tossed off a quick, "See we are not disturbed," to them before marching through the door right on the heels of his bodyguard.

What am I going to do?

If he could avoid a war he would, short of giving up the west to this renegade archmage. He didn't know much about Heramiir other than his reputation as an incredibly powerful Gift user, and he'd only ever met the man personally at his ascension ceremonies. Erian knew that was the first thing he would have to remedy. He led the nine members of his council down a short path and over to a shaded tundra which afforded a dozen high backed wooden chairs, each carved from a single piece of polished wood and gilded with silver. The intricately sculpted and matching furniture was set out in a circular arrangement and had been a gift from Terall, the current Arborii ambassador, when she had first come to his court many years ago.

Of them all, only she had permission to enter this place without him present. As she had told him once long ago, an Arborii away from the trees is an unhappy Arborii. And while it would not harm her to be away from the Emerald Sea, she said the small forest one of his ancestors had planted here was at least a minor taste of home. Besides, she had proved herself an ally and a friend many times over the years, not that she looked her age. Erian himself didn't mind getting old, but he sometimes wished humans could do it half as gracefully as the Arborii race managed despite their somewhat alien features.

He motioned for the others to take their usual seats, which they promptly did, Terall hesitating slightly as she deftly threaded her long flexible tail through the gap at the back of the chair.

"So let me see if I understand the situation correctly," Erian said bluntly once they were all settled.

"Archmage Heramiir has staged a successful rebellion in Miralthrall and turned the loyalties of the college there from my rightful authority to his own. Furthermore, he has an army at his disposal which has also turned against me, and is commanded by Archmage Nereth, one of the greatest military commanders in living memory. Does that about sum it up, Tolmarak?" he asked, allowing just a hint of the anger he felt to show through his voice.

"Yes Sire," Tolmarak answered with as little emotion as possible, "To the best of my knowledge that is correct."

With a grimace, Erian looked around the circle at his closest advisers.

"Thoughts?" he asked, opening the floor up for any who wished to speak.

"We must strike back now," the Teraliv envoy announced emphatically before anyone could speak. "If we take what forces we have and march now we will gain the element of surprise and deny Heramiir the chance to consolidate his position. The archmage will not be expecting us to mount an attack until the last snows of winter's dusk have melted here, meaning a late spring campaign once we've marched from Aramar to Miralthrall." He sat back in his chair, scanning the others' expressions for signs of support.

"I thank you for your advice Droik," Erian said even as he discarded the idea. For one, he didn't have enough men in the city to march on such a large target sooner than a phase from now. Second, even if he ordered the march at that time, his army would be mired in dawn of winter's snows soon after they arrived at Miralthrall, and that was assuming the snows didn't arrive early, or his men late.

While the notion of catching Heramiir off guard was appealing, it wasn't worth the risk to his own men who would be in for a long harsh winter on the enemy's doorstep. Besides, Miralthrall had never fallen until now, and if he could avoid a direct siege of the city, he would.

"What say the Arborii?" he asked when the others remained silent.

"Terall?"

Terall looked up from her thoughts and her black eyes, larger than any human's, appeared slightly startled for a moment.

"Perhaps an envoy," she eventually suggested, "I understand your wish to dissolve this rebellion, but the safety of the western border must be upheld at all costs. A civil war could allow the dark nations the opportunity to weaken our defences enough to break through and reclaim much of the western provinces. Possibly even as far as the Cloudburst Cliffs."

She was right of course. Erian had already thought of that himself, but he wasn't sure sending an envoy to a rebel leader was the right approach. It seemed to him that showing a weak hand initially in this situation would be an open invitation for others to take the same actions in the future. Also, he wasn't sure he wanted to legitimise Heramiir in the eyes of the western population by addressing him in an official manner.

Unfortunately, that only left him with a very limited set of options. Assassination might be possible. It was a more preferable option than open warfare. But without knowing exactly why the other magi were following Heramiir in his treason, Erian immediately realised he could wind up creating a martyr if Heramiir's support was genuine, and not coerced. Still, it was something to be considered if nothing else presented.

"Forgive me if this sounds pretentious," the white-haired Duke of Keral said in his quietly confident voice. He was the eldest member of the council at nearly ninety, except perhaps for Terall, whose age was anybody's guess, but the old noble was still vigorous despite his advanced years.

"It seems to me while a civil war must be avoided if at all possible, a show of force will be necessary either way if the magi of Miralthrall are to be convinced to relinquish the lands they have already taken."

"Which begs the question," Archmage Tolmarak broke in, "If we can avoid a war, what will be done with the magi who have joined Heramiir against you?"

The eight other heads of the council swivelled from Tolmarak to the king as he shifted uncomfortably in his chair. There was a complete moment of silence except for a blue jay which had landed just beyond the tundra and was busy warbling out a song to whoever had the time to listen. Erian spent the moment gathering his thoughts before answering.

"It will depend on the role each has played. For those forced to join or those who act as agents for us, perhaps an amnesty, although it would once again depend on the roles they have played. For the ones who willingly joined him after he rebelled, I think five or ten years of border duty would be appropriate."

He looked away then, but soon returned his eyes to look his friend in the face.

"I'm sorry Tolmarak. I know he was once your apprentice, but Heramiir, Nereth and any others who initiated the actual coup will have to be declared renegade and charged with treason. As much as I hate to waste such talent, I can't let the general populace think armed rebellion is a tolerable offence."

"I see," Tolmarak replied noncommittally.

Erian had known his advisor long enough to notice the slight tightening at the corners of his eyes and the way he sat that little bit straighter in his chair. He would accept the matter because his king had ordered it, but he also wasn't happy about it.

"And if it comes to war?" Tolmarak asked eventually.

"The same," Erian replied, this time without hesitation, "For those who survive."

Tolmarak stood from his chair and was plainly about to launch into a lecture about how the magi were the backbone of their defence against the dark nations, and how any civil war would lower their already slight numbers. All of which he was keenly aware of.

Erian forestalled it with an upraised hand.

"Peace, Tolmarak. It has not yet come to that. Let us see if we can avoid it all together. The first thing we need to do is find out more about why Heramiir has incited this rebellion. Right now, we do not understand his goals, or even what his motives are. Is he after power? Land? Is he still loyal to Jeranon or has he sided with the dark nations?" There was an intake of breath from the Duke of Aritah at that possibility.

"I want each of you to devote some of your resources to answering these questions. No military campaign can be planned until we know whether the dark nations are involved, and I don't think I need to detail the dire consequences for any of you if they are."

"If they are," the young Duke of Vaross said anyway, "We could be facing the largest war Jeranon has ever seen without the support of our western armies or any defences west of Midway, either man-made or natural."

"Which is precisely why we must make every effort to see it that does not come to that," Erian repeated.

"I have ruled Jeranon for over forty years, and in that time the dark nations have made some of their most aggressive attacks in a thousand years. Yet we have always prevailed against even the most ruthless of adversaries. I will not end my reign by watching all we have worked for turn to ashes because of one man's greed!"

"My Dukes and distinguished emissaries, I must now ask you to send word to your respective duchies. It is my fervent hope we can avoid the war we all see looming at our doorstep, but if there is no other way to make Jeranon whole again, then war it shall be, and we must be prepared. I would ask that each of you return to your lands and conscript every fifth man between fifteen and thirty years of age. They are to report to Aramar for training as soon as can be arranged."

"But what about the harvest," Duke Timon blurted out, interrupting the king. The short dark-haired noble in his middle years was from the duchy of Lansia in Jeranon's northeast, where the vast majority of the region's economic wealth revolved around the grains and other foodstuffs grown or found in its rich, fertile farmland.

"Most of it should be collected by the time the conscription parties reach the outlying districts," Erian said thoughtfully as he paused for a moment, staring off into the distance.

"Also send out an order with the message that the harvest is to be completed on schedule no matter who has to work the fields. With fewer workers and magi available to enhance the yields, we probably won't get a full crop next year, and we can't afford to lose this one as well."

That brought an unhappy nod from Duke Timon. Erian knew a civil war would throw Jeranon's economy right out the window, but right now there wasn't much he could do about it. Keeping his people fed was the top priority and keeping his kingdom whole was a close second. Keeping the general population prosperous was something which might have to be put on hold, as much as it galled him to admit it.

There were resigned nods from the other Dukes, which Erian expected, but he wasn't finished giving out orders yet.

"Tolmarak, I want you to send out loyal magi with the recruiters. Empty the college if you have to, but find me every last citizen with the Gift and bring them to Aramar for training."

"Yes Sire," Tolmarak said, and Erian thought he even sounded pleased. Come to think of it, Tolmarak had never been happy about the order for the magi to curtail their searches of the country, looking for those with potential to use the Gift. Erian hadn't been too thrilled about giving that command either, but there hadn't really been any choice given the situation at the time. Still, this gave him the perfect excuse to rescind the order, and if the nobles didn't like it, they would just have to fight their wars without the support of the battle trained spell casters of the college.

Finally, he turned toward the two emissaries.

"If we go to war, can I expect aid from your peoples?" he asked of the two ambassadors.

"The Teraliv have always aided you when you've called!" Droik nearly shouted, but then Droik always nearly shouted, except of course when he actually was shouting.

"For three thousand years since your people came to these shores the Teraliv race has stood with the men of Jeranon against the dark nations of the west. All here are aware our mutual enemy has been gathering their strength this past decade. We assumed it was in preparation for a major campaign against us, but if that assumption proves true and they launch it now, we could be caught completely off guard," he intoned, waving his short arms emphatically through the air.

"I will ask my king for his aid in fighting this Heramiir if you wish, but I think my warriors would be more useful to all of us in keeping the dark nations on their side of the border."

As much as Erian hated to admit it he knew Droik was right. No matter what took place in Jeranon itself, the border with the western nations had to be protected.

"Ambassador Terall, what assistance can we expect from the Emerald S..."

Tolmarak gasped and sat bolt upright in his chair.

"Is something wrong?" Erian asked quickly as his friend stared off into space, his eyes seeming to look directly through the garden wall. Tolmarak stood absently from his seat as though his mind were somewhere else, then shook his head twice as if to clear it. He strode purposely towards the outer wall of the castle grounds and placed his hands on the vine-encrusted mortar.

"Such power," he whispered just loudly enough to be heard as he followed something only he could sense through the thick, high wall which separated the garden from the street.

By now, Erian, along with all the others, was getting extremely curious as to what the leader of Aramar's College of the Arts was doing as he traced his hand along the palace wall at the speed of a slow walk.

Abruptly he turned, "I must go now Sire, my apologies but this cannot wait," and without another word he was off at a dead run, or the closest thing he could manage at his age towards the door which led back into the palace, his silver-lined cloak rippling out behind him as he went. There was a slamming of a door and one of the royal guards stuck his head around the corner to make sure everything was all right before closing it again, using a more sensible amount of force than the archmage had a moment before.

"I told him he should have gone before we left," Droik shouted with a laugh as he slapped the dark-haired Duke Timon on the shoulder.

Erian gave the short Teraliv envoy a sidelong glance and the young Duke of Vaross laughed unashamedly while most of the others tried to hide an assortment of smirks and grimaces.

"Anyway," King Erian said, trying to bring a semblance of order back to his military council meeting.

"What of the Arborii? Can I count on any support from your people?" he asked, and just like that everyone was serious again.

"Your friends in the Emerald Sea stand ready to assist you if it becomes necessary, on the condition you first attempt a peaceful solution to this situation," Terall answered carefully.

"Agreed," Erian said without hesitation. With Tolmarak gone, that seemed about all he could decide with the current information. He would move his pieces into place and then attempt to open a dialogue with this renegade archmage, if only to give him the chance to surrender without further bloodshed. Failing that, he might very well be calling on both Terall and Droik's people for support before very much longer. Any civil war which had the two nexuses for the College of the Arts on different sides would be long and bloody. Erian knew in his heart that if Heramiir had fallen far enough to side with the dark nations, then it was the beginning of the end for Jeranon's freedom, and probably that of the Arborii and Teraliv as well. All of them together had enough trouble holding the western nations beyond the Dark Iron Mountains. If Heramiir had dissolved the vital line of defence that the border afforded, Jeranon would be laid wide open to any attack their enemies committed to.

As much as Erian wanted to avoid a war, that possibility was far too pressing to be ignored. If the worst came to pass, he would need every able-bodied soldier and conscript in the field, well trained and ready to fight.

It still might not be enough.

"Go back to your duchies. Begin the conscriptions, collect the harvest, and prepare for war. I want all of your levies in Aramar no later than the end of summer's dusk," he told the assembled Dukes in no uncertain terms.

It was asking a lot he knew, but as they stood to leave, he knew he would soon be asking a great deal more.

"Stay a moment, Raymon. I have one last order for you, and I'm sure you're not going to like it."

As the others left the garden, Duke Raymon waited patiently in front of his chair, and as Erian began to speak, he found himself hoping he wasn't making a terrible mistake.

'There is something beautiful about the sea, though today the stench of the severed claws we took as trophies from the monster we fended off make it slightly less so...'
Excerpt from the log of Captain Torell

CHAPTER 4

REVELATIONS

As Crest unfurled its great mainsail and pulled out of Aramar's docks the following morning, Jayden stood at his usual place on the foredeck beside the sleek swordfish figurehead. The sun was out and Jarvis was bellowing orders to the men in the rigging while a crisp wind had blown in to give them a firm push down the Camar River, sending them northeast towards the open waters of the Sea of Dreams.

Jayden looked over at the forested south bank, wondering idly what lay behind the dense wall of trees which denoted the boundary of the Emerald Sea, beyond which he had never ventured. As the wind settled for a moment, the distant sound of a man yelling carried faintly to Jayden's ears. He turned to see what the commotion was about and was surprised to see the chubby little harbourmaster running after them on the north bank, shouting something at the top of his voice.

The specific words weren't distinguishable from the rapidly increasing distance, but the fat little man suddenly began jumping up and down and waving his arms to hold

Jayden's attention. Once he realised he'd been seen he began motioning in an exaggerated manner towards a distant figure.

Jayden followed the harbourmaster's gesture and spotted a man who had walked right out onto the cusp of one of the larger military piers, which were still abreast of the ship.

Jayden had no idea who the stranger was, but he appeared old. The man was dressed all in black save for a silver-lined cloak which fanned out beside him as the wind picked up, grasping at it and trying to tug him sideways off the dock into the river below. The old man stood composed, unaffected by the weather in what seemed a slightly unnatural way.

An Archmage?!

Crest was a big ship, but as the stranger stared at them from the precipice of the dock, Jayden had the uncomfortable feeling he alone was being focused on, although the distance was far too great to clearly see the man's eyes.

The distant figure bowed his head for a moment, and Jayden thought he must have chosen to forget about whatever errand he was on. But when the stranger looked up again his lips began moving, and although there was no hint of a shout, Jayden heard every word as though he were standing not two feet away.

"You are one of us. Tell me your name."

For a long moment, Jayden just stood there, before eventually remembering to breathe as he repeated the archaic question in his mind.

For as long as the histories recorded, that question had been the first thing a mage would say to someone they found who had the Gift, but was not yet trained.

But if he were being asked, and as he looked around the deck, he realised no one else seemed to have heard the voice as they went about the usual tasks of sailing a ship this size, that would mean...

For long moments he stood, watching in disbelief as Crest moved further away from the pier and the archmage astride it.

It couldn't be. He'd been tested by a mage when he was ten years old and the woman had told him he had absolutely no ability in the Gift. He had been crushed at the time as his childhood dream of becoming one of the magi was denied him in an instant. Eventually, he'd gotten over it and begun training on board Crest to take over as captain of the family's flagship when his father eventually retired.

As he looked at the cloaked archmage who still stood awaiting his reply, a story he had once heard floated up through his numbed mind about a child who had been denied entry to the college during his testing. That child had later developed quite a strong talent for the Gift and been immediately admitted. It was said to be very rare, and those few who found their talent later than most were always among the most powerful of magi, almost as if their talent had been given time to mature before becoming active.

But I can't be one of those, can I?

Those lucky few found with the Gift each year were taken to the College of the Arts in either Aramar or Miralthrall, depending on which of Jeranon's duchies they resided. They spent their lives learning the mage's arts and defending Jeranon against the dark nations of the west, not to mention any other threats of a less than natural origin.

Not the life everyone would choose, he was sure, but all *his* life he had dreamed of becoming a mage, of travelling the world and being at the centre of events which would never so much as touch the far-flung Anchorhead Promontory on which Grandell was situated. Even when he had failed the testing, he had still daydreamed of what it might have been like.

Better to live in the real world than one made of dreams, his mother had always said. What he had never told her though was that it seemed to him that living with no chance to achieve your dreams wasn't much of a life.

If this was for real though, then more than anything he wanted to take this chance. If he had been on the docks the matter would already be settled. All citizens with the Gift were taken to the College of the Arts for training. However, the timing of their departure gave him a unique chance to make this decision for himself. He could simply remain quiet, anonymously sailing away, a random sailor on a ship headed east. If he chose to answer the archmage's question, it would indelibly commit him, his entire life to the college. While he wasn't afraid of what that would mean, he wished he didn't have to make such a swift decision.

Still unsure what to do as the archmage's figure receded, his thoughts turned to Rhianna and their plans for escape. He had gone into Aramar against his father's will, arriving back at Crest just moments before the captain had returned, because he still wondered what he would do for a living once they escaped.

Dael would be able to find them at the college, but perhaps that wouldn't matter? If anyone could shelter them from the wrath of a petty noble it was the spellcasters of the college.

Once that occurred to him the decision was easy. It was everything he needed, everything he wanted. He looked the diminishing figure on the docks right in the eye before he could overthink the situation any more and spoke softly so none of the crew would hear him. For some reason he couldn't explain, he was absolutely certain the distant archmage would hear his words as easily as Jayden himself had a moment before.

"I am Jayden Torell, of Grandell."

The full import of what he'd just done hit him as the black clad stranger spoke his final words, there could be no going back now.

"I will find you, again. Be ready," the distant figure told him before turning to walk back up the long pier and meet the fat little harbourmaster as the now out-of-breath man came puffing up to his side. The pair walked along the pier in animated conversation which Jayden could no longer hear before the archmage mounted a fine-looking horse and headed back towards the city while the harbourmaster went about his business.

Jayden couldn't take his eyes from the mage's back until Crest rounded the first bend in the river, then suddenly found himself having to grip the handrail to hold himself upright as an inexplicable wave of dizziness washed over him.

"You all right Jay?" Jarvis asked abruptly enough that he jumped a foot off the deck.

"Whoa, easy there boy, you be as pale as a sheet. And your hands be shakin'!" The hulking first mate added in sudden concern.

Jayden looked around sickly, half stunned by what he'd just done, and still reeling from the sudden dizziness.

I'm going to be a mage!

His hands refused to stop shaking despite balling them into fists in a futile attempt to hide it.

This must be the quickening, he realised abruptly. It was a sickness that was said to last for days once a new mage used the Gift for the first time.

But how? When?

The archmage had talked to him from the shore, clearly using the Gift to do so.

Did I somehow contribute to that when I gave him my answer?

It seemed unlikely that he could have done so without knowing, but right now Jayden's spinning head would let him consider the subject no further.

"I don't feel so good," he admitted as he slid down the side of the figurehead to sit on the polished wooden decking.

"Boy!" Jarvis bellowed, and the ship's boy appeared as if on cue.

"That was bein' a bit fast Es, you'd better not have been eavesdroppin'!" he shouted, then followed the scolding with, "Fetch Benson and don't be takin' all day about it."

"Yes Sir!" Esdern answered as he slid down the ladder to the main deck and scampered inside the hatch.

"I don't know what's wrong," Jayden said in answer to Jarvis' previous question once Esdern had left them alone, "Maybe I'm just seasick."

Jarvis gave him a withering glare; he didn't enjoy being lied to.

"I don't want to talk about it just yet," Jayden said decisively as he once again tried to stop his hands from shaking, this time by running them roughly through his windblown brown hair.

A mage, me?

He still couldn't fathom it as he rested there against the figurehead, his eyes closed to ward off the spinning.

It changed everything. The entire picture he had in his mind of how his life would turn out had just been altered, and suddenly all his childhood dreams of travel and adventure came rushing back in to fill the void.

Apart from any other consideration, if the archmage reached him before the wedding was scheduled, it might not even be necessary to leave Grandell in a headlong rush away from Dael's guards.

He sat for a while, staring at the shore as the surrounding districts of Aramar slid past slowly, and fought his rebelling stomach while Crest made its way down the Camar towards the distant sea. His hands continued to shake, and he felt as though the entire world were spinning on a different axis, but right now he needed to think. Jayden knew his father wanted him out of Grandell for his own safety, and he instinctively recognised that if he told him what had just happened, David Torell was perfectly capable of turning the ship around right now and delivering him to the college personally. Just to keep him away from Dael.

That wasn't something Jayden could allow.

Being away from Rhianna for the last phase had been bad enough, and he had a feeling the return trip would feel even worse. As much as he didn't relish the prospect of lying to his father, Crest was his fastest way back home and so his 'sickness' would have to be seen as just that, at least until they made it back to Grandell.

After what seemed like hours, his father arrived with the ship's healer. Benson was a short man with a receding hairline, he was also a full member of the Herbalists and Apothecary's Guild. The pair were accompanied by Esdern, whose curious expression had now been replaced by one of concern.

"Are you all right son?" his father asked as the healer knelt beside them and began his examination.

"I don't feel right," Jayden answered groggily as the rail thin Benson examined his eyes and ordered him to cough.

"Say 'ahhh'," Benson directed in his wispy voice, and Jayden complied, feeling like a fool as he became aware that a few of the sailors up in the rigging were watching the proceedings.

His father must have seen him look, because a moment later he looked up himself and bellowed, "Back to work, men," before returning his attention back to Jayden, and Benson's practised ministrations.

The skeletally thin healer frowned for a moment before prodding at his throat and turning Jayden's head from one side to the other.

"Have you eaten anything the rest of the crew hasn't shared?" Benson asked dubiously, and grimaced when Jayden answered truthfully that he hadn't.

He stood and walked a few feet away with David in tow to say something which Jayden couldn't quite make out over the sound of the wind and his own sudden tiredness.

But after only a few moments the pair returned, and Benson knelt down again.

"Can you walk?" he asked seriously.

"Yeah," Jayden replied weakly, "But probably not in a straight line."

Benson raised a slightly amused eyebrow, but didn't hesitate to reach around his back and help Jayden to his feet. He ended up taking most of his weight as Jayden's legs immediately buckled.

"Come on, we'd better get you below," he said while David moved in to support Jayden's other side.

Even through the vast weariness which had overcome him since his brief contact with the archmage, he couldn't help but feel embarrassed when they had to pass him down off the foredeck like a piece of cargo and cart him across the main deck to the hatch which led below.

With a fair amount of effort, the pair managed to carry him down the corridor and into his own cabin where Benson told him in no uncertain terms he needed to rest. A sentiment which Jayden whole-heartedly agreed with as his father helped him remove his boots and jacket, and guided him over to his bed where he flopped down onto the covers and was asleep mere moments later. The last thing he heard as he fell into a troubled slumber was Benson saying quietly to his father that he wasn't sure what sickness afflicted him, but didn't think it was life threatening.

Good, Jayden thought as the darkness took him.

They wouldn't be returning to Aramar after all.

*   *   *

They were back down by the river. He and Rhianna were passing a lazy afternoon skipping stones across the surface while Dael stood a little apart, aiming at a nearby tree he claimed. Although Jayden was sure he was trying to hit the huge beehive which hung high in the branches.

I must be dreaming, he thought foggily as he turned his head towards a commotion a little way up the river. A few of the local fishermen had dragged a huge carp out of the water and were busy congratulating themselves on the catch.

There was a sudden darkness, as though someone had thrown a heavy sheet over his eyes. It was accompanied by a swift jolt of fear as he panicked, then just as jarringly he could see again, only now the scene was different.

He was a small child again, standing in the captain's cabin on board Crest and staring at the huge map which dominated the port wall.

"One day I'll go to all those places," he said to himself as he waited for his father to finish his shift and come below decks to see him.

Again there was the darkness, and after a moment of disorientation, a feeling of dread overtook him as he found himself in the middle of a forest, thick foliage on all sides and only a dim sun overhead to break up the shadows which crowded around. Behind him he heard a snort from the great boar he'd been tracking and froze in fear. It had circled around, hunting him right back. He spun, bringing his spear in line to meet the boar's furious charge as it crashed through the undergrowth towards him. It hit the end of his weapon at full speed and the spear was wrenched from his grasp as the beast smashed into him, just missing his leg with an old and splintered tusk.

Again there was black.

This is turning into a very strange dream, he thought as he waited for the next segment to begin. These were all pieces pulled from more than a dozen years of his life in an apparently random order, and abruptly it struck him as strange that he was able to think at all. He rarely remembered his dreams when he woke, to say nothing of consciously participating in them.

He was riding a horse at the head of a vast column of singing men, the sun beating down upon them as they crested a hill flanked by a pair of enormous rectangular stones set on either side of the road.

Blackness again. That one was no memory of his. The thought only held him a moment though. The blackness was different this time, and somehow even more disconcerting than before. There seemed to be something else in here with him. Almost like a whisper he couldn't quite hear.

He stretched out his hand in a furious motion and a searing ball of flame hurtled from his fingertips, incinerating the side of the barn. A man jumped an impossible distance sideways to escape and hit the ground rolling.

The darkness returned, only this time the whispering was a bit louder. He could nearly make out the words as he strained to hear them.

He crept through an underground cavern large enough to fit a small city. Ahead of him were a dozen inward curving pillars of blue and red flame surrounding a beam of solid white light flecked with gold which ran from floor to ceiling and shed light over half the chamber. He signalled his companions to remain behind. They had played their part well, but there was nothing they could do to help him now.

Darkness swallowed him again, and this time his straining ears caught a snatch of the whispers which seemed to be coming from all around him. "...of dark aspect..." they seemed to say, "...pain shall tear his soul asun..." And then he lost it again.

With frightening speed the things came at him and Jayden ducked under one of the creatures' arms, which suddenly turned into a tentacle and grabbed at him as he went past, clipping his shield instead. He launched a fireball at it, the intense heat evaporating a hole right through its chest, but with an oceanic roar the thing sucked more water up from the river at its feet and was whole again within moments.

Blackness returned, and with it Jayden felt a rising sense of panic. "...destroy all that which stands..."

He could hear the snatches of words more clearly now, and truth be told he'd had more than enough of this dream, which was rapidly descending into the realms of a nightmare.

He had managed to reach the river through the press of battle and looked desperately around, his clothes were spattered with human, and other creatures' blood, but the worst was yet to come. He searched the field for one man, a mage, and his only true opponent. All was chaos at the heart of the battle, and he barely ducked under the swing of a double-headed axe which should have taken off his head. Reflexively he sent out a gout of flame in the Imbic's direction, causing the great brute to back off and look for another fight as it staggered away, its armour still burning in a few different places. Jayden turned towards the river once more, and mounted astride an enormous black stallion, he saw him. The first thing he noticed were the piercing green eyes.

"...only thought is of betrayal..." the next darkness whispered without a pause, then a few seconds later, "...fate shall be decided..."

Suddenly the darkness changed.

He was standing in the huge cavern again, but it was different now. The column of white and gold had disappeared and only the dim light of the fiery columns which stood at its heart remained to illuminate his way. He traversed the distance to where the column of light had been and stood at the centre of the gilded diagram which was etched into the ancient floor. He truly had no idea if this would work or not, but he had to take the chance. "All shall be forgotten," he muttered nervously as he gathered all the power he could for this one final spell. There was no point waiting. If he died, then he died. Even if he survived, he would be changed forever, so he wasn't nearly as concerned as he probably should be. One way or the other his life as it was would end, now. He shot his hand up into the air and with all his might struggled to activate the great machine. It wasn't enough. He strained to gather more power and added it to the flow. There was a sudden noise from deep under the cavern and a blinding light surrounded him. He screamed.

He woke suddenly, still screaming until he realised he was back on board Crest, safe in his own bed. His door flew open without warning, and his father and Benson came rushing back in. David glanced around before asking if he was all right, while Benson sat on the side of the bed and began another, and this time far more thorough, examination.

"I'm fine," Jayden tried to assure them, slightly less dizzy, but even more embarrassed than before as Benson finally finished.

"I just had..." he hesitated, feeling foolish.

"Had what?" his father asked calmly.

"Nothing," he muttered, "Just a nightmare. That's all."

His father grinned, though not condescendingly.

"I see," was his only reply as he motioned for Benson to leave him be.

"Try to get some rest," the healer ordered once again as he left the cabin.

"Rhianna?" David asked with concern once Benson was gone.

"Strangely enough, no," Jayden replied. "Just a very odd dream."

His father nodded and went as far as the door.

"Benson's right Jay, get some rest. If it's still on your mind in the morning, you know where to find me."

Jayden only nodded as his father closed the door behind him. He doubted he would still remember the disturbing dream by morning, but as tired as he now was, he lay there for what seemed like hours, turning the bizarre images over in his mind and wondering where he had come up with such rubbish.

The idea of him leading men into battle was ridiculous, and if he ever saw that beam of white and gold light again he wasn't about to go anywhere near it.

His thoughts chased themselves round in circles for hours, until finally, near sunset, he fell into a deep but uneasy sleep.

*   *   *

Jayden stretched, blinking to adjust his eyes to the morning light as he came out onto Crest's main deck. The dizziness which had beset him after talking with the archmage back at the capital had been gone by the time he woke the next day. The weakness and shakes had persisted almost a week though before finally leaving him in some semblance of peace, and good riddance to them. Unfortunately, the strange dream, although never repeated, even now refused to leave his mind, causing an odd uneasiness in the pit of his stomach every time he thought on it.

They had made good time since leaving Aramar nearly a phase ago, and after briefly surveying the landmarks along the coastline he realised they should reach Grandell harbour in only another hour or two, three days ahead of schedule. His father had been as good as his word, and according to Jayden's calculations he still had over five weeks to plan and attempt the escape before the Ginfron's earliest deadline for the wedding was reached.

The wind had freshened, and the sky had turned a murky grey-black during the course of the day, but above him the sails were full, and the singing of taut lines could be heard as he made his way across to the prow.

He was not looking forward to this next encounter. He had played the scene over and over in his head a thousand times over the last few weeks, trying vainly to make it come out all right. But when it came right down to it, he could always see the look of disappointment in his father's eyes. Despite all his attempts, Jayden still had no idea how to tell the man who had raised him that in all likelihood this would be their last day together. He planned to try convincing Rhianna to wait until the archmage arrived, but the wedding was drawing closer and the odds were good she would insist on leaving immediately.

If she will even talk to me at all.

In truth, he knew there was a good chance that

tomorrow or the next day he would leave Grandell with her for good. Together they would try to escape to Aramar, where the College of the Arts awaited him, and no one had any interest in the minor nobleman Dael of Grandell, or what had happened by the river last spring.

Reaching the front of the main deck, Jayden climbed the steeply slanted ladder to the foredeck. As he reached the top, the familiar sight of his father greeted him, standing legs parted for balance and arms crossed, just behind the swordfish figurehead.

As the salted spray from an errant wave caught him, Jayden realised a certain sharpness in the air which spoke of clouds about to open up.

The wind grew brisker around him.

Crossing the foredeck, he went to stand beside the burly man, still trying to think of a way to tell his father he was leaving Grandell for good.

*   *   *

David Torell stood on the foredeck of Crest, watching the impressive storm clouds forming up ahead.

He was deep in thought as Jayden came up beside him and stood quietly, something obviously on his mind.

"Looks like we're in for some bad weather," David said without taking his eyes from the ocean.

Jayden nodded reflectively.

"Do you think it will delay our arrival in Grandell?" his son eventually asked.

"I would have thought you of all people would not be so eager to get back home," David softly probed.

"It's not Grandell I'm eager to get back to," Jayden

muttered under his breath.

David nodded sagely and Jayden turned red, clearly he hadn't meant that last comment to be heard.

"I know you two think you're in love," David said with a sigh as he turned to look his son in the face, "But there is nothing you can do about it. Rhianna has been promised to Dael, and however fine he has split hairs on the matter, I have it on very good technical advice the marriage is, unfortunately, legal. In a little more than a phase, Rhianna will be the next Countess of Grandell. It has been lawfully, if not morally, arranged."

"Yes, arranged," his son shot back, "And without her consent!"

David sighed.

"I know, but it has always been that way with the nobility Jayden. You know that."

"Nobility!" Jayden whispered, his voice low and fierce.

"Her great auntie married into a minor noble house. There isn't even a single blood tie!"

Once again David sighed in resignation.

"I know that too, Jay."

As he spoke, the first small droplets of rain began to patter down against the timber decking.

"Boy!" he shouted, once again becoming the captain.

Esdern came scrambling up the ladder to the foredeck a moment later and stood at attention.

"Bring the men their coats."

As the boy scrambled back out of sight, a quick look at Jayden showed that his son had plenty more to say on the matter.

"Come inside," David ordered. They were both off watch, and he moved away from the prow, expecting

Jayden to follow. Whatever his son was going to try, it would be better if he found out here and now where the men were loyal to him.

As the two of them crossed the main deck, they exchanged greetings with Jarvis, and David ordered him to send word when they were entering Grandell harbour.

They continued inside, the sound of the wind and the first mate bellowing orders fading as they moved further below and headed for the captain's quarters.

Only when they had entered the cabin and secured the latch behind them did he speak again.

"Out with it boy."

Despite what Jayden had already told him, he knew his own son well enough to know he hadn't yet offered up whatever news he had come out on deck to tell him. Abruptly, David found himself wondering what could weigh so heavily on Jayden's mind that he would use his problems with Rhianna as a lead to broaching the subject.

Jayden looked down at the smooth polished decking of the cabin floor for a moment, sorting his thoughts, and when he looked up again, David knew he wasn't going to like whatever it was his son had to say.

"I'm leaving Grandell. Rhianna is coming with me."

So that's it.

David had resigned himself to something like this happening phases ago, but to hear the words spoken aloud still cut to his heart.

"You can't," he found himself saying.

"Dael doesn't care about you. If you take off by yourself I think he would be just as happy to see you go. But mark my words Jayden, if you try to leave Grandell with Rhianna at your side Dael will have armed men after you within a day."

A silence borne of shared knowledge descended around them. Outside the hull, the gentle sound of the rain splashing against the deck could be faintly heard over the sound of the waves as they slapped against the wooden planking of the ship. For a moment the two men stood listening, each knowing the words which would be spoken next.

"I know," Jayden said at length. "But I must try."

David looked intently at his son, and for just an instant he thought he caught a glimpse of the man Jayden was so quickly becoming.

It's something in his eyes.

"When will you be leaving?" David asked as he stood, turning his gaze out the small window the captain's cabin afforded.

"Tomorrow most likely," Jayden said quietly, "As soon after nightfall as we can arrange."

David nodded. This must be what Jayden had been planning since before they had left for the capital.

"I was hoping to borrow some supplies," Jayden said, breaking the train of thought.

David's eyes narrowed thoughtfully at the request. If Jayden really intended on going through with this, he needed to see just how serious his son was about the whole thing, for both Jayden and Rhianna's safety. Right now was probably the best opportunity he would get.

Turning fully towards the window, he turned his back to his son, watching only Jayden's reflection in the polished glass which kept the now constant downpour outside.

"No," he said simply, "If the count found out I had helped Rhianna to escape, and he would. The young fool might take it into his head to exact some form of retribution from your mother or sister."

The reflection in the porthole showed Jayden flinch at the thought, and it made David wonder whether he truly was prepared to deal with this whole situation.

"Or did you think once Grandell was out of sight it would all just go away? It won't you know, and we will be left here to live with the consequences of your actions."

He didn't want to be cruel, but if the boy couldn't even handle a dressing down by his old man, there was no way he would be able to deal with Dael's guards.

Perhaps it would have been better for everyone in the long run if he'd marooned Jayden back in Aramar until this entire mess was settled. It had been a tempting option when he had fallen ill shortly after leaving, but with absolute certainty he knew his son would not, could not, have forgiven him after the promise he had made, and that had stayed his hand. Now he wondered if that estrangement might not have been the best possible outcome to this whole disgraceful affair.

"So what do you propose," Jayden responded stiffly, "That I just allow the woman I love to be forced into marrying a man she loathes because of her foster parents' greed?!"

"Of course not," David replied with difficulty, as he turned back towards his son, "But if you go through with this your resolve must never waiver. Dael will use every trick he has to get Rhianna back, and lying to you is the very least of them. If you do escape, you must never return to Grandell Jayden. No matter what you hear."

Silence fell, but the determined look on Jayden's face never changed, and David silently accepted his son would go through with this insane plan no matter what he said. And when it came right down to it, he knew there was no way a pair of youths on horseback could evade Dael's professional trackers.

He wanted more than anything to help Jayden and Rhianna escape to somewhere they could be happy and live in peace. However, what he'd said before about Dael taking retribution on Lyssa or Miya would more than likely come true if he did. There just weren't any good options here.

He sighed as he moved to sit in the bolted down chair which stood behind his desk, trying hard to convince himself Jayden could handle the situation.

"If this is all the time we have, we shouldn't spend it arguing," David offered with grudging acceptance.

"Tell me son, where do you plan to go. How will you make a living for yourself and your new wife? I assume that's what you have in mind. Have you asked her yet?" he demanded suddenly, the words coming out in a rush as the possibility occurred to him.

"Not yet," Jayden replied with just a hint of a grin, "But soon."

Jayden halted for a long moment after that admission, plainly attempting to gather his thoughts.

"There is something else I have to tell you."

David felt his own face take on a pained expression.

"Go on," was all he said aloud though.

Jayden looked at the ground for a long moment, but finally spoke.

"A few weeks ago, when we sailed out of the capital, I saw the harbourmaster running after us along the waterfront."

"And you didn't think the captain needed to know?!"

David interrupted, startled.

"At first I wasn't sure he wanted us," Jayden continued defensively, "But then he began pointing at a pier and jumping up and down as though he had red ants in his breeches. I was about to let Jarvis know, but then I saw what he was pointing at. It was a man dressed all in black, except for a silver-lined cloak, standing right at the tip of one of the deep draught piers. He looked at me in the strangest way and then he looked away. When he looked back though I could see his lips move as if he was talking normally, and I could hear him as though he were standing right there on the deck with me."

"An Archmage?!" David exclaimed in consternation. "What did he want?"

Jayden looked down at the deck again for an instant before meeting his eyes.

"He said, 'You are one of us,' and then he asked my name."

For a long moment David just sat there in shock, his mouth moving several times before he could make the words come out.

"But… but you were tested, the mage said you had no ability in the Gift at all."

Jayden nodded his agreement, "I know, but archmagi don't come down to the docks to tell tales to passing ships either," he replied.

David sat bolt upright in his chair. "Did you tell him your name?" he asked intently, knowing his son's entire future depended on this answer.

"I did."

"Then you've sealed yourself to their order for life," David told him bluntly, though privately admitting he was not disappointed.

"I know," his son replied just as seriously, "But whatever life awaits me in the college almost has to be better than the one which awaits me back in Grandell. Besides, with the college's support, Rhianna might just have a chance at making a clean break with Dael after all."

There didn't seem to be anything to say to that, so the two of them just sat for a while, listening as the rain pounded a steady rhythm against the hull.

"That's why you got sick the day we left Aramar," David mused, "I've heard rumours that happens when a mage uses the Gift for the first time. I've never seen it myself before though. No wonder Benson couldn't work out what was wrong with you."

Beyond the window and the rain, David was just able to make out the fuzzy darkness of the coastline as they sailed past the familiar shores of this home stretch of the Jade Coast.

"I don't suppose I can convince you to hold off leaving until the mage comes to Grandell for you?" he asked wearily, although he was already sure of what the answer would be.

His son was full of surprises today though.

"My hope is that I can convince Rhianna to do just that. To wait and see if he makes it to Grandell before the wedding is scheduled, though I have no real confidence she will be happy to do so. Even if she is willing, if the time gets too close, we won't have any choice but to leave without him."

"I see," David said again, with a growing sense of dread. At best this mysterious archmage might be a few days behind if he'd found a fast ship. If he were coming overland though, he would be considerably further away.

"You've chosen a difficult path Jayden. What if the mage arrives in time but refuses to help Rhianna escape?"

There was a moment then when his son's face appeared startled, but the determined look returned after a moment, stronger than before.

"Then I will refuse to cooperate with him. Even if he uses force to bring me to Aramar, he can't compel me to learn from the magi there, or become a loyal servant of the king."

David shot up out of his chair and crossed quietly to the cabin door, unlatching the small lock and flinging back the timber frame to look out into the corridor.

After satisfying himself that no one had been listening, he closed and re-bolted the door and strode back to his chair where he sat slowly, deliberately, and as calmly as he could.

Leaning forward intently he forced his hands to unclench and placed them on the table, face down.

"Boy, if any number of people heard what you said just now, especially those loyal to Dael, you could find yourself at the wrong end of a noose. I hope your plan works, I really do, but be more careful of what you say, and even more so when and who you say it to. Not even one of the noblemen who oppose Dael's methods would hesitate to have you hung for treason against the crown."

"I know that, I didn't mean…"

"Of course you didn't, but Dael would need little more excuse to see you dead than the words you just spoke out of hand."

There were footsteps in the corridor followed by a timid knock at the door and then Esdern called out.

"Excuse me Captain, but the first mate requests your presence on deck."

"Thank you Esdern, I'll be there presently."

"Aye Sir," the youth replied before his footsteps could be heard scampering off toward the end of the hall where the hatch leading to the main deck was located.

David stood, followed quietly by his son.

"Jayden, whatever happens I want you to promise me you won't do anything... rash," he said after a moment's hesitation.

"You mean like running off with a nobleman's betrothed?" Jayden asked with a humorous smirk which David couldn't help but return before becoming serious once more.

"I mean like getting yourself killed. I want to see you happy Jayden, but even more than that, I want to see you alive. Perhaps that's selfish of me, but I guess that's a father's right."

"I won't," Jayden told him solemnly, "I have too much to live for now."

After a final moment of intense study David nodded slightly.

"Good. Then let's get up on deck."

Patience is a virtue, until it is not.
Arborii proverb.

CHAPTER 5

ONE SHINING MOMENT

The pier was hard to make out through the driving grey sleet which now filled the sky. Crest had entered the sheltered waters of Grandell Cove just in time to take shelter from the rising sea, but despite the calmer water, inch wide hailstones now pelted the hull as Jayden attended to his tasks. He couldn't help but feel sorry for the men in the rigging as he saw them tying off sails and securing lines with fingers half frozen by the unusually heavy, and numbingly cold rain.

As they returned to the deck, the captain bellowed over the sound of the storm for the rowboats to be dropped. Jarvis nodded once to acknowledge the captain's order before calling some of the crew to help, then slipped over the side into one of the two twelve seat craft which would pull Crest the final few spans towards the dock. Under normal conditions Jayden knew either his father or Jarvis could have the ship moored in their sleep, and even he was getting good at the precise manoeuvres a ship as big as Crest needed to dock safely.

These were anything but normal conditions however, and with visibility dimmed to almost nothing there was no point risking a collision with the pier.

It was only just after midday by Jayden's estimation, but the sun was nowhere to be seen, not even as a bright patch in the unrelieved grey of the storm clouds above.

He wiped the cascade of water from his face and peered into the soggy darkness in the direction he knew the shore to be. Even at this range, the pair of dim yellow and red lanterns which marked the end of the pier were all that could be seen of the long wooden structure. Jayden guessed they were no more than thirty spans away at most, everything else was a haze. A quick look over the side showed him the water below was an inky black, although unmarred by any sizeable waves. The driving rain itself was the problem, and had completely soaked through the neck and sleeves of his heavy, oil-treated coat since coming back out on deck.

The rowboats had pulled them half the distance towards the dock when he was finally able to make out the pylons as an indistinct blackness in the blur of wind and rain. The sky was the darkest he had ever seen it during the day and Crest thundered with the sound of eyeball sized hailstones hitting the deck on every side. It was more than a little unnerving.

From the afterdeck, a sailor gave a yell which was barely audible over the hail and occasional roar of thunder, and Jayden turned to see his father already rushing over to the wheel. The sailor piloting the ship was now lying on the deck unconscious, bleeding profusely from a large cut on his head where a huge hailstone had hit him squarely in the temple.

Looking around, Jayden spotted Esdern crouching near the hatch and shouted, "Get Benson!" at the top of his voice. Esdern looked at him quizzically, clearly unable to hear the command over the violence of the storm, but as he sent his gaze to where Jayden was pointing, he gave a thumbs up before rushing below to find the healer. Jayden rushed over to help the injured man, kneeling beside him and applying pressure to the unconscious man's wound while kneeling over him to keep the downpour off his face. There was a sudden bump as Crest reached the dock, though not enough to unbalance him, and then lines were being thrown over moorings as sailors made themselves busy fastening Crest to the pier as quickly as they could. No one wanted to be out in this weather a second longer than was absolutely necessary to get the work done.

The storm continued raging around them as strike after strike of lightning began illuminating the harbour and cliffs on either side for a split second at a time.

He could feel from the gentle swaying of the vessel that the waters in the cove were almost still, except for the squall stirring the few small waves which made it past the harbour mouth to froth.

That was about the most violent the ocean ever became in here, and why the docks were located in this particular cove even though there were much bigger and deeper inlets only a few miles up the coast.

Trade by shipping was the lifeblood of Grandell's economy, and the sure anchorage this little cove provided was well known by any man who had sailed more than a year or two on the east coast of Jeranon. Some people said the inlet was once altered by magical means to ensure the water would always remain calm, but those were just stories told by old drunks to pass the time of day, and no one took them seriously. Normally the ship would be unloaded as soon as they arrived in port, but with this much rain, hail and darkness there was just no way the work could be safely carried out.

Something hard and cold smashed into Jayden's arm, and for a moment it went completely numb. For an instant the memory of that day in the river, and the tortured walk back to Grandell carrying Rhianna on a foot numbed from the cold came rushing in as he stood massaging the site of the impact with his still usable hand. After a few long moments though, feeling slowly returned, accompanied by a bad case of pins and needles. Jayden picked up the offending hailstone and threw it overboard with an annoyed grunt. Benson had come on deck in the meantime, looking severely put out at having to be outside in the howling storm while most of the sailors rushed below to gather up their things. He told Jayden to remove his hand and inspected the wound before instructing him to hold the man's head still while he wound a bandage around and around until the blood flow had been stemmed.

With the ship now stationary, David left the wheel and came to help them.

"Open the hatch," he ordered as he and Benson picked up the still unconscious man. Jayden moved as fast as he could to the main hatch without slipping on the soaked deck and opened it long enough to let the others pass the sailor down between them. As soon as they were through he joined them, slamming the hatch closed as quickly as possible. Unfortunately, there was now a large puddle near the hatch that Esdern would have to clean up.

"How is he?" David asked Benson once most of the outside noise was left behind.

"Provided he wakes up soon he'll be fine in a day or two," Benson replied with only a small amount of concern on his face. "But I need to get this wound properly sown up or he'll have a nasty scar."

David nodded and the two men carried the sailor into the nearby infirmary room while Jayden held the door for them.

After the man had been placed on a utilitarian bed, Benson assured them he could take it from there, and Jayden and David left the healer to work in peace.

"May as well pass the word for everyone but dock crew to go on home until morning," his father said once the door had closed behind them a moment later.

"I have a few things to finish up so I'll remain on board. Unloading is out of the question for the moment, and there's not a lot more we can do until this storm eases off a bit. By the looks of it that might not be till tomorrow at the least, so you can head home as well."

Jayden nodded his agreement, knowing his father would have asked him to remain if he'd needed aid dealing with the injured crewman, or anything else.

"Okay, I'll let mother know what's happening," he called to his father, already heading towards the hatch to give Jarvis the word. Fortunately, he ran into the first mate before he had to go outside. The hulking man was already coming to see what the next orders were, given the unusual situation. Once he'd relayed his father's orders, Jayden headed back to his own room to gather the few things he'd brought with him on the trip. He quietly gave the door the password as he reached it, then pushed it open to reveal the small cabin.

The few items his father had brought him before they left, with the exception of his sheathed blade and leather purse, were already bundled in a sack on his bed. He tied both loose items on under his sodden coat before picking up the bundle full of clothes and other various items and slung the sack over his shoulder. Glancing around one last time to make sure he hadn't forgotten anything, Jayden took a deep breath as he thought on what he now had to do. He left the small cabin, locking the door behind him as he headed back up on deck.

If anything, the weather seemed to have worsened in the few minutes he'd been below. The sky was no longer dark grey but the pitch black of a clouded, moonless night, and Jayden shivered as he came back into the chilling rain which continued seeping through the neck hole of his still soaked coat.

The smooth wooden decking of Crest was magically warded to repel the rain, but he still had to watch his footing as the constant downpour kept renewing what the decking sloughed off. Even at this distance the lanterns on the pier were hard to make out through the torrential downpour. After shielding his eyes from the driving rain though, he was able to find his way to where the gangplank was being augmented by two burly sailors wielding a catch-rope. The men didn't look happy to be stuck out in the rain and hail. Nonetheless they were taking their job of making sure no one fell between the ship and pier as they crossed the treacherously rocking piece of wood seriously. One of the sailors threw the rope to him as Jayden approached. He fastened the slipknot around his right wrist and held the length of it as he traversed the bucking gangplank down onto the pier. Relieved he hadn't needed it, but glad it was there all the same, he loosened the rope from his hand and threw it back to the sailor with a nod of thanks before turning towards shore.

In the time it had taken him to reach the dubious safety of the long wooden pier, the driving rain had soaked him through. From the increased weight of his small sack of belongings, he could tell they too had been subjected to the saturating assault of the storm.

With every part of him drenched already there didn't seem much point in hurrying to where the carriage was kept. Not to mention that with only the black silhouette of the dock against the white froth of the waves below to guide him forward, it was worth the extra care.

The wind gave him a sudden shove towards the edge of the pier and nearly sent him tumbling into the inky blackness of the cove. He only avoided the fall because the wind shoved him violently back in the opposite direction a moment later. As soon could plant his feet securely he hurried toward the safety of the shore, stumbling forward until the marker lights finally came into sight on the still invisibly storm-wracked coast.

This is ridiculous!

Despite another, thankfully less violent shove from the wind, he made it on to dry land without further incident.

If it can still justifiably be called 'dry', he thought as he ran a cleansing hand over his face, removing the rain for all of about half a second.

Despite his earlier idea about not needing to hurry since he was already drenched, the constant thundering of the rain and hail hitting every part of his body was starting to get more than a little irritating. He began to jog towards the building where one of his family's carriages was usually kept.

The door was unlocked as usual, there weren't enough carriages in Grandell that anyone could steal one without being noticed immediately by the local townsfolk, especially since all the prominent families painted them with their merchant sigils. But as he slipped inside, he found both horses and carriage were nowhere to be seen.

He couldn't quite credit the idea someone had made off with the carriage in such muddy conditions, which only left a member of his family or someone acting on their orders. Either way it was an irritation he didn't need as he slipped back outside, unintentionally leaving a spreading puddle of mud and water in the entrance. He shut the door tightly behind him and headed away from the docks at a half jog. He really didn't want to be out in this weather for the next hour, but since there wasn't a great deal of choice in the matter he kept going. The rain coursed through the black sky, hammering at him while the wind continued its attempts to bully him to the ground whenever he least expected.

The small houses on both sides of the street all had their lanterns lit inside, and Jayden soon found if he walked straight up the middle of the road, he could just make out the glow to either side. He used it as a marker to keep moving in the right direction as he sloshed his way up the flooded street.

It was better than nothing.

*　　　*　　　*

Even as Jayden moved away from the docks, another ship, this one much smaller and sleeker than Crest, was just pulling up on the other side of the same pier. It was challenged by the sailors who still waited miserably on the dock for the last of Crest's crew to disembark. As it slowed to a halt, an impossibly bright, Gift-wrought lantern was lit on board the newcomer's ship, illuminating the pennant bearing the flame and dragon Sigel of Aramar's College of the Arts.

The two sailors looked at each other as the smaller ship threw ropes over the dock moorings of its own accord and came to a perfect stop just out from the pier.

"Fetch the captain, Wallace!" the higher ranked of the two sailors ordered his companion, "He'll want to know about this!"

As the remaining sailor kept a close eye on the mage's ship, and no one else in their right mind would dare to fly a college pennant from their mast, he looked on in disbelief as a portion of the hull seemed to reach out for the dock and latch on, forming a path from ship to pier which looked a great deal steadier than their own rocking gangplank.

Oblivious to the howling wind and driving rain, the sailor's attention was now firmly rooted on the spectacle before him.

He had always thought of Crest as being a good balance between master shipbuilding and Gift-wrought enhancements, but this sleek little college ship was something else entirely.

He continued his vigil, willing something else to happen now that the ship was properly moored.

*   *   *

Archmage Tolmarak could hear the rain pounding even with the deck-hatch still closed. He had appropriated this college ship, 'Sling' it was called, and sailed from Aramar as soon as he could arrange for the men and supplies to be loaded, he would need them to carry out the king's conscription orders. He hadn't been particularly surprised at the results of the council meeting after he'd left, only that Erian had ordered such a massive build-up of forces to deal with the threat. And yet, if the worst occurred, if Heramiir really was working with the western nations, he was grudgingly forced to admit that it still might not be enough.

Tolmarak had brought a hundred veteran soldiers and his own personal mageguard contingent with him to help with the conscriptions. His own task was to seek out any citizen with potential in the Gift and return them safely to the college for training. That being the case, his first stop of course was Grandell, where possibly the most powerful student he had ever discovered awaited his arrival. He had realised immediately this Jayden, whose aura he had felt through the Palace Garden's wall, and again at Aramar's docks where he had only just tracked the boy's aura down in time after having searched the capital all night, surely had to be one of those very rare people whose talent hadn't developed until much later in life than most. There was simply no other way someone as powerful in the Gift as he could walk freely around Jeranon for so many years without being noticed by half a dozen different magi, even in this far-flung province.

Tolmarak thought it likely that if he was correct about Jayden's potential in the Gift, someday the boy would join the ranks of the archmagi. If his intellect proved as powerful as his talent for the Gift, and Tolmarak could only wish for such an outcome, the possibility existed that the boy might even be trained to take up a position as leader of one of the two college's someday.

Though if that ever occurs it will be many years after I have met the black lady, he thought wryly.

Unfortunately, that possibility also assumed the boy survived the coming war, and there was no longer any real doubt in Tolmarak's mind the current crisis would come to exactly that. Of course an envoy had to be sent just in case this dispute could be settled peacefully; but if Heramiir truly had the loyalty of Miralthrall's magi, Tolmarak held out no real hope they would be dissuaded from their course in time to avert a brutally fought and bloody civil war.

None of that is a concern for right now though, he reminded himself, focusing on the task at hand. He could feel the strength of Jayden's aura somewhere on the shore ahead, and it was hurrying away. Sling's captain had reported a three-masted ship entering the cove just ahead of them, and Tolmarak thought it was likely the same vessel Jayden had been aboard when he had first seen him a little under a phase ago. The huge ship the boy had been aboard would have needed to make an exceptional run to travel so far in such a short time. Sling was one of the college's best ships though, and even with several days of bad weather early in the trip they had caught up with Crest in good order.

Now all he had to do was find the boy in the worst storm he had seen in a great many years, and prepare him to fight a war that even Tolmarak wasn't entirely sure they could win.

Gathering a mere fragment of his power he shaped the air above him into a dome that would move as he did, and reached out to open the deck-hatch which would lead him into the storm.

*   *   *

"Jayden! Jayden!"

For a moment he thought his mind was playing tricks on him. As Jayden turned from trudging up a street pounded to mush by the force of the constant rain, he was slowly able to make out the features of the person who was desperately calling his name over the howling of the storm.

"Genna!" he shouted back, waving a greeting which she ignored as she rushed to reach him through the nearly foot deep mud. She slipped as the slush which had once been a road stubbornly refused to relinquish its hold on one of her feet, and before she could react she was thrown face down in the mud with a splash audible even from where he was standing. She didn't stay down for long though. Before he could close even half the distance, Genna had scrambled back to her feet and continued her headlong charge at where he was still making his way towards her. She didn't even bother to go back for her shoe.

There was something not right about all this, and a second before the muddied, red-headed girl reached him, he was able to see her expression clearly for the first time.

"Thank the Maker you're here!" she sobbed hysterically as she collapsed against him, obviously close to exhaustion.

"Genna, what is it?! What's wrong?!" he shouted, half over the rain, and half because something immensely cold and heavy had just settled itself deep in the pit of his stomach.

Although she was exhausted and crying, she pushed

herself away from his steadying hold long enough to look at him face to face, and what he saw in that instant was enough to confirm all his worst fears a hundred times over.

"It's Rhianna, you've got to help her!" Genna screamed over the rain and wind.

"Dael has moved the wedding up to today and Rhianna is being escorted around the clock by his personal guard so she doesn't try to escape again."

"What!? She tried to escape on her own?" Jayden exclaimed, even as a hot stab of guilt sliced through him.

"But she knew I was coming back for her once Dael thought he'd won."

"The last she saw of you was the day before Crest sailed out! She thought you'd just left her here!" Genna screamed furiously, but even through the rain he could see she was still crying.

"She didn't get my message?!" He shouted as the cold thing in his stomach worked its way even deeper.

How could I have been so stupid! How could I...

"There's more," Genna interrupted before he could finish the thought, "I was having lunch at home today when, when..."

"When what?!" Jayden shouted more loudly than was truly necessary, but he had to find out what had happened. Storm or no storm he had to get Rhianna out of Grandell immediately, and the thunder and rain could follow Dael into any of the nine hells they chose if they tried to stop him.

"When what?!" he shouted again, and this time Genna seemed to snap out of whatever horrific memory she was immersed in.

"She came to my door, drenched to the bone and

holding a filleting knife so tightly her hands were pure white. But not even this storm could wash away the blood that covered her from head to foot. She just stood there, shivering as she told me she had killed both of the guards Dael had set to keep her prisoner in that dead tone she's taken on ever since you left."

"What happened Genna? Is she safe?" Jayden interrupted. The rest of the story could wait. He had to get to her now, before Dael's dead guards were discovered.

"I tried to bring her inside, I did. But then a patrol spotted her from across the street, and from the looks of them they already knew about the murders. But Rhianna didn't leave straight away. She looked at me in the strangest way and whispered that she would not marry Dael. Then she turned to the soldiers and brandished the knife at them and screamed like some kind of animal. She waited until they were almost on top of her and then she screamed 'I will not be Dael's slave! Not Ever!' and ran back into the storm with the entire patrol right on her tail."

Jayden felt chilled all over. It had nothing to do with the storm.

What have I done?

His rucksack fell unheeded to the cold muddied ground.

"Did she get away?" he asked a moment later as the question managed to penetrate his horror at Genna's vivid retelling.

"I think so," she replied as she wiped the ever-present rain away from a face already washed spotless from her fall in the mud a minute before.

"Before the storm swallowed them up, I think she was pulling away from them. If she could have kept that pace up for a few minutes they wouldn't have been able to follow her in this," Genna sobbed hopefully.

"But she could be anywhere. You have to find her Jayden. When I saw her, she didn't even have a cloak. If she stays out in this storm for more than another few hours she'll be dead before Dael even has a chance to find her."

A snatch of conversation filtered through his distressed mind from the last time he and Rhianna had talked, sending another stab of guilt and shame down his back that threatened to break him right then and there.

Not while I have you, the crystal-clear memory of Rhianna's voice whispered tauntingly into his mind.

"I think that might be what she intends," Jayden said quietly as the cold heavy thing in his stomach began to writhe, making him feel as though he was going to empty its contents in one enormous lurch.

"Genna, go to my house, and if no one is watching get two horses ready. I think I know where Rhianna might be, and if I do find her we are going to be leaving in a hurry. He turned away from the red-headed girl to whom he owed so much, but then stopped.

"Dael won't be pleased you helped us, if you want to get a third horse ready, you would be a welcome companion."

He didn't know if he should have made the offer, it might even put Genna in more danger if she accepted than if she stayed. But it was done now and there was no more time to be wasted.

Without another word he turned and ran in the direction of the cliff top path as fast as the sucking mud, which was once the main street of Grandell, would allow. He cursed himself for a fool with every step, hoping desperately that her life hadn't been saved last year only to have her go through all she had endured since then, and now lose it because he'd lacked the courage to stay in Grandell and see their escape plans through to the end.

*   *   *

Tolmarak stepped out into the raging storm. The small ward he had set a moment before deflected the rain and hail away from him as he crossed Sling's gently rocking deck and moved down the gangplank onto a soaked wooden pier which looked to be in very good repair. Once he had found Jayden and scanned the town for any others with potential, he thought he might return here and spend a few hours investigating the Gift-wrought construct that kept the water in this little cove almost calm despite the dire storm which threatened to wash away half the town. It was a minor matter, but he had never seen a construct designed in exactly this manor before, and if he wasn't mistaken, it had to be a thousand years old at the least.

Something like that is always worth a look, he thought as he was stopped by a middle-aged man in the uniform of the huge ship docked across the pier from them.

"Welcome to my dock, Archmage," the man said respectfully, "You may of course remain here for as long as your business requires."

"Thank you, Captain," he replied as he continued past the drenched man who turned to fall in beside him. He had no real interest in continuing the conversation, or in the captain's permission, and captain he must be if called this pier 'his' dock. No simple crewmember would lay

193

claim to such a thing without cause. At any rate, it served nothing to make the man angry, so Tolmarak allowed the captain to walk alongside him for a few moments longer.

"Might I ask what your business is here in Grandell?" the captain asked curiously.

Few people had the nerve to question an archmage about his business, especially out in the provinces where the magi were still held in some regard by the general populace. It caught him a little off guard.

Tolmarak halted on the rain-pounded pier and the captain followed his lead.

"It is my own," he answered as he began to walk again, leaving the soaked but straight-backed man behind.

"Is it because of Jayden?" he heard the man call over the storm before he had gone more than a half-dozen steps. He stopped again, waiting just long enough for the captain to catch up, before continuing down the pier.

"He has told you," Tolmarak surmised as they neared the shore.

"He is my son," The captain replied as they kept moving towards the lanterns which marked the coastline.

"Will he come willingly?" Tolmarak asked as the boy's aura abruptly veered away from its previous path at the speed of a quick run.

"Yes, he wants to become a mage," the captain told him at length, "But there is a problem…"

"There always is," Tolmarak sighed.

"Very few of those found with the Gift are happy to just pack up their homes and lives and take up residence in the college. So, what particular condition does Jayden wish to place upon us before we can teach him our ways?"

'It can't be this easy,' the captain's expression seemed to

say as he turned a startled look towards the archmage.

Tolmarak caught the glance and smiled.

"Whatever you have heard, Captain, we are not kidnappers, nor slavers. What point would there be in training these young people to be magi if they were not loyal to the king and to Jeranon once we were done?"

The captain continued to look at him, and Tolmarak could see the excitement growing in the man's eyes. He had a feeling it meant Jayden would ask for something big.

"I see you already know what your son's demand will be," he observed, making the big man blink.

The rain continued to pound down around them, skipping away from Tolmarak and drenching Mr. Torell. The captain seemed not to care as they left the pier, the man motioning him to a small building nearby where he said his carriage was kept. The carriage was nowhere to be found though, so the two of them continued up the main street on foot. It wasn't long before Tolmarak felt the need to employ a basic earth spell to harden the ground in front of them as they walked along the mud churned street, and their journey became easier.

The deep darkness the storm had brought with it was starting to itch at Tolmarak's senses, and he abruptly found himself wondering whether the rain and wind were an entirely natural phenomenon. Certainly no human hand was involved. Someone powerful enough in the Gift to employ it at this level would be able to be felt from miles away, and none of the western sorcerers were close enough for this kind of mischief. Tolmarak shook his head as he discarded the thin line of reasoning.

He must be getting jumpy in his old age if a simple storm gave him the jitters. He wondered idly what Adriaan would say if she knew. Always a practical woman, she had been born without so much as a wisp of Gift talent. It hadn't taken him long to realise all those years ago that underestimating her in almost any way was a serious mistake indeed though.

Tolmarak shook off the sentimental thought and concentrated for a moment on locating Jayden, who had moved even further away from where he had been.

"Do you have any idea where your son is now?" Tolmarak asked impatiently as the rain intensified even further.

"He should be nearly at home by now!" The captain shouted over the sudden torrent of water which made even the stalwart captain bow his head.

Tolmarak guided the rain away from him with a thought, and the captain looked up appreciatively at the storm clouds which could no longer touch him.

"He appears to be running, in that direction," Tolmarak said as he pointed towards the east of town.

"Are you sure?" the man asked incredulously.

Tolmarak just looked at him patiently for a moment. It was enough.

"My apologies Archmage," the captain amended, "But there is nothing out there except the forest and the hills.

At that piece of information even Tolmarak frowned.

"Nevertheless, that is where we will find him," the archmage said as he set off in the direction he had pointed.

*   *   *

Jayden continued to run. He stumbled on a tree root which had been revealed to the outside world as the rain stripped away the surrounding dirt, but managed to recover his balance in time. He slowed for a moment, then gave a shrug since he couldn't really feel any pain due to the cold starting to numb his extremities.

"Keep going," he muttered to himself as soon as he had caught his breath a little.

The top of the path was in sight now and another blast of wind nearly knocked him off his feet as he left the protective cover of the trees and headed out along the most dangerous section of the track.

The cliff edge was obscured by rain and darkness, but out to sea he could make out an incredible lightning show which he would have loved to watch on any normal day. He made sure he stayed well back from the sheer edge as he started north. Every few seconds he had to stop and blink as a particularly bright flash of lightning would temporarily blind him to the otherwise murkily dark surroundings. The numbing wind constantly caught at his clothes, trying to drag him off his feet again and again, but he would allow nothing to keep him from his goal.

Eventually his dogged persistence paid off as the dark mass of the boulder came into view. He began to carefully place his feet on the tiny protrusions which were the only way up. The water cascading down around him didn't make things any easier, nor did the tingling ache which filled his fingers whenever he put his weight on them. With a bit of care though he soon neared the top without mishap. He was about to place his hands over the leading edge of the plateau when the sound of a shout reached him over the thundering of the storm.

"Rhianna!" he yelled as he threw caution to the driving wind and vaulted up the last span of the crevice to catch the lip of the boulder, before hauling himself up on top. As he turned from his awkward position to face the main part of the cliff, he was shocked to see a pair of heavy boots standing not two feet from his face. The man they belonged to was huge and thickset, but most unnervingly, he was wearing the livery of Dael's personal guard, and he held a drawn sword in his hand which he obviously wanted to use.

"Kill him," Dael's imperious voice commanded from somewhere on the plateau, and Jayden knew he was in trouble as the guard lifted his sword in anticipation of the strike.

There was no way he could get to his own blade with it pinned beneath him as it was, and Jayden suddenly noticed that this was the same man Rhianna had humiliated on their return to Grandell the last time he had seen her. The man gave Jayden a condescending smirk as he began his strike and Jayden spun away from the blade without thought, kicking out desperately at the guard's legs as he did so, even managing to connect with one.

Steel rang on the stone where his head had been a moment before, but the man didn't quite go down from Jayden's blow. He fell heavily on his knees, his sword skittering away across the plateau as the unexpected fall, coupled with the jarring recoil of his own strike made him lose his grip.

The guard gave him a predatory smile and jumped back to his feet all too quickly as Jayden rolled away, nervously drawing his own blade. He knew how to fight with the thing in general terms, but this would be the first time he'd had to use it on another person outside of a practice session. With a start, he caught sight of Dael and another guardsman over on the sea-facing side of the plateau, and in his moment of distraction, the big guard charged.

The man had drawn another sword from somewhere and Jayden was only just able to parry his first crushing overhead swing. He fell painfully to his own knees in the process. The guard then reversed his attack and swung low with a sweep of the sword intended to split him from crotch to stomach. Again, Jayden barely managed to get his own blade between himself and his opponent, the force of the clash jolting him back up to his feet. He jumped back from the next swing and watched as the big guard overbalanced at the lack of resistance, taking a fraction of a second to recover before he attacked again.

A sudden thought came to him as the guard smiled his mocking smile and gave another crushing stroke Jayden was only just able to deflect, not because of its speed, but simply due to the sheer force. He began to back subtly towards the cliff with each meeting of blades as if he weren't aware of where it was. From the big guard's expression, he was doing a convincing job as he took another quick combination of blows on his blade which nearly sent him staggering too far. Jayden looked back for a moment, pretending to notice the edge of the cliff for the first time, then went on the offensive. He aimed several wild blows at the guard which the swordsman easily deflected with his superior strength and skill. The rain continued to course down around them as the big guard began to push him back towards the cliff edge again, each impact sending a jolt through his arms which matched the timing of the ringing of steel.

With the barest glance back, he saw he was already in as good a position as he would get for this. The instant the heavy-set guard aimed his next crushing overhead swing Jayden ducked back, causing the man to overbalance again as his sword swept past the point he'd expected to meet resistance.

Jayden didn't hesitate. He rushed in past the man's guard and grabbed the front of his tunic with both hands, allowing his own sword to fall forgotten to the stone plateau. With an almighty pull he forced himself to fall painfully backwards onto the stone, pulling the surprised guard forward with him as he planted his feet in the man's stomach.

Extending his legs with as much force as he could muster, Jayden sent the guard vaulting over his own prone form and off the edge of the cliff where his horrified scream rapidly faded into the background noise of the storm.

Jayden regained his sword and his feet as quickly as he could, stunned his idea had worked, which also meant he had just killed a man, even if it was in self-defence. He knew it had been a stupid risk, but he also knew he had almost no chance of beating a trained swordsman with that much physical strength in fair combat. He looked around the plateau, putting the dead man out of his mind as much as he could, and was horrified to see what had kept Dael and the other guard out of the fight.

Backed up against the edge of the cliff Rhianna stood poised, the filleting knife still clutched in her hand and the front of her dress covered in blood. From the defiant way she stood, he didn't think it was hers though.

The remaining guard was clutching a wound on his arm as he wearily tried to circle the cornered girl, but Rhianna was having none of it and with a quick slashing motion opened up a new tear in the guard's uniform, this time across the chest. The guard suddenly reached in, ignoring the second slash he took from the deadly knife and managed to restrain her from doing any more damage as he squeezed her wrist until she was forced to drop the weapon or have the joint shattered from the pressure. With a shout Jayden rushed across the waterlogged plateau with his sword aimed high at the second guard's neck. Neither of the men seemed to have noticed he had disposed of the other guard. Jayden had just enough time for a single thrust before Dael came to his senses, whipping out the rapier he always carried and diverting Jayden's blow so the guard holding Rhianna merely lost his grip instead of his head.

*   *   *

Rhianna stood stock still for a moment as she saw for the first time exactly who it was that had been struggling with the other guard.

He came back!

Genna had counselled her to wait all along, but as the long days after Jayden's disappearance dragged on without word, a little voice in the back of her mind had tried hard to convince her that he really had abandoned her. That he had chosen to save himself at her expense. Eventually, with no word forthcoming and Dael growing more obsessed with her by the day, she'd felt she had no choice but to escape on her own, and just as Jayden had told her they would, Dael's trackers had found her before she'd been gone two days. They had brought her back to Grandell where Dael had ordered her placed under guard both day and night by his personal soldiers. For her protection of course.

I should have known Jayden better than that.

Despite that persistent little voice, even as she'd fled Grandell she had never quite been able to completely reconcile that the man she loved, the man she had known most of her life, would simply abandon her. Now she knew she was right as he locked his antiquated Oo'vi blade with Dael's splinter thin rapier.

A heavy hand on her arm brought her spinning back to the present as a sheet of brilliant lightning lit up the sky, followed immediately by a deafening crack of thunder that shook the entire plateau. She spun, punching the guardsman hard along one of the two deep slashes she'd forged in his chest. The man groaned in pain but didn't relinquish his hold, instead cuffing her in the temple hard enough to make her see stars. There was a moment when everything went too dark, and she felt the guard renew his restraining hold on her arms, but then another flash of lightning seemed to reflect a little too brightly from one of the deeper puddles near her feet. It drew her eye.

The filleting knife had come to rest at the bottom of a shallow trough, if she could just get to it.

*   *   *

Jayden narrowly dodged away from another flourish as Dael hunted him across the plateau. In spite of his desperate defence, there were several thin gashes across his arms and chest where Dael's blade had landed hits, and Jayden found himself unable to keep up the frantic pace of thrust and parry Dael was setting.

He was starting to get worried as Dael, grinning maliciously, scraped another glancing hit across his cheek with a deft flick of his blade, and continued to advance.

Jayden knew he was outmatched by the young count's sword skills and was forced to stop backing off and stand his ground as he neared the edge of the cliff.

Dael made a few more deft strokes which all resulted in red stripes that burnt like fire across his arms before voluntarily backing off, and Jayden was faced with the unmistakable truth. Dael was playing with him, and had been since their blades had crossed on his first swing at the guard. The count himself stood confident, barely out of breath and with not a mark on him. He seemed oblivious to the driving rain and the fickle wind which still tried to grasp at them both as they stood silent, watching each other for any hint of a new attack.

"Well met Jayden!" Dael called over the clamour of the storm, "Beautiful day for a wedding is it not!"

Dael laughed at his own tasteless humour, then launched another assault that drove Jayden right to the very edge of the cliff.

Jayden threw himself desperately to the side to avoid going over the edge, and was rewarded with a long gash down the side of his leg for his efforts. He heard Rhianna desperately call his name as he scrambled away from Dael's advancing form.

The count slowly followed him, making lazy sweeps with his needle thin sword to stop him from getting to his feet.

Jayden kept a grip on his sword as he fled from the flashing rapier Dael was menacing him with. He knew he had to end this quickly, but how? Dael was far faster with his weapon than he was, and the count also had years of training behind him from the best teachers and swordsmen both the military and the Armsmen's Guild had to offer.

He had to get rid of that advantage if he was going to survive the next few minutes.

If only I knew how to actually use the Gift.

Pushing aside the useless thought, he realised with a growing certainty that the only reason he had made it this far was that Dael was enjoying playing with his latest victim. Had he wanted to, he could have ended the fight any number of times already.

That arrogance might just give him a chance, if he could survive long enough to use it.

He scrambled to his feet under the cover of a wild swing and waited for Dael to close. In the corner of his eye he could still see Rhianna desperately struggling to free herself from the guard's restraint, and he briefly considered making a dash across the plateau to help. As Dael abruptly advanced again though he was forced to discard the idea, knowing he wouldn't make it halfway there before Dael's rapier found its mark.

He paused as the young Count of Grandell approached, not backing off this time, and as Dael closed, he flung the serpentine blade with all the strength he could muster sideways at Dael's legs, forcing the count to leap awkwardly out of the way or have them cut out from under him. The throw was good and Dael's sudden jump sent him far enough off balance for Jayden to charge him without being skewered. With all his strength Jayden grasped Dael's wrist as they fell and smashed it hard onto the rocks with a satisfying thud. He didn't think it was broken, but it didn't really matter as the needle thin sword went skipping through his fingers and over the forest end of the plateau.

While Jayden had been busy disarming him, Dael had managed to get his other arm free, and although it was the count's left hand that landed a blow on Jayden's gashed cheek, it still sent him reeling away in pain. The two combatants regained their footing on the slippery surface as quickly as they could and faced off again, Rhianna's struggles becoming more desperate under the iron grasp of the second guardsman.

"Very well done Jayden!" Dael shouted abruptly, the constant thunder making it hard to hear what he had to say, though Jayden wasn't all that interested anyhow.

"I would not have thought you had it in you to disarm me. Tell me fisherman, why do you fight so hard for another man's bride?" he shouted gloatingly, "Can you not find your own?"

Jayden knew there were a hundred responses he could make, but he needed a second to recover his breath, and the wounds on his chest and limbs were stinging fiercely as the rain and wind continued to pound in on them.

"Think about it this way Jayden. I am a Count, ruler of all I can see, and then some. You on the other hand are a glorified farmer, who has the potential to become a fisherman if your father ever dies and leaves his pitiful little boat to you. Even if you managed to kill me, what could someone like you possibly offer her," he asked, pointing to where the guard was still busy restraining the struggling, and by the look of it, now half crazed Rhianna.

The sight made Jayden's blood boil, but it was obvious the guard had orders to restrain her, not to do harm, and taking his attention off Dael right now would be a fatal mistake. So as hard as it was, he forced himself to turn away from Rhianna and pay attention to the far more deadly foe in front of him. He looked the young count up and down slowly and it made him almost physically sick to remember he had once called this loathsome, power-hungry tyrant a friend, even if they had been only children at the time.

"Speak up farmer. Perhaps she would like a grape?" Dael laughed contemptuously.

He knew Dael was trying to make him angry enough to lose focus, and Jayden wasn't about to succumb to his plan. On the other hand, there was probably a good chance the same tactic would work on Dael himself; the count certainly had a volatile enough nature to make it worth a try.

"I can only think of one thing," Jayden shouted back over the storm, "She loves me, and I love her. For all your influence, all your money, and all your threats. You are absolutely impotent in that regard."

For a second there was no response other than a burning light suddenly kindling in Dael's eyes.

"I see. Well, that's really quite rude Jayden. I'm going to kill you now."

And then he charged.

Jayden set himself in time, but at the last second Dael whipped a wicked, hooked dagger from behind his belt and slammed it into Jayden's chest.

Rhianna screamed as he fell back off the tip, but it seemed to Jayden the knife hadn't made it past his ribs or he would surely be dead. Dael looked at the blade in astonishment and Jayden saw the tip of it had broken off, then felt sick as he realised it was probably still stuck in the rib it had just shattered.

Dael snarled and threw himself at Jayden. He tried to roll out of the way, but he wasn't fast enough and the now tipless knife bit deeply into his arm as he struggled to hold the count off long enough to do some damage of his own. He managed to get a solid punch into Dael's crotch with his good arm before staggering up and away as the pain in his chest began to intensify. Jayden wasn't sure if it was the rib or whether the knife-tip had broken loose in the wound, but he found his head swimming as he staggered towards Rhianna and the remaining guard, who was now having a great deal of trouble restraining her. He was almost there when he saw her look up and scream.

"Jayden. Behind you!"

He turned just in time to see Dael raise the knife, and without hesitation plunge it down hard into his chest, and this time he knew it had penetrated his ribs by the sudden blinding pain in his chest as well as the triumphant sneer dominating the count's twisted face.

He stood for a moment longer. Then as the world began to waver, he found himself on his back, able only to see the clouds pouring rain on him from their inky darkness. As his head rolled to the side, he was just able to make out the end of Rhianna's struggle with the guard as she finally managed to slam the back of her head into his nose hard enough to loosen his vice like grip. She elbowed him hard twice in the wounds along his ribs, making him double over in pain, and then dived for the puddle by her feet. She took hold of something and with all her strength drove it up through the guard's chin and into his skull.

The big man slumped to the ground without a noise,

sliding off the edge of the cliff they were far too close to, taking her only weapon with him.

*   *   *

Without thought Rhianna rushed over to where Jayden was lying on the cold stone of the plateau and knelt down beside him, knowing even as she did that there was nothing she could do to help. The hilt of the knife was still sticking out of his chest and a dozen or more sizeable gashes across his arms and chest were constantly being cleaned by the unceasing torrent from above, making it impossible to determine just how much blood he had lost. She forced herself to speak to his unconscious form, though to tell him what she didn't know. Only that she had to say something, before…

Something hard and cold slapped her on the side of the head. She was knocked backwards, towards the edge of the cliff, and when she regained her senses, she saw Dael kneeling over Jayden and gripping the hilt of the knife embedded in his chest.

"NOOOO!" she screamed even above the sudden crack of thunder which tried to drown her out.

Dael placed his other hand unheedingly on the hilt and looked up at Rhianna's horrified face.

"Yes," he said simply, and tore the shattered knife from Jayden's prone form, causing him to convulse and cough up a huge mouthful of blood before falling limply back to the stone, barely breathing.

Something seemed to break inside her as Dael stood above Jayden, holding the knife out so very casually for the rain to wash clean of his childhood friend's lifeblood. She couldn't breathe as she watched Dael's silent adulation over what he'd just done. Couldn't move as she watched him watching Jayden's last few laboured breaths, even knowing she needed to escape while his attention was not on her. But as she came to her senses and tried to leave, she found she couldn't do that either, not while he was still alive. So with a sinking feeling in her stomach, she began to rise from the plateau one last time.

In Dael's other hand Jayden's serpentine sword was now firmly grasped. The count must have retrieved it while she was fighting with the guard. He'd hit her with the flat of the blade she realised as she climbed unsteadily to her feet. Dael continued to stand over Jayden's limp form for another moment longer, obviously savouring the sight of his fallen friend. As Rhianna stood, he seemed to notice her again, almost as if he'd forgotten she was there.

He began to move toward her with far too bright a look in his eye which showed her once again, and all too clearly just how mad he really was, but there was nowhere to go. The part of the plateau she was standing on was right out at the point. Behind her and to either side the drop was enormous, and in this poor light she couldn't even see the rock-strewn ocean she knew to be far, far below. The wind continued to whip at her as it tore its way up the cliff, plastering her sodden clothes to her body and half blinding her with strands of her own hair.

When Dael finally reached the outcropping she now stood on he stopped, the blades in each of his hands held ready, but not pointing at her.

"You know Rhianna," he said casually, as if making idle conversation, "I've put up with a lot from you over the last year or so."

For a second Rhianna thought she had heard wrong as she stared in horror at the tipless knife Dael had used to kill the man she was sure she would have married, had he asked. But that could never happen now, and that same knife which had destroyed her last chance for a happy future was now pointing towards her.

"If you had just accepted your fate, and being elevated from a lowly peasant to a countess is not such a terrible one I should think. My guards would still be alive, and so would he," Dael accused as he motioned to Jayden's still form, lying forgotten on the cold stone of the plateau.

"Do you see how much trouble you've caused everyone?" he asked as he took a step towards where she was standing.

"Now come here, this nonsense has gone on long enough. If we start back now, I think we can still get you cleaned up in time for the ceremony to be held at sundown."

Rhianna stared at him in disbelief as she saw something out of the corner of her eye which filled her with hope. It might have been just the light, but for an instant she could have sworn Jayden had moved. More than anything she wanted to run to his side, to see if it was true, but knew instinctively if Dael realised he wasn't already dead, Jayden would soon pay for her mistake with what little time remained to him.

"I grow tired of your stubbornness Rhianna, so I will say this just one more time. Come to me. Now!"

"I will not marry you Dael! Not now! Not ever!" she shouted back at him through the thundering storm.

"Yes, you will," he replied smugly, "The Maker's priest will do whatever I say. And I say he will perform the ceremony. Besides, you have nowhere to run. You can't get past me and back to Grandell before I do, and even if you did get away, you would soon be brought back to the keep by my guards, just like before. There is no escape from this Rhianna. By this time tomorrow we will be man and wife, and all of this will be but an unpleasant memory which changed, nothing."

As he finished his little speech Dael stepped up onto the protrusion where she stood, and as she took an involuntary step back, she felt her foot slip. She wheeled her arms for balance and only barely regained her footing instead of going over the edge, which she suddenly realised was right behind her now.

With growing desperation, she wondered what to do next. Beyond Dael's menacing gaze she could just make out that Jayden had moved again. Slowly, and obviously in agony he was dragging himself to his feet. Maybe he hadn't been hurt as badly as they both thought. Even as the notion occurred, she knew it was a lie, but one she would cling to for all she was worth.

She wanted to call out, to tell him to run, but in his present condition she was astounded he could even stand, and there was no chance at all he could outrun Dael in the inhospitable clifftop terrain.

At any rate, Dael couldn't be allowed to know he was alive, and yet the count would see Jayden as soon as he turned around.

Dael took another step, completely intent on his target. In a moment he would reach her and pull her back from the cliff, at which point he couldn't fail to notice Jayden slowly advancing despite the seeping wound in his chest. How he could walk after losing so much blood she did not understand, but it was painfully apparent that walking was about all he could do.

She needed a distraction, and although calling Jayden's name would do the job, if she couldn't take Dael on herself after that, her gamble would surely result in Jayden's death, and this time she knew Dael would make sure.

As she searched vainly for some other way to distract the mad count, he took the final step up onto the ledge where she was perched and smiled a smile which never reached his eyes.

She had run out of time, and she suddenly realised no matter what she said to make Dael lower his guard for that one crucial second, he couldn't fail to notice that Jayden was still alive at some point in the fight she was about to begin. But with both of those blades pointing at her she needed a distraction, and she needed it now.

"Jayden, No!" she screamed over the sound of the storm as a huge strike of lightning blinded them all for an instant.

As her sight returned a moment later Rhianna screamed again, but this time in rage as she caught sight of Dael, knife hand upraised as he spun on his heel to throw the broken dagger towards the badly wounded man. Jayden was still hobbling his way towards the count, a look of purest fury on his face which was shown up clearly by another burst of light from the onyx clouds above.

Without hesitation Rhianna threw herself at Dael as he released the knife, and the two of them tumbled to the ground, Dael losing his grip on Jayden's sword as it slid across the plateau and away from either combatant. Rhianna tumbled into a deep puddle, and as she scrambled out again, she realised despairingly she had twisted her ankle to the point where she was barely able to stand. How she was going to stop Dael now she had no idea, but the demoralising thought was wiped clear an instant later as she heard Dael's mad laughter rising above the storm.

He was still sitting where her tackle had felled him not two spans away, but her attention was deflected instantly to where he was looking at the crumpled form of Jayden. The broken knife protruded from his stomach as he lay, gasping for breath which would barely come. But even with all his injuries she saw his eyes were still focused. She could see his mouth moving as she hobbled painfully to his side, but the words were too quiet for her to hear above the pounding of the storm. Rhianna knelt, cradling his head in her arms as she put her ear to his mouth, trying to hear what he was saying. She knew he had only a few moments left now, but he refused to let her calm him as his lips continued to move weakly, trying to tell her something. There was so much she had to say, to tell him before…

The rain was quickly being replaced by tears running down her face, but there was no time for that now, Jayden was still trying to speak, and if he didn't calm down she knew it would steal away the last few seconds he had left.

With nothing more than force of will alone he reached out feebly with fingers numb from the storm and loss of blood to take her hand one last time.

"R… Run," he breathed in a gravelly whisper as his pain-filled eyes locked with hers, then closed as he slumped back to the stone; and if he was still breathing this time then not even she could tell.

As she knelt on the cold stone, still holding Jayden's lifeless form, a heavy hand grasped her shoulder and dragged her roughly to her feet. She lashed out wildly, not knowing or caring if Dael had once again gone to retrieve Jayden's serpentine blade. With sight dimmed by the rain and her own tears, she realised after several blows that his hands were empty of steel this time and immediately pressed her attack, throwing punches and kicks at him at an ever increasing rate. For a moment she thought she was winning as he backed up a few steps, but no matter how frenzied her blows became, Dael blocked each strike with ease. He held his ground for a moment as Rhianna's fury continued unabated, then backed off a few more steps, prompting her to follow if she wanted to continue the attack. Rhianna was all too glad to comply, and before she knew it they were halfway around the plateau.

Suddenly Dael moved, striking her in the midriff with the speed of a viper, and felling her with the single powerful blow.

Rhianna sprawled on the ground, winded badly but far too wild to care as Dael stood over her. She picked herself up with a snarl and once again threw herself at him, the count easily deflecting the maddened blows as if she were nothing more than an unruly child. After another few swings he reached out, clearly growing annoyed with the unabated assault, and took hold of both her hands, giving her a shove that once again sent her tumbling roughly to the stone.

She landed on something hard, and with a start she realised one of the many stones which adorned the ancient plateau had broken loose at last.

Rhianna grabbed at the double fist sized rock and threw it as hard as she could, catching Dael squarely in the chest and knocking him off balance long enough for her to regain her feet. She rushed at him, landing blow after blow around the murderer's head and chest, but this time Dael wasn't playing. With a punch that sent her reeling he knocked her back, then aimed a kick at her head for good measure, sending her sprawling towards the very edge of the plateau. Rhianna scrambled to her feet as Dael approached, struggling to catch her breath, but then he stopped.

His lip was bleeding and his left shoulder looked a little stiff.

He isn't even breathing hard! she thought despairingly. Rhianna herself could hardly stand on her twisted ankle, which she had completely forgotten during her frenzied attack. The pain and weakness of the injury was rushing back with a vengeance now that she had a moment to think, and the few blows Dael had bothered to strike at her still had her head spinning.

It was then, as she looked into his calculating eyes with her own panicked ones that she finally realised the truth. There was no way for her to stop Dael doing whatever it was he chose right then.

Not without you, she thought in anguish as she once again caught sight of Jayden's lifeless body.

"No more Rhianna!" Dael shouted angrily from a few steps away, "Come with me now of your own accord or I will beat you senseless and carry you back to the keep. Either way is fine with me!"

Rhianna just stood there as he spoke, terrified now because she knew he could do exactly that if he wanted. If their fight had only achieved one thing, it was to prove that.

Except that Jayden is dead because of it, a little voice wailed in the back of her mind.

"I will not marry you Dael," she whispered hoarsely, horrified as she backed away as far as she could from the slowly advancing count.

"Really?" Dael replied coldly.

"Look around you Rhianna, you've run out of options," he told her in his most condescending tone as he moved warily towards where she stood.

With a quick glance around, Rhianna saw he was right. Behind her the cliff edge loomed as the rain continued its torrential downpour, disappearing into the darkness as it fell from the ebony clouds to the indistinguishable sea a thousand spans below. In front of her Dael stood like an avatar, his arms crossed as the storm crashed down around them, apparently of no consequence to him as he stood waiting for her to decide. After only a few seconds though he advanced again, slowly and warily.

In case he has to restrain me again, she supposed.

As Dael came within range, she saw to her complete amazement that Jayden's arm was moving, reaching out for her. It was a fact not lost on Dael. But the sudden flush of joy she felt was short lived as it became clear that just that simple act had used up the little remaining strength he'd been able to gather. Jayden's arm slumped back to the ground, and although his eyes remained open, she knew with certainty he would not move again. She wanted to be with him, but if he hadn't already, then in a very few moments he would be lost to her forever, and she knew beyond any shadow of a doubt that even if she could get to him, there was nothing she could do to save him now.

Dael smiled a cold smile as he turned his attention back to her, reaching out his hand in a mocking imitation of

Jayden as he closed the gap between them. She wanted to back away, but the edge of the plateau prevented her from moving. There was nowhere left to go as Dael took the final step between them.

Not while I have you, her own voice echoed in her mind.

"Come with me," Dael said, his voice cutting smoothly through the thunderous sound of the storm.

Everything her hope had been built upon was gone, but there was still one thing of which she was certain, one thing she could control.

"I will not marry you Dael," she told him, suddenly calm. The count looked at her quizzically for a moment before shaking his head at her stubbornness.

She looked back over to where Jayden lay, the light in his eyes was almost gone now as he lay prone on the wet and bloodied rock of the stone plateau which overlooked the Sea of Dreams.

She didn't know if he could hear her or not, but the vague look of panic which quickly grew in his mortally wounded eyes showed he had read her clearly enough.

She locked gazes with him one final time as Dael reached out to take hold of her.

"I'll always love you Jayden," she said, and stepped back over the cliff.

*   *   *

"RHIANNAAAA...!" Jayden screamed, hacking as he began coughing up blood. Even moments away from death he managed to force himself halfway to his knees and crawl a few agonising inches towards where Rhianna had disappeared, before the darkness which had been gathering at the edges of his vision reached out and took him fully.

*　　*　　*

Dael just stared at where his future wife had thrown herself off the cliff in confusion, before turning away. He couldn't quite credit what he'd just seen.

A pity, but it didn't really matter he supposed, he could find another girl to become countess easily enough. She wouldn't be Rhianna, but perhaps this time he would look for better stock.

He walked over to where Jayden lay, intending to retrieve what was left of his knife from the fool's dead body, but as he was about to pull it from Jayden's lifeless stomach, he noticed the very faintest of movements which told of a breath being taken.

"Well look at that," he said to himself, amazed his childhood friend could take such a set of wounds and still have life left in him. He considered retrieving his knife anyway, but that would certainly send Jayden on his way. So he sat on the stone beside Jayden and waited, watching as the last few seconds of his life ticked away.

"Jayden!" an unexpected voice screamed from the forest side of the cliff.

Dael looked up in time to see a dark form in a silver-lined cloak wave a hand and send him sprawling over to the other side of the cliff. He tried to rise as the two newcomers rushed to Jayden's side, both out of breath as they skidded to a halt. For some reason he was unable to move so much as a finger.

Dael saw for the first time once he stopped struggling

that it was Jayden's father who accompanied the unknown archmage. That made sense, he had expected David to intervene in his plans once he returned from the capital. If the archmage had come on official business of King Erian though, surely he should be awaiting Dael's pleasure in the keep, not traipsing around the forest with Jayden's father on a night such as this.

It was a bit of a mystery, he thought as he pushed the night's events to the back of his mind. And there was nothing he liked more than intrigue. So as the archmage feverishly worked on Jayden's wounds while David glared promises at him from where he knelt by his fallen son's side, Dael watched.

Perhaps this game wasn't quite finished yet after all.

He who laughs last, has outlived his enemies.
Northmen saying.

CHAPTER 6

VENGEANCE

As he woke, the first thing Jayden heard was the sound of his own scream.

Rhianna was dead. She had thrown herself from the cliff, and this time there was nothing he could do to save her.

The repeating nightmare which had plagued him since losing consciousness on the plateau refused to let go as he struggled to make sense of his surroundings.

Where he was, he didn't know. It wasn't his home, but neither was it one of the keep's many cells.

His hand flew to his stomach, and then his chest, feeling for a wound that was no longer there. In his dazed state he thought he must have missed it. As he moved his fingers tentatively down the unbroken skin, he noticed his arm was whole and free from the deep cuts Dael had inflicted during their struggle. He groaned again as salty tears ran anew down his face. No natural remedies could have healed his wounds so perfectly. The archmage had arrived.

Just not in time to save Rhianna.

He lay there for a long while, his senses strangely deadened until finally, after what must have been many hours he felt himself curling up into a tight ball on the thin mattress which kept him insulated from the canvas floor.

A tent? he thought, finally able to wipe the tears from his eyes and take a muted kind of interest in his surroundings. *How did I get here?*

He hadn't been in any condition to make the journey himself, and he knew Dael wouldn't have spared him.

With a start, he suddenly realised the torrential rains of the night before had stopped, and the sun was shining strongly on the roof of the tent. It was daytime now, and Jayden noticed the sounds of men and horses moving around beyond the canvas walls.

He couldn't help but wonder whether they had just started, or if his mind had just been ignoring them until now. The next thing he noticed was that the hooves of the animals were striking stone, not grass or dirt, making him wonder exactly where he had been taken, and how long he had been lying here unconscious.

Wherever it was though, however long it had been, he had to find Dael and repay him for Rhianna's murder.

The count might not have actually struck the killing blow, but Dael was in every way responsible for forcing her to leap from the cliff when she knew full well there was no possibility she could survive.

He had more than sufficient grounds to petition Duke Timon to sanction Dael, but the only woman he had ever loved was dead at his childhood friend's hands. The law hadn't been there to protect Rhianna when she was alive, and he saw little reason to abide by it now that she was dead.

No matter how long it takes, I swear by the Maker you will pay for her death in blood.

The thought of taking vengeance on Dael lent him

strength. As he tried to sit up though, a sudden wave of nausea hit him, accompanied by a creeping blackness at the edges of his vision and a muffled ringing in his ears. He sat motionless for a long minute, taking deep, rhythmic breaths until finally his vision cleared, and although he still felt sick to his stomach, the danger of blacking out seemed to have passed.

As he looked up again, Jayden noticed for the first time the pitcher of water sitting on a table beside his mattress. He reached over thankfully and poured some of the clear liquid into a glass which lay waiting on the embossed tray which held both items. There was no food to accompany the drink, but he felt too sick to keep anything down in any event. As the water loosened his parched throat it seemed to make him feel slightly better though, and he poured a second glass as he examined his surroundings in a little more detail.

He didn't think he was a prisoner. It seemed unlikely he would be housed in something as insecure as a tent if that were the case. Apart from the mattress and table, and a small pile of clothes nearby which he recognised as his own, the tent was bare, offering no further clues as to his current situation.

He was dressed only in his small-clothes, and as he reached over to the small pile of belongings, he saw the shirt and breaches differed from the ones he'd been wearing last night.

As he pulled the grey shirt on over his head, he remembered it was one he'd left at home when they'd sailed for Aramar. That must mean someone from his house knew he was here, wherever here was, and had brought it for him to wear. Another thing he didn't think would be allowed if Dael did in fact have him.

Good. He pulled on the pair of beige breaches which had been left. It would be easier to get away from wherever he'd been brought and take vengeance on Dael if he didn't have to throw off any guards who might have been waiting outside the tent.

Something metal being dropped onto stone nearby gave him a start and drew his attention to the outside world. The sound of men and horses had continued unabated since he'd awoken to them, and Jayden wondered just what he would find when he emerged. He quickly tugged on his boots, the last item in the pile, and looked around the suddenly empty tent. Except for the pitcher there was absolutely nothing he could use as a weapon, even the table's legs were too short to do any real damage, and he doubted he could carry the round pitcher inconspicuously.

He decided against it and went to the tent's entrance. Surely he could find some kind of weapon once he got inside the keep. He knew that was where he would find the murdering count, but first he had to get away from here. Moving slowly so as not to attract undue attention, he lifted the door-flap back a bit to peer outside.

What he saw made little sense.

The first thing he noticed was that he was still in Grandell, and the tent he had been sequestered in was perched just on the edge of the stone-paved town square which sat opposite the keep itself. Across the square, scores of men, some in Dael's livery and some wearing what he recognised as the colours of the Aramarian garrison itself, were busy loading carts with what looked like provisions for a lengthy trip. What that was about he had no idea.

In another part of the square, a long trestle had been set

up and two of the men dressed in the livery of Aramar's guard were busy interviewing a lengthy line of townsmen. By the looks on most of the crowd's faces, they were less than happy to be there.

A little girl of seven or eight summers suddenly emerged from the crowd and ran up to one of the men waiting in line, who was obviously her father. She quickly handed him something before hugging him tightly around the waist and dashing off again through the crowd and out of sight. Jayden couldn't help but stare at the child's long blonde hair as she disappeared. It was done in the same style which Rhianna had favoured when riding, loosely tied back by three ribbons each about a foot apart from the others. The thought that he would never see that again clenched his hands into fists and once again blurred his vision with tears. To distract himself, he began studying the crowd in earnest. Despite all the commotion in the square there were no silver-lined cloaks to be seen in the throng, and no one seemed to be paying him an undue amount of attention right at this moment.

He took a chance and quietly emerged from the tent, attempting to look as though he had every right to be there. He walked across the square as quickly as he could on still unsteady legs, acting as casually as possible as he made his way to the dense gardens which surrounded the hulking keep. Somehow he reached it without anyone raising an alarm, and once there he found a tall hedge to wait behind and think about his next move.

Waltzing in the front gates was out of the question. The guards would be on the lookout for him, and if he tried to slip past them, the chances were too high that they would pick him up before he even made it through the door.

There was a bolt hole he knew of though which led from the innards of the keep to the forest around the other side of the structure. He and Dael had used it many times to sneak out from under the old count's watchful eye when they had been children.

Jayden felt his hands once again clenching in rage, but he forced himself to take a breath and calm down, for now.

The bolt hole had its exit inside one of the large hedges on the forest side of the keep. He had no idea if the tunnel was still sound, or if Dael had placed guards on it, but if he could just make it there without being seen he might stand a chance.

After a tense minute, once he was sure no one had noticed him leave the tent, he headed off around to the back of the keep, trying to keep as many of the trees and hedges as he could between himself and the huge square stonework that formed the central defence of Jeranon's east coast. He was sure he would find Dael somewhere inside the stone fortress.

He kept a close look out as he traversed the distance around the keep's wall and entered the outskirts of the forest behind the enormous stone structure, but it was unnecessary. Whatever was happening in the town square was occupying everyone's attention, and he made it to the large hedge without a hitch. He stood listening for a minute, breathing hard and feeling weak all over, but all he could hear were the calls of birds and the gentle wind rustling through the forest canopy. If there were any guards, they were stationed inside.

The hedge was an unruly looking thing, about ten feet wide and six high, and appeared for all the world to be a simple wild grown plant, unless you knew better. As

Jayden parted the intertwined branches with difficulty, he pushed his way into a small cleared area in the middle of what was actually four carefully planted trees pruned to give the illusion of it all being one tangled mess.

Jayden dropped to his knees and scratched away the thin layer of dirt and debris that covered the trapdoor, and with a sharp tug pulled the wooden plank right off the decayed inner latch which should have held it closed. He was a little surprised Dael hadn't fixed it since becoming count.

As he stood above the partially open doorway Jayden smiled grimly, if there were guards inside, they knew he was here now and would be rushing out to meet him this very moment.

Let them come.

He almost wanted an encounter, but after an uneventful minute Jayden decided no armed men were going to swarm out of the hole after all. He swung the trapdoor open the rest of the way, finding it strange the bolt hole was in such a state of neglect.

Perhaps Dael doesn't think he needs an escape route? Jayden reasoned as he dropped down into the small hole to land on wobbly knees, wavering for a moment before gaining his balance and closing the trapdoor behind him.

More likely he's too arrogant to do the work himself, and too paranoid to reveal his secret escape tunnel's location, he corrected after a moment.

Whatever the true reason, he was just as glad to have a way into the keep that didn't involve storming the front gates.

As the trapdoor clicked shut above him, the darkness became almost absolute. Jayden waited until his eyes slowly adjusted to the thin crack of sunlight still able to make it through both the thick hedge and the trapdoor above, and after a minute it was just enough. He took two steps forward and then ran his hand along the right wall of the tunnel at head height, finding the torch and bracket exactly where he remembered it to be. By the feel of the cobwebs which surrounded it, he didn't think the implement had been used since the last time he'd been down here.

It was the work of a few moments to locate the small box which held pieces of flint and steel, and with a practised hand he quickly had the torch shining its burnt orange glow along the confining walls of the bolthole's tunnel.

Despite the thickness of the webs there was no sign of the spiders which made them, and Jayden breathed a faint sigh of relief. He didn't have much of a plan yet, other than finding his way into the keep and killing Dael. It was crucial that he find a weapon before confronting the count. In his weakened state Jayden knew he couldn't beat the man in a prolonged hand to hand fight. Despite that formidable obstacle, the fact he had made it this far unopposed encouraged him to keep working his way down the ancient tunnel, burning the cobwebs out of his path as he went.

The tiny crawl way which led under the keep's fortified walls had always seemed big enough before, but it had been years since he'd been down here, and Jayden realised he had grown since then. Now the dirt-edged tunnel nearly brushed his shoulders on either side, while the roof loomed just above his head. It took some time, but eventually he came in sight of the staircase which led up to the primary part of the keep.

As soon as the stairs began, the walls changed from dirt to stone, and an old metal handrail on the left side of the passage appeared. The stairway widened out enough so he could walk normally, although he still wouldn't have wanted to try to get two people through it at a time.

Up and up he went, the stairs quickly beginning to take their toll on his still weakened legs. Jayden knew he must be in the keep by now, although he hadn't yet passed the first exit.

He stopped to listen when he finally reached the first door. It wasn't a door from the outside, just an anonymous section of wall unless you knew the trick of opening it. The sound of chains rattling and a prisoner's plea to be released accompanied a metal door being slammed.

Jayden knew he had reached the entry to the lowest underground level of the keep, where the cell block which housed Dael's prisoners was located.

He kept climbing. He wasn't unmoved by the man's pleas, but for all he knew the prisoner was every bit as guilty as Dael himself, and Jayden would only get one chance at surprising the count. If he stopped to help this man now, he would most likely be captured or killed, and even if he weren't, the alarm would be raised as soon as someone noticed the prisoner was missing. So as he approached the next doorway, he put the unknown prisoner from his mind for now and listened.

The muted sound of guardsmen gambling issued through the entry, confirming to Jayden he had finally reached the barracks level. He waited for a moment, but the noise remained at a constant volume and he realised the men must be sitting in the same room the door opened onto.

Jayden ground his teeth. He had been hoping to sneak

into the barracks, which was certain to have at least a few decent weapons in it and arm himself as best he could. That was out of the question now though, and for an instant he almost reconsidered going ahead with his plan.

The dim light of the torch flickered, and suddenly all he could see was himself lying on the cold wet stone of the plateau, watching helplessly as Rhianna disappeared over the edge of the cliff.

He gasped in a quivering breath, and from the other side of the wall he heard one of the guardsmen say, "Hey Tommy, you just hear something?"

"Bahh, it's just the rats again," the man who must have been Tommy answered to Jayden's dim relief.

"It's your bet," he added a moment later, affording Jayden the chance to creep soundlessly away from the door and up towards the next level.

He quietly sidled up to the next door panel and put his ear gently against the cold, mossy stone. Through it he could hear a cook bellowing orders to the kitchen staff, and Jayden immediately knew he was on the ground floor of the giant stone keep. He and Dael had used this exit many times when they were children to pilfer food from the kitchens.

It was possible he could find some implement there to use as a weapon, but with the staff in full working mode he knew he could never do it unseen, so reluctantly he continued on.

The keep had nine levels, two below ground which housed the cells and barracks, and seven above ground besides the tower and siege turrets. The next four landings he listened at were all filled with the voices of people passing him unawares as they hurriedly went about their business. The whole of Grandell must be in an uproar he decided. Whatever the guards from Aramar were doing down in the town square was only a part of what had caused all this commotion. If he didn't know better, he would have sworn the entire town was preparing to just pack up and leave.

At any rate, he knew he wasn't going to find any weapons here, so he kept climbing the stone stairwell towards the second top floor of the keep. Once again, he nervously put his ear to the door and listened. There was no sound at all for a full minute, and Jayden stopped to consider his next move. Dael's quarters were right above him now, and he still had to find a weapon before confronting the count. Silence still reigned on the other side of the doorway, but just as he was about to try opening the hidden panel, the sound of voices reached him dully from somewhere down the corridor.

"Have you heard the latest?" Jayden was able to make out through the thin stone as he snatched his hand back from the release.

"I'm sure you're about to tell me," a second voice tiredly answered.

The two men came to a fortuitous halt almost directly on the other side of the wall and the first voice continued.

"You know how the count had us running all over town in that storm a few days ago looking for that girl he wanted brought in for questioning?"

Jayden gave a start at that. He'd assumed it was only the day after...

"Well, it turns out some of the boys from the north tower heard the count talking with that archmage from Aramar, and from what they heard, the count actually caught up with her on top of the cliffs. Reckon she must have stumbled across an old goat path or something. Anyway, while he was trying to convince her to come back with him, that Jayden guy that her and the count used to hang around with years ago bursts up onto the plateau and tries to kill them all."

"All?" the second voice responded, "You mean the count and his guards, don't you?"

"Well yeah. Anyway, from what I'm told, he disarmed Sergeant Valek and sent him over the edge and down into the sea. Can't say I'll miss him. But word is that while Jayden was fighting with Dael, that little hellcat Rhianna managed to stick Fredrik with that same filleting knife she used on Allan and Lee."

There was no audible response to his statement, but Jayden could imagine the man's expression from the gossiper's next comment.

"Yeah, I know, who would have thought old Freddy could be bested by anyone, especially an untrained girl. That's four of our men dead at the hands of those two, but here's the thing. Dael didn't kill either of them."

"That's not what I heard," the second guard replied in a strange tone.

"Then you heard wrong," the first voice interrupted.

"When Dael killed Jayden, Rhianna threw herself off the cliff, only Jayden wasn't dead! Apparently he was mortally wounded and just about gone, but then out of nowhere that archmage turns up with Jayden's old man and uses the Gift to heal him. Now he's recovering over in one of those tents the Aramarian's set up down in the square."

"So what you're saying is that it's just the count's word against Jayden's about what really happened up there," the second guard shrewdly answered.

There was silence for a long minute after his comment, although the lack of footsteps warned Jayden the two men were still outside the doorway.

"Look, I just follow my orders. I don't really like Dael any more than you do you know, but who would you believe, the count or the murderer," the first man asked.

"What difference is there?" the second man grimly returned. "I knew Rhianna a bit, enough to know she would not have killed those guardsmen unless she had no other choice. I can't imagine what Dael did to make her take her own life, if that's even true, rather than go down fighting."

Jayden suddenly knew he had to talk to that second guard alone. He absolutely had to find a weapon, and if not an outright ally, that second voice might at least be sympathetic to his cause.

"Well, at any rate, the Aramarian's should be gone in a few days and things will get back to normal I suppose. The sooner that archmage takes that Jayden guy away from here the better. He has the count riled up something chronic, and that's no good for any of us."

There were footsteps leading away from the other side of the door, but after a moment Jayden realised only one pair was leaving, and he didn't know which one. Again he waited for a full minute, listening intently, but there was not another sound. If the guard on the other side of the wall belonged to the second voice, he might convince the man to give him some aid. On the other hand, if it was the first guard who had stayed, he would raise the alarm as soon as Jayden cracked open the secret door. Either way there was only one of them, and he had to get a better weapon than this old torch before confronting Dael.

Jayden found himself hoping it was the first guard. He couldn't take any chances on the garrison being alerted to his presence, which meant he had to disable the man quickly, whichever one it was. He reached out to the release lever, gripping the torch like a club, and tripped the small mechanism which swung the door open a few feet. There was a muffled yell as it collided with the guardsman, who must have been standing right next to it Jayden realised as he jumped around the corner and swung his improvised weapon at his opponent's head.

The torch went high and guttered as the guard was shoved out of reach by his impact with the door. Jayden was forced to follow as the man frantically crab-walked backwards a few steps, giving himself enough room to draw his blade, but not to regain his feet. Jayden launched himself at the man, knocking the sword aside with the heavy iron-bound torch, disarming the off-balance guard.

The old iron connecting with the sword rang through the corridors, and when Jayden reflexively looked up to see if anyone had heard, he felt a foot come crashing into his left shin, toppling him towards his opponent. He landed heavily on the carpeted stone of the floor. With a grunt he staggered back to his feet in time to face off with the guard, who was no older than he was Jayden was surprised to note. The man drew a knife from a hidden sheath on his belt.

"Who are you?" the guardsman demanded, his eyes flickering towards the secret passage which had remained open during their brief scuffle.

For a moment Jayden considered diving back into the passage and slamming it behind him, but knew if he did so the guard would raise the alarm as soon as he moved.

There might be another way though. The man's voice was that of the second guard.

The young man advanced cautiously, wary of the iron-bound torch which Jayden still held as it trailed a thin wisp of smoke into the keep's air. He seemed unconcerned with the sword he had dropped, but since it was a few paces down the corridor behind him, Jayden would have to get through him to reach it anyhow.

"What that other guard told you is true," Jayden said rather than waste words on an introduction, "Dael was responsible for Rhianna's death, and for that I promise he will not see the dawn."

There was a moment of silence, and Jayden was sure the guard was about to call for reinforcements, but he lowered the knife and a strange light kindled in his eyes.

"You're Jayden?" the guard asked in a voice every bit as quiet as his own had been a moment before.

There didn't seem to be any point denying it at this stage, but he kept the torch raised as he spoke.

"Yes. I heard you tell the other guard you knew Rhianna, is that true?"

"It's the only reason I haven't called the entire garrison down on you already."

There was a brief moment while the two men studied each other, each taking the other's measure as they decided what to do next.

"What do you intend to do?" Jayden finally asked, as much to get things moving as to break the suddenly awkward silence. He couldn't stand out here in the corridor all day without some other guardsman walking past, and he didn't trust his luck to find him a second guard who would keep his presence a secret.

"Tell me what happened to Rhianna," the guardsman ordered instead, "And I want to know the truth. All of it, or so help me I will call for reinforcements before you can take the first step..." he said, snapping his fingers for emphasis.

Jayden was sure he was going to anyway, but something in the man's voice stopped him from trying for the secret doorway before it could happen. So, with a deep feeling of misgiving he stayed in the corridor to talk to this strange guard. A guard Jayden abruptly realised who was risking his own neck by not turning him in as soon as he'd jumped out of the hidden passage.

"All right," he grudgingly replied, "How much do you already know?"

"Only that Dael had arranged a marriage between himself and Rhianna, and then a few days ago she went wild, killing her minders and running off into that storm without so much as a cloak."

"Then you don't know anything," Jayden told him bitterly.

"Dael bribed her foster parents into allowing the match despite Rhianna's implicit objections. But he didn't know that we, Rhianna and I, were planning to leave Grandell so she wouldn't have to go through with the marriage, despite the documents having already been drawn up. Dael was watching us closely though, so I left... I left," his voice caught in his throat as he remembered letting his father talk him into sailing to the capital and back when Rhianna had never needed him more.

"It was supposed to throw him off the scent, to make him think we'd both given up, that he was getting his way. When Crest returned a few days ago during the storm, I ran into a friend who told me what you just said about

Rhianna killing the two guards to get away. She'd done it because Dael had moved up the wedding to that day and she was desperate to escape. I guessed she would head up to the cliff top. That's where she always went when she needed some time alone. When I arrived, I found Dael and two of his men had managed to get there ahead of me. The moment I reached the plateau Dael ordered one of the guards to kill me. I had no choice but to fight."

He stopped to look at the guard's reaction, but the young man's face was as grim as a mask, so he continued.

"There wasn't time to escape, there wasn't time to think. I had to kill him to save my own life, but when I went to help Rhianna, Dael attacked me. He was too good. I couldn't keep up with his blade and although I managed to disarm him, he pulled a knife from somewhere and stabbed me in the chest."

Jayden halted, gently running his fingers over where the wound had been a few days before.

There was still more to tell, but he didn't think he could make himself relive it all again as he saw the storm wracked plateau, perfectly detailed in his mind's eye.

"How did she die?" the guard asked after a moment, and although he was furious, his voice was still hushed for privacy.

"Tell me!" he whispered fiercely, causing Jayden to blink in surprise.

Perhaps the young guard standing in front of him dressed in Dael's grey and maroon livery actually had known Rhianna, and not just known of her, he thought with genuine surprise.

Strangely, knowing that made it easier for him to continue.

"Dael pulled the knife out of my chest and I lost consciousness. When I came to, he had her backed up against the edge of the cliff. I tried to stop him."

"After taking a knife wound to the chest?" the young guard asked incredulously.

Jayden gave a futile shrug.

"It didn't do any good," he returned, before taking a breath and finishing the account.

"I was only a few steps away when he spun, throwing the knife at me and taking me in the gut. I saw Rhianna fighting with him as I lay there, forced to watch but unable to move. She never had a chance. I told her to run, but she wouldn't leave."

His breath became ragged as the memories came flooding back in full force.

"Dael was toying with her the whole time. When she finally struck a blow which hurt him, he put her down hard, forcing her right back to the edge of the cliff. He told her they could still be married by sundown and that she had nowhere else to go now that I was dead. He even told her it was her fault. And when she finally saw she couldn't fight, or even escape, she did the only thing Dael couldn't stop her from doing."

He stopped, unwilling to share the words whispering through his mind, the last thing she had said to him; the words he knew which would haunt him until the day he died.

"She threw herself over the edge," the guard supplied dully when Jayden did not continue. "She never was one to give up when she wanted something. I guess that went for when she didn't want something as well."

The guard stepped back a few paces and picked up the

237

sword before Jayden could react, placing it in its sheath on his waist.

"As I said, I knew Rhianna, but if I were to go with you now the guard due to relieve me in about a minute would find my post empty and raise the alarm."

Jayden couldn't quite believe what he was hearing.

"Will that take you to Dael's chambers?" the guard asked suddenly, pointing to the doorway which at some point had swung almost closed.

"Yes," Jayden answered, finally deciding he could trust this unusual guard, at least to a point.

"Take this," he said, holding out his knife hilt-first and offering it to Jayden, who gratefully took it.

"I would give you my sword, but anyone who saw me would notice it was gone," the guard whispered.

"What about the knife?" Jayden asked, suddenly concerned for the man's safety. If he failed, Dael would come looking for whoever's blade he had used.

The guard pulled his uniform top up a bit to reveal a hidden sheath sticking out from his trousers.

"Not so easily noticed," he said with just a hint of a grin, "Now go, before my replacement arrives."

Jayden nodded as he opened the door wider, then stopped.

"I won't forget this," he promised, then slipped back into the darkness, closing the door behind him with the still smoking torch in one hand and the guardsman's knife in the other. Now it was time to even the score.

He headed silently up the blackened hallway's last lengthy flight of stairs until he came to the end of a passage which backed onto the count's private suite. After all, this was who the bolthole had been designed to protect. Behind the secret door he could hear two voices arguing through the thin stone of the concealed entrance, one was far away from the wall and muffled, he couldn't make out who it belonged to. The other was Dael's, and from the sound of it he was as close to the passage's entrance as the guard on the floor below had been.

I never even asked his name.

The sound of his former friend's voice sent a thrill of fury down Jayden's spine, and all the anger and grief which he'd just barely been holding in since awakening in the tent a few hours before rushed to the surface in a sudden burst of cold energy. Taking a good grip on the knife and torch he reached up slowly, savouring the moment, and tripped the mechanism.

'This alliance born of our desperate collective interest shall not quickly be severed. Let us therefore no longer mourn, but celebrate the spilled blood which has forged these bonds toward a greater future…'

Excerpt from the 'Treaty of the Realm' signed by the three monarchs at the outset of the wars of founding.

CHAPTER 7

WYLL

As the secret entrance swung outwards, Jayden kicked it as hard as he could to add to the door's momentum. An incredulous cry issued from the other side, and Jayden smiled grimly as he started moving, knowing he'd hit his mark.

Before Dael even finished yelling, Jayden leapt from the passage, following the door's progress as it swung into the room. With the speed of a startled cat he moved around the obstacle as it rebounded back towards him, weapons ready only to find Dael sprawled on the carpeted floor, a shattered glass of red wine staining the rug beside him. Even as Jayden raised the guard's knife in his off hand, he smashed the still smouldering metal torch down on the count's arm as hard as he could, stopping Dael's rushed attempt at reaching his rapier. There was an audible snap as Dael's arm gave way to the solid iron, and he cried out in pain.

Jayden took another step forward and dropped to his

knees on top of Dael, causing the count to howl again as Jayden sunk them deep into his stomach, winding him badly.

"For Rhianna," Jayden whispered as their eyes finally met, and then brought the knife slamming down with all his strength.

For a long moment his mind refused to acknowledge what was happening as time seemed to grind to a halt, but eventually he realised his mind was not the problem, his arm was refusing to move. Again and again he tried to bring it down, to strike the killing blow, but it was no use. Incredibly, his arm was somehow stuck in mid-air, and all his attempts to remove it from its invisible prison were not achieving a thing.

With a sick feeling in his stomach Jayden twisted around, looking over his shoulder to see exactly whom the second voice he had heard from the passageway belonged to.

As he intuitively knew he would be, Jayden saw the second man standing next to a chair by the roaring fireplace. His expression was as stern as his clothing, which consisted of functional black pants, a matching shirt which appeared oddly uniform-like and some of the finest quality shoes Jayden had ever seen. All of it was covered, except at the front, from neck to ankle in a pitch black, silver-lined cloak.

"I can't let you do that, Jayden," the old man told him bluntly. Without so much as a blink or crooked finger, the knife and torch ripped themselves out of his hands and went sailing across the room via what must have been the Gift, and came to rest on a chair beside the archmage.

"Quite frankly I'm surprised you have the energy to even stand yet. Your wounds were... severe."

"The thought of his death lends me strength," Jayden growled as he once again tried to free his captive limb.

Tolmarak glanced at Dael with a look of what might have been anger as Jayden spoke. In a moment it was gone though, and Jayden was forced to watch in despair as Dael shoved him off and climbed painfully back to his feet.

The count gave him a broad grimace which Jayden knew would have been an arrogant smirk if Dael wasn't still winded and pained by his broken arm, which he was now holding protectively across his chest.

"If you'll be so kind as to release him Archmage, I will take it from here," Dael ordered. Even as with his off-hand he awkwardly drew the needle thin rapier which was never far from his side.

"I don't think so," the archmage told him in exactly the same tone he had taken with Jayden. The rapier sailed across the room at the archmage's behest to join the knife and torch on the plush chair beside the white-haired mage. Dael took a menacing step towards the old man, but only one, since he found himself abruptly caught by the same invisible force which had hold of Jayden's arm.

"Don't think for a minute you can intimidate me boy," the archmage told him icily.

"You may have the poor people on your lands terrified of your power, but to me you're just one more minor nobleman grown far too arrogant for his own good."

For an instant Jayden thought Dael was about to object as his eyes turned cold, but after a moment more of straining against his invisible bonds the count instead chose to relax. He must have realised there was little else he could do, short of politely asking for the archmage to release him, and there was no way he was going to do that.

"Give me your word you will not attempt to kill him again and I will release you," the archmage said as he turned his attention back to Jayden.

Jayden shook his head in refusal as he once again fruitlessly attempted to free his arm.

"Release me then, and I promise not to harm the boy, even if he did break into my private quarters and try to kill me," Dael told the archmage in his most placating voice.

"Forgiveness is a virtue after all," he finished with a grin.

Jayden found himself growling wordlessly as he continued trying to free himself.

The archmage shot the count a glance full of rebuke and Dael found his jaw abruptly clamped shut by the same force which had hold on the rest of his body.

Dael's eyes glittered with hatred as he stood there, bound and unable to do anything now but wait and watch.

"Jayden, stop straining against the bonds," the archmage told him pointedly. "You can't break them, but you can hurt yourself if you tear a muscle or dislocate a joint by twisting too far."

Jayden continued to struggle now that Dael was not an immediate threat, concentrating his full attention on whatever had hold of his arm. He wilfully ignored the archmage's warning, risking injury until finally, for the briefest of moments, his hand seemed to slip.

*   *   *

Tolmarak's eyes widened in shock as Jayden continued to dissolve the construct through sheer force of will, his arm moving by degrees as the magical bond weakened.

He doesn't even know what the spell is, or how it's constructed! How is he doing this?

Even most of the fully accomplished magi back in Aramar couldn't have neutralised this spell, simple though it was, when cast by an archmage as dominant as he. Certainly none of them could have done it without training. This common merchant's son was powerful in the Gift almost beyond belief, more so than even Tolmarak himself, and the archmage knew he was counted among the very strongest of magi currently living.

During his lifetime he had only encountered a handful of equals in the Gift. Two had been human and one an Oo'vi high shaper who would have defeated him in battle if it hadn't been for a young protégé of his called Nereth, who had turned the tide just in time. That had been many years ago of course. Now Nereth had declared rebellion against the king, leading the army of the only man Tolmarak had ever known who was clearly stronger in the Gift than he.

This boy Jayden will be a power to be reckoned with, Tolmarak thought as he watched his spell begin to fragment under the boy's intent will. Tolmarak had sensed his aura long before the boy had entered the keep from one of the lower levels, no doubt through a bolthole leading to the concealed entrance he had kicked open. That would cause problems for him in the future as Tolmarak well knew from experience. Anyone with the Gift put out an aura that other Gift users could sense, even those of the western nations, and the stronger in the Gift you were, the larger an area your aura covered. The problem was that Jayden was so strong in the Gift that every mage within a mile of the boy would be able to sense exactly where he was at any hour of the day or night. It made him a prime target for his enemies.

Before being recalled to Aramar to take up the position as leader of the college there, Tolmarak had briefly taken leave from his other duties to help train the newly promoted Mage Heramiir. As a result, he had spent a considerable amount of time in the renegade's company, and knew with certainty that this boy in front of him was probably the only person in the world who could match Heramiir strength for strength with the Gift. Unfortunately, Heramiir had nearly fifteen years of training and practice in battle magic and other more arcane arts to complement his raw strength.

For right now though, Tolmarak could see Jayden was losing focus even as the spell came unravelled. As his arm jerked free from the restrictive magic, the boy lost his balance. He fell roughly to the carpeted floor near where the count's shattered wineglass had spilled its blood red contents, which no doubt the talented young mage would consider a poor substitute.

The boy tried to stand again, but could only make it as far as his knees as he looked hatefully up at Dael's motionless form.

Not surprising really.

The fact Jayden was still conscious after taking so many wounds so recently and now using an element for the first time not in a simple exercise, but a task which would have taken many newly elevated magi quite some training to accomplish was nothing short of amazing. Jayden had already unknowingly used air when he had communicated with Tolmarak at Aramar's docks. Now having dissolved the spell of air and spirit which Tolmarak had been holding him with, something which by all rights the boy should not have been able to do, that only left him with fire, earth, and water.

With an obvious effort, Jayden used the wall as a support and climbed slowly to his feet, a shard of the shattered glass clenched stealthily in his fist. Tolmarak saw it in time though, and as Jayden staggered towards the immobile count, he used a delicate spell of air to extricate the sharp glass from Jayden's hand without cutting him.

"He deserves to die," Jayden said, sinking shakily to his knees. The exertion and adrenaline surge of the last few hours had caught up to him at last, and even the boy finally sensed he was in no condition to match power, or even wits with him at the current time.

Tolmarak crossed the distance to where Jayden was kneeling, struggling against the effects of using the new type of magic. He swayed and then braced himself against the floor with an outstretched arm before he could succumb to the deep exhaustion which almost always resulted from using a new part of the Gift. It wasn't the days of sickness that followed a new magi's awakening, but it would drain him to the point of apathy until the next morning at least.

"If I let you kill him now, in cold blood, you will become exactly that which you hate," he told the boy quietly. As Jayden looked him straight in the eye for the first time, Tolmarak almost thought he might have reached him at last. But then Jayden's eyes fixed on a point beyond him and with a cry the boy staggered to his feet, lurching toward a wall covered in trophies and relics from ages past.

"Jayden," Tolmarak warned as the boy reached up to take hold of an ancient sword.

"This is mine!" Jayden snarled as he gripped the hilt of

a long serpentine blade and took a step back towards Dael.

"That piece of filth must have taken it from me on the cliff top," he shouted, his arm outstretched and pointing the blade menacingly at the count.

"Is it not enough for you to kill your only childhood friends?! You have to rob them as well!" Jayden screamed, and when no response was forthcoming, the boy ripped away the spell which held Dael's jaw closed.

"Answer me!"

Tolmarak had seen a lot during his long life, but the ease with which this untrained boy had just torn apart one of his spells was frightening. He would have to take him firmly in hand he realised, or Jayden might become more of a menace than a help in the coming years.

"How can you live with yourself? How can you sleep at night after the things you've done?" Jayden shouted again, clearly at the end of his strength.

"Quite well actually," Dael replied as he arrogantly lifted his chin.

With a snarl Jayden lifted the sword over his head with both hands and Tolmarak was forced to disarm him once again. He called the Oo'vi relic across the room with the Gift to join the other weapons on the chair as Jayden began a furious charge at the count.

"Stop doing that!" Jayden screamed as he reached out his hand, and his will, to bring the serpentine blade back across the room.

For a moment Tolmarak was forced to actually make an effort to counteract the boy's magic, though he was very careful not to let it show on his face. Eventually Jayden's focus faltered though, and what little strength the boy had rallied seemed to flee with it.

Even so, Jayden stared at the archmage for a long moment with hate-filled eyes before finally accepting that getting his hands on a weapon was not going to happen. Without any other options, Jayden turned his attention back to Dael, striding up and stepping so close his lips were almost touching the loathsome noble's ear.

"Sleep well then, 'Count' of Grandell, and never forget that one day when you wake with a bright blade at your throat, it will be my hand that wields it."

With a quick punch to Dael's midriff the boy turned and stalked past Tolmarak, giving him an ominous glare as he picked up his serpentine blade and exited the room.

Tolmarak waited until the young man was safely around the corner before allowing himself a deep sigh of relief. If the boy ever found out how close he had just been to overpowering an experienced archmage before he had even begun his training, Tolmarak despaired of ever winning him over to the king's service. The boy was clearly dangerous, but with that much innate ability he might also be the only Gift user in the entire world who could take Heramiir on in a straight fight.

Unfortunately that made him vital to the coming war effort, and Tolmarak knew his training would have to be rushed ahead for Jayden to be of any use to the king's cause. If not for that, Tolmarak would have considered having a group of magi put a powerful ward on the boy to stifle his abilities until he had shown he could be trusted. Now that he had discovered the Gift he would inevitably employ it again, especially given how quickly he had learnt to manipulate the bonds of the spell which Tolmarak had used.

Tolmarak abruptly wondered what the boy had been

like before the events of the last week, and whether he was naturally brutal, or if it was just his anger and grief at what had happened that night on the cliff. Still, while the boy's nature might be in question, his power certainly wasn't, and with war brewing, strength such as his couldn't be left unchecked. He would have to be dealt with carefully Tolmarak decided as he exited the count's quarters, almost forgetting to release Dael's remaining bonds in his hurry to catch up to the boy. He would have to take Jayden under his wing personally if he hoped to gain his trust and loyalty. After seeing what he just had, he couldn't help the sneaking suspicion that achieving that goal might be more important to the future of Jeranon, than the conscription of every other man on the promontory.

*   *   *

Dawn had broken an hour past, and the men Tolmarak's soldiers had picked out from the townsfolk to form Grandell's levee of conscripts were saying their final goodbyes.

Those wealthy enough to own or have just bought horses capable of making the lengthy trip were checking equipment or tack before mounting their steeds, while Jayden sat waiting on his own horse, Strider. Normally he would have been comfortable in the saddle. Today he found himself unconsciously shifting between a half limp slump which threatened to send him hurtling to the street if anything spooked the beige stallion, and a stiff, straight-backed posture which made him appear as unyielding as the stone statues which decorated the border of Grandell's main square. The sky overhead was a murky grey which trapped the day's heat and made everything stick. The flies had come out for the summer as well, further adding to the irritable manner of those with nothing left to do but wait for the long march to begin.

Little more than a week had passed since Dael had killed Rhianna, and Jayden still found it hard to think about anything but the cliff top plateau as he waited for the column to begin moving. As he sat here, he had discovered that by allowing his thoughts to drift to the past, far to the past, he could ignore the present, and the man who stood not fifteen feet away to his right. He could almost feel the cold steel of the serpentine sword which sat in its sheath on his belt. It was all he could do not to draw it and cut Dael's heart out as the count stood conversing fitfully with the captain of his guard.

If Jayden thought there was any chance at all Tolmarak would not stop him again, he would have leapt off Strider's back and charged straight at Rhianna's murderer. The guards and the hundreds of witnesses who filled the square to bursting were not a concern. But he couldn't even do that. The archmage had made himself painfully clear once Jayden had woken the night after breaking into Dael's apartments. He had told him that while his previous attempt had been pardoned, if he tried to commit murder again now that his initial shock had worn off, Tolmarak would see him locked away in a prison where not even the Gift could help him escape.

If Tolmarak had threatened to let him hang, Jayden didn't think he would have cared, he no longer worried about dying, or living for that matter. But if he tried to kill Dael and failed, and the archmage locked him away for the next twenty years, he would not be able to exact vengeance on the man he had once called a friend. That particular thought burned him all over again as he sat there, waiting, trying not to lose the last fragments of self-control which remained to him.

The sun continued its infinitesimal march across the morning sky.

The storm which had opened up so heavily above Grandell a week before had long since gone. It had now been replaced by another set of clouds, leaving the sun to shine dimly through their cover as it continued trying to dry out the still soggy ground below. And still they waited.

Tolmarak himself sat astride his grey warhorse, positioned not at all subtly between Jayden and the part of the town square where Dael was still conversing with his captain.

No doubt to prevent me from causing any more trouble.

He didn't care about the archmage's caution though; it was unnecessary. Once the archmage had told him that he would personally conduct his training, Jayden had decided he would go to Aramar with Tolmarak and become a mage, although he'd had no intention of letting Tolmarak know it. Keeping the old man on edge these last few days was the least the archmage deserved for not allowing him to take his vengeance.

Jayden knew he could bide his time at the college, learning all they could teach him, and discovering more himself. Only once he was in a position to have a genuine chance at overcoming Dael's forces would he return here and execute the Count of Grandell for the crimes he had committed.

As he sat, silently seething at the sight of Dael walking unchained and free, he noticed the archmage staring at him. He knew Tolmarak considered him little more than a boy, yet he thought the archmage looked ready to pounce the instant he tried to move, as if unsure he could stop him in time. Jayden stared back a moment too long and gave the archmage a cold smile, which prompted the old man to give him an unimpressed shake of the head.

There was a sudden commotion on the side of the square facing the Keep, which attracted both his and the archmage's attention. A lieutenant wearing Dael's grey and maroon livery was leading two of his soldiers out towards the count, and Jayden was shocked to see they were dragging another guard between them, one who had obviously been beaten. He was still struggling weakly in their grasp when the small group of guardsmen reached Dael and his captain. The lieutenant saluted smartly, then took the prisoner by the hair, lifting his battered head up for the count to inspect.

Jayden gasped loudly enough for the archmage to look his way and see the startled expression on his face. Their eyes locked for a moment, and when Tolmarak turned back towards the count and his guardsmen, Dael was already pointing a knife threateningly at the prisoner with his one good arm. By the looks of it, it was the same blade Jayden had used the other night to try to take his vengeance with, and Jayden saw Tolmarak nod almost imperceptibly to himself in understanding.

Dael was clearly aware the knife Jayden had burst into his rooms with had been obtained from this guard, and by the furious look in his eyes, he now knew the guard hadn't put up much of a fight.

"Dael will kill him without so much as a trial for thinking he helped me," Jayden said calmly, but loud enough for Tolmarak to hear.

"If you truly wish me to commit my life to the college, show me that its leader is worth following. Save him."

*   *   *

Tolmarak turned back to face Jayden and saw him sitting perfectly still astride his beige stallion, his agate hard eyes giving a weight to the request that the words alone had not.

The archmage nodded slowly before dismounting and walking over to where the count and his men were still harassing the prisoner, and without pause placed himself between the beaten man and the knife wielding count.

"What has this man done?" he asked, already knowing the answer, but wanting to see what Dael's response would be.

"Be gone mage, this is none of your concern," Dael spat back as he tried unsuccessfully to stare Tolmarak down, his pride obviously still injured from being trussed up and gagged the other night.

Even so, that was not a tone one took with an archmage, and Tolmarak was not about to let it pass when coming from such a power hungry, self-important minor noble like Dael. He'd healed the man's broken arm later on the night Jayden had broken it, and so felt no compunction in binding the arrogant young count from neck to toe with a constrictive spell of air which would keep him immobile. He purposely made it different from the one he knew Jayden could manipulate, and then with his left hand took the knife from Dael's grip.

"You would do well to remember your manners around me," Tolmarak told him.

"I am an Archmage, leader of the college at Aramar and advisor to King Erian the Third, Defender of the East and Heir to the house of Savani. While I am here, I speak with his voice and his authority."

"Release him," Tolmarak ordered the guards who were still holding the prisoner.

The two burly men looked at each other for an instant and then at Dael for confirmation. It wasn't forthcoming, and Tolmarak didn't care. He sent the two guards sprawling with a sharp blow of air to each before looking the prisoner up and down. Despite having been soundly beaten, the man didn't look like he had sustained any permanent injuries, and his bones appeared intact. Tolmarak waited until the haggard guard pulled himself upright, then watched as the young man tore the emblem of Dael's house from his uniform and threw it to the stone at Dael's feet.

The count was livid, his muscles standing out beneath the ethereal bonds as he struggled vainly to break away from Tolmarak's invisible grip.

"You're a dead man Wyll!" he snarled, the spittle flying from his lips reminding Tolmarak of nothing so much as a rabid dog.

He turned his back on the maddened count even as the man's tirade continued, and saw the two guards he had shoved with the Gift had picked themselves up, and were now looking at each other and at their lieutenant for instructions.

"Have one of my field medics clean you up Wyll," Tolmarak told the beaten soldier whose name he now knew, "And don't concern yourself with this. You're under my protection now," he finished, inclining his head towards Dael's still struggling form.

"Oh, and Wyll, do you have a horse?"

The young guardsman nodded painfully, "Yes Archmage," he answered respectfully, "But he's on my family's farm a few miles south of here."

"Good. Captain Ravenburg!" Tolmarak called.

Wasting no time, a stocky Aramarian officer in the black uniform of the mageguard guided his horse over to where the group was standing.

"Orders Archmage?" the captain inquired crisply.

"See that Wyll here is outfitted for the march and send some men to gather his equipment and belongings from the keep. Also, as soon as one of the healers has looked him over, go with him and retrieve his horse from his family's farm, then return here with all speed. Dismissed."

"Aye Sir!" the officer saluted, and then set off at a brisk pace with Wyll trying to keep up at a half limp, his right leg causing him no small discomfort. Tolmarak found himself wondering whether the man was in a fit enough state to ride, or if he would need more care than the medic in his mageguard unit could easily provide. He had never specialised in the healers' arts other than the battlefield triage that all magi were required to learn as part of their training, training that had undoubtedly saved Jayden's life not ten days gone. Still, Wyll's wounds were minor compared to that and Tolmarak could take care of them himself if need be.

Then he heard something behind him which shocked him to the core.

In the midst of his ongoing tirade, Dael had actually had the nerve to threaten him. Him! One of the most powerful archmagi in Jeranon and advisor to the king no less.

This little man badly needs to be taken in hand. He turned to face Dael, the count going slightly pale as he realised the archmage had heard every word.

Tolmarak did his best to study the so-called noble as though he was some offensive kind of bug, which wasn't too far from the truth Tolmarak realised with a sneer.

Without warning he pulled the invisible bands tighter around Dael until not even his muscles could be seen twitching beneath the bonds, and the count's breathing became shallow and rapid.

Tolmarak moved closer to the enraged man until his own white hair almost touched the count's face.

"You think to threaten me!" he whispered coldly, "When I return to Aramar I make you this promise, in my report to the king on the state of his cities, Grandell's will not be a favourable one. Now, little man, let me teach you something about threats. If you co-operate with me completely from this point on, I *may* allow you keep your patent of nobility."

He waited for a moment to let that sink in.

"But if you threaten me again, in fact, if I so much as see you again... If I find out you have tried to take any form of retribution against these men or their families, or their friends, or their holdings, or in any other way, I will make it my personal business to see King Erian rescinds your position and demotes you to the status of peasant. I will then find the deepest, darkest hole in Jeranon and leave you in it to rot. Or perhaps I will just give you over to the peasants of Grandell whom you have so obviously been mistreating since coming into your father's title. I wonder how they would treat you once the protection of your position was stripped away."

By the time he was finished, Dael's eyes were a mixture of outrage and terror. With a shove of air Tolmarak released the bonds and sent the arrogant count sprawling to the ground for everyone to see, and indeed he noticed the entire town seemed to have stopped to watch Dael being put in his place by the old archmage.

Nothing ever changes, he thought in disgust as he turned his back on the count. Threaten these minor nobles' lives or their livelihood and they just went back to whatever they were doing, but schemed against you as well. Threaten their status however, something most of them had taken for granted since birth, and they usually fell into line quickly enough. He strolled back over to Wind, his smoke-grey steed, and with a reassuring pat on the nose mounted the war-trained horse. With a single tap of his knee Tolmarak guided him over to where Jayden was still sitting atop Strider, watching the exchange with some small amount of satisfaction.

"Thank you," Jayden told him stiffly, before falling silent again.

Together they watched as Dael marched back into the keep by himself, thwarted. With Dael's departure, it was obvious Jayden knew that his chance to reach Rhianna's murderer was irrevocably gone. He hid it well considering the circumstances, but it was clear the boy was only just barely keeping himself in check.

As Dael walked through the gate, he took a swing at one of the guards he was passing, dropping the man to his knees as he continued without a backward glance. He never broke stride as he was lost to their view, hiding inside the stone fortress which was supposed to be the source of Grandell's protection.

A very short time later, the mageguard captain rode up to Tolmarak with Wyll at his side on a borrowed horse and reported that all was ready for the rest of the men to begin their march. Tolmarak nodded and Wyll and the captain rode off again, this time to the south of town towards his family's farm where the young guardsman would presumably saddle up his own steed and say a quick goodbye to his family.

"Lieutenant Bickerall," Tolmarak called once the pair had left. A few moments later a tall man, also in the unrelieved black uniform of the mageguard, with massive shoulders and a neck like a tree trunk presented himself before the archmage.

"Give the order Lieutenant, move the infantry out."

"At once, Archmage," the sizeable man replied as he jogged back to the column and began shouting orders to the Aramarian soldiers, who in turn each kept their group of conscripts in line.

As soon as the column began to snake its way north, a heartening cheer went up from the assembled crowd. By the looks of it, most of the town had come to bid a final farewell to family and friends before they marched off to war.

"Lieutenant Bandell," Tolmarak called as soon as the noise died down.

"Form up the cavalry and move out. I'll join you on the road as promptly as I can."

The bowlegged lieutenant gave a crisp salute and began shouting orders at his men, who brought the mounted conscripts into line even as Bandell himself mounted his own steed at the head of the column. There was a moment of confusion as two of the villagers' horses took enough of a dislike to each other for one of the riders to be thrown to the ground. The animals were separated, and a rather bruised young man remounted his horse with an embarrassed wave to the soldier in charge of his unit.

Within moments everything was back in order, and with a disapproving shake of his head, the dour lieutenant gave the order to begin the long journey north to Clairemont. He had sent Sling sailing ahead to prepare the far-flung population centres of the promontory for the column's arrival. From what he had seen in Grandell, he no longer trusted the mayors and minor nobles of the region to carry out the conscriptions and gathering of resources to his satisfaction. So now they had to waste time marching around the Anchorhead Promontory making sure the king's orders were implemented smoothly. After all, it was a lot easier to ignore or try to lie to an outrider than it was to do the same to a small army led by an archmage.

For a day or two Tolmarak had considered sending Jayden back to Aramar on board Sling when it departed yesterday morning so he could begin his training at the college. After the episode in the count's chambers though, he had decided against it, choosing instead to keep the boy close while Jayden was at such a crucial stage of his development as a mage. For now, it would be safer for all concerned if the boy stayed under his own watchful eye. Besides, he could teach Jayden the basics of the magi's art while they were on the road. The next few phases promised to be long and uninteresting as they made their way along the promontory's winding roads and then marched back to Aramar. Teaching Jayden would at least help pass the time. With any luck, he might just be able to get the boy's mind focused on the training, instead of killing Dael, and the war he would shortly be asked to fight in aid of his king's cause.

The last few days since his abortive attempt on Dael's life, Jayden had become withdrawn. His frustration and anger had become more inwardly focused, so even though he hadn't spoken a word of complaint in days, the boy had wound himself up as tight as a spring. Tolmarak was starting to fear that one day soon he would simply snap and discover in a rage he could overpower his teacher. If that were allowed to happen, Tolmarak feared Jayden would head back to Grandell to finish what he had started the other night, irretrievably wiping away any progress they had made in the meantime, and probably getting himself declared renegade in the process. At all costs he had to devise a means of avoiding just such a situation occurring.

Which left him the question of what to do with Wyll. The young man had demonstrated initiative and independence of thought when he had gone against his liege and given that knife to Jayden. Unfortunately, Tolmarak still wasn't sure whether the other trait he had shown was courage or treachery. Despite Tolmarak's dislike of Dael's methods, the boy was a guard, and had no doubt sworn an oath of service to the man he had aided Jayden in trying to kill.

He wasn't sure whether it would be a good idea to throw the two of them together on the long march ahead. He had a hunch they could become fast friends, but they might also feed each other's desire for revenge, and that was something he emphatically did not want. Still, after all that had happened, he knew Jayden had to have someone to talk to besides a gnarled old archmage such as himself, and this Wyll might just be the man for the job.

Perhaps it would be for the best.

Eventually he decided to make the two young men ride together for the first few days at least, then see how things panned out from there.

It wasn't too much longer before Captain Ravenburg and Wyll came riding back up the street, and only then did Tolmarak realise just how long he must have been lost in his thoughts.

He turned to look at Jayden, but the boy was still sitting his mount with practised ease, eyes focused on some distant memory, and Tolmarak was glad to see that much of his nervous, almost manic, energy had drained away now that Dael had left the square.

The crowd that had come to see off their friends and loved ones had all but dispersed, and as the two riders he was waiting for came to a halt before him, Tolmarak couldn't help but admire the flawless white stallion Wyll rode, which glistened a deep chocolate brown below all four of its knees.

"Ready on your command, Archmage," Ravenburg said in a deep tone as he reined his mount to a halt.

"Very well Tarrent," Tolmarak replied familiarly to his mageguard officer as he took a last look around the square. The tents and the men he had brought with him to Grandell had all gone now, and the statue-lined square was once again as clear of obstructions as it had been when he'd arrived more than a week before.

"It's time to go," he said to Jayden, and then with a flick of the reins asked his own mount to begin walking across the empty square toward the north end of town.

Without a word, or any visible gesture, Jayden moved

Strider around and fell in beside him, his eyes cold and his chin raised as they crossed the square and passed the towering stonework of the keep.

Next to Jayden, Wyll guided his white steed through the streets of the town with a comfortable ease, and Tolmarak again wondered where the boy had come across such a rare beast, and if he even knew the true nature of the creature he rode.

Captain Ravenburg rode a smoke-grey warhorse similar to Tolmarak's own, looking around at everything as he passed, alert for trouble as always as they made their way out of the provincial seaside town.

"Did your family not come to see you off?" Tolmarak inquired delicately after they had ridden through most of Grandell with no sign of Jayden's parents coming to bid him farewell.

"I told them not to," he replied. "We've said our goodbye's already."

Tolmarak had allowed the boy to spend the last few days in his own house after recovering sufficiently from his first use of spirit magic, Jayden's mother insisting Tolmarak also stay on as a guest.

He knew Jayden's business here was anything but finished, though even the boy seemed to have accepted there was nothing more he could do about it at this moment. Yet as they passed the final row of houses marking Grandell's northern border, it was clear Jayden was having to work hard to keep control of himself as he left his birth town behind in the dust.

A very few minutes later the sound of hooves pounding the solidly packed dirt road behind them reached the ears of the riders, and they turned as one to see a small solitary figure riding an unsaddled horse towards them at a full gallop.

The group stopped as soon as it became clear they were the rider's target. The others watched as Jayden jumped down from Strider's back before taking a few long steps to where the young girl had leapt from her own mount, rushing forward to meet him. Both Wyll and Ravenburg shared a curious glance to see if the other knew what was going on. Tolmarak just sat patiently on his horse, knowing from the last few days of guesting with Jayden's family that the approaching rider was David and Lyssa's youngest child, Miya. Tolmarak couldn't help but smile as the little girl quickly closed the distance between them and caught her older brother in a tight embrace, only standing back long enough to give him something. Jayden placed it in a hidden pocket inside his shirt before hugging her tightly again and carrying her back over to the dappled mare she had ridden in on just moments before. With only a little effort Jayden lifted his little sister back onto her horse and placed a gentle kiss on her forehead before saying something the others couldn't hear. Then he made her promise to go back home, which after a long moment of fretting she eventually did. Gripping the horse's mane in both hands she turned the animal sharply away from the group at a canter, which turned into a gallop a few strides later as she fled back along the dirt road towards Grandell.

"My sister, Miya," Jayden said to the two soldiers who were still looking at him quizzically as he remounted his steed.

"Come on," Tolmarak said in a not unkindly fashion when Jayden once more had his seat, "We've a long way to go before we catch up with the column, and many more miles to cover beyond that before we can rest."

Jayden nodded reluctantly as he turned Strider away from Grandell for the last time, and as the small group of soldiers and magi made their way slowly northward along the road to Clairemont, Jayden and Wyll turned their backs on the town they had lived in all their lives.

The sun began to rise higher in the heavens and the morning's clouds melted away to nothing while they rode, and although the young guardsman Wyll would occasionally give a regretful look over his shoulder in Grandell's direction, Jayden never did.

'If it can be imagined in sufficient clarity, created with sufficient strength, focused into reality by one's connection to the Gift, it can be done.'
Excerpt from 'The Gift', one of the few surviving tomes written pre-cataclysm.

CHAPTER 8

THE MAP AND THE BOOK

It was well after midnight, and scores of candles flickered in gilded wrought-iron candelabras positioned at each corner of Archmage Nereth's study, casting a bright yellow glow over the map-covered table at its centre. Paintings hung suspended from bronze hooks which had long ago been embedded in the stone walls, while other, less identifiable items were meticulously placed on recessed shelves cut directly into the walls. A vague smell of smoke hung in the air.

Nereth stood behind a vast wooden table staring at the largest of the maps. He had placed stone weights on its corners to stop the parchment re-rolling itself into the cylindrical position it had occupied for a great many idle years. The ancient parchment told of a time when Jeranon had ranged little further west than a few garrisons above the Cloudburst Cliffs, although the map extended all the way to the border of the Dark Iron Mountains. At least half the towns and villages which currently stood in Jeranon were unmarked, while many others which no longer existed were positioned with great accuracy, the ill-fated city of Harverness most of all.

The map had been made by a master, of that much Nereth was certain. He'd just spent the last two days riding the roads outside Miralthrall, taking his own measurements, and the map matched them perfectly. It was a priceless treasure to a general such as he, and only one of many he'd uncovered from the vault beneath the restricted section of the college library.

Staring at the map, he knew he'd made the right choice all those years ago when first deciding to back Heramiir's bid for power. It was true, he'd had his own motivations for doing so, namely removing the king's restrictions on experimentation. The treasures recovered from the vault these last few weeks alone however would have been enough to justify his actions over the years even without that, and there was so much more down there still waiting to be codified.

For the last hour, servants had been coming in and out of his study carrying the buckets of dirt Nereth had instructed them to cover an enormous marked out area of floor with.

The map in front of him was far too fragile to risk damaging with use, and constructing a copy would be necessary in order to utilise it properly.

He turned to look at the cordoned off area and nodded to himself.

"That is enough," he told the servants who were depositing the latest trip's worth of dirt onto the floor.

He was about to send them away so he could work in peace, but at the last moment changed his mind. Some of the Giftless still weren't happy about the magi taking control of Miralthrall. Until they settled down, it wouldn't hurt them to see a small demonstration of what a mage could do when they set their mind to a task, or to understand that not all of the Gift was about fire and death.

He waited a few minutes more while the procession of servants entered and deposited their bucketloads into the marked rectangle. As each man or woman finished their task, they drifted over to the far wall to wait with the others, milling about but not disturbing the silence. When the last bucket of dirt had been strewn across the floor Nereth walked a circuit of the flagged area to make a final inspection before proceeding. Everything appeared to be in order, so he returned to the long wooden table where the ancient map laid waiting in a strong pool of candlelight.

What he was about to try would be complex and draining, even for an archmage of his skill.

At least the first part will be the most demanding.

He could attend to it while his strength and concentration were at their peak.

He spread his hands out over the map, the black enamel of his gauntlets nearly brushing the table, and began. The yellow candlelight was swept away as Nereth covered the parchment with a shining layer of spirit magic, its pale blue light pushing the slowly dancing shadows across the room in its wake. Nereth closed his eyes to concentrate on the sensation of his spell more clearly as the glowing enchantment brushed against the profoundly subtle raising and lowering of the ink where each fresh colour had been applied. He then ever so gently began to manipulate the spell as he found each line. With the patience of a master jeweller he pulled sections of the spirit spell upward so they matched the intricate patchwork of topographic markings layered over the print of the land.

His mind searched over the lay of the map, making minute corrections to the spell as he went. The height of each hill had to be exact, every stream and forest accounted for. The detail of the parchment itself was amazing, and the mental effort required to copy it all so precisely began to tell. Nereth worked for long, painstaking hours before he was finally done, and when at last he opened his eyes, it was no surprise to see that dawn was perhaps only an hour away. He checked the spell repeatedly to find any mistakes or regions he might have overlooked, but eventually accepted that he had done the job right the first time, and sighed with relief. The hardest part was complete, and now it was time to transfer the completed spell from the table to the floor. With a minimum of fuss Nereth waved the spell across the room and settled it perfectly into one of the flagged corners of the dirt pile which the servants had prepared. With the utmost care he began stretching his creation along the borders of the marked area, making sure to keep all its dimensions accurate, until a corner of the spell precisely met each flag.

The beginnings of a smile twisted Nereth's lips as he worked a simple mix of earth and fire magic to fuse the dirt beneath the stretched-out spell. The room became warm, and a bead of sweat rolled its way off Nereth's brow and onto his black enamelled plate armour. He would have to wrap this up soon, even with all his mental training he was not immune to the effects of creating such a complex construct. The mental stress of maintaining sufficient focus all night was feeding his growing headache, which in turn would soon be bad enough to impede his focus. At best he would have to let it go at that point, to continue would be to risk losing control of the spell, causing it to implode with wild and unanticipated consequences. But for now he could continue.

Once the dirt had solidified into a single solid mass Nereth closed his eyes once more. Using an earth spell Heramiir had shown him years ago, he expanded the mass upwards until it encountered, and fit snugly into the mould of the spirit spell he had just so painstakingly constructed. When he was finally finished the task, he walked a slow lap around his work and inspected every detail again before allowing the spell to fade. Without its pale blue glow to fill the chamber the room suddenly dimmed. Most of the candles had burned down hours ago, and a good portion of the light which remained was coming from the pre-dawn haze now staining the horizon through the massive glass windows overlooking the countryside beyond Miralthrall's walls. Nereth filled the room with a bright, natural coloured light, and it was a measure of his fatigue that he had to blink several times to adjust his eyes to the brightness which sprung out of nowhere.

Turning his attention back to the map he used the Gift once more to create a detailed, though far less complex layer of spells. This time they overlaid each region of the map with the illusion of the grassland, rivers and trees which were shown on the ancient parchment. With a wave he sent it over to the barren map on the floor and after resizing it, anchored the illusion to the dirt itself, turning the physical structure into a large and immobile arcane object which would power the illusion for many years to come. Creating a persistent piece of arcana like this would have been a serious matter mere weeks ago, with endless procedures, delays and permissions required, if it were allowed at all. Now he could just do it. Nereth smiled in satisfaction as he referred to a far more recent map he possessed. With a few more minutes of effort he grew and anchored miniature villages, towns and cities which represented all of Jeranon's population centres across the new map, as well as the castles along the border, until at last it was done. After a deep breath he looked up from his creation to find the sun was just beginning to peek up above the eastern horizon, so he let the remaining spells fade and stood back to admire his handiwork.

Another bead of sweat worked its way down an inch of his forehead and he wished for nothing more in that moment than to simply swipe it away, to feel the salty wetness of it on his hand as any normal person would have done. But no, even that simple pleasure was denied him. A moment of stupidity, one moment of arrogance in his youth, and he would feel nothing ever again underneath the massive suit of armour which had fused with and replaced his skin from the neck down.

Thank the Maker I wasn't wearing a helmet that day.

Old King Erian had been livid, but had foregone a prison sentence in favour of having him walk the halls of Miralthrall's college, forevermore a living testament as to why the ban on experimentation with the Gift existed in the first place.

He carefully wiped away the sweat, his head feeling the cool pressure of the gauntlet's enamelled metal, his hand feeling nothing at all.

"You may go," he told the servants whom he abruptly noticed were still standing over by the far wall. He had completely forgotten they were there, which was the point of having servants in the first place he supposed. They must have been waiting all night, watching while he went about his work. That was what he had wanted though, and it was good to see that even if they were not yet loyal to him, they were at least obedient.

As they filed out of his study, Nereth turned his back and went over to the enormous windows which covered the eastern side of the room. The sun was just beginning to rise on another day, and the night's activities had gone without incident leaving him tired, and with a headache, but otherwise alert. He heard the door close behind the last of the servants and carefully rubbed his eyes to clear his head.

"Impressive," Heramiir's expressive voice sounded from behind him.

Nereth spun, startled. He must be more tired than he'd thought, not to have noticed the archmage's approach. Heramiir's aura could be felt like a background hum whenever he was anywhere near the college structure, but still... A sly grin tugged at Heramiir's lips when he saw Nereth's startled expression, and as the younger archmage looked between the ancient map on the table and its three-dimensional copy on the floor, he allowed himself a quiet laugh.

"The red book holds some interesting secrets does it not?" he said jovially as Nereth reached out at him with the Gift.

"The master showed me how to translate the eleventh page this morning. I believe you will find it most interesting."

Nereth frowned as he discovered Heramiir had

somehow managed to mask his aura, and withdrew the probing finger of spirit magic. The probe showed it was intact, but even at this distance Nereth found himself blind to the archmage's Gift. It was a little disconcerting.

Almost like being in the presence of one of the Giftless.

Nereth decided to test this new ability of Heramiir's, so he gradually closed the distance between them, straining to catch any hint of the archmage's aura. When he was little more than two spans away, he finally caught the subtle feeling which announced the presence of another with the Gift. Yet the sensation was different, twisted in some disconcerting way.

As soon as he was rested sufficiently, he would have to examine the book again. The creature Heramiir called 'the master' only allowed them to translate the leather-bound volume it had gifted him one page at a time, and not in consecutive order. It was frustrating beyond reason because the sections contained in its yellowed pages were often longer than a single page, denying them the whole process of a spell. In one case it even teased them with a heading 'Transportation through the Gift,' whilst not giving any details because the heading was written underneath the end of another section which finished near the bottom of a page.

What exactly 'the master' was, Nereth was not yet sure, save that it wasn't human.

Heramiir had only divulged to him last year that he had been in contact with a creature that lived under Miralthrall's basements since before they had begun plotting nearly a decade ago. The archmage had also explained that it would only allow him to meet it face to face once they had successfully conducted the coup.

Nereth had always known Heramiir wanted power at almost any cost. Even so, these revelations coming so soon after they had openly declared themselves against the king had made him less than happy.

In his search though the ancient scrolls he'd liberated from the college's vault, he had developed certain suspicions about what this being was, and suspicions like the ones he now harboured needed to be confirmed, or hopefully, discounted.

Whatever the creature's motives though, and he wasn't sure even Heramiir knew the truth of that, the red book it had given them was a priceless treasure. Or it would be if they could read the cursed thing. The book seemed to be warded in some fashion none of them knew how to dispel, and attempting to translate it without the master's help had been an exercise in futility. Unfortunately, knowing how to translate one page of the book didn't mean you could read it all. In fact, the ward seemed to change the text every time a new paragraph was uncovered.

If the information in its pages wasn't so valuable it would be a great joke to give to someone I really didn't like.

"Yes, most interesting," Nereth returned eventually as he came to stand on the other side of his long wooden desk, atop which the original copy of the map still lay, unfurled and weighted at the corners.

Being able to mask your aura was something the college had been trying to perfect for decades with little success. Eventually the experiments had been abandoned when the old king had died, and his son Erian decided he didn't want magi walking around Jeranon who couldn't easily be identified.

"How goes the campaign?" Heramiir asked, changing

the topic abruptly, as he was sometimes inclined to do. Nereth was used to the archmage's seemingly erratic conversation though. It was a product of the man's ability to compartmentalise a vast array of topics in his mind, so Nereth simply changed his train of thought and answered.

"I have been here all night replicating this map, but the last report I received indicated our forces now have control over the garrisons on the cliffs as well as the city itself. Parties have been sent out to take the nearby towns and I don't expect any serious resistance from the peasantry at this point."

"Good. What about Karver and Danarel?" Heramiir asked, referring to the cities immediately up and down river of Miralthrall.

"Karver fell within hours of the initial assault," Nereth reported blandly.

"Danarel however, and precisely Earl Forstann, has managed so far to hold off the legion I dispatched. I believe they neutralised two of our magi with some kind of deception involving a trained deer and a poisoned letter. The messenger wasn't there when it happened, and his details were sketchy at best. The only solid information we have is that before they were killed, our magi reported there were no others with the Gift in range of their senses."

He fell silent, waiting for the archmage's response. For a long moment there was nothing, then Heramiir slammed his fist down hard onto the table between them, even in his rage taking care to avoid the ancient map.

"Which two?" he seethed, his right hand still balled into a fist.

"Kraytho and Belasin," Nereth answered quickly, "Both

were trained in battle magic and experienced in the field."

"Perhaps you could tell me Nereth, how a commander with no access to the Gift can not only take on but defeat two fully trained and experienced magi when we have the element of surprise?" Heramiir demanded.

"I expect either a merchant or peasant must have reached the cities before our soldiers, since both Karver and Danarel were walled up tight when our troops arrived."

"I see," Heramiir replied, the rebuke clear in his voice.

"What steps are you taking to correct this matter?" The archmage asked as his eyes strayed to the map adorning the wooden surface of the table.

"Another legion has been dispatched with three archmagi in support, they should link up with the original force sometime tomorrow. I have ordered Danarel be taken more or less whole and Earl Forstann brought back here alive if possible. We are still short of talented commanders to hold the western border while we engage the king's army next spring. I imagine Stonekeep would be an important enough assignment to keep him tied to that castle. Besides, if he is willing to defend his city against even his own countrymen, I think we can trust him not to let a western army into Jeranon."

He had privately considered having the man publicly executed in retaliation for the deaths of the two magi he had sent to Danarel, but right now was not the time. He needed men who could command the garrisons along the foothills, who while not necessarily loyal to him personally, would defend Jeranon against any force sent over the mountain range which marked the kingdom's border.

Those who were loyal to the new order would be

needed come spring, when the king would no doubt send his army west as soon as the snows melted. Nereth had no intention of being caught between the old king's force and an attack by the western nations.

The men of the northern plains to the west of the mountains were trained from the time they could walk to be heavy cavalry or infantry, and they excelled at attacking a given target. The first time he had fought them though, he had stumbled upon the fact that once forced to defence their discipline became a touch and go kind of thing. Years later, when he had encountered them a second time it was to lead a defence of his own countrymen. As luck would have it, he had been only a few hour's ride away when they struck, and although he had not arrived in time to save the village, after a day-long pursuit his men had run the raiders to ground. The plainsmen had turned to face his troops once they knew they'd been spotted, and after blunting their attack with his magi he had sent his own cavalry out wide of the enemy charge to flank them from both sides. With the pikemen in the middle to protect his spellcasters he had corralled the Northmen with gouts of rock spewing upward from behind them to cut off their retreat. The rest was history and a thousand knights of the northwest plains had been routed and sent packing that day, back across the Dark Iron Mountains, the few which had escaped his trap anyway.

The Imbic warriors of the far west however were a far more formidable foe to the Giftless. Their minds were slower than the other races and almost any trap was effective against them. Nevertheless, Nereth had seen an Imbic mutation take a ballista bolt to one of its five arms and just break the shaft in two to stop the excess being jolted in battle, as a strong man might do if hit by an arrow he couldn't easily remove.

For some reason, the Imbic race didn't seem to include any sorcerers in its makeup, or at least if it did, they had never been seen on this side of the mountains. Yet Nereth had always respected their strength and unpredictable nature, and he refused to be caught off guard by labelling them mindless brutes.

The greyskins directly to the west of the mountains had always been the most aggressive of the four western nations, with nearly half the attacks over the last hundred years having been initiated by them. The Augrahl commanders could be devious, and the untold numbers of Nostahl they could bring to the field always made them a dangerous enemy. By themselves, the diminutive Nostahl weren't much of a problem. However, a few hundred small bands of the three foot high creatures roaming the countryside trying to outflank you and get at your supply lines were almost impossible to contain when used as a distraction by a larger force, especially in the tall grasses of Sammorand.

The Augrahl Shaman were no laughing matter either. Thankfully, few of them survived the brutal training inflicted upon them. Unfortunately, that meant the ones who lived to face the armies of Jeranon were always exceptionally strong in the Gift. He had almost been killed by one in his first combat with the greyskins, and that battle was about as close as he had ever come to defeat. Too many of his men had died that day, but the attack had been driven back. In the aftermath, the enemy commander, minus most of one of the horns which adorned their leathery, elongated heads, had taken what was left of his force back across the mountains. It wasn't really a retreat, but then it hadn't really been an attack, simply a probe to test the border defences south of Stonekeep Pass.

Stonekeep Pass was located near the centre of the Dark Iron Mountain range. The gap in the mountain wall had been formed by some devastating ancient earthquake, and was the widest and easiest way to cross the border between east and west. It was the only place from the Western Waters in the south to the Great North Ocean at the other end of the range that an army could march through with only minimal consideration for the terrain. Its western end however was right on the Augrahl Imperium's doorstep, and they had their own fortifications in place to defend the opening in their side of the mountains which rivalled even Stonekeep's towering presence.

Unfortunately, whilst being the most aggressive of the nations who opposed Jeranon, Nereth had never considered the Augrahl Imperium to be the most dangerous of the empires which his people referred to as the western or 'dark' nations. That title went strangely enough to the smallest of the races beyond the mountains. Far to the southwest, beyond even the lands of the Imbic lay a forest protected by the black spells and incantations of its inhabitants. The few rangers who had returned from that deep into enemy territory over the centuries had brought strange reports of trees a mile high which moved as the sun departed, the entire forest shifting its borders each night, or moving altogether whilst only the moon stood witness. Most of the reports conflicted to a degree, yet one thing they all agreed on was that the Blood Forest was alive it some way it had absolutely no right to be, and possibly even aware.

Whether it was a true life or the result of the spells which the Oo'vi inhabiting it had placed upon the mighty trees over the course of millennia was anybody's guess. One thing was certain though, when the Oo'vi attacked they were ruthless and thorough. They excelled at fighting on foot and their magicians were even more adept at the darker arts than the magi of Jeranon. Their only real weak point was that they lacked any kind of standard cavalry, but then they hardly needed them with their natural speed and stamina.

"This is the map you took from the vault?" Heramiir inquired, and Nereth wondered how long he had been standing there, lost in thought before the archmage had spoken.

"Yes," Nereth replied after a moment, "It is flawless."

Heramiir began to study the map himself, running his hands over the yellowed parchment, just above its age-worn surface.

"I know this map has lain in the vault for at least fifteen-hundred years," he said at length, "But when I look at it, it seems somehow familiar. It's as if I've seen it before, a long time ago."

Nereth studied Heramiir unobtrusively. The archmage had been acting... not unpredictably, but certainly out of character since they had taken Miralthrall. It was nothing he could put his finger on yet, but there were several minor items he had noticed, and when added up they were beginning to concern him.

Perhaps it was simply the stress of conducting a coup and carving a new empire out of the old, but Nereth suspected it was something more. Too many things had occurred for it to be coincidence.

After another moment of study Heramiir turned his attention away from the map and crossed the sizeable room to stand before the giant windows which looked out over Miralthrall.

"As soon as we are finished here, I will be leaving you for a time," Heramiir said as he stared thoughtfully out at the view.

"Do what you can to solidify our hold on the west, but make sure we are ready to meet the king's forces come spring. Also, don't make any overt moves against Archmage Poller until I return, unless he forces the issue of course. On another matter, I want Hassan in the field by the end of the week. Have him make our presence known in some of the outlying villages. If he does well, use him to attack Stonekeep. I don't think I need to remind you the garrison there is large enough to cause us trouble on our flank if the western nations don't keep them occupied over the course of the next summer. Also, once you have the castle secured, it might be in our best interests to have word reach the king that Hassan is working for us of his own accord. But I'm sure you've already thought of that," Heramiir finished with a frown as his eyes were drawn back across the room to rest squarely on the ancient map still adorning the top of Nereth's table.

"There is something strange about that map. I want you to put it back in the vault once you're finished," Heramiir ordered.

"There is something... compelling, about it."

Nereth knew precisely what the archmage meant. When he'd first unrolled it in the vault which held the college's most valuable relics, he had put the yellowed parchment aside for later filing. As the day had worn on though, even as he uncovered more of the Gift-wrought treasures which the ancient cellar housed, he had found himself more and more frequently looking over his shoulder, glancing at it as if to make sure it was still there.

Finally he had taken the map from its temporary home and unrolled the ancient parchment to find a name scrawled in black ink down in the bottom left corner, a corner which was currently being covered by a large stone paperweight.

"It almost feels the same as when the master calls to me," Heramiir mused quietly as he returned to the table.

Nereth had a hard time keeping a grimace off his face at the comment. He had needed confirmation of an idea he'd had, and Heramiir had just handed him the exact thing he was hoping would not come to pass.

"How much do you know about this creature you call 'the master'?" Nereth tried to ask casually.

Heramiir looked up from the map then, frowning thoughtfully as he did.

"I know enough not to call it 'creature'," he said at last, and Nereth thought he detected the tiniest bit of strain in the archmage's voice.

"Yes, but how much do you really know about its goals, its ambitions?" Nereth tried again. Now that his private suspicions seemed to be confirmed he could afford to be a little bolder. Heramiir had not taken well to his criticising the master when he had first been told, but Heramiir's own comments about the map seemed to indicate the creature was not as benevolent as it appeared. The name on the map had been written by a mage who had lived two thousand years ago, and yet the magic imbued in its parchment still seemed undimmed by the passage of time, as did the blackness of the name. That mage was still remembered today as the most infamous in college history. Nereth knew from the secret annuls which only the few archmagi who were most accomplished in the darker arts were allowed access, the mage in question had died alone, executed in the very cell he was being held in, screaming that he had to return to his master.

"I know it has given us the means to take this city," Heramiir angrily returned.

"And what has it asked in return?" Nereth questioned. The last thing he wanted was to provoke Heramiir, but he had to get the younger archmage thinking about the creature's motivations.

"So far, nothing," Heramiir replied.

"But now that Miralthrall is ours the master has finally summoned me to meet him face to face, as he has always maintained he would."

Nereth was about to try again, but Heramiir continued before he could speak.

"Do not think I am ignoring your warnings old friend. You would not hold office as my general if I did not respect your intellect. But so far, the master has kept every promise it has made. Our knowledge has already benefited from the writings in the red book, uncovering arts we had never even conceived of, and perfecting others like shielding an aura which we had been working on for decades."

Nereth considered Heramiir's intent stare for a moment as the younger man spoke, and reluctantly dropped the subject. He would not convince Heramiir today, he could see that now. Hopefully by the time the archmage returned from his meeting with the master, Nereth would have more evidence to back up his suspicions and could try again.

"Just be careful," he told Heramiir, as if the most powerful archmage in college history were his own little brother.

"Of that you can be sure," Heramiir replied, "No one knows better than I just how powerful the master truly is. I have no intention of upsetting it when we meet."

"When will you return?" Nereth asked to change the subject.

"I don't know," Heramiir replied with a frown. "I'm not sure how far it is, or even why I've been summoned. That's why I wanted to get this last briefing out of the way before I left. No matter what happens, I will return in time for the spring campaign."

Nereth hesitantly nodded, not sure how to take this sudden news. Heramiir's extended absence so soon after they had taken the city could create several difficulties he could immediately identify.

"I trust you'll keep the others in line while I'm gone?" Heramiir asked casually.

"Of course, Archmage," Nereth replied in a tone fit for speaking to his superiors. A tone he was rarely required to use anymore.

"Everything will be ready and in place by the time the snows melt."

"Excellent," Heramiir replied, "Have Deshara send me a report if I'm not back by the end of the week, and each week after if necessary."

Nereth nodded his agreement, but otherwise held his tongue, there was only one subject he felt needed to be discussed, and Heramiir was obviously in no mood to have the master's motivations questioned again right now.

"Oh, one last thing," Heramiir said as he turned his

back to the table, "Has Korvith left for Aramar yet?"

"I imagine so Archmage. He had planned to depart today at first light," Nereth said with a frown.

Of all their scheming and planning, all the risks and gambits he and Heramiir had planned over the last years to bring them to this point, Korvith's mission was the one that troubled him the most.

The Giftless were of little concern to him, there were so many that they bred like rabbits. The magi however, they were a different matter altogether, and apart from their talent, their rarity made them precious. He didn't relish the idea that some of them would have to be killed if the spring campaign was to be a victory. Ordering Korvith to assassinate enough of them to keep a good portion of the others home when the army marched had been almost as difficult for him as if he had ordered his own finger cut off. He'd done it anyway. Otherwise, come spring the king's army would leave Aramar with most of the college behind them no doubt, and then Nereth would have no choice but to destroy them all, if his own forces weren't overwhelmed first. Either way, Jeranon's might would be weakened to a point where the western nations could swarm over the mountains at their leisure.

"And he understands the import of what he is to do?" Heramiir asked with a sigh.

"Yes Archmage. That is why we chose him for this mission."

Heramiir nodded.

"This killing of our own, I do not relish it Nereth. If there was another way I would take it. But if such an avenue exists, I do not see it."

"Nor I," Nereth replied, "But if this is not done, I fear it will be at the expense of all we have worked toward this last decade. When the king marches against us next spring we could find ourselves caught between his full forces and a possible incursion by the western nations. We cannot win a war against both those armies at the same time."

Heramiir nodded solemnly. "As always my general, you speak wisely. Let us hope Korvith also treats this task with the gravity which is its due."

Heramiir studied the map for a last lingering moment before pushing away from the long wooden table.

"As of now Nereth, I leave you in charge of Miralthrall, until such time as I return."

"Of course, Archmage," Nereth said with a bow.

Heramiir flatly watched him for an instant too long and then turned, his Gift-wrought cloak swirling about him like an angry thunderhead as he left.

When at last the archmage's footsteps were safely out of earshot, Nereth breathed a sigh of relief. For an instant, just before Heramiir had left, he'd been sure the archmage had been giving him some kind of warning. It was a thought that would have made him break out in a cold sweat if he'd had skin capable of doing that.

I guess we both need to be careful, he thought as he took away the small statues pinning down the corners of the map. When he lifted the one from the bottom left corner of the parchment, he placed his gauntleted hand on it to stop the old paper re-rolling itself into the shape it had occupied for more than a dozen centuries, and stared. Even after all this time the ink in which the name was scribed was fresh and black against the yellowed, age-worn parchment. The name itself was short, six small letters and two short syllables which had thrown a kingdom into chaos and darkened the name of every mage for a hundred years afterwards.

"Eldrik," Nereth whispered as he traced the ancient calligraphy with his fingers. He had begun to suspect the creature Eldrik had died raving about all those years ago was one and the same with Heramiir's 'master'. With Heramiir's assertion about the map's pull feeling the same as when the master influenced him, it seemed Nereth's assumption was correct. The question was what the map's significance was, and why it had been invested with such powerful magic that traces of it remained nearly two millennia later. He shook his head, there were still too many pieces missing from the puzzle for him to figure out its shape just yet, though it was not something he was willing to leave too long. His instincts told him this would come back to haunt him if he let it slide, so as the day wore on, he began to scrutinise the map more thoroughly with the Gift than he had the previous night. He stopped to break fast when a servant entered with his morning meal of steaming porridge and a platter of fruits. Nereth instructed her to leave his meal on a chair as the entire length of the table was covered with various items which were the current objects of his study. Or at least they had been until he'd found the map.

All day he toiled over the ancient parchment, interrupting himself only just long enough to see to his other duties, which today included learning the spell to mask his aura, which was unsurprisingly complex. Then he would have to show the others in Heramiir's inner circle the process and order Deshara to contact Korvith with the information, which would be of immeasurable help to his task in Aramar.

As twilight inevitably darkened the sky, he decided to try one last thing before turning in for the night.

He needed sleep badly, and his headache had not improved after the exertions of the last twenty-four hours, but a fresh idea had just occurred to him, and Nereth knew he would never sleep until it had been tested to his satisfaction. So he waited tiredly as the sun sank below the horizon and the darkness of night returned to the countryside, bringing with it the strengthening of the spirit realm which would aid his intended spells. When night had fallen fully, he began to delve into the map with a dagger of spirit magic, different from the one he had used the night before and much less complex. He drove the powerful spell deep into the fabric of the print, trying to penetrate the ancient spells the thing was covered in. For a long moment they held, resisting his every effort to probe the secrets he knew the parchment must hold. Then with a jolt the probe slid through, and with a sudden feeling as though he were falling from a great height, Nereth found himself standing in a region of flat grassland punctuated only by a stout nearby hill. With a start he swore, cursing himself for being so careless that the map's enchantment had been able to draw him in so completely.

This is incredible! I've never seen such a convincing illusion.

He looked around quickly but there didn't seem to be any immediate peril. Ready to explore, he drew the earth up in a fifteen foot high mound next to him in case he needed to find this spot again, before proceeding to climb to the top of the nearby hill which was the only feature in the otherwise endless sea of grass.

It wasn't until he reached the top that he realised how wrong this all was. If this was, as he'd assumed, some kind of illusion, then he was still back in his study and seeing a projection around him. The problem with that line of reasoning however was that there were no hills in his study, so what had he just climbed?

He could see the sun was still visible in the sky and wondered how far west of Miralthrall he was supposed to be. When he'd driven the dagger of magic into the fabric he hadn't paid nearly enough attention to the corresponding location on the map. As he looked out over the vast open lands of what had to be the Sammorand Plains, he realised that there were no visible landmarks to help him gauge where this exact spot lay. Yet nowhere else in Jeranon could you find ground this high and look from horizon to horizon seeing nothing but the ten-foot-high grass which defined the region he now found himself in.

He knew he wasn't actually here, he couldn't be, despite feeling the exertion of climbing the short, steep hill. Of all the six races, only an Oo'vi high shaper could transport themselves with magic, and even then, only themselves. That a piece of arcana could be powerful enough to replicate the feat was more than he could credit, even for Eldrik. Another clue was hearing the soft metallic clinking of his plate armour which he'd warded shortly after the accident to always remain silent. As he felt the breeze push gently against his face, he took a deep breath, content for a single moment to simply watch the grass stems swirling in patterns below as the currents of air whispered across their surface. With a start, he thought he heard the sound of an argument coming from somewhere in the distance, and walked a few steps to the east to get a clearer look over the side of a rocky outcrop.

As he rounded a boulder, he saw a roadway had been

cut and cleared long ago, running through the plains and travelling just past the far edge of his vantage point. On it, a caravan of travellers was having some debate about whether they should continue on for another hour or make camp in the hill's shelter, although dusk was only now beginning to descend on the open plain.

Nereth wondered where he was supposed to be, so he continued down the other side of the rocky hill until he came to a place where the whole side of it had fallen away in some earthquake long ago.

Subconsciously employing a simple spell of air, he leapt nimbly off the edge and landed lightly on his feet, twenty spans below. He proceeded to the road without a second thought and walked the short distance to the caravan.

At first the two travellers, who were still having their good-natured but animated discussion on whether to continue took no notice of his approach, but then a small boy with bright red hair came jumping out of the caravan to look around. When his eyes swept past Nereth, who was only a few paces away now, he didn't even blink, continuing to play as though he weren't even there.

Nereth had never bothered to try understanding children, for obvious reasons he could never have any of his own. Even so, the boy's behaviour still struck him as odd. Surely even one as young as this would call the others if he saw a cloaked and armoured stranger approaching them in the middle of all this... nothing. With a shrug Nereth closed the final few feet to where the discussion was continuing unabated and stood in front of the pair for a second while they ignored him. Feeling vaguely irritated he went to tap the thin man on the shoulder and was shocked to the core when his hand proceeded right through the man's body and out the other side. Still the discussion continued obliviously, and it quickly became apparent neither they, nor presumably the boy, knew he was here.

Nereth strolled around the pair, studying them until he heard a loud hissing from behind. He turned to see what was causing the commotion and was confronted by a grey and black tabby cat, its back arched and tail lashing furiously as it tried unsuccessfully to stare him down.

"So... you can see me, can you?" Nereth asked as the young red-headed boy walked over and picked up the cat, trying to soothe it as it kept its eyes locked on where Nereth was standing.

He moved a few steps sideways but the cat's gaze never faltered, following his progress with unblinking eyes as it hissed again.

So, not an illusion, or an echo message...

"What's wrong with the cat?" the thin man called from behind him.

"I don' know da', maybe he saw something?" the boy replied as he took the cat back inside the covered wagon.

Nereth found an amused grin on his face, but at any rate he now had a good idea of what the map had originally been designed for. In a way he was here, though not in the way he had assumed.

He had used scrying devices before, but the momentary glimpses the ones that the magi of Jeranon could painstakingly construct didn't come close to this wonder. This device was a treasure beyond compare. The only problem was that it was linked to the creature Heramiir knew as the 'master', a creature which had almost two thousand years ago directed the most powerful mage in college history to stage a rebellion which had nearly torn the kingdom apart. Even in Eldrik's time its motives had not been revealed, but whatever they were, it was becoming apparent now that it appeared bent on that same goal again.

The pair of travellers had climbed back onto the front seat of the caravan by this time and were busy getting the horses moving. The boy's assertion the cat might have seen something lurking in the long grass seemed to have settled their discussion once and for all.

Nereth watched them go for another moment and then with the same spell he had used to enter the map's magic he tried to create a slight tear and break free. The transition was easier this time, though he still felt a moment of disorientation as he found himself back in his study at the college building in Miralthrall.

Despite his extreme fatigue, and the headache which came crashing back in as he sat in a nearby chair, he smiled in genuine cheerfulness for the first time in what seemed like ages.

He had both learned how to mask his aura and unlocked the ancient map's secret, a magic which hadn't been seen since Eldrik's time. For a general, the pair of revelations were about the greatest two gifts he could have hoped for. He would have to study the map much more thoroughly over the next few days, but for now all he wanted was a good night's sleep. Having been up for thirty-six hours, and using the Gift for a lot of that time, he was ready to drop. As he left his study, he renewed the wards on the door and closed it manually with his gauntleted hand. His headache was now pronounced enough that he didn't even bother with even that simple spell of air as he headed towards his quarters on the upper level of the college building. The day after tomorrow Hassan would leave, and quite a few of Nereth's concerns would go with him. If there was to be an uprising against Heramiir's new order, Nereth would put money on Hassan having a pivotal role in its inception. Still, that was why he had spies even among the veteran guardsman Hassan was sure to pick.

None of the villages he was going to assign Hassan to bring into line had any particular tactical significance, but Nereth had other reasons for choosing those locations. Unless he was very much mistaken, Hassan would soon find himself bound to his new oath and hunted by the king's men as a traitor. Again Nereth smiled, he was sure Hassan was intelligent enough to understand the ploy, not that he would appreciate it. By the time they came up against Stonekeep a few phases from now, Hassan would be firmly in his grasp, and glad for the protection at that.

Nereth laughed softly to himself.

Today has been a superb day, and tomorrow promises to be even better still.

'Uncertainty clouds decision. Certainty clouds the conscience. No battle is without casualties.'
Excerpt from 'The precepts of Battle' by General Shaw, written after the war of Eldrik's rebellion.

CHAPTER 9

SEAL COVE

"Enter," Nereth called from behind the long wooden table which housed the current objects of his study. As the door swung silently open, it revealed to him the form of Colonel Hassan.

The veteran soldier entered the room slowly and took his time looking around before coming to stand directly opposite the desk, arms crossed lazily in anything but a proper military stance.

The black enamelled plate armour Nereth had no choice but to wear remained silent under his silver-lined cloak as he stood deliberately, choosing to ignore the unspoken insult.

With the barest hint of air magic, Nereth dried the ink on the parchment he'd just written.

Apprentices and newly raised magi sometimes spent years perfecting incantations and gestures to create in their minds the intent and focus that forming a working spell required. He was long past that stage though, and a simple picture in his mind's eye and a wisp of the Gift was all he needed for most things these days.

Once the spell was complete, only then did he turn his attention fully to the man he had summoned.

"I have no wish to serve you," Hassan defiantly pre-empted him as he folded his arms more tightly across his chest, "You are a traitor to the rightful king, and eventually you will have to answer for that crime."

Nereth watched the scarred soldier, frowning for a long moment before deciding to reply to the obvious taunt.

"Perhaps," he replied slowly, "But for now at least, I am in command, and we both know you will follow any order I give you. You are too well aware of the consequences to do otherwise."

The corner of Hassan's mouth twitched, and his hands curled briefly into fists, but that was his only response.

"Your orders," Nereth continued as if nothing were amiss, "Are to travel to the outlying villages of Seal Cove, Railain and Nestarn in that order, and convert them to the cause. You may choose two hundred men to accompany you. I will also be sending along one of the newly promoted magi to support your efforts. On arrival at each of these locations you will subdue the local populace by any means necessary. I'm told each of these villages has a population of less than a thousand, so you shouldn't have any trouble."

"By subdue, I suppose you mean kill?" Hassan demanded.

"By subdue, I mean convert if at all possible. But they must be made aware that there is a new order in the west. Surely a commander of your talents can do that without resorting to a slaughter."

"Of course I can. When?"

"Tomorrow at first light. All your equipment and

provisions will be arranged, and the mage I have placed under your command for the duration of the assignment will await your arrival at the south gate. All you need do is gather your men and carry out your orders to my satisfaction."

"And that's all?" Hassan asked with a frown.

Clearly the colonel had managed to convince himself Nereth was going to send him on some horrific rampage of destruction. One he would have to complete or forfeit the lives of his men and their families, not to mention his own.

"No threats? No ultimatums?" the soldier guardedly asked.

Nereth couldn't help but laugh.

"We can go through all that again if you like," he replied, "But I find repetition dull, so let's just skip it since we both know how that conversation will go, and what its result will be. If it makes you feel better, leave here with all my imagined threats and ultimatums in your mind if not your ears. Perhaps they will help justify that you are as willing to carry out the orders of a... what did you call it before? Oh yes, the orders of a traitor, as I am to carry out those passed down by Heramiir. Of course, if doing so makes *me* a traitor..."

Hassan stared hatefully at him for a long moment, clearly furious at the parallel.

"You are dismissed," Nereth cheerfully told him before Hassan could bring himself to speak again.

*   *   *

Hassan pivoted stiffly and strode through the door, which through the Gift had already been opened for him.

Fine, he thought as he walked away from Nereth's study. *If that's what the traitor wants, that is what he'll get.*

It was a great pity for the archmage though that he hadn't been specific about whose cause Hassan was to convert them to.

For the first time since Heramiir had taken the city, Hassan felt a grin stain his normally severe face.

*　　*　　*

It had been nearly a week of hard riding since Hassan and his men left Miralthrall on Nereth's orders. He was on schedule however, and so was not surprised when the scouts reported they were about to come into view of Seal Cove, a tiny town nestled against the rocky beaches of the coast to Miralthrall's south. Hassan called a halt and his two hundred men formed up around him.

They were all exemplary soldiers, men he'd served with before. Even so, he fully expected the archmage's threats had swayed one or two to keep an eye on him.

Of course that didn't even take into account the newly elevated Mage Nereth had sent along.

The boy is little more than a teenager, Hassan thought as he watched Derrack rein his mount in to one side. The young Gift user was uncomfortable on his horse, and Hassan was sure he had never been escorted by soldiers before. He was constantly gawking when Hassan ordered the men to drill with blades or bows after they made camp each night, and it wasn't earning him any friends.

What Hassan was planning to do in the village ahead would have to remain a secret for now. Right at this moment he wasn't even sure if he would get the opportunity to put his plan into motion, or in fact if he should.

He knew what he wanted to do was right, and the only way he could continue to fulfill his oath to the king, but there would be a price to be paid. Worse though, it would likely not be by him directly, but by others who would carry out his instructions. Despite being a seasoned commander, Hassan found himself nervous about the day ahead. More nervous than he had been in a great many years in fact.

Once the men had gathered around, he looked them over before speaking.

"Whatever we encounter in the village ahead, I mean to leave here once our mission is completed with zero civilian casualties. There will be no slip-ups, no accidents, and absolutely no looting. Whatever their current attitude, these men, women, and children are not our enemies. They are neighbours, and our countrymen, and I will sentence any man who does them harm for the appropriate crime. They will not be happy to see us, they will likely resist, they may even provoke us with force. Remember your training and remain calm, you are all better armed and trained than even the most aggressive of those we may meet. You are authorised to defend yourselves if need be, but only to the necessary extent."

Hassan looked around again, privately glad to see more than one face relieved at his orders.

"All right," he nodded in satisfaction. "Let's go."

After the moment's respite, he turned his mount and set off, quickly cresting the nearby ridge and coming into view of the village. A few minutes of steady riding later and they passed the outskirts of town where single-storey stone houses with slanted tile roofs seemed to be the norm. As their column passed through the main street, much of the local populace went into hiding, but they reached the village square without incident and he called for a halt.

When no one came out to meet them, Hassan took a moment to survey the surroundings. The south side of the square sported an open parkland, while the east was taken up by a series of market stalls which had been abandoned by both customers and vendors as soon as his men rode into the square. The North side was lined solidly with good quality two-storey housing broken only by the road they'd entered the square from, and that only left him with one other option.

"Have the men set a perimeter and wait for my return," he ordered Jarl, who was never far from his side.

He dismounted and stepped up onto a solid wooden porch populated by several tables with large umbrellas over them. After crossing the unoccupied space, he entered the double-storey tavern which dominated the entire west side of the square, apart from the border of the parklands which was taken up by the continuation of the King's Road.

The day was clear and hot, and only a set of cords strung with wooden beads to keep the flies out covered the doorway of the tavern. Hassan moved them aside with one hand as he entered the well-lit but rustic construction, listening to the soft clicking noise as the beads fell back into position once he moved inside.

"Can I help you?" a portly barman inquired as he looked Hassan's uniform up and down with a frown, noticing the outstretched hand holding an unblinking eye which was the emblem of Miralthrall's College of the Arts.

Nereth had ordered the quartermasters to remove the waterfall device of the former duke from every soldier's uniform shortly after the coup, and replace them with these.

"I believe so," Hassan returned more jovially than he truly felt as he surveyed the otherwise empty room, "Tell me good sir, who is the mayor of this town?"

"That'd be old Luke," the barman answered with a frown, his hands surreptitiously straying behind the counter.

"And where might I find him?" Hassan asked when no further information was forthcoming.

"Right here," an elderly voice announced, accompanied by the sound of a footfall on the tavern's stairs.

"Welcome to my inn, Colonel."

For an instant Hassan had the overwhelming feeling that he recognised the old man as the mayor made his way awkwardly down the stairs and into the main room, but just as quickly the feeling was gone.

"You are Heramiir's men, yes?" the old man asked as he motioned Hassan over to a table in the centre of the room.

"Sit down," the tavern's owner commanded when he didn't immediately comply, and Hassan couldn't help but admire the air of authority which hung around the mayor like an insubstantial mist.

The man the barkeep referred to as 'Old Luke' waited until he obeyed. His light armour clinked as he took a seat at the table, and the mayor pulled out a chair soon after and sat stiffly on the opposite side.

"I presume you are here to make it clear to us just how long Heramiir's reach is?" the old man asked without preamble.

"Word reached us less than a week after the coup," the mayor continued, "I wondered how long it would take that traitor to send out parties to bring the local townships into line."

Hassan nodded as he noticed the barkeeper unobtrusively, but keenly listening to their conversation, he shot the man a withering glance which old Luke picked up on.

"Leave us," the mayor instructed, turning back to Hassan without waiting to see whether he'd been obeyed.

With only a slight hesitation the portly barman untied his apron and left the tavern without a backwards glance, his departure followed soon after by the sound of a closing door at the far end of the hall.

"Now you can say whatever it is you didn't wish Benny to overhear."

At Hassan's rueful expression the old man gave a soft rasping chuckle.

"I served in my king's army for close on forty years son, nearly half of them spent at Stonekeep Castle. I didn't get to be 'old Luke' by not using my wits, you understand?"

"I'm beginning to," Hassan replied with a slight grin, liking the old man despite what he would have to do if the mayor of Seal Cove rejected the plan he was about to bring to his attention.

"I was sent here on orders by Archmage Nereth to subdue your town and convert it to Heramiir's cause. Failing that, I think you know what I have been ordered to do," Hassan told him bluntly.

"I see," Old Luke said as he stood from the table and walked with a slight limp around the bar to fill two large ceramic mugs from a keg which rested against the wall.

"It's a funny thing," the old man said as he returned to his seat, sliding one of the foaming mugs across to Hassan.

"Once upon a time, long ago, I served in the household guard of Miralthrall's old Duke Kellesan. He was a wily man and taught me much of the skills of the battlefield."

The mayor paused to take a deep draught of his ale, which Hassan joined in gratefully after a week on the road, then continued.

"One year a young guardsman was sent to us from Aramar, from King Erian himself we were told. When he arrived, he was assigned to the duke's household guard. Soon though, his prowess with the blade and knowledge of tactics saw him promoted as an officer at Stonekeep Castle, just in time for it to be assaulted by several legions from the western nations. I was surveying the defences for the duke at the time, so you see it happened that I watched with my own eyes as the Augrahl shamans blasted their way through the outer gate. The secondary wall fell soon after despite the best efforts of our troops. I tell you from where I was standing it looked as though we would have to retreat into the main yard itself. But then a young man in Kellesan's livery cut his way across the field and rallied our men long enough to push the enemy back, all the way through the gates and outside the walls to where our archers and siege machines could do their work with only minimal harassment. Anyway, the day was won, and the young guard went on over the next two decades to gain the respect of just about every soldier placed under his command. Not to mention gaining himself a reputation as one of the king's finest officers and a loyal defender of the realm. After what I saw that day I made it my business to follow that guard's career over the years, and I must say that rarely have I seen a man fight with such courage or loyalty to his king."

Old Luke paused again to take another long swig of his ale before placing the mug back on the table with a clunk.

"Whatever do you think happened to him, Hassan?" the old mayor of Seal Cove asked him suddenly, causing Hassan to sit back in his chair, an astonished expression on his face.

"I never thought you of all people would turn traitor after all this time."

After a long moment of study, Hassan realised with an embarrassed grimace just who this old man was.

"Berengail, Sir Luke Berengail?" he asked at length, not quite believing his luck.

The aged mayor gave a slight grin and a nod, and Hassan's face became thoughtful as he realised the old man in front of him was possibly the best ally he could ever have hoped for.

"At your service," the old mayor responded cautiously. "If you wanted to talk privately for the reasons I think you do. I should warn you though Hassan, it's just old Luke now, I'm far too frail to be running around and waving my sword at people, no matter how justified the cause."

It was more than a shock to learn that the legendary Berengail knew who he was. Every soldier knew of this man's exploits in driving back the dark nations over the course of several campaigns. Those stories and others were a good part of the reason he himself had signed up for service as a young man. Hassan smiled slightly, if the crafty old knight would lend his aid, his plan might actually have a chance at succeeding.

"So, you will remain loyal to the king? You will refuse

to bend knee to Archmage Heramiir's rule, even knowing the consequences?"

Berengail agreed without hesitation and ruefully smiled.

"Son, my body is old now and frail. If I got down on my knees at my age, I doubt very much I would ever have the strength to stand on my own two feet again."

There was a long moment of silence as they sat tensely on either side of the rough wooden table, each of them intently studying the other.

"Good…" Hassan replied eventually, "Good. Then I would say that we two have a lot of work ahead of us if we are to restore Jeranon to its proper order and help King Erian reclaim the west from Heramiir and Nereth's treachery."

Hassan sat anxiously for a moment, but old Luke finally nodded with a grin and raised his mug, which Hassan emulated in deep relief.

"To His Majesty the King," Old Luke uttered, and once Hassan softly but fervently echoed the toast, they both drained their mugs and placed them back on the table.

"I must see to my men soon," Hassan said with a frown.

"I trust them, but there is a newly elevated Mage with us and we cannot afford to make mistakes here. If we do, the consequences will be far worse than a simple matter of our two heads on the block."

Old Luke looked up at the roof in thought for a moment before shrugging.

"Send your men out to gather up the outlying farmers and property owners so you can make a grand announcement, and order the mage to search the area for any candidates with the Gift. That should be convincing enough to give us a few hours to plan things so we can all keep our heads on our shoulders. Or most of us at any rate," the old mayor added with a grimace.

Hassan nodded. Not everyone they would enlist into their underground movement was likely to survive.

"Well, the day is waiting," Hassan replied as he stood from the table and moved towards the door of the inn, "Remain here while I send my men away."

No one could be allowed to see them alone without good reason or suspicions might be stirred further down the track. In the kind of game they were about to embark upon, Hassan suspected even those suspicions would be lethal.

Old Luke got creakily up from his chair and took both mugs back behind the bar where he filled them to brimming again as Hassan left the inn through the swinging beads hanging in the doorway.

He returned to his men and gave Jarl his orders in the most frustrated tone he could feign.

"That stubborn old fool," he ranted so his men would overhear. "He doesn't even believe that there's been a coup! Round up every villager within two miles and bring them here before sundown so I can address them all at once. Derrack, take a squad for escort and scan the region for any latent Gift users."

Soon enough his men broke up into their respective squads and were leaving to fulfill their orders while Derrack chose one apparently at random and began a search of his own.

With that taken care of, a few minutes later he waved the bead curtain aside and re-entered the inn with a vague frown still etched across his forehead.

"Problems?" Old Luke asked as Hassan crossed the floor and took the full mug which he indicated.

"No, I told them you needed some convincing, and I think they bought it once they heard the orders," Hassan replied as they both returned to the table.

"Then what is it that's troubling you?" the old knight asked as they took their seats.

For a moment Hassan's eyebrows rose, and he couldn't help but grin at the old man's calmness at what they were about to attempt.

"All right," Hassan said after a long moment of thought, "Here's what I think we should do."

*   *   *

It had been a long hard week of riding, and this last day of scouting the countryside around Seal Cove, gathering up the locals and sending them on their way to the town square had been an unproductive one as far as Derrack was concerned. They were just leaving the last homestead to head back to town and Derrack hadn't found a single person with Gift ability all day. He wasn't too surprised though. This close to Miralthrall it would have been hard for anyone to avoid contact with the magi on the long-term basis necessary for hiding a talent. Although he didn't like to complain, he thought it was a bit of a waste of time. With the soldiers gathering up everyone in the area he could have just waited until they were brought to the town square and then scanned the crowd. Still, Archmage Nereth had placed him under Hassan's command for the duration of this assignment and he knew well enough to follow the archmage's orders, even if Nereth's other instructions had been a little vague.

He still wasn't sure what to make of Heramiir's new order. As far as he could tell nothing much had changed in his everyday life since the archmage had declared his bid for power. His lessons had continued as always, although some of his classes seemed to be slightly more in depth now than they had been before the coup. On the other hand, he had just been given his first assignment since being promoted to Mage.

Maybe I'm just not high enough in the magi's hierarchy for the full impact of the rebellion to affect me yet, Derrack thought with a grimace. At any rate there wasn't much he could do about it even if he wanted to. He knew he should have left Miralthrall when Heramiir had given them the choice, but something had stopped him from trying, and now it was far too late. By staying, he had inadvertently thrown his lot in with Heramiir and his followers, and he doubted the king would have much patience now even if he did decide to try and make his way back to Aramar.

He had heard whispers around the college that it would be war next spring when the king would no doubt come with an army to reclaim his lost land, and Derrack was worried. He knew if it came to that it would mean fighting other magi, and most of them would probably have far more experience than he did. So each night since leaving Miralthrall he had practised using the Gift without speaking the complicated strings of words which allowed him to actuate the spells. So far, he'd had only very minor success, but it was a start. Besides, he had every intention of working as hard as he could, so that he would be ready to defend himself by the time the king's army marched across Jeranon to confront them.

He followed the column of troops he was accompanying as they walked their mounts slowly back to Seal Cove. Some of the youngest children and the old or crippled were mounted on the soldiers' horses as they led the local people to their destination. It was slow going, but not as slow as if all the peasants had been forced to walk themselves.

The shadows had stretched long by the time they reached their destination, and the other parties had already returned with their charges, filling the square to capacity. The soldiers of the squad he had chosen helped the last group of peasants to dismount before leading the animals away and quickly remounting.

From inside the inn which lay across the square, Derrack could make out the sounds of an angry conversation that went on for some time before Hassan finally came back out and nimbly climbed up onto a wooden crate.

*   *   *

"People of Seal Cove, hear me well!" Hassan shouted so his voice would reach the crowd over the sound of the rustling trees on the south side of the square, "We have come here today for one reason. To see your village become part of the new order."

"Long live the king!" someone in the crowd nervously called.

Who it was Hassan couldn't see, but inwardly he smiled.

"Yes, long live the king," he repeated after a long moment, "But not here. Whether or not you recognise his authority, Archmage Heramiir is now the foremost power in western

Jeranon, and he will tolerate no opposition to his rule."

The crowd began to murmur this time, but there were no specific comments called back, and Hassan was a little relieved. He really didn't want to make any examples of these loyal, hardworking people, but for everyone's good he had to get them to accept Heramiir's rule, for the time being at least.

"We will not bow to Heramiir," the old mayor answered stubbornly as he emerged from the inn.

"If you're not careful old man, this entire village will suffer for your obstinacy," Hassan replied coolly.

"Don't make the mistake of crossing the archmage," Hassan called to the crowd, "My orders are to convert Seal Cove by any means necessary, and at the end if you will not cede control of your town, to destroy it."

That was a lie, but it would get them angry and a little scared, which was what he needed right now.

There was a hushed silence over the crowd at that pronouncement, and Hassan could see several villagers looking around nervously at the ring of soldiers which now lined the square, hemming them in.

"I don't want to do that though," Hassan told them in his most reasonable tone, "My deepest desire is to accomplish my mission and leave here tonight with no further disruption to your existence. In the morning when you wake, the only difference you will notice will be the college flag flying from the town's pole instead of the king's emblem. Is that really such an unreasonable price for peace?" he finished with a shrug.

"You have until the sun goes down fully to decide. When you're ready, send your mayor in to tell me your answer," Hassan instructed the crowd as he jumped down from the crate and went back inside.

He knew the villagers were likely to choose to follow the archmage with his men still lining the square. Now all he could do was wait and see if Sir Luke's reputation was worth its salt as the old mayor played his part in their hastily devised plans. They had both known any kind of open resistance was out of the question for now. Without knowing exactly whom either of them could trust just yet to help implement their plans, old Luke had come up with an idea to divert any suspicions which might have arisen as to why they had been in closed talks for most of the day.

Hassan waited for a long time inside the inn as he took a seat opposite the beaded doorway. He heard angry shouts erupt and then die down again and he knew old Luke was making his well-conceived speech about remaining loyal to the king in the face of the archmage's treachery. A speech which was shouted down by the frightened crowd of unarmed civilians. The conversation went on for long minutes as the sun disappeared behind the horizon in a cascade of burning clouds. The deep blue of night soon took over the sky and the stars began to creep out from their daytime hiding places.

He was just about to go out when a despondent looking mayor entered the inn, giving him a wink once he was safely out of sight of the crowd.

"As mayor of Seal Cove, my people have instructed me to cede control of this village to the archmage's forces and relinquish my authority to you," Old Luke said loudly enough to be heard from outside the building. "But for myself, I will not bow to Heramiir's treasonous commands," he finished proudly. Even though none could see him but Hassan, there was still a dangerous gleam in

309

the old knight's eye which indicated that this part of his speech at least, was truth.

"Are you ready?" Hassan whispered with a frown, and when Sir Luke nodded without hesitation, Hassan took him roughly by the shirt and pushed the old mayor outside.

A hush had fallen over the assembled villagers as they listened to the conversation taking place inside, and when Hassan came out, roughly pushing old Luke before him, there was a fearful murmur from the crowd. Despite the difficult position the mayor's vocal opposition of accepting the archmage's rule placed the whole town in, there was a palpable concern for the old man's safety. Regretfully, Hassan pushed him roughly to his knees, trying not to let it show on his face, and drew his broadsword from the scabbard on his back.

There were several cries from the crowd and Hassan waited a few moments for effect before pivoting on his heel and swinging his blade down hard on a chair beside the door, sending splinters in all directions.

With a wrench, he pulled free from the wreckage an arm's length strip of wood and held it high above his head for the crowd to see.

"Derrack, light this," he ordered the young mage, who was looking more and more apprehensive by the moment.

From the young man's troubled expression, he knew what was about to happen, but with a gesture and a frown he obeyed the order, as Hassan had been sure he would.

"You have chosen well," Hassan shouted to the assembled villagers as he held the now flaming brand aloft.

"All of you except one that is," he said with a

contemptible glance down at the mayor, who had yet to regain his feet.

"You should have accepted the archmage's gracious invitation while you had the chance."

The old mayor just looked at the flaming brand in despair as he shook his head from side to side.

"So be it then old man, reap the reward of your stubbornness."

Hassan turned with a frown and flung the fiery brand up onto the inn's second storey roof where it rolled for a moment before settling into the thatch. Within seconds the flame took, and a vicious black smoke began pouring from the building, casting an even darker stain against the night sky. The villagers looked on in disbelief while old Luke just sat there in front of it, head lowered in dismay and unable to watch.

With a motion to Jarl, his lieutenant walked purposefully across the square to the flagpole and lowered the king's standard. After removing the now outmoded flag, he replaced it with that of Miralthrall's College of the Arts before raising it to attention and stuffing the royal emblem into a bag.

Hassan nodded and smiled as if pleased at the sight, then gave the order to mount. He vaulted up easily onto his black charger after placing his sword back in its scabbard and taking one last look around.

The villagers were still staring at both him and the roof of old Luke's inn, which was now blazing out of control as he ordered his men to form up and ride out. He stayed where he was, motioning Derrack to remain with him as he waited another few moments for the soldiers to form up on the other side of the square.

He stared at the blaze consuming the inn's roof for a few seconds more before shaking his head.

"Oh, put it out," he told Derrack in as condescending a tone as he could muster.

The young man glanced at him in surprise, but then hurriedly made a series of gestures which soon had the flames hissing and sputtering as if untold buckets of water had suddenly been dropped on them. Within moments the flames disappeared altogether and the black smoke pouring off the roof thinned as Derrack finished whatever it was he was doing. The young mage nodded that he was finished, and Hassan called out to the crowd.

"Follow Heramiir, or I'll be back," he said with a meaningful look at the crowd.

He turned his steed sharply away from the square and with Derrack at his side, cantered out of Seal Cove to meet up with the rest of his men.

It was already dark, but the road here was good and the moon was shining brightly tonight. Hassan kept the men moving until they reached the small brook he had seen in an empty field a few miles out from town on the ride in.

He hoped old Luke's inn hadn't been damaged too badly in the blaze. He had been surprised when the old knight had suggested it as a way to avoid suspicion about what they were planning. When Hassan had baulked, Berengail had told him slyly that he had been saving to replace the thatch with tile for some time anyway, and eventually Hassan had given in. Now that it was over, he had to admit it had been a most effective display. He kept repeating the scene in his mind as they rode, eventually satisfied that if he had been watching their little drama from in front of the inn, he wouldn't have suspected the mayor and the colonel who had nearly burnt down his livelihood were conspiring together against Heramiir's new order.

Hassan eventually gave a small sigh of relief. He was sure nobody knew what they were up to, and while Heramiir still had control of his family, and those of his men, that was the most important thing.

"Something wrong?" Jarl asked as he moved his bay stallion alongside Hassan's own.

"Just glad I didn't have to kill anyone today," Hassan answered truthfully.

He wanted to tell Jarl what he was planning, and the Maker only knew how badly he needed allies for his plan to work, but right now he couldn't risk trusting anyone, not even his oldest comrade. Not that he thought the man was untrustworthy, but he just couldn't take the chance. Not yet. The only reason he had been so open with old Luke was that when he himself had been younger, and only new to the king's service, he had always looked up to the knight's deeds and exploits as a kind of role model for his own. The man's reputation was legendary, and right now Hassan knew that would help him recruit people who could be counted on in a crunch, the kind of people who could keep their mouths shut.

After another half hour's ride, they reached the brook he had seen that morning and Hassan called a halt for the night. He ordered the camp be set up and sentries posted, although he allowed the men some respite in the form of not having to drill this evening. There probably wasn't anything more serious around here than the odd wolf or wild pig to threaten them, but Hassan was too long a veteran not to be prepared for the worst. In quick order he oversaw the construction of the camp, the men taking care of their horses, and the lighting of fires for the cook to prepare their dinner and for the men to stay warm by. Once all his obligations were met, he went to sit by his own fire at the centre of the small area. Hassan waited until the cook brought him a bowl full of the thick meat and vegetable soup which formed a staple of their field diet, along with a spoon and a piece of flatbread to soak up the juices. After thanking the man, he waited just barely long enough to not burn himself on the soup, and then fell ravenously on the steaming meal.

He was just cleaning out the thin wooden bowl with his last piece of bread when Derrack came over.

"Do you mind if I join you?" he asked guardedly.

Hassan had never shared the innate wariness most people seemed to have of those who could use the Gift, at least he hadn't until the coup. He nodded curtly while he finished his meal and wondered what was on the young man's mind.

"I wanted to thank you," the young mage said after swallowing several mouthfuls of the incredibly hot soup.

Hassan raised an eyebrow and cocked his head to one side.

"For letting me put that man's roof out before we left," Derrack continued.

"When I was little, I lived in a small town called Clearbrook, it's near the border to the west. One day our village was attacked by a band of Nostahl which had managed to sneak through the mountain patrols, as sometimes happens. We could usually repel them with ease, but this one time they made it all the way into town and set most of the buildings alight before we could drive them off. We thought everyone had gotten out in time, but in the confusion someone must have counted wrong. It wasn't until we heard the screaming that we realised one of the villagers had been left behind, trapped on an upper floor. It should never have happened."

He stopped speaking for a moment, gazing regretfully into the flames of the campfire as Hassan had seen so many of his longest serving soldiers do from time to time, thinking on old battles gone wrong.

He watched the young mage with a thoughtful frown, but didn't interrupt the boy's thoughts as he continued to stare at the flames.

"I don't know if there was anyone in that inn today," he finally continued, "Probably not. But I'm thanking you for making it so I don't have to wonder."

Hassan just looked at the boy for a moment before inclining his head in acknowledgement.

"Look," Hassan said, deciding to be honest with the young mage, at least about this. "Despite Nereth's threats, I have no intention of massacring civilians. Especially not to gain the objectives of a self-confessed traitor like Heramiir. When he asks for your report, you can tell him I said so."

"Archmage Nereth ordered you to do that?" Derrack replied incredulously.

"My orders are to convert or subdue Seal Cove, Railain and Nestarn by any means necessary," he told the young mage as he set his bowl and spoon down on the ground a little too hard.

"I guess the lives of the common folk just aren't as valuable to our new leaders as those of the magi. Sorry if that spoils your illusions kid, but that's just the way it is, now."

"So, what happens if the villagers force the issue?" Derrack asked at length.

Hassan gave a grimace which quickly turned into a scowl, "Heramiir holds several thousand of our men, and more importantly their families, and mine, hostage inside Miralthrall's walls. Their lives depend on my cooperation in Heramiir's schemes," he said as he met the young man's eyes.

They sat and regarded the fire in silence for a moment after the exchange, Derrack's bowl laying forgotten in his hands. After a while, the mage looked up at him with fierce determination.

"Colonel, I should warn you not to order me to kill civilians. I may be a mage, but that doesn't mean I'm a butcher and if you do give that order, I will simply refuse, in front of the men if I have to," the young man said in a rush.

"You will follow any order I give you while you are under my command. Those are your orders from Nereth himself!" Hassan informed him stonily as he locked eyes with the inexperienced mage.

After a long moment he drew back though, picking up his empty bowl and spoon before standing and putting his free hand lightly on the young man's shoulder.

"But rest assured Derrack, I mean to see that order is never given. Now finish your food and get some rest, we have a long ride ahead of us before we reach Railain, and I want to be long gone from here by the time the sun clears the trees."

*   *   *

Derrack nodded as Hassan left to wash his utensils in the shallow brook, then did as he'd been instructed. He finished his own dinner and followed the colonel's example, washing his bowl and spoon before heading to his small triangular tent and tiredly crawling into the sleeping roll.

It had been a long and difficult day on the back of a week of hard riding, and now that he was lying down Derrack found he was unbearably tired. He yawned as his mind wandered off to sleep, but before he did, he couldn't help thinking Hassan must have gotten it wrong. Surely Archmage Nereth wouldn't hold thousands of woman and children from his own city hostage to ensure one man's cooperation.

It was true what he had said to the colonel though. He really would refuse if Hassan ordered him to kill innocents. Derrack hoped it wouldn't come to that though. The look in Hassan's eyes just before he'd left had convinced Derrack that the colonel had been telling him the truth, at least about his own family, and that would make him desperate to succeed.

The colonel must have guessed that he had been ordered to keep watch on him, but despite everything, the man had treated with him fairly since leaving Miralthrall, and Derrack found himself liking the solemn officer. Even though it was painfully clear there was no love lost between the colonel and the archmage, it was hard for Derrack to reconcile the things Hassan was saying with his own experience. That Archmage Nereth, one of his most respected teachers since childhood, not to mention the man who had first discovered the Gift in him could be doing the terrible things Hassan accused him of was hard to swallow. And yet he was forced to admit that some slight part of him did believe it. Nereth was nothing if not efficient. One thing was certain though, where most men would have fobbed off a potential spy, the colonel had gone out of his way to address Derrack's concerns tonight.

As he fell into an exhausted sleep, Derrack wondered if maybe he was seeing the slightest sliver of how Hassan had garnered his legendary reputation for gaining the loyalty of his men.

At first we couldn't understand what these creatures were that the Maker had infested our world with. Mortals, he called them.
Excerpt from the red book.

CHAPTER 10

THE WELL OF TEARS

Come! The voice boomed in Heramiir's mind, even as the now familiar section of wall peeled back to reveal the circular passageway beyond.

There was no need to answer the master's call as he crossed the threshold between the deepest of Miralthrall's basements and the catacombs below. He knew full well the power that resided beneath Miralthrall could sense exactly where he was.

The dank passageway was as overgrown with filth as it had been the first time he'd come down here all those long years ago, and Heramiir found it necessary to watch his footing on the slippery moss which covered every surface.

The section of wall slid closed behind him. The darkness which abruptly encompassed the tunnel would have been absolute, if not for the pale, shining blue ball of light he'd had the foresight to call up with the Gift as he stepped into the maw-like opening.

"Where are you?" Heramiir called into the blackness beyond. He knew from experience that untold miles of mazelike catacombs lay before him. Trying to find the master without the powerful being's aid would be an exercise in futility, one he no longer had patience for.

Heramiir's skin fairly tingled with anticipation, after all these years of plotting, of hiding in the shadows and waiting for just the right moment to strike, his rebellion had finally come to fruition.

The master had always maintained that once Miralthrall was under Heramiir's direct control, it would allow him to meet it in person, and now he had been summoned. He could barely imagine what arcane secrets the master held, and yet he couldn't help but worry at the creature's seemingly endless power, which exceeded even his own powerful talent for the Gift by so very much.

To his annoyance, Nereth's questions kept circling through his mind.

What are its goals, its ambitions?

He trusted Nereth as much as he trusted anyone, but doubts about the master were something he could do without right now. When he returned though, he would have to make time to find out why his general had been so intent on pursuing this matter.

He pushed those thoughts to the side as he reached a fork in the passage, the tunnel to the left led slightly up and the one to the right angled sharply downward. Both disappeared into blackness within a few steps.

Heramiir thought for a moment before continuing. The correct route was almost certainly the one which led deeper into the catacombs. It would be a simple matter to try it, but he had run afoul on previous visits of the traps laid all about this place to stop wanderers from making their way easily through the tunnels, and had no desire to do so again.

He had wondered about those ever since the master had

led him down here that first time to find the red book. He knew the being was powerful enough to repel any trespassers without the need to rely on the childish but deadly ambushes which dotted the hallways and intersections down here. But if the master hadn't set them there to keep people away from him, someone else must have put them here, possibly for the same reason. Heramiir wondered who had dared to set the traps in the first place, and why the master hadn't cleared them away centuries ago.

A disturbing possibility presented itself. If he was correct, it meant at one time, and possibly still today, there had to have been another creature like the master, or at least something else as powerful.

He was still standing in front of the fork in the corridor when the master's voice ordered him onward once more.

"I don't know the way," Heramiir called into the blackness.

There was a moment of disconcerting silence, but eventually a brilliant blue tongue of flame appeared in the left-hand corridor, blinding him with its brightness. For long moments Heramiir blinked as his eyes adjusted to the glare. He let his own light spell fade as his vision finally cleared, then approached the blinding blue light, stepping back again as the intense cold radiating from the mystical flame chilled him to the bone. Without warning or fanfare, the strange apparition drifted away down the corridor at the speed of a slow walk, lighting the blackness as it went.

Follow, the voice called from out of the cold flame, and Heramiir had no real choice but to obey. For hours he followed the flame's steady pace through the catacombs beneath Miralthrall, never stopping, never slowing down, because as soon as he did the strange blue light would quickly leave him behind, its speed never altering as it made its way inexorably towards the master.

*   *   *

Heramiir was parched. He had no idea how long it had been since he'd entered the catacombs, but three lengthily spaced meals had passed as he wandered after the master's guide.

He had conserved his water as best he could for the trip underground. With no idea the journey would be this long or gruelling though, the canteen at his belt had now run dry and there was insufficient moisture in the air down here to refill it with the Gift. Heramiir found himself in desperate need of rest. He watched as the cold flame took yet another turning downward and determined to ask for respite if the cursed thing continued much longer. He plodded on after the magical flame on blistered feet which he couldn't even stop for long enough to perform a basic healing on.

Just as he was about to call out to the master that he had to rest, a sound came out of the depths which lifted his spirits sufficiently to force him onward just a little further.

As he plodded his way into the next chamber, Heramiir came into an immense cavern fed at one end by a waterfall crashing down out of the darkness above, continuing without interruption into an ebony chasm far below.

He had begun to hate the cold flame as he traversed the catacombs, but as he followed it out onto the ledge, its relentless motion ceased. Heramiir took two more steps before his exhausted mind registered what had happened. He stopped abruptly, relieved beyond words as he trudged his way around it, crossing the small distance to the edge of the precipice which butted up against the underground falls. Lowering himself to his hands and knees, he knelt out over the chasm to immerse his head in the fringes of the thundering icy spray.

When he had drunk his fill and refilled his canteen to brimming, he moved across to a dry part of the ledge and sat for a moment. He removed his shoes painfully and performed the simple spell which would see them healed in only a few moments rather than days. As soon as the pain from his countless broken blisters subsided, Heramiir found himself utterly exhausted. Too fatigued to even care if the frozen flame moved again while he slumbered, he moved far enough away from the edge to be safe, put his pack behind his head, and slept.

*   *   *

When he woke sometime later, Heramiir was still tired, though no longer bone-weary as he had been before resting. He glanced around and with some relief saw the flame was still exactly where it had stopped, still shimmering, but otherwise immobile as the rocks around it. It was impossible to tell what hour of the day or night it was, and Heramiir found he had lost all concept of time since entering the tunnel which led from Miralthrall's basements into this labyrinthine cave system. A system in which he realised he was now hopelessly lost.

He searched quickly through his pack and pulled out some trail rations after taking a long drink from his canteen, which he once again filled from the icy falls. By the time he had taken a privy stop and slung his pack back over his shoulder, the cold flame had already begun to move. With a tired sigh Heramiir once again followed it through yet more of the caves and tunnels, all of which had long since blurred into one in his mind.

On and on he followed the flame through the underground caverns until he once again felt weary and sore from travelling, although at least this day, or whatever stretch of time passed for it down here, his feet hadn't blistered.

After what seemed like forever, the cold flame led him to a change in the natural formation of the maze. The walls here were straighter, though in poor condition, and as he headed down this latest corridor Heramiir suddenly realised that he was standing on the ancient remains of a shallow staircase. As he rounded a bend, the tunnel began sporting decaying pillars at common intervals along either side, reaching up to form sinister arches overhead as they met every fifteen feet or so where the stairwell descended another step. There were no rails or guides along the way, and Heramiir was glad for the bright glow of the magical flame as he stepped around fallen debris, and over the cracked carvings of whatever alien race had constructed this wretched sanctuary so far below the surface of the world.

He was forced to stop abruptly as the cold flame died without warning, and for an instant, an uncharacteristic panic seized him. Without the master's aid he knew he would never find his way back to the surface, but even as the thought occurred to him, Heramiir realised he could still just barely see the ground in front of him.

There must be a source of light further up the tunnel.

His heart still hammering, Heramiir decided against calling up a light of his own. The glow from ahead was so dim it would be lost completely if any other illumination came into play.

With that in mind he watched his steps as he descended the decayed stairway. His caution was unnecessary though as there were no more of the constant side tunnels to get lost in as were found in the natural caverns. He followed the ancient stairwell for what seemed like hours as the dim glow gradually increased in brightness, allowing him to move much more quickly than he had when the ice-cold flame had first winked out.

The shallow stairway widened out, and as Heramiir stepped down for what seemed like the thousandth time he was suddenly half blinded by a shining light in the distance which had been covered until now by the gentle curve of the corridor.

The light ahead was red and blue. As he hurried towards it, he saw the horizontal and vertical slashes of brilliance were leaking in through an impressive set of carved wooden doors which had long ago fossilised into stone.

As his eyes finally adjusted to the glow, he studied the frieze on the ancient doors and couldn't help the little thrill of fear which ran down his spine as he wondered, not for the first time, exactly what it was he was dealing with.

Carved on each of the doors were three symbols, and each of them was a rune of impressive power unless he was very much mistaken. The top rune looked like a vaulted arch with an inverse chevron cutting through its centre, although what it symbolised Heramiir had no idea. In the middle of each door, partly obscured by the thick petrified bar which held them closed, a stylised letter C was carved. Encompassing it was a larger backwards C, which in turn was eclipsed by a third C even larger than the second.

Heramiir stared at the rune for a long time before his lips compressed, and he found himself frowning in displeasure. These runes were not to be trifled with. He could feel the Gift emanating from them even now, but he had absolutely no idea what they meant. Under normal circumstances, he loved nothing better than to study some magic he didn't yet command. But these doors blocked his way, and he knew with unshakable certainty that the master was waiting for him just on the other side.

With another frown he moved his gaze down to the last of the runes which looked like nothing so much as a withered tree, naked of its leaves and uprooted from the ground, lying on its side.

The thick bar which blocked the doors also carried the same runes from left to right, and Heramiir was loath to touch it without knowing exactly what they had been designed to do.

Come! the master's voice boomed in his mind, giving Heramiir a start as he continued to survey the runes.

"What of these runes of power?" Heramiir asked it with a grimace, his bright green eyes flashing in the dimness as his inspection gleaned no more useful information.

"Will they try to stop me if I enter?"

The master laughed a mocking laugh and took his time before responding.

I have studied them for millennia, but they are in a language even I do not know. You must open that door Heramiir. All the answers you seek lie in this chamber. Now enter! If they are a danger, I will do what I can to protect you. But be wary, it was not I who placed them there, and the one who did wished me only ill.

Great, Heramiir thought. Someone powerful enough to openly wish the master ill had placed three unidentified runes of extraordinary power on the door sealing his chamber.

Still, he hadn't come this far only to be stopped by his own trepidation. With a thought to the master Heramiir readied himself, clearing his mind and gathering as much focus and clarity as he could before placing a wisp of earth magic on the petrified wood of the bar. He was careful to avoid the set of carved runes.

He waited a long moment in tense anticipation, but nothing happened, and eventually his heart slowed back to a more normal pace. With another calming breath he trailed a tiny wisp of spirit magic into the bar and again waited for a response, one which never came.

Beginning to feel a little more confident, he touched the bar with a burst of air magic. When no response was forthcoming, he used the Gift to quickly lift the thick bar of petrified wood away from the door and place it to one side of the rubble strewn corridor as he studied the ancient doors themselves.

He considered the petrified wood for a long minute before deciding the bar hadn't been hiding any information he hadn't already seen. The middle runes were now fully uncovered, and for good or ill, they were the same as the ones on the bar which had been obscuring them for countless neglected years.

Still unwilling to touch the actual doors physically, Heramiir reached out and gave them a slight push of air to see what would happen. Somewhat anticlimactically, the only response was for the petrified wood to swing back an inch or two, letting in more of the red and blue light.

Deciding it was time to take a chance, he pushed the huge double doors back quickly with a powerful gust of wind. As the ancient entrance parted, the multicoloured light from beyond nearly blinded him.

When his eyes finally adjusted to the brightness of the chamber, Heramiir found himself at a loss. The immensity of the sight before him held him entranced for long minutes as he studied the master's chamber, struggling to understand what he was seeing.

Beyond the rune-inscribed doorway lay a cavern of immense proportions, and even this brightly lit he was unable to make out the roof, nor the far side of the chamber. He stepped quickly through the doorway. There was no response. Normally this would have interested Heramiir greatly, but at the moment his attention lay elsewhere.

In what he presumed was the centre of the massive cavern lay a circle of enormous shining red and blue crystals. Each stood at least a hundred feet high as they reached for a ceiling indistinguishable in the darkness. The glittering spires themselves were leaning slightly inwards towards the very centre of the cavern's roof, the outside of each crystal angling inwards to taper off to what Heramiir was sure would be a razor-sharp point up in the distance. But the score of crystal sentinels were not what had so caught hold of Heramiir's attention. At the absolute centre of the cavern, and the sparkling red and blue circle of teeth, was a brilliant shaft of light which set the crystal structures shining white for most of their inward length. The reflected glow showed up dozens of fissures on each pillar where they appeared to have shrivelled or dehydrated like an over ripe apple. That wasn't something crystal did, which made Heramiir even more curious as he took a few tentative steps towards the outside of the circle. The shaft of light at the heart of… whatever this vast construction was, reached from floor to ceiling where it disappeared into a hole created especially for it.

Or perhaps by it, Heramiir thought uneasily.

As he approached the circle, he realised he had judged its size wrong. From the rune-inscribed doorway he had assumed the closest spire was only about a hundred spans away, but as he finally approached the nearest one, he realised that it must have been more than half a mile. The shaft of light cast a long reflection off the midnight-blue, shining marble floor, and Heramiir realised the cavern's surface must be slightly convex since the reflection seemed to be aimed only at him, even when he tried moving aside.

When he finally came to a halt between the closest of the enormous crystal spires, Heramiir could only stare at the magnitude of the construction. He had thought where the spires changed angles on their outward facing side had only been a few spans off the floor, but now that he was closer he realised with wonder that a three-storey building wouldn't have been so high.

Come! the master's voice called in his mind as a blazing object right at the heart of the brilliant white shaft of light seemed to pulsate slightly for a moment. The shaft itself never changed though, and the rings of more intense illumination running diagonally up and around its surface like motes of dust in the sunlight never altered as Heramiir hesitantly stepped inside the circle of spires.

"Come, kneel before me," the master called, giving Heramiir a start as it used its own bass voice to speak with him for the very first time.

Heramiir promptly obeyed as he tried to keep watch on the blinding object at the centre of the column of light, but was soon forced to look away as his eyes began to sting and water.

"Well done, Heramiir," the master said in deep satisfaction.

"Twenty thousand years I have waited, but you are the first to heed my call and make it this far. Your reward shall be great."

"Thank you, Master," Heramiir replied as he struggled to take in what the creature had just told him.

What kind of being can live for twenty thousand years? he thought in wonder.

"Do all of your kind live so long?" He asked, fishing for any information he could glean about the powerful individual before him.

"Sometimes."

Heramiir's lips thinned in annoyance at the vague answer, but he held his tongue and waited for the master to speak since there was little to be achieved at this point by gaining the creature's ire.

There was a lengthy pause in which Heramiir had nothing to do but wait, still kneeling on the midnight-blue marble floor which he suddenly realised was being warmed by something underneath even this deep level of the subterranean caverns.

After several minutes of silence, Heramiir grew impatient with the master's delay, and eventually he stood. If the master had that little interest in him then Heramiir had no intention of kneeling before the creature like a lowly servant.

"Why have you called me here now?" he asked when there was still no response.

"I wish to teach you," the master informed him in his own deep voice, "And when you are strong enough, you will free me from this place so I can hunt down the one who imprisoned me here all those long centuries ago."

With those words, everything fell into place. It explained why the creature had first led him down here during his initiate and each time since. It explained why such a powerful being had remained down in these caverns for all this time. It even made sense why the master had cleared the traps out of his way when he'd led him to the red book. The master was a prisoner, and needed his help. There were only two things which still troubled Heramiir about all this. First of all, who had placed the strange runes upon the entryway? If it had been the master's captor Heramiir didn't think he would have survived walking through the ancient portal. If not the master's jailor though then who, and what were the pointless runes designed to do in the first place since they were so clearly still active?

The other matter on his mind could be cleared up easily enough he supposed, so he once again addressed the shaft of light where the master was trapped.

"Why did I have to take Miralthrall before you would meet with me?" he asked with a thoughtful frown.

When the master answered, its voice sounded as though it were giving a shrug inside the shining prison. The words were enough to chill Heramiir though, and make him wonder if he had done the right thing in coming down here by himself after all.

"It is mine," the master told him, "I wanted it back."

So… that's what you are…

"You're one of the builders," Heramiir breathed in awe.

"Not a builder!" the master's voice boomed, both audibly and inside his mind, "The builder. This whole world is mine, was mine to shape as I saw fit. Miralthrall is my home! At least until I was betrayed and imprisoned here by the only other I had ever truly trusted!"

The abrupt fury in the master's voice alarmed Heramiir, and he did his best to move away from this obviously dangerous subject.

"What is it you wish to teach me?" he deflected.

"I will find her, yes I will. The prophecy must be fulfilled after all. You will release me soon, and then I will find her, wherever she is. Oh yes, wherever she is. She was never as powerful as I, never. Never! I was betrayed, yes I was, but I will not be tricked this time, oh no, no no," the master ranted even as the blood drained from Heramiir's features.

How he had never seen it before he didn't know, but as he tried to back away from the shaft of light, the master began laughing senselessly, and in that one horrified moment Heramiir realised the absolute truth. The creature before him was utterly, completely, mad.

"You aren't going anywhere Heramiir," the creature called before a crippling pain began shooting through his head.

Heramiir dropped to the warm floor, insensate. As he lost consciousness, he thought he could hear singing echoing around the cavern as a childish melody chased him into darkness.

"Not long now, not long now, gonna get out yeah not long now," the creature merrily chanted over and over again, long after there was no one to listen but itself.

AUTUMN

'The imagination of a child is a wondrous thing, the ability to see the world not as it is, but how they wish it to be. This visual imagination is a critical component to the training of any new mage, and why they must be taken at such a young age.'
Excerpt from 'The Gift'.

CHAPTER II

A PARTING OF WAYS

It was another muggy morning at the tail end of a sweltering summer that refused to loosen its grip.

Technically, summer's dusk had ended a few days back, supposedly turning the cycle of seasons towards dawn of autumn's lush hues and setting the trees alight in red and gold. Instead, the foliage all around was brown, and seemed dry as tinder to Jayden's tired eyes.

For many interminable days the column had marched down this road as it made its way west, until finally, on this particular morning, those at the head of the long line of conscripts rounded a bend in the well-travelled highway. As the forested hilltop before them crested and gave way, it revealed a pair of granite monoliths straddling the stonework path on the downward slope.

Some of these men had been marching for phases, all the way from Grandell up to the north tip of the Anchorhead Promontory and back. The huge marker stones beside the king's road filled them all with a great sense of relief despite the early heat of the day. The news spread through the column, which was now over ten thousand strong, and the small army began to pick up speed as they rallied themselves for the final stretch of the march. They had walked or ridden over three hundred leagues to reach this point, past dozens of the roadside monoliths which marked the major roads of Jeranon at precise intervals of five leagues apiece. Despite, or perhaps because of their aching feet and dust-covered clothes, the sight of these particular marker stones, engraved as being the last before the road reached Aramar, was enough to start some of the men singing.

It was an old travelling song, one which turned quickly into a raucous ballad as a good part of the column joined in.

Jayden didn't feel much like singing as he rode in his customary place with Wyll near the front of the column.

As his eyes searched out this newest horizon with what little interest he could muster, he felt an abrupt chill as he recalled the strange dream he'd had aboard Crest after using the Gift that first time.

Although Strider never broke pace, Jayden could only stare up at the stone pillars in sudden trepidation as his heart raced, and remember the panorama from that dream.

He was riding a horse at the head of a vast column of singing men, the sun beating down upon them as they crested a hill flanked by two enormous stones set on each side of the road.

He had never been on this hilltop before, Jayden was certain of that since he'd only ever been to Aramar by ship. But as he examined the marker stones and the surrounding lands, there was no denying they seemed to match up perfectly with those in his dream. What that signified he had no idea, but the day appeared outwardly peaceful, and there was no sign of imminent danger.

He had assumed the strange dream to be a figment of the sickness which had taken him after using the gift for the first time. Now he didn't know what to think as he stared all around at men going on about their business as though nothing out of the ordinary were happening, and to them he suddenly realised, there wasn't.

Perhaps I should tell Tolmarak about it?

A strange dream brought on by exhaustion was one thing, a strange dream after using the Gift for the first time which came true, at least in part, might well be something far more significant. Yet he didn't entirely trust the old archmage. Tolmarak hadn't yet lied to him that Jayden could tell, but the man who was leader of the College of the Arts, not to mention the king's personal advisor, had priorities which went far beyond his young apprentice's best interests. Besides, the latter parts of that dream contained a variety of images he would rather not revisit, something he was sure the archmage would insist upon if Tolmarak became aware of the circumstances surrounding the vision.

Since it still seemed that nothing was in fact about to disturb the peace of the day though, he couldn't help but wonder why he would dream of this moment at all, or if how that might be possible. Perhaps it was some strange echo of memory.

Strider snorted, breaking Jayden from his train of thought as a particularly large fly landed on the horse's nose. For one endless second, Jayden's heart hammered in his chest as he sensed something dire about to occur.

Strider shook the pest off and continued walking along the road, far enough now that Jayden's perspective had changed. The surrounding land no longer matched the dreamscape which had floated so clearly to his mind a moment before, and Jayden stewed in puzzlement as to exactly what had just occurred. The column proceeded on its way, the men he travelled with neither aware nor affected by his odd mental revelation.

The oppressive heat of the last week had lifted somewhat this morning with the arrival of a cool breeze from the south which blew in from time to time. It was a relief, if only a small one, as the damp air continued to bond clothing to flesh and make the long march an arduous task for those on foot. On the other hand, the dust from the roadsides wasn't nearly as bad as it could have been, and putting these final marker stones behind them was enough to lift even Jayden's spirits, despite whatever else they may have signified in his dream.

As the column continued down the hill, Jayden looked out over the vast valley stretched out before him. In the distance to the southwest, a vast woodland of vibrant green extended as far as the eye could see. Copses of gold or sometimes red trees punctuated the forest as they reached out above the surrounding canopy of the Emerald Sea. The Camar River was also visible from this height as the huge waterway ran its course through the forest, and once it emerged, flowed hard against Aramar's southern edge, its silvery blue water reflected by the baking sun overhead.

In all his trips to the capital on board Crest, Jayden had never gotten as far as that forest. His father had made a few runs to some of the Arborii towns near the river a few years ago, but Jayden wasn't yet part of the crew at that time. He had always wanted to meet an Arborii, more to see if the stories were true than anything else, but since most Arborii tended to stay near their forests, he'd not yet had that chance.

Ever since childhood he'd always had an interest in exotic places and times long past. He had always been most fascinated by the stories of the cataclysm which had destroyed Jeranah in its entirety. The Desolate Fleet had been forced to sail away from their homeland and into the unknown without maps or sufficient supplies. It should have been a death sentence, but somehow they had found their way to this continent. With the help of the oppressed Arborii and Teraliv nations, they had forged an alliance and driven back what were now known as the 'dark' or western nations during the wars of founding.

Those interests were a product of more innocent days, and in his own past now. Whatever future he still had awaited him down in the valley, within the marbled stone walls of the college.

Strider snorted, disrupting the train of thought before it could firmly take hold, and Jayden patted the beige stallion's neck as they continued down the plantation girdled road. The few moments of shade from a nearby orchard were a blessing from the Maker himself as the rest of the column crested the hilltop, continuing down the final stretch of road in the archmage's wake.

Aramar itself was visible in the distance now, its slate grey walls rising high above the three and four-storey buildings built outside the main city over the course of three thousand years.

As his mood slipped again, he watched in silent lethargy until he could finally make out the forms of thousands of men digging trenches around the borders of the enormous city. He sat a little straighter in the saddle as he observed them going about their tasks, and for the very first time the reality of what was happening intruded upon his mind, slicing cleanly through the isolation he'd wrapped around himself since the night of Rhianna's murder.

I am going to war.

Not today, but soon. Tolmarak had been telling him exactly that since shortly after his attempt to take vengeance on Dael, but it had never seemed real until this moment.

Next to Miralthrall itself, the capital had already been the second most fortified city in all of Jeranon. For the king to order a new outer wall constructed, Jayden realised with a start that he must have serious concerns about the upcoming campaign.

Whatever the magi could teach him, it would be best to learn it as expeditiously as he could.

The song of the men behind him reached a crescendo and lost all coherency as the conscripts cheered loudly, upsetting some of the horses. Strider just snorted again and kept walking down the gentle decline behind Tolmarak's grey warhorse.

"So that's Aramar," Wyll breathed in astonishment as he took in the sight of the city for the first time.

Jayden nodded as he considered the former guardsman who had ridden with him over the past couple of phases. He wasn't sure whether to call him a friend, but Wyll had helped him back in Dael's keep, and in return Jayden had convinced the archmage to stop Dael from killing him. Since then, on the long trip around the Anchorhead Promontory and down through the main mass of the continent, Wyll had been an agreeable enough companion. He had even respected Jayden's request during their first day on the road not to question him again about the events on the cliff top that night back in Grandell.

Abruptly it hit him, once they had finished riding all the way down the long decline into the valley, they would enter the capital and everything he knew would change once again. He respected Archmage Tolmarak, but the old man wasn't a friend. Almost everyone Jayden had ever known was back in Grandell, and he couldn't return there until he was ready to deal with Dael once and for all. Wyll was about to be sent off to a barracks the Maker knew where to train for the coming conflict, and Jayden harboured little doubt that with this many men being drafted to the king's army, it was unlikely the two of them would meet again any time soon. With the war most likely coming next spring, this might even be the last time they spoke.

With that in mind Jayden edged Strider closer to Wyll's horse, Socks, and sighed, "I'm sorry I got you into all of this."

Wyll turned to regard his serious expression for a moment before nodding in acknowledgment of Jayden's sentiment.

"I admit, I was annoyed with you at first for not finishing Dael off. If you had, I could have stayed back in Grandell with my family and friends. Now that we've been on the road for so long though, I think it's finally hit me just how small and provincial Grandell truly is. I'd be lying if I said I was in any hurry to go back, even were it possible," he finished with a grimace.

They rode in silence for a time as the column moved ever nearer to the crews of men digging out the trench for the new wall's foundations.

"Do you ever feel like your life is totally out of your own control?" Jayden asked as he stared out at the untold scores of men labouring at the king's project.

"Not really," Wyll responded with a thoughtful frown.

"Except?" Jayden prompted when Wyll remained uncomfortably silent.

The young guardsman gave him a sideways glance and a smirk.

"You're going to laugh," Wyll told him ruefully as he reined Socks in closer.

"I doubt it," Jayden replied.

*　　*　　*

Wyll studied his travelling companion for a long moment before deciding to answer. Jayden had been quiet and disconnected for most of the first phase of their journey. It hadn't been until they'd left the Anchorhead Promontory behind for good that the apprentice mage had begun to show a little more openness in his conversation. Still, Wyll could hardly blame him for taking a while to get his head back together after what he had been through at Count Dael's hands.

Although Wyll knew he himself would never have harmed Rhianna, he still couldn't help but feel as though he was in some part responsible for the count's misdeeds.

After all, he had been in Dael's service while those events had taken place.

Shaking off the guilty thoughts, he turned to Jayden and took a leap of faith.

"All right," he said finally, voice pitched so only the two of them could hear.

"Ever since I was little, I've been having this dream. Sometimes I get it for days or weeks in a row, and other times entire phases can go by without it occurring at all."

He checked to see if Jayden was going to roll his eyes or dismiss what he was saying as rubbish, but his companion only nodded to himself in a vaguely unsettling matter, so Wyll continued.

"In my dream I see a stone building, overgrown with vines and cracked deeply with age. It's some kind of temple I think, but not like anything any human ever constructed. I walk out into a… magnificent clearing, and the doors open. They're huge and carved with a rune that looks like an uprooted tree lying on its side without any leaves, and don't ask me how I know it's a rune, I just know it is."

He could see he had Jayden's full attention now, and that made it a little easier to go on. He rarely told people about his dreams, but in the last few phases he had found he could speak to the young mage on just about any topic without Jayden criticising or making light of what he had to say. At least that was the case on days he could find a subject which would garner more response than a yes or no answer. Naturally, he steered clear of bringing up Rhianna's name, or the events which were still so obviously close to the surface of the young mage's mind. Apart from that one constraint though, he had quite enjoyed their time on the road, travelling at the head of the column with Jayden, Captain Ravenburg and Archmage Tolmarak for company.

"And then what?" Jayden asked, more curiosity showing on his face than Wyll could remember seeing since they'd left home last spring with the king's recruiting party.

"There's a pause, once the doors have fully opened," he continued.

"In my dream at least, it seems as though the entire forest is holding its breath, waiting for something, and then from the shadows a woman steps out of the building."

Jayden sighed in exasperation and shook his head.

"I should have known," the young mage muttered, but Wyll wasn't finished.

"No, it's not that kind of dream," he said with a laugh.

"This woman, whoever she is, is as tall as I am, and slender. In my dream she always wears a midnight black dress that comes down to her ankles and matches her hair, which is hanging loose and almost as long. She talks to me, and although I can never quite make out what she's saying, somehow it still makes sense. I've never understood what the dream means… Maybe it doesn't mean anything," he admitted at length.

"But you think it does."

Wyll slowly nodded his agreement and waited, but Jayden didn't seem inclined to say any more about it.

Normally Wyll would have let it go at that, but the apprentice mage had rarely shown so much interest in anything, and Wyll was disinclined to let the vague spark of character the topic seemed to have kindled go out that easily.

"Why the sudden interest Jayden, what do you dream about?" he asked, instantly regretting it as his companion's face turned a sickly pale colour.

"I'm sorry, I shouldn't have..." he apologised, but the damage had already been done as Jayden began to stare off into the distance once more.

He had been like this on and off since they had met, and Wyll was well used to his companion's bleak moods by now, although he still did what he could to alleviate them. Sometimes Jayden would just stop responding though, as if the rest of the world had ceased to exist around him. It was no longer surprising when it happened, though it was still a little disconcerting.

Sometimes Jayden could be this way for minutes, or on a few occasions, hours, but this time he seemed to pull himself back to awareness with a visible effort and surprised Wyll by answering his question.

"When I can sleep, I dream of caverns filled with shining light, and walking through the midst of battle searching for a mage whom I know I must kill, and a voice that whispers things to me I can almost understand. But in the dream I know that when I finally do, when it all makes sense, my life will be at an end. That's what I dream of, when I'm asleep."

Wyll had no idea what to say to that, but then a thought occurred to him, one he had to ask, although fervently hoping he wasn't pushing too far.

"And when you're awake?" he asked softly.

Jayden's only response was to slowly twist his body in the saddle and stare far past the horizon towards the northeast, in the direction Wyll knew Grandell had to lie.

He nodded to himself in understanding.

"When the time comes, I'll go with you," he offered.

"No," Jayden cut him off, "When the time comes, I'll go alone. But… Thank you for the offer," he finally added as he turned back to stare at the approaching city, Jeranon's capital, Aramar.

They travelled in silence for the next few minutes as they watched the city, and the workman digging out the foundations for the new wall grow closer. Sometime later, a messenger came riding up from the capital to speak with Archmage Tolmarak, who conversed privately with him for a few seconds before ordering Captain Ravenburg to bring the column to a halt.

Eventually the archmage turned his grey warhorse and motioned for Jayden and Wyll to join him, which they both did as the order to stop was passed down the long line of men.

"I'm afraid this is where we must leave you Wyll," the old archmage informed him once they arrived.

"From here I leave your training under Captain Ravenburg's expert direction, but I'm afraid this will most likely be the last time Jayden or I see you for quite some time."

Wyll nodded in acceptance. He'd expected this was why the archmage had called them to join him so close to their destination.

"Perhaps our paths will cross again someday, Archmage," he answered respectfully.

"If the Maker wills it," Tolmarak answered, although Wyll got the distinct sense the archmage thought that an unlikely outcome.

"Well," Wyll said as he turned to face Jayden, "I doubt you'll change your mind, but if you ever have need of my sword or my service for another task, seek me out."

Apart from the fact that he now realised he considered Jayden to be a friend, he had no real intention of spending the rest of his career in the regular guard. He could no longer return home to his family's land and take over as he'd been intending after a few years of service, but there were other options. For one, it was well known that serving in the mageguard was a fast track to promotion as well as being a lot more exciting than regular soldiering duties, even if it was considerably more dangerous.

"I will, Wyll," Jayden said with just a hint of a genuine smile, which was about as close as he had come since Wyll had met him back in Grandell.

The sight was enough to make Wyll grin, and he held out his arm in the traditional gesture of a parting expected to be for some time amongst friends. Wyll was pleased when Jayden didn't hesitate to return the gesture by grasping his arm firmly above the wrist, which Wyll returned.

From the corner of his eye Wyll saw Tolmarak raise a snowy eyebrow in surprise, but watched with what Wyll was sure was a little more interest than he'd previously been displaying.

"Until later then, Archmage," Wyll said to Jayden, who for once gave a rueful grin.

"Until later, General," Jayden returned with something closer to a full smile this time.

Wyll nodded as they released each other's forearms and heard the archmage tell Captain Ravenburg to see he was properly trained, and to take the column to whichever training camp the messenger from the city showed them to.

With that done Tolmarak gathered up the small group of Gift users he had gathered on their journey, and once again turned to Jayden.

"It's time to go. Your training awaits," the archmage informed them as he turned his steed, Wind, towards Aramar's giant gates and cantered down the home stretch without another look back.

For a second, Jayden and Wyll looked at each other before Strider began frisking. Jayden calmed the horse before speaking again.

"Take care of yourself Wyll. Don't go trying to be a hero, all right?"

Wyll's face became sombre as he nodded.

"That goes for you too," he returned, "Now get going or Tolmarak'll be gone before you catch up.

Jayden looked down the road as the archmage's group moved further away, and nodded.

"Till next time," Jayden said, then nudged Strider into a gallop with very little effort as he raced down the road to catch up with the others, who had already reached the first row of buildings.

Captain Ravenburg finished conversing with the messenger a moment later and then came back over to Wyll.

"May as well keep riding with me until we get to the camp," he directed, before turning and bellowing for the column to move out one last time.

As the men and horses began to walk once more on tired feet, Wyll looked down the street at where Jayden was just riding out of sight between a large alehouse and a blacksmith. He couldn't help but wonder if he would ever see his friend again, or whether the coming war would separate them permanently. He hoped not, but it was out of his hands now as the messenger left the king's road and headed off towards the fabled Emerald Sea, which covered much of the lands southwest of Aramar.

Oh well, whatever will happen, will happen, he thought, already speculating on what mysteries must be hidden beneath that dense foliage, and wondering just what exactly the next few phases would hold in store.

*   *   *

Jayden caught up with Tolmarak's small group on one of Aramar's outlying streets. He reined Strider in, matching the archmage's pace as he settled into his now customary position beside the old man with his short, snowy hair and silver-lined cloak.

Jayden had rarely seen the city from this angle. Usually when he came to Aramar on board Crest, he spent most of his time in the city proper, or at the great markets which stood outside the walls.

But as they travelled the clean, wide streets, Jayden found he couldn't shake off the melancholy which had descended on him as soon as he had passed the first rows of three-storey stonework houses. The last time he had been in the capital he had been searching for somewhere to settle once he and Rhianna escaped cleanly away from Dael and his trackers.

If I hadn't gone to Aramar on my father's advice, Rhianna might still be alive.

His ability in the Gift wouldn't have been discovered by the archmage either he admitted, but truth be told, that seemed a trivial thing in comparison.

A gasp from behind him pulled his attention back to the present, and he was startled to see that after rounding the last corner, the palace was now just ahead. He must have been even more deeply submerged in his thoughts than usual for him not to notice their passage through the giant gates and bailey which protected the inner city.

There were several other exclamations of wonder as the children who made up the group caught sight of the palace fortress for the first time. He was abruptly reminded that apart from himself, the oldest of the apprentice magi Tolmarak had found on the journey was just fourteen years old.

Even that was unusual according to the archmage, and Jayden had the uncomfortable feeling he was going to spend his next few years training with a bunch of children gathered from around the country. At nearly twenty-one summers himself, that idea didn't appeal. Not that he had anything against them, but he was fairly sure he wouldn't have much in common with them either. Still, he would put up with whatever he needed to in order to learn the mage's arts. Completing that task so he could return to Grandell and take his vengeance on Dael was all that mattered.

He knew he should be more concerned with training for the coming war, but right now he couldn't make himself look past finishing what he had started that night in Dael's keep.

Eventually they turned down a wide street near the palace and were greeted with yet another sight which had most of the children exclaiming in delight. At the end of the road, past its own wall and gates, was what looked like a giant seashell spiralling up to a point more than a hundred spans above. Around the structure stood a cryptic circle of marble columns which supported nothing but air, each one carved with the likenesses of dragons in flight beneath the flaming Sigel of Aramar's College of the Arts.

"Welcome to your new home," Tolmarak said to the group as he turned to smile genuinely at the children, most of whom looked excited at the thought of living in the giant structure.

A few minutes passed as they rode across the stone-paved college grounds, through the circle of columns and past a goat tethered to a post in the middle of the yard. Eventually they arrived at the double front doors of the college building itself, which were again carved with the dragon in flight and flame sigil, before dismounting at Tolmarak's request.

Once everyone was back on the ground, they all stepped up onto a sprawling stonework porch covered by a flat roof supported by six of the carved stonework pillars the builders had obviously favoured. The large wooden doors to the building stood wide open as they approached, and the doorframe itself seemed to glow a pale jade with some inexplicable light

Tolmarak walked right up to the edge of the doorway before whispering something to it, then turning back to them.

"When you walk through this door, do not be afraid," he said, "The voice you hear will not harm you in any way."

There were a few worried frowns from the children, but no one said anything, so Tolmarak continued.

"Allow me to demonstrate," he added, before turning to step through the door.

There was a tinkling sound like wind chimes, and a wispy voice which seemed to come from nowhere, and yet also all around them, spoke.

"Welcome back Archmage, you were hoping for two, but the one you have with you makes five."

At that, Tolmarak stopped and a broad smile broke out on his deeply lined face as he turned back to the group.

"Thank you, Tammy," he said to the doorway, "I've brought some fresh students for you to read."

"Step through one at a time please," Tolmarak instructed as he turned back to the children, "And listen to what Tammy says to you. Over the years I have found her talent, and her advice, to be without flaw."

The door pulsed brighter at Tolmarak's words, and the old archmage smiled again in response as he motioned for the first of the children to enter.

Jayden didn't know the little girl's name, but the strange doorway called it out as the child passed the threshold, listening to the oracle's words before walking further into the chamber beyond.

Next was a boy of no more than ten summers which the door identified as Hank, before telling him to listen to his dreams as much as his ears.

Jayden decided to wait until last as the second oldest in the group, a short red-headed girl named Jodie, was told she should begin learning the language of the dragons. When she asked why, the doorway's response was that telling her now would ruin the surprise. Jayden couldn't help but let a tiny grin escape as the girl walked away, obviously put out by the so-called oracle's lack of candour.

After that came Elouise and Sam, whom Tolmarak had discovered at Henmar's Point. The Archmage had been astounded when he'd discovered the siblings were both quite strong in the Gift. Apparently that almost never happened.

Elouise was told to hold back her curiosity until she could master the Gift, while Sam was encouraged to integrate his ability in the Gift with his talent for making things with his hands.

Finally, after all the remaining apprentices had gone through, it was Jayden's turn, and as he stepped up to the portal the voice spoke, stopping him before he could enter.

"Stand before me, Jayden of Grandell," Tammy's chiming voice commanded in an entirely different tone.

Jayden saw Tolmarak's eyes widen in surprise, and found himself more than a little concerned that this was something out of the ordinary, even for the canny old archmage.

"For many long centuries I have awaited this day Jayden, so hear me well. The very world itself stands at a precipice the likes of which has not been seen since the time of the builders' demise, and you will be the wedge on which the scales turn. Heed the prophecy when you find it, listen well to your dreams, even though they are only a fragment of the whole, and find the meaning of the symbols. Together these three will see you through the dark time ahead. They will see us all through."

Jayden could only stare in silent bewilderment as the oracle finished speaking, his expression mirrored on Tolmarak's weathered face.

"Step through," the old archmage told him abruptly, and Jayden obeyed, hastily walking through the doorway whilst keeping a firm eye on it as though some enormous spider were crouching on its surface, waiting to drop on his head.

Again, Tolmarak looked surprised as the oracle gave no response to his passing, except to briefly flare brighter than normal before settling back to its dormant state.

There was an intense moment of silence as the group of children, and especially Archmage Tolmarak, studied him as though seeing some strange animal for the very first time. But since Jayden had no idea what to do or say he just shrugged, which seemed to break the silence wide open as the apprentices all began talking at once.

"That's enough, children," Tolmarak said in his calmest tone.

A pair of servants came to meet them, exiting from a door built into the side of the winding marble staircase which ran up the perimeter of the sizeable room, leading to the upper levels of the college.

"Please show these new apprentices to rooms and have their things brought up," the archmage instructed as the servants approached. He held Jayden back as the others were led up the winding staircase and out of sight, most with only a backwards glance for Jayden as they left.

"Come with me," Tolmarak told him as he walked the few steps back to the strange doorframe and then passed through it again. There was no response, and after a moment Tolmarak turned to stare at the oracle in concern.

"Come through," he said at length, and then watched closely as Jayden walked under the frame. Again there was no reaction, so this time Tolmarak tried calling its name.

They waited there in the pre-dusk for several minutes, listening for a reply while Tolmarak grew more agitated by the second.

"Tammy, if you can hear me at all, give me some kind of sign," the archmage implored, but he might as well have been speaking to a normal door of wood and metal for all the response he got.

Eventually Tolmarak approached the oracle and ran his hands down the surface of the polished frame, but still there was no response.

"Come on," the archmage finally said to Jayden with a frown, "I'd better take you up to your room."

"What's wrong with 'Tammy?'" Jayden asked, feeling a little guilty as they approached the base of the wide spiral stairway which led to the rest of the college. He hoped he hadn't broken it, whatever 'it' was, even though he didn't think he'd done anything different than the other apprentices. Tolmarak seemed genuinely fond of the strange presence, and besides, Jayden wanted to find out how it knew about his dreams.

"I'm not sure," Tolmarak grudgingly replied.

"In all my years here, Tammy has never failed to make a reading or answer me when I've called. That she should make such a dire prediction and then fall silent... I fear it can only bode ill for us."

The two of them passed several landings as they climbed the staircase, Tolmarak showing no signs of his age as he set a pace which had Jayden breathing a little harder than normal. When they finally came to the fifth floor, Tolmarak left the stairs and headed down a brightly lit, austere corridor before taking another hall to the right and stopping outside a door. He pushed it open to reveal a small but clean room with a desk, cupboard and dresser with drawers, and a bed made of polished redwood. On the far side of the room was a window with green linen curtains which overlooked the palace district of Aramar. Further south, the Emerald Sea was visible past the city in all its verdant splendour.

"This will be your room for the time being, but don't worry, your quarters will improve once you attain the rank of Mage and Archmage respectively. If you have the discipline to apply yourself that is," Tolmarak added seriously.

"No matter how powerful you are, you will not be allowed to continue here if you use the Gift irresponsibly or to flout the laws of our kingdom. Understood?"

"Yes Archmage," Jayden replied. He thought Tolmarak might already suspect what he was planning to do once he had learned enough about the Gift, but the last thing he wanted was to confirm it for the old man before he could even begin.

Tolmarak gave him a flat gaze which said all too clearly he knew Jayden was only saying what he wanted to hear, but in the end chose to let it pass.

"I know it's only early, but try to get some sleep. Your lessons will begin tomorrow and you will need all your strength and awareness. I'll have someone send up your luggage in a few minutes as well as a hot meal," he continued distractedly.

"If you have questions about the college building, I'm afraid they must wait until the maid arrives. There is something I must see to now, but get some sleep and wait here until I summon you for your lesson," Tolmarak said, growing visibly more distressed as he spoke.

"Is something wrong?" Jayden asked carefully, not wishing to anger the old archmage.

"Yes, but it doesn't concern you right now so have something to eat and then sleep. I'll see you tomorrow," he said before turning and leaving the room without another word. The door swung closed behind the archmage and Jayden found himself alone in the small room that was apparently to be his new home.

He supposed he was officially an apprentice mage now, though he'd been learning the basics of Gift theory for the duration of their march to Aramar.

He should be excited, but he wasn't. He had every reason to believe that things would get better now, that the world would open up to him as it never could have for a common merchants' son. Yet as he sat in this small undecorated room that was supposed to be a home, Jayden didn't think he'd ever felt so alone.

Admittedly due to his own fear that the archmage would refuse to teach him, he couldn't even confide to Tolmarak that despite his genuine interest in learning about the Gift, he still didn't feel any different than he had that first day as they'd left Grandell behind. Which was to say tired, sad, and very, very angry.

He pulled the curtains the rest of the way back and stared out at the bustling city below. Now that he was finally alone, he no longer needed to pretend. He let his shoulders slump as the all too familiar sadness washed over him again. His gaze ran over the anonymous buildings of the capital for lack of anything better to do while he waited unenthusiastically for the food the archmage had promised. Maybe then he could eat something, then try to sleep, and have another wretched day without Rhianna, and without vengeance, over and done with at last.

*   *   *

"Welcome to camp five boys, hope you be likin' your new home," the lieutenant on guard duty called in a thick Sunset Isles accent as Wyll and Captain Ravenburg crossed the gate line of a sturdily constructed wooden palisade a few hours later. The palisade all but filled an enormous natural clearing within the Emerald Sea itself, each of its seven sides lined with what appeared to be rows upon rows of barracks and other necessary structures. Across the central yard there was even what looked to be a massive stable next to a well-equipped armoury, complete with its own smithy.

"You received our advance riders?" Ravenburg asked the lieutenant who had greeted them so casually a moment before.

"Aye Sir, got your dorm assignments right here I do, and who be teaching 'em," he responded, handing the mageguard captain a clipboard thick with sheets of paper scrolled with line upon line of small but precise writing.

"The first number be the buildin'. One, two, three, four or five," the lieutenant said, pointing to each of the barracks in turn, "The following numbers be the room assigned to each squad."

Ravenburg nodded his acknowledgement, scanning the sheets before taking the pencil off the top of the board and scribbling out a name, replacing it with Wyll's, before adding the other man's to a squad at the end of the list.

"Do you have enough men to get everyone settled?" Ravenburg asked the gate guard evenly.

"Aye Sir, there be no problem on this end. Just leave 'em with us and we'll be takin' care of the rest."

"Very good Lieutenant, carry on."

Wyll listened with interest to the conversation between the soldiers, and when Ravenburg returned he went to speak, but was cut off brusquely by the stocky officer.

"I know what the archmage said, but I don't have time to train you myself, so I'm leaving you in Karthael's squad. He's as good a fighter as I've ever seen and he knows how to teach his skills to others. Believe me when I say he will do a better job preparing you for the coming war than I could at the moment."

"You're going back to the city then?" Wyll asked, unexpectedly nervous now that he was clearly on his own.

"Yes. I am the head of the mageguard after all. I wouldn't worry about it though kid, you've already been noticed by the leader of the College of the Arts and made friends with one of the most promising young recruits in the last hundred years."

"You think we'll meet again?"

Ravenburg's opinion seemed to be just the opposite of the archmage's, and Wyll was glad to hear it after all these weeks on the road getting to know Jayden and Tolmarak and the shrewd captain beside him. Soldiers from camp five were already streaming through the gate and replacing the Aramarian troops in preparation for their departure.

"I'd count on it," Ravenburg said with a small grin. He turned his smoke grey warhorse with a satisfied nod and shouted the order for his men to form up and ride out, which they did with precision once they were free of the large crowd of conscripts.

While Wyll had been talking to the captain, the gate lieutenant had been pinning the assignment sheets up to a large board just inside the gates, and was now returning to the front of the milling column.

"Listen up!" he shouted above the talk of the idle conscripts.

"I'll be lettin' you inside in groups, so be bein' patient. Make your way to the boards and be findin' your name and room assignment before movin' on. The number beside your name is bein' your barracks and then your room number. Those of you who be havin' horses should be takin' them to the stables on the far side of the compound before reportin' to your rooms. Anyone who can't be readin' should be reportin' to Private Mendleson over by the lists for assistance. Finally, this will be takin' some time, so be patient. I'll be havin' water passed down the line, but dinner won't be bein' served until you're all inside. So, let's be getting' this done," he called as loudly as he could.

"Okay, first twenty," he said to the pair of guards set to counting off men.

Having been at the head of the column with Captain Ravenburg, Wyll found himself in the first group allowed inside the camp. He headed over to the boards to find his name, which wasn't hard since the captain had scribbled it in his own writing and the hurried mark on the neatly written page was easy to locate. He saw his number was four twenty-two and his instructor named Karthael, just as Ravenburg had said. With that in mind he headed across the massive yard towards the stables, and when he arrived a few minutes later he dismounted, giving Socks an affectionate pat on the nose. Untying his saddle and bags he lifted them off Socks' back, prompting the white stallion to snort in appreciation and nudge him with its huge equine head. The horse lifted one brown foot and then another as he stretched, walking a few paces in a circle before returning.

"Can I take your horse Sir?" a little stable boy asked hesitantly from behind him, and Wyll turned to regard the child who was surely no more than nine or ten summers at the most.

"Will you be able to handle him safely?" Wyll asked with a frown. Socks might have a good temperament, but should the stallion decide to be wilful then Wyll was certain there was no way this boy could control him.

"Maybe I should go with you," Wyll suggested, and knew he'd said the right thing by the relieved look on the boy's face.

"Thank you, Sir," the stable boy said earnestly, "Where are you billeted?"

"I'm in four twenty-two," Wyll replied, and then told Socks to follow, which the horse obediently did as the boy led them into the warren-like stables which were already full to brimming with horses of all sizes and descriptions.

"Does he always listen so well?" the boy asked as he led them down a long row of full stalls.

"Only when he feels like it," Wyll replied, receiving a playful nudge from the horse in return, "But sometimes I swear he understands more than any animal should."

There was a haughty snort from behind and the boy looked at Socks in amazement.

"You see what I mean. Anyway, don't call me Sir, I'm Wyll. What's your name?"

"Andrew," the boy replied shyly.

"Well Andrew, don't take this the wrong way, but why were you assigned to take horses when you're not big enough to control them if something goes wrong?"

"Everyone else is busy already," the boy answered stoically.

"Usually I just feed 'em and keep the stalls clean, but with everyone arriving today," he shrugged.

"You like horses?" Wyll asked as they arrived at a free stall with the numbers 4-22 branded into the back.

The little boy nodded enthusiastically in response.

"Yeah, my dad, he's the head groom here, even said he would get me my very own one for my next birthday. Isn't that great!"

"Sure is," Wyll responded with a grin, "Socks here was born to one of my father's mares when I was only a little older than you, and I've had him ever since. If you take good care of him I might let you ride him sometime."

There was a disapproving snort from Socks and Wyll couldn't help but grin.

"Maybe he'll let you ride him sometime," he corrected, and was surprised when the white stallion lowered his head for Andrew to pat. Usually Socks didn't let anyone touch him except Wyll, which his father had always maintained was because Wyll had been there at the birth. Yet Wyll didn't think that was it. His father had been there as well, and Socks had never let him within ten feet without a struggle. It had been something of a mystery back home as to the horse's parentage, as his colouring was completely different to the beige's and black's which made up Wyll's father's herd. Wyll himself had always suspected it had been a wild stallion, not one of his father's stock that had broken into the enclosure where Socks' mother was kept. Whatever the truth, there had always been something strange about the horse that he couldn't quite put his finger on.

"Andrew, where are you boy? Come on, there's work to be done!" they heard called good naturedly from somewhere down the stalls.

"I'd better go," the boy said as he gave Socks another pat and then left the stall at a run.

Wyll sighed wearily and put his gear down. He took the large brush out of his saddlebags and started rubbing Socks down as the large horse began chewing on hay which appeared to have been prepared and left sometime earlier in the day.

When he was finally finished, he gave Socks another affectionate pat, picked up his gear and admonished the white stallion to behave, earning him a nip on the arm in response once his back was turned. He gave the horse an unamused glance and left the stall, closing the wooden barrier as he went.

He followed the long stable rows back the way he had come and made his way outside into the fresh air. Dusk was taking hold of the dawn of autumn sky. With a quick look around, he located barracks number four and spent several minutes crossing the compound to reach it. He walked along the rows of rooms until finally arriving at a door with the number twenty-two painted roughly in white across the top lintel.

With a quick twist of the doorknob he opened the unpolished wooden door, swinging it back to reveal a plain room with just enough space for the five two-storey bunks which were the only proper furniture the room held. As he stepped inside, Wyll noticed that under each set of bunks a pair of hastily constructed wooden chests waited. They were little more than crates by the look of it, but still sufficient to hold the few belongings the conscripts had been allowed to bring with them from the Promontory.

As the door swung closed, Wyll was startled by the scraping sound of a knife being drawn across a whetstone behind him. He turned to the right, looking back to see where the sound was coming from. A short man with fiery red hair was propped up on one of the top bunks where he couldn't be easily seen from behind the inward arc of the door.

"Hi, I'm Wyll," he finally said when the little man just continued sharpening the knife with a comical grin on his face.

"Bosric," the short man answered as if that were all the explanation required. He held up the knife to inspect its edge before making it disappear up his right sleeve with a flourish.

"Well, I guess we're in the same squad then," Wyll observed as he placed his saddle and bags on the bottom bunk on the opposite side of the doorway. Without further discussion he dragged one of the wooden chests out from underneath the bed and unpacked the contents of his bags. In a remarkably short time he was done. He closed the chest and slid it back under the bunk as the door swung open to reveal a pair of large men, both with short cropped brown hair and so similar in appearance they almost had to be brothers.

The one in the lead stopped for an instant and blinked as though surprised to find the room already occupied, but then hurried to the far wall and claimed the top bunk while his brother took the adjoining one on the left.

"I'm Sarran. This is my younger brother Charran," the big man who had claimed the bed against the far wall said without preamble before turning back to where he was stowing his gear. The second of the heavyset men turned around to look at both Wyll and Bosric before nodding and turning to follow his brother's example, prompting Wyll to wonder whether the pair always acted as much alike as they looked.

He glanced up at Bosric who just looked at him with that same ridiculous grin before the short man turned and pulled a bizarre face at the backs of the two newcomers, drawing an involuntary laugh from Wyll.

Sarran, the older brother, looked back with a frown, but Bosric had once again taken up his comical grin and was busy pulling another long knife from his belt which he slowly ran across the whetstone.

The two brothers were still unpacking their things when the door once again opened and a hulking ebony skinned man walked through the door. In one giant hand he carried his saddle, and in the other his bags, which looked as though they were about to burst, although the dark-skinned giant didn't seem to be having any trouble with their weight. The other thing that caught Wyll's eye was the double-bladed axe, mounted on a five-foot shaft of ironwood and banded about with steel, which was strapped to his back in a readily accessible sling. He glanced around the room, included everyone in a single nod of greeting and proceeded calmly across the room to put his things in the chest next to Sarren's, claiming the lower bunk against the wall farthest from the door.

When he was finally finished, he turned around to face the others who were milling about the room, keeping to themselves for the most part while they waited for something to happen.

Soon enough the sun was fully set and the line of conscripts still stuck at the gate were growing impatient as they waited to eat and then rest in a warm, if not entirely comfortable bed for the first time since leaving the Promontory.

Eventually though, the rest of their squad members arrived as a long and awkward hour passed. What brief talk there was in the room centred around the coming war and when dinner would be served in equally serious tones.

Wyll began to study the others in earnest as the last of the men arrived. Apart from those who had already settled in, there was a tall man with short brown hair who introduced himself as Brendan. He was a guardsman from Silvertown, a fair-sized city in the mainland's south, and he seemed as unsure about the reason for his sudden change of billet, having apparently been in the camp for some weeks, as the others from the Promontory were about having him there. Along his face and arms ran a myriad of tattooed symbols which Wyll couldn't help but study as Brendan went about the business of unloading his gear.

After that was a black-haired man of average height who gave the room a furtive glance before moving inside to claim a place on the bunk below Bosric, where he couldn't easily be seen when the door swung open.

There was a pause of about twenty minutes then, and if it weren't for the three empty beds still occupying the room the men might have thought no one else was coming. But finally, the last of the unknown squad members arrived one after another, causing the compact room to bustle with activity for a few moments as they stowed their gear.

The first was a thickset man who carried himself as though he knew what his weapons were about. Weapons that included a light, but functional hand axe with an intricately carved haft which the left-handed man stowed beneath his pillow. When he was done, without even a single word to the others, he lay down on his thin mattress and fell into a deep sleep.

The next through the door was a short man, though not as short as Bosric. He carried his bag of belongings and saddle, but didn't appear to have any weapons on him as he packed away his gear on the bunk below Brendan's. When he was done, he introduced himself as Kienan and soon had most of the men laughing with a ridiculous story which Wyll was almost certain he'd made up on the spot.

Finally the door swung open one last time to reveal the final member of the squad. He was an unremarkable man at first glance, except for his hair, which was shaved clean apart from a raven black topknot which fell past his shoulders. He took a moment to look around before entering the room, sizing up the inhabitants. Without a word he moved fluidly to the bunk below Charran's, which was the only one left. With a minimum of wasted movement he packed away his few belongings, which were comprised completely of weapons or riding gear, and then unstrapped a longsword from the harness across his back before sliding it under the bed.

The sense of anticipation became even more acute as the last of the conscripts made their way through the outer gate, and a few minutes later the dinner bell was rung. All of the men except the left-handed conscript, who was still fast asleep, exited the room in haste to search out the evening meal. There still wasn't much talk amongst them, but Wyll suspected that would change over the next days and weeks. After all they would be spending enough time together.

Perhaps I shouldn't try to make friends with these men, he thought abruptly, before firmly pushing the notion aside. After all, they were training to go to war and there was a good chance at least some of them wouldn't come back. Even so, if he himself were to die Wyll realised, he wouldn't want his last days filled with the company of strangers. With that realisation he decided to try and get to know them all, and this evening's meal seemed as good a place as any to start.

Pride in one's accomplishments is understandable. Pride in one's abilities is acceptable. Pride in one's self is arrogance.
Avsanian Proverb.

CHAPTER 12

KARTHAEL

When the sun crested the surrounding forest canopy the next morning, Wyll had already been awake in his bunk for some time.

He considered himself to be an even-tempered man, but as he'd groggily opened his eyes an hour before, he'd been surprised the rasping noise coming from one of the men across the room hadn't long since woken the others.

That's it!

Just as Wyll was dragging himself out of bed to wake the snorer, the barracks door was shoved aside to admit the harsh morning sunlight and the silhouette of a very thin man. A very tall, thin man Wyll realised as the newcomer ducked his head under the doorway and entered the room.

"Get up!" the intruder bellowed.

The other men all woke at the commotion and began swinging groggily out of their bunks, one by one standing at attention on the cold wooden floor. All except Seth, who had leapt from his bed the instant the door began to open.

The tall man, Wyll finally made out as his eyes adjusted to the glare from outside, was not in fact a man at all, at least, not a human one.

All his life he'd heard travellers' tales of the Arborii who lived in the Emerald Sea. He had never really expected to meet one though until the guide sent from Aramar had led them under the forest's shelter yesterday afternoon. Still, it seemed wisest not to make any stupid comments at the moment, so Wyll waited as the others dragged themselves from their bunks and into a state of semi-wakefulness.

Seth was first.

There was nothing particularly imposing about the man. He wasn't a giant like Marad and he lacked Sarran's scarring or Brendan's tribal tattoos, yet there was something unsettling about him. Without so much as a sideways glance, Wyll's top-knotted roommate seemed to be aware of everything nearby, even to the spider making its silent way down the bedpost behind him.

Despite his snoring, Marad wasn't the last out of bed. That honour went to the dark-haired Kienan, along with the newcomer's ire.

"Get yourselves dressed!" the Arborii ordered, his long slender tail swishing in displeasure as he waited, statuesque, until every member of the squad donned the uniforms which they had received last night after dinner.

"My name is Karthael," he said in a more normal tone, his short grey and white fur being ruffled by a breeze from outside.

"As you can see, I am Arborii, born in the Emerald Sea and raised as a hunter from the day I could walk. For the better part of the last forty years I have served in a ranger battalion which helps keep the nations of the west beyond the Dark Iron Mountains. I also hold the rank of colonel in the king's army, and make no mistake, this is not an honorary title. I have been placed in complete control of your training and you will refer to me as 'Instructor' at all times. That is the sole reason I am here. I will instruct, while you will allow yourselves to be taught. This is in your best interests for two outstanding reasons. First, because you are here to be trained for war, and as soon as the snows melt that is exactly where you are going. Second, any man who doesn't pull his weight will be assigned to a penal battalion that will be first to assault Miralthrall's walls when the time eventually comes."

At that statement there was more than one furrowed brow and concerned glance between the men from the Anchorhead Promontory, though no one spoke aloud.

The men's expressions were not lost on the instructor though and he gave voice to a pained sigh.

"You," he said, pointing at Kienan. "Has no one told you why you are here?"

"Only that there is war in the west, Instructor. As to the specifics, we have only rumours," the black-haired man answered. "Have the dark nations invaded as far as Miralthrall?"

A predatory grin worked its way onto Karthael's face.

"If only it were so cut and dried," he said, almost to himself.

"No, so far as we know the western nations are not involved at this point. The Archmage Heramiir of Miralthrall has staged a rebellion."

He waited a moment for the murmurs to die down and then continued.

"At this stage Heramiir controls Miralthrall and most of the surrounding countryside. With the aid of the magi there, by next spring we expect him to be in command of most of western Jeranon."

There was a long moment of shocked silence which Karthael allowed them, but eventually the Arborii continued.

"That is why I must ask each of you for your best efforts over the coming phases on not one, but two fronts. Your training will be your first concern, and given the restrictive timeframe, that regimen will be demanding enough for any of you. In addition, however, the king has ordered an outer wall built for Aramar. Each unit of soldiers and trainees is to spend two days a week on its construction."

There were looks shared around the room, but this time no one said anything as the seriousness of their situation rapidly settled in.

Karthael stepped further into the cramped room and gave them each a cursory examination.

"At least the march here seems to have kept you all fit," he remarked with approval.

"All right, first things first. I'm told you all have good horses so I assume you can all ride with some amount of proficiency?"

There were nods all around and a "Yes Instructor," from Kienan, so he continued without delay.

"Next question, and I don't care if you learned from a master swordsman or if it was hunting game on your farm. Do any of you have any weapons training?"

There was no surprise for Wyll when Seth raised his hand in a half wave of acknowledgment, nor when the heavily tattooed Brendan nodded. In fact, of them all, only Kienan and Tauman professed to never having received any form of formal weapons training.

"We'll start with you," Karthael said, motioning towards Seth. "Tell me your name and what training you have."

"My name is Seth." the top-knotted man replied matter-of-factly, "I prefer to fight with twin Drakheras or a single Longsword, and I can hit a moving target with a longbow at a hundred and fifty paces."

Karthael's brow climbed during Seth's brief speech, which was the longest Wyll had heard him make since they'd arrived the night before. It was difficult to tell what had caused the instructor's reaction however, whether at the mention of the Drakheras, whatever they were, or the strange accent Wyll had been trying without success to place since Seth's arrival.

For an instant he glimpsed something fleeting in Seth's manner as Karthael scrutinised him, something akin to the tang of salt in the air just before the ocean is sighted. As quickly as it came though, the moment passed, leaving Wyll wondering if he had imagined the entire thing.

As he scrutinised the dangerous man, Karthael moved until he stood toe to toe with Seth, looking down, but after a final moment of consideration the instructor turned away and said, "So you're him. Very well, continue around the room," he added as he nodded towards Marad.

The big, dark-skinned man looked a little startled at being chosen, but then said his name.

"I can fight with a spear some," he continued. "But I prefer an axe or a mace."

He shrugged, "Heavy weapons suit me better than knives or swords."

Karthael nodded to himself, making mental notes as he sized them all up.

Next in line was one of the two large, brown-haired men who Wyll now knew were in fact brothers.

"I'm Sarran. I don't know any blades but since I was ten years old I've been practising the quarterstaff with my brother," he told Karthael as he pointed to Charran, who was next in line. "I tried learning to use a sword once," he added with a far off look on his face.

"I wasn't very good at it," he amended, absently running his fingers along one of the many scars which decorated his arms.

"I'm Charran, Sarran's brother," the next man said without a pause, "I've been practising the quarterstaff as well."

The two men looked almost identical, and Wyll couldn't help but wonder whether they really were as dense as they sounded. Perhaps, as with some of the more isolated farming families on the Promontory, they'd simply never enjoyed the benefit of travelling more than five miles from the place of their birth before being conscripted to give them any culturing. Despite having lived miles from Grandell himself, Wyll's parents were well travelled in their youth and encouraged him to do the same. He hadn't realised how rare that perspective was until speaking with several of the men whose families were more rurally based during the long march.

Karthael grimaced at the brothers' remarks, and Marad rolled his eyes while Wyll tried not to smile. A fine bunch of soldiers they would make, so far only two of them could use the same weapon.

"What about you?" Karthael asked the tallest of the conscripts.

"Brendan Sir," the man replied, "I've been in the guard

for eight years, stationed at Silvertown before I volunteered to join the conscripted men."

"Why did you volunteer?" Karthael interrupted the brown-haired soldier who was only a few inches shorter than himself, and quite a bit bulkier.

"Back home my youngest brother was accepted into the duke's guard," Brendan told the Arborii in a crisp voice which suggested he was well used to reporting to his superiors.

"Less than a phase later the recruiters came to Silvertown and my brother was chosen as part of the detachment. I was able to convince the commander of my garrison to let me take his place. I figured my experience would give me a better chance of surviving once we got to the front, Sir."

Karthael gave a slight nod of approval.

"And your training?" he asked in a neutral tone.

"I was in the heavy cavalry detachment in Silvertown, Sir. I am proficient with the lance, sword and bow, both on foot and mounted."

"Good, if all that's true you can help me drill the others."

Next in line were Kienan and then Tauman, both of whom Karthael skipped since they had already declared they had no real martial training. After them Karthael came to the shortest man in the group, barely five-foot-tall with bright blue eyes and hair the colour of fire. He had a wild look about him despite nothing being immediately out of place.

"I'm Bosric. You can keep your swords and bows. I won't be needing them," he announced in an imperious tone which visibly annoyed the instructor.

"Well I'm sure the master weapon-smith will be pleased to hear that before he wastes his time," the Arborii replied as he took a step towards the much shorter man, who barely reached his grey-furred shoulders.

"Tell me, O great master Bosric, how are you going to defeat the king's enemies without a sword or a bow?"

"With a knife of course," the little man replied a bit too cheerfully.

"A knife," Karthael repeated, considering. Although Wyll thought he was only humouring Bosric as he crossed the remaining distance between them, "And are you any good with your knife?" the instructor asked with another grimace.

There was just an instant while Wyll blinked, and when his eyes reopened the little man had the point of a thin, gleaming dagger pressed hard enough against Karthael's throat that its point was lost in the instructor's fur.

"I'm the best knife-man in Jeranon," he whispered cheerfully into Karthael's furious face.

With an abruptness that shocked everyone in the room Karthael flung himself into a back flip and kicked Bosric's wrist with perfect aim, sending the knife thudding up into the ceiling where it remained embedded, quivering with the impact.

The instructor landed on his feet after completing the lightning quick somersault and grabbed Bosric by the tunic, lifting him off the hardwood floor. A quick twist sent the shorter man flying headfirst through the open doorway, but just before he hit the dirt, Bosric changed his fall to a roll and came nimbly to his feet. With a speed no human could have matched Karthael followed, lifting the much shorter man off the ground again before growling, "The next time you draw steel on me will be the last!"

Bosric just hung there in Karthael's grasp, not limp, but not struggling either.

"Of course it will," the much shorter man answered glibly, "Next time I won't stop at the skin."

With an inhuman strength Karthael flung Bosric back through the doorway and into the dorm room where the much shorter man caught a bedpost and used his momentum to change course and land on one of the bunks.

Karthael came striding back into the barracks a moment later with a face like a thundercloud.

"Even a well-placed knife thrust takes a moment to kill," he growled as Bosric scrambled back to his feet.

"In that time I could easily return the favour."

The short man nodded, climbing down off the bunk as the other conscripts watched the exchange with avid interest.

"I'd still be past your guard," was all the short man said as he grinned back at the instructor, apparently none the worse for being thrown across the room, twice. Strangely enough though, Karthael acknowledged the nod with a not entirely disrespectful one of his own before turning towards the two remaining conscripts in the group.

"I'm Wyll from Grandell," he introduced himself before the still riled up instructor had to ask.

"I've been in the guard at Grandell for half a year and had basic lessons with a sword, both on foot and horseback. I can fire a short bow accurately when mounted, but I only have experience hunting game."

For a moment Karthael watched him. The instructor appeared to be waiting for something, but since Wyll had nothing more of relevance to add, it seemed prudent to let the Arborii make the next move.

"It's a start," Karthael told him at length, "And you?" he asked the final member of the group.

The thickset man standing beside Wyll reached into his pocket and pulled out a thin slab of something white and smooth like marble. Along with it came a stick made from a substance which resembled compressed charcoal with a handle running most of its length.

Karthael's brow furrowed as he began to write, but after a few seconds of effort a line of text appeared on the slab and Karthael cursed as he read it.

'My name is Cale. I have no tongue', was scribed in flawless script across the slab. A few seconds more and a fresh line had replaced the old text.

'I've been in the guard for three years and am skilled with a lance and an axe. In my hometown I won all three tournaments I entered.'

"Interesting," Karthael replied as he quickly changed what he'd been about to say, "I thought the tournaments were only for the nobility?"

The slab was once again cleansed, and this time Wyll saw that the left-handed Cale did it by holding his thumb against the top left corner for a second. The writing simply melted away, and he realised the slab must be some form of arcana constructed with the Gift. It must have been worth a fortune.

'I am the fourth son of the Squire of Green Hill County,' he wrote in his precise hand, 'but I think you are much more interested in my tournament record than my lineage.'

Once more Karthael sighed.

"Can all of you read?" he asked the group, and this time there were nods all around.

"Well, that's something at least," he muttered, "What a bunch of misfits."

He looked around the room one more time while shaking his head in a very human-like gesture.

"I must have offended one of the generals again."

Glancing around the room Wyll wondered if the Arborii officer wasn't right. Apart from Seth, Marad and Brendan, none of the men in the group looked particularly imposing, and Wyll couldn't see any immediate reason they had all been assigned to the same squad. He found himself abruptly hoping he wasn't going to war with a unit of leftovers which couldn't be placed or fitted easily into other companies.

"Bring your saddles, leave your weapons. Let's go see your horses," Karthael said without further delay as he ducked back under the doorway.

After grabbing the things the instructor had mentioned, Wyll found himself blinking rapidly as he walked out into the early morning sunlight. The shadows were still long on the ground, but already it was getting warm and the clear blue sky promised a hot day to come. As Wyll's eyes adjusted, he got his first chance to have a really good look at his new home. Around the edges of the vast natural clearing, a wooden palisade had been imported from without the Emerald Sea to stand guard between the camp and the surrounding forest which towered above the training site on all sides. From what he had seen last night on the way in here there were six sets of buildings which were complete. One was the stables, and another the armoury and mess, but the barracks themselves were arranged on each wall of the camp as ten rows of buildings, each fifty rooms wide, with a fifth set undergoing final construction. When the final structures were finished, it would complete the symmetry of the seven-sided courtyard. Some quick mental calculations told Wyll that when this camp alone was finished, it would be capable of housing twenty-five thousand men. With a low whistle Wyll remembered the gate guard's greeting the previous night, *'Welcome to camp five boys, hope you be likin' your new home.'*

The very idea the king planned to recruit over a hundred thousand men into the army was one Wyll had a hard time getting his head around. Grandell itself had been home to little more than ten thousand if you included the surrounding homesteads, and Wyll wondered what that many people all gathered together would even look like.

What have I gotten myself into? he thought as they followed Karthael across the courtyard towards the stables.

The immense building they were headed for was easily the largest structure in the compound. It looked at least as long as any of the rows of barracks and was three times as deep. Of course, the horses would need more room than the men he realised. They passed a squad of recruits who had already mounted up and were beginning a drill under the expert eye of what looked to be a veteran cavalryman. As they continued walking, Wyll watched the horsemen divide into two groups and begin charging at one another from a short distance. As they met, they smashed their curved wooden practice sabres high and low against each other as they galloped past and headed to the end of the line where the other group was waiting.

Cale held out his writing slab for Wyll's inspection.

'A novice drill,' was written derisively on the pad. Wyll couldn't help but raise his eyebrows as another pair of horsemen clashed halfway between the two groups. One of them lost his grip on the heavy wooden sword, which brought an immediate tirade from the instructor and a wordless snort from Cale.

'He won't last,' was Cale's only comment before once again cleansing the pad.

After a few more minutes they eventually crossed the distance between their barracks and the stables, which were on opposite ends of the camp. The courtyard itself was about a mile wide and just as deep, and as they neared their objective, he could see several other squads of men being led out onto the field, most by only a single veteran soldier. The one exception being on the other side of the courtyard where a short man who Wyll quickly realised was of the Teraliv race was waving a double-headed axe at a group of soldiers who were copying his strokes.

"Bring me the mounts for squad four twenty-two," Wyll heard Karthael say to a waiting stable boy, who immediately rushed off to find the correct horses.

They waited in silence for the next few minutes as Karthael left them and walked some distance over to the main gate.

"What's he doing?" Sarran asked as they watched their Arborii instructor, who had taken up a position at the centre of the fifteen-foot gate which was open and manned by a squad on either side.

"Whatever it is, he's done it before," Brendan replied as

the gate guards gave him an acknowledging wave and then ignored the Arborii as he stood motionless in the middle of the roadway.

Half a dozen stable workers appeared a few minutes later with their horses, and as Wyll took Socks' reins he patted the white stallion on the nose, receiving a playful nip in response.

From the moment Socks had been foaled he had been Wyll's horse, and there had only been a handful of others in Grandell that could keep up with him at a run. Rhianna's own mare, Jolly, had been one of them. The first time he had met her had been on the south heading Sea Road which eventually led from Grandell down to Damerette. She had challenged him to a race between the point and the place where the road divided. It had been a close thing, but Socks had just beaten the leggy mare to the post and Rhianna had seemed shocked that she and Jolly had been bested. She had congratulated him though, and they had ridden together, chatting for a while before she returned to Grandell while he continued on his way towards the farm where his family lived. Wyll had never come so close to losing a race, and he remembered how Socks had always seemed a little put out with the graceful mare the few times the two horses had come across each other after that.

"I suppose we should saddle the mounts," Brendan said, bringing him back to the present. Marad nodded his agreement, and once they had begun the rest of the squad quickly followed suit. Wyll went about the business of attaching the saddle and tack to Socks' back before standing back a step to see everything was in order. It was funny Wyll thought. He could hardly ride any other horse, but Socks had never thrown him, and when they ran it was as if the otherwise white stallion's partly brown legs were an extension of his own. Not even the wind could outpace them.

He had no idea why that should be the case, but the last several years had shown it to be true. It was that more than any matter of ownership which made Socks his.

When he was finished, he gave Socks another pat on the nose, but this time the stallion seemed oblivious to the touch. The horse's huge black eyes were locked on something behind Wyll's back, and as he turned, he saw Socks wasn't the only one transfixed. The other horses were also staring at the same thing Socks had seen, and then all at the same time they began to move. Socks gave a gentle tug on his reigns to free them from Wyll's grip and walked over to take a place in the centre of the precise half circle the other nine had formed. Wyll just gaped at the horses' incredible behaviour for a minute before recovering himself enough to spin around and see what had caused the implausible performance.

As Wyll turned, he stopped, staring at the sight before him. Karthael was returning from the gate on the back of a willowy stallion so white he expected it would have made freshly fallen snow look dull. The horse looked like a normal beast, but the way it gleamed even against the brightness of the morning sun suggested there was something more to it.

When Karthael finally re-joined the group, he swung down off the steed with the ease of long practice and watched as Socks knelt down on one knee and lowered his head to the ground.

Karthael's steed seemed to study the other horse for a

long moment before strolling forward on its graceful legs to stand directly in front of Socks.

"What is going on?!" he heard one of the others ask from behind.

It was a question Wyll would have asked himself if he hadn't been so intent on the spectacle being played out in front of him.

Karthael looked up and addressed the group.

"Si'aik," he said, pointing towards the magnificent white stallion, "Is of the Rahara, the race from which we believe your human steeds descended many millennia ago. They have been on this continent longer than you have, and are very different from the domesticated horses your ancestors brought with them on the desolate fleet. Though not so different that they cannot interbreed. Whose horse is this?" he asked, pointing at Socks.

"Mine, Instructor," Wyll answered without taking his eyes from the animals, "His name is Socks."

"Socks?" Karthael repeated in a manner which sounded almost offended.

"Well Wyll, it would appear Socks is Rahiri, a half blood, a direct descendant of Rahara and more common stock."

Wyll nodded thoughtfully as he watched Socks stand back up to his full height while Si'aik seemed contented with whatever Socks' display had been. He thought about what Karthael had said and decided the instructor was right. It would explain a great deal if Socks' sire had been of the almost mythical Rahara, the fey steeds it was said that would tolerate only an Arborii to ride.

"All right, listen up men," Karthael announced as though nothing out of the ordinary had occurred, once more demanding the squad's attention.

"This camp is over three miles around the perimeter, so this is what we are going to do. When I tell you to ride, you will exit the camp via the main gate. When you are clear of the compound, you will head in an eastward direction around the palisade and ride hard until you return to the gate and this position here."

He pointed at a short painted pole sticking out of the compacted dirt near where they stood.

"I will pursue after half a minute. If I am able to tag any of you before every member of the squad finishes the course, or if I return to this post before even one of you, the entire squad will receive extra duties. Do I make myself clear?"

There was a chorus of acknowledgements, and then Karthael gave the order.

The men scrambled into their saddles and within a few moments they were heading for the gate at a full gallop.

As he rounded the gate and left the compound, Wyll gave a glance back at Karthael, who was still standing beside Si'aik, calmly watching the others leave the camp. Turning his attention back to the course ahead, Wyll determined not to be the one who caused the unit the exertion he was sure 'extra duties' would entail, and quickly outdistanced the others by several lengths.

He couldn't help but smile as he leant low over Socks' neck and felt the wind rushing through his hair. The ride from Grandell had been long and arduous, and he was still tired and sore from phases in the saddle. In all that time though there had been no chance for him to simply ride. Not at more than the slow walk the column had been forced to maintain so those on foot could keep up. Socks seemed glad of the chance to run as well, and within moments the rest of the squad was left far behind, almost out of sight around the curve of the wooden palisade.

When he realised he was about halfway around the camp Wyll reined Socks in, though the horse barely needed the break, and turned to wait for the others to catch up. Before the rest of his squad came into sight though Wyll heard their shouts, and when they finally appeared it was with Karthael, easily sitting the Rahara steed without a saddle, only a few lengths behind. Even as he watched, it was clear the instructor would catch them in less than another minute. The horses owned by his squad were all good stock he had noted when they'd been brought out by the stable hands, but they just couldn't compete with the Arborii steed which Karthael was riding.

"Ready Socks?" Wyll asked with a grin. He doubted he could outrun the instructor, but Karthael had already nearly caught the others, so there wasn't much point in holding back.

With a slight pressure from his knees, Socks leapt ahead and raced straight towards the middle of the squad's loose formation. Wyll bent low over the saddle and hoped the instructor wouldn't see him through the group of men and horses.

As he passed the squad, he saw that Karthael was right behind them. The instructor was so intent on the last moments of the chase that Wyll was able to thread between Tauman and Charran's horses and dart past the instructor, giving Si'aik a teasing slap on the rump as the horses thundered off in different directions. With a whooping cry he looked back, turning Socks in the opposite direction from where Karthael had angrily left off chasing the others, who were regaining their lead as fast as they could. Wyll finished his half circle and headed out into the no-man's-land between the palisade and the surrounding canopy of the Emerald Sea with Karthael in close pursuit. From this angle he could see the others were far enough around the course that Karthael surely couldn't catch them now, even with Si'aik as his mount. The instructor was closing with him though, and Wyll once again bent low over Socks' neck as he urged the stallion straight on into the forest. Trees flashed past in quick succession, and Wyll began turning Socks back in the direction the camp. Ahead of him was a huge moss-covered boulder which had a strange tree growing from a split in its side, and Wyll figured going around the right of it would put him on a straight line to his target. He chanced a glance backwards and saw Karthael only a length or two behind, and with a tug on Sock's reins changed the course of the stallion's gallop to take him away from the instructor and around the far side of the boulder. As he veered off, Wyll saw Karthael take the bait, ducking low under a branch and heading around to the right, where he would cut Wyll off in moments.

With as sharp a tug on Socks' reins as he ever needed to give, Wyll pulled the horse up short and reined him around a hundred and eighty degrees and galloped off in the other direction.

From behind him he heard a furious curse as the Arborii instructor realised his mistake, then the steady drumming of hooves once again picked up from his pursuer. Wyll bolted for the edge of the forest, and after threading through the final line of trees saw the gate was still nearly a quarter way around the palisade from where he was heading. He burst out of the undergrowth at a full gallop,

Socks leaping over a fallen oak with little difficulty and plunging onward towards the end of the course. When he finally approached the open gate, he could see the others dismounting in the distance and then Bosric pointing at him frantically as the others turned to watch.

When Sarran began motioning as well Wyll looked over his shoulder and got a start when he saw Karthael's intent form only a single length behind.

"Come on, we're almost there!" Wyll shouted to the mostly white stallion.

With a snort, the tiring Socks gave one last burst of energy which carried them to the gate ahead of Karthael but didn't gain any ground. There was only a hundred spans left now and Wyll looked back at the grinning form of the instructor as he closed the distance even further. The squad was all cheering, except for Seth, who watched with silent interest as Karthael's horse drew up level with Wyll's own.

The two riders were bent over their mounts, the instructor intent on beating him now instead of simply tagging him. Both horses galloped the final stretch for all they were worth as several of the squads training around the area stopped to watch the mad dash of the Arborii instructor on his fey steed, and the fresh recruit who was just barely keeping pace.

As they reached the last fifty yards Si'aik stuck his head out in front of Socks, and without any urging from Wyll the Rahiri mount strode ahead even faster than before. For a moment the two horses stared at each other sideways in an unfriendly manner and then returned their eyes to the target, both straining to reach the post before the other. The wooden marker loomed up between them, forcing the horses to separate. Both riders frantically urged their mounts onward until instants before they reached the mark, Socks gave one last surge and put the contest to an end as he outdid Si'aik by a hand.

A cheer went up from the conscripts and even the dour Seth managed a smile as Karthael and Wyll both slowed their mounts and walked them for a few minutes to cool the steaming horses off without cramping.

There were congratulations all around for Wyll as he finally dismounted and joined the others, and then sudden silence as Karthael did the same.

The Arborii instructor gave voice to an annoyed sigh as he studied Wyll, who was still flushed with the excitement of his victory.

"Congratulations Wyll," Karthael finally said at length, "Si'aik and I have never been beaten before, and we've been doing this for a great many years."

"Thank you, Instructor," Wyll replied, then couldn't help but add, "Socks and I have never come so close to defeat. I think it was that more than any doing of mine which gave him the necessary strength at the last."

Karthael nodded graciously before turning to address the whole of the squad.

"Who can tell me what this man's most obvious mistake was?" he said, pointing at Wyll with a single black claw.

There was a moment of silence as the men realised Karthael was asking them a serious question rather than putting the young conscript down because he had won.

Eventually Brendan ventured, "He left the squad," in his deep rumbling tone.

"Correct," the instructor replied, "And his most significant act?"

"He came back?" Charran suggested.

"Yes, he came back, but more importantly he showed initiative, putting himself in harm's way to get the rest of you out of trouble."

Wyll couldn't help a half grin as Bosric gave him an amiable cuff on his shoulder, which was level with the short man's head as the Arborii instructor continued.

"And what was my mistake?" Karthael asked with a slight grimace, looking each of them in the eyes.

A few seconds of silence passed as no one wanted to be the one to criticise the instructor, but then Bosric stepped forward with a grin and did a full forward somersault in the air before declaring, "You chose to make a show of it instead of taking the easy and assured victory, Karthael."

The little man with the wild red hair stepped back into the row of soldiers without another word and waited for a reply, though his ever-present grin never faded.

Karthael just stood there, looking at the impertinent little man for a moment before barking a curt laugh.

"Quite right Bosric, I couldn't have put it much better myself," he told them at last.

"You are all soldiers now, whether you want to be or not, and getting the job done is what soldiers are about. Never seek glory in battle. If you ever have the chance to obtain your objective or gain victory in an assured but unspectacular way, take it. Unless your orders are explicit or to the contrary of course."

A runner came up to Karthael and said a few words Wyll didn't catch before the instructor acknowledged him and sent the boy on his way.

"Come with me. It appears the master armourer is

ready to take your measurements now," Karthael ordered as he set off towards the huge smithy building.

"Bring your horses, they'll be needed as well."

Both Brendan and Cale nodded in understanding and Wyll caught Seth giving a vague frown before Marad glanced his way and mumbled, "Looks like we're going to be heavy cavalry."

"What makes you say that?" Wyll asked.

The huge dark-skinned man just looked at him for a moment.

"Can you think of another reason the armourer would require our mounts?"

After a moment Wyll shrugged as he shook his head from side to side.

"Strange choice though," the gigantic man continued after a moment, "I mean, it'll suit me and a few of the others well enough, but Bosric and Kienan just don't have the muscle and reach to pull it off."

He fell silent with a frown then, and Wyll once again thought what a strange collection his new squad was. The men ranged from Brendan's height and Marad's mass all the way down to Bosric, who was little over five feet tall. From his brief time spent with the squad so far, Wyll knew that some of the men like Seth and Brendan were sharp of wit and tongue, while Sarran and Charran were just the opposite. He still wasn't entirely sure about Bosric's state of mind. Then there was the level of their skills, ranging from Kienan and Tauman who lacked any martial training, all the way up to Seth, Cale, Brendan, Bosric and Marad. Those men looked as though they knew exactly how to use the weapons they had carried into the dorm room the night before, and had done so many times, even if each of them did use a different type of steel and discipline.

Wyll hadn't been in the guard long himself, only a little more than half a year before the recruiting party had come to Grandell in fact. In that time, he had trained with several weapons and found a simple two-handed sword suited him best. It was a strange thing he thought. When he fought with fists or heavy weapons such as maces or hammers, his blows were often jerky and inefficient. Something about the tempered steel of a well-balanced sword made his movements much more fluid, feeling more like a dance than a brawl. His instructor back in Grandell had commented on it one time, saying that if he were any more graceful he would make him train in a dress. It had been one of the nicer things the horrible old man had said the entire time Wyll had been in the guard. Still, the wrinkled old tutor had known exactly what he was about when it came to the weapons rack. Wyll had eventually come to realise that remark was the closest the old man would ever get to giving him a compliment.

When they finally reached the armoury, Karthael pointed to a short line of soldiers waiting their turn for a heavily muscled man with a head as bald as a badger and a moustache wider than his face to take several measurements. He called them out to a scribe who was already sweating despite the early hour, while writing them down on a nearby pad.

Wyll moved to join the line with the others. While he waited, he watched the many weapon-smith's working the forges, hammering out swords, knives, armour, and other less obvious constructions for the coming conflict.

Eventually the line moved forward as the master

armourer finished his task and called brusquely for the next man to step forward, which he impatiently did.

With a look at the bored expressions of the soldiers at the front of the line, Wyll settled in for a long wait. With some small amount of interest, he watched one of the smiths attach a hilt to a long-bladed sword which would be nearly as tall as Bosric when finished. A few long minutes passed until finally the line moved forward once again. Now there were only eight more men left in front of him.

Wyll sighed.

'We are all unique. It is our most common attribute.'
Excerpt from 'The Nature of Man' by Tyrnius, High Priest
of the Maker at the time of Eldrik's rebellion.

CHAPTER 13

STEEL AND SORCERY

Jayden slowly opened his eyes, and for the first time in the long phases since Rhianna's death, the nightmares which plagued his sleep each evening failed to jolt him out of bed. Not that the dream tonight had been any less disturbing. This morning he simply felt as though every drop of sweat had been wrung from his body, leaving him as worn out and misused as an old dry sponge.

Light slanted in the small window between where the green linen curtains didn't quite meet, and he realised the bed sheet was tangled around his left leg. Kicking it free, he swung himself wearily off the sweat-soaked mattress and poured a cup of water from the covered pitcher on the desk. He downed it in a single swallow and poured another, which he drank a little more slowly as he ran his hand through his damp and matted hair. When he finished the second glass, which was still cold from the night's blessedly low temperature, he replaced the cup on the tray and wondered what he was expected to do now.

It was his first full day in the College of the Arts. Tolmarak had told him last night to wait here until he was summoned for his lesson. The old archmage had seemed remarkably distracted as he'd all but fled Jayden's room however, and neglected to say exactly when that would be.

A quick look through the crack in the curtain showed the sun only now peeking its way into a cloudless dawn of autumn sky. The hour was early, but Jayden had a feeling the archmage was not one to allow much of the day to pass in idleness.

Whenever the summons came though, he decided the day's activities would likely be undertaken more appropriately with more than just his nightclothes on. With that in mind, he opened the dresser to thankfully find everything he'd brought with him from the promontory packed neatly in the drawers. One of the maids must have come in after he had fallen asleep last night and arranged his things. Apparently they weren't much for privacy here. He poured more of the water from the pitcher into the wash bowl beside it, and used a wet towel to rid himself of the layer of sweat his nightmare had left behind. A few minutes later after drying off and dressing in his customary tunic and trousers, Jayden stamped his feet into his well-worn boots.

With nothing left to do but wait and think, he found himself unwittingly taking the bottom draw out of the cupboard which held the few meagre belongings he'd been permitted to haul across the country on the baggage train. He wanted to put it back, but his eyes were drawn to the blood-stained shirt which lay concealed in the cupboard's base. He'd hidden it there last night, and as always, once he saw it he had to take it out and stare at it.

He had run across it in the refuse pile at home the day after his attempt to take revenge on Dael. For reasons he couldn't quite explain, he'd been hoarding the torn and bloodied piece of cloth ever since. From time to time, his hand would mechanically stray towards the ruined shirt, his fingers running along the jagged tears where Dael's knife had pierced both it and his flesh.

I should just get rid of it, like Tolmarak said.

In his mind's ear, he could hear himself for the ten thousandth time screaming again as Rhianna fell, but he knew better by now than to try to block out the memories by closing his eyes. That just let him see it again as well. The archmage had told him the ragged shirt would act as a kind of catalyst, connecting him to the events on the cliff top as long as he held on to it. As much as it galled him to admit it, Jayden was starting to believe the old man was correct. The visions were much stronger when he held the proof of Dael's treachery in his hands, and yet something compelled him to keep the old shirt close.

A peremptory knock sounded at the door and an instant later it swung wide open, causing him to jump and face it as the unexpected movement startled him.

The torn shirt remained firmly gripped in his hands as Tolmarak strode into the room with little or no regard for his privacy, and the archmage noticed the bloodied scrap of fabric right away.

For a moment Tolmarak stopped and glared at the ragged piece of cloth, then sighed in resignation.

"When I told you to be rid of that, I did so for your own good. I know you dream of taking revenge on Count Dael for what he did that day. The plain truth is that when the time comes, I for one will not oppose you short of a royal decree, though others will. For now though, you have to put it aside."

"I can't do that," Jayden told him fiercely.

"You must," Tolmarak replied, his intractable tone now a match for Jayden's.

"The entire kingdom hangs by a thread. Rebellion has been declared in the west by one of the strongest archmagi Jeranon has seen in almost two millennia, and the western nations have become too quiet over the last several years. War is coming Jayden, I can feel it in my bones. All that remains to be seen is where and when the pieces will fall."

"So you keep saying," Jayden replied, "And when our enemies do take the field, you want me to fight them for country, for king, and for you, and kill as many of them as I can before they do the same to me. I no longer have any problem with that task."

Without warning, Tolmarak snatched the bloodied shirt from Jayden's hand.

"If the king is not able to find a peaceful solution before this rebellion gets out of control, then this," he said as he waved the ragged piece of cloth in front of Jayden's face. "This atrocity to which you hold so tightly will be but one among millions. The western nations will swarm over the Dark Iron Mountains like a flood as soon as they realise Jeranon is no longer united against them. On that day, our kingdom, which has existed on these shores for almost three thousand years, will be ground into dust."

Jayden glared as he snatched his shirt back from Tolmarak, even as the archmage continued to stare him down.

"Let me make something perfectly clear to you Jayden. If this develops into a full-fledged war between the east and western provinces, you can be sure Heramiir will bring the magi of Miralthrall into the conflict. When that happens, the king will order the college at Aramar to intervene. Even if we do manage to defeat Heramiir's armies and subdue the opposing magi, Jeranon's military will be weakened to the point where we may no longer be able to hold the dark nations beyond the border!"

"You would be well advised to put your personal feelings aside and help me do my job, which is to see you develop your talents as fully as possible before the fighting begins. You will not survive to take your vengeance otherwise. Now come with me," Tolmarak ordered as he turned and walked away from Jayden, who shoved the bloodied shirt back into the base of the cupboard.

Leaving his small room, Jayden caught up with the white-haired archmage and fell in beside him, his pride seething. Yet something Tolmarak had said a moment ago had rung a bell in his mind, though he couldn't quite place it.

"I thought you were the leader of the college here in Aramar?" Jayden eventually questioned him as they travelled down the interminable length of the college's mazelike corridors.

"As you well know. Why mention it now?" Tolmarak returned brusquely as he continued to stride through the building, clearly still irritated by their previous conversation.

"Isn't it also true that you are advisor to King Erian?"

"What of it?" Tolmarak asked again, his tone now a mixture of annoyance and mild curiosity.

"And you will be taking enough time from those duties to instruct me?"

"You, and a few others," the archmage confirmed as they continued.

"Why?" Jayden asked, stopping just in front of Tolmarak, forcing him to halt momentarily as well.

Moving around where Jayden was standing, Tolmarak motioned him to continue as he spoke.

"Some things are more important than others."

When Jayden tried to question the archmage further he chose not to answer, continuing instead to their destination, which as it turned out lay just around the next corner, and up a wide flight of marbled stairs.

*   *   *

As they made the quick ascent, Tolmarak could see the boy's face becoming darker by the moment. While the grief mostly seemed to have bled away on the long march back to Aramar, every few days he would still fall into a dark or depressed mood which Tolmarak had no idea how to counter. At such times, the boy would become unresponsive, aware of everything around him certainly, but unresponsive nonetheless. Now was not the time though. Today would mark the beginning of his new life as a mage, and with war looming just over the horizon he intended to push this class of students harder than any he had taught before. He hoped they could handle it. The five of them were the strongest of the untrained Gifted the recruiting parties had found over the previous phases, and unbeknownst to them they would play a pivotal role in the coming years, whether they wanted to or not. He had no desire to manipulate them, but he also couldn't credit that Heramiir would just leave them be while the conflict raged, not with the strength of Gift each one of them possessed.

With the door to the study just ahead he stopped, turning to face the most powerful of his young pupils.

"Inside this door are four other students whom I will also teach. You would do well to make them your friends Jayden, for you will be together as long as you are under my instruction. If you survive the coming war, you will likely know each other for decades after that."

For a moment he held Jayden's gaze until the younger man eventually looked away.

"I will try," Jayden muttered stiffly.

It would be all he would get at the moment, and Tolmarak was glad for that much as he pushed the door open with a wrinkled, sun browned hand.

Some magi felt it necessary to do everything with the Gift, even to the point of opening doors ahead of themselves. Tolmarak had always disapproved of such practices, he hadn't survived all these long years by being physically weak, and neither had anyone else he knew of either.

There was no lock on this door, so Tolmarak simply pushed against the latch which held it as he stepped forward into the sizeable room beyond. The chamber he had requisitioned for his class' use was shaped like a large octagon, and as far as he knew it was the only one of its type in the building.

Inside the room, four of the five chairs he had previously placed in a semi-circle facing his own seat had been pulled out of position. However, they were now occupied by the other students, who were taking their ease while waiting for him to arrive.

"If you please," Tolmarak said with a motion toward where the chairs had originally laid.

Before long the others had dragged the heavy wooden

seats back into position and Tolmarak took his own place at the head of the circle. He sighed.

"Jayden, come over here please," he said as he saw the youth still standing half a step outside the doorway. When there was no response he turned to see what was keeping the young man from Grandell. With a quick glance at where his stricken gaze lay, the archmage stood, immediately crossing the chamber to block Jayden's view of the room.

"What is it boy?" Tolmarak demanded.

Jayden's face was a mask, his features a bloodless white, "What's wrong?"

Instead of answering, Jayden just turned and walked woodenly out the door before slumping against the wall and sliding to the floor with a blank expression on his face. Tolmarak followed him quietly and when he saw Jayden wasn't going to move any time soon, he squatted down beside the young man despite his aching knee and waited.

"She..." Jayden eventually managed to speak with a shudder.

"That girl, in the room... She looks exactly like Rhianna."

Tolmarak cursed silently, this was the last thing he needed with the demands on his time already so great.

"Which one?" he asked as patiently as he could, though with the way the last few phases had gone he scarcely needed to. Only one of the three women in the class was close to Jayden's age, and of course she would have to be the most powerful of the four others. She was nowhere near as powerful as Jayden in the Gift, but then only the Archmage Heramiir was. This girl was far closer to being on a level with Tolmarak himself.

Nevertheless, Lady Firerose, the daughter of a minor nobleman from the north was still exceptionally strong, and Tolmarak had no time to split the two of them up so he could teach them separately. As it was, students with the strength these five possessed would normally have been given their own tutors from the outset. The standard practise would be to teach them individually so the other students wouldn't hold them back, or feel compelled to try stupid or dangerous things to keep up with their peers.

With war looming over the horizon though, every mage who could be spared was busy constructing the new outer wall the king had ordered built around the capital. They also had to find time to attend to their own duties and studies in battle magic, not to mention teaching the students who had not yet attained the rank of Mage. As much as Tolmarak would have liked to make things easy on Jayden, he just didn't have the luxury to teach both him and the young Lady Firerose the way it should be done.

"Jayden," he said quietly, and for once the boy looked up at him, not having sunk into his own private misery when reminded of Rhianna's untimely death, and spoke.

"If I didn't know better, I could think they were sisters, twins even. Except for the colour of her hair," Jayden added.

"I have to go back in there, don't I?"

"I'm afraid so Jayden. Just as soon as you're ready," Tolmarak answered, trying to hide his surprise.

"I wish I didn't have to force the two of you together, considering... But time is against us. I only have enough hours in the day to teach all of you at once, though I freely admit that is not normally how it is done with students of your strength."

Jayden nodded wearily in acceptance, though it seemed wrong to Tolmarak that the boy should choose now to capitulate so readily. It was as if seeing the young noblewoman had shocked him deeply enough that the last shreds of defiance he had wrapped so closely around himself since Rhianna's death had suddenly unravelled.

Without further prompting Jayden got slowly to his feet, though his face betrayed no spark of emotion, and silently walked back to the door, not even pausing as he went inside.

Tolmarak found himself deeply troubled by the simple display. He ignored the familiar twinge of pain his knee gave him when he straightened, and followed the young man into the classroom which he knew would become a second home to all of them over the next few phases.

As Tolmarak re-entered the room, all was silent as Jayden took the only empty seat left in the semi-circle. Tolmarak couldn't help a grimace as he watched Jayden sit stiffly, his eyes straight ahead so he wouldn't have to see the girl in the plush chair next to his who reminded him so much of his lost love.

Tolmarak had yet to meet the others, having only been briefed about them by Archmage Dallenkin this morning. He had wanted to get all this out of the way last night when he had ridden in. Unfortunately, the accident which had occurred as he showed Jayden to his room had required all other considerations to be suspended while he arranged for the fatal events to be kept from the collective students' notice.

His investigation had uncovered little about the freak

accident, but Tolmarak wasn't ready to let it go just yet. He was sure the Gift had been used in some fashion to pry the large stone from the roof where it had remained solidly ensconced for untold years. The mortar around the missing block had still been strong, and he had fused the stonework back into its place with the Gift during the small hours of this morning. News of the death would inevitably get out, but so long as none of the servants or Magi who had come running to help disobeyed his order not to talk about it to the students, Tolmarak was fairly certain the specific details had been contained from the younger apprentices.

He hoped he was just being overcautious in his old age, but there was something about the accident which struck him as being more than just a tragic, but natural occurrence.

With a start Tolmarak realised the students were watching him, quietly waiting for him to say something to get the class underway. All except Jayden, who was still staring woodenly at the wall ahead of himself.

"Welcome to the College of the Arts," Tolmarak began in a voice rich from years of teaching his pupils and dealing with insufferable nobles.

"As of now you begin your instruction into the unseen things of this world, you begin your instruction as magi."

"Most citizens of this realm," he continued after a moment, "Will live out their lives in ignorance of even the simplest of truths you will learn here. For most magi who pass the training, especially ones with as much potential in the Gift as you five have, a life fraught with perils and danger awaits you at the end of your studies. But it is also a life filled with wonder and excitement. Great deeds can and must be done by those few who have the strength and conviction to put their power, and more importantly, their very spirits to the test. But I warn you now, this path to greatness is not for everyone. Less than one in ten of those who attain the rank of Mage have the courage and the raw power to follow this calling and become recognised Archmagi, though all of you have easily enough strength. The skills for this undertaking I can teach you, but the courage, the spirit and the sheer determination you will need should you choose this course can only come from within."

There was a moment of hushed silence as his students tried to take in those words, although Jayden seemed disinterested. When no one else was game to speak, Tolmarak decided it was time he introduced himself to the others.

"For those of you who do not already know, my name is Tolmarak. I have been an Archmage here for nearly forty years and I am now head of the college at Aramar. In addition, I have the responsibility of being King Erian's advisor on all things relating to the Gift, and other more arcane magics of which you will learn in due course. That is all you need know about me for the present, other than that I will be your teacher while you are here. For now, I would know more about you. I apologise for being so unprepared, but urgent matters have had me tied up since I returned to the college last night. As a result I know little about you other than your names. You must be Billy," Tolmarak said to the only other boy in the class besides Jayden.

"Why don't you tell us a little about yourself, where you come from, that kind of thing?"

The blonde-haired boy, who couldn't have been more

than ten years old, nodded nervously before beginning.

"Hi, I'm Billy," he said.

Tolmarak smiled encouragingly for him to continue.

"I grew up in Silvertown before I came here. I used to run errands for the head of house at the keep."

"Aren't you a bit young to have been working?" Tolmarak asked in mild surprised.

The slight boy just shrugged.

"My father was lost at sea before I was born and my mum died of the coughing sickness when I was five. The head of house at the keep offered to take me in a few phases later and give me a place to stay if I would run errands for her. I didn't like it much, but it was better than the streets."

"Well," Tolmarak said, a little taken aback by the orphan boy's bluntness, "One thing I should make clear to you all is that the magi of Jeranon are in very short supply. For every child born with the Gift there are at least ten thousand without the necessary spark. There are so few of us that we have no choice but to look out for each other as if we were ourselves part of one big family, especially when outside these walls. I don't expect you to fully understand that yet Billy, for now I ask you simply to believe it. Now, which of you fine ladies is Nadeara?" he asked, his gaze moving between the three young woman who made up the balance of the room.

"That would be me," the oldest of the students replied.

Tolmarak had initially thought someone must have made a mistake when he'd been told about her age. Nadeara was in her mid-twenties, fully twice as old or more than most new magi, with straight black hair ending just above her shoulders and deep blue eyes that seemed at odds with her olive complexion. She seemed unconcerned as she sat at ease in the centre chair of the five which Tolmarak had provided. From long experience he knew that here was a natural leader, one would do well in the coming years if she applied herself to the training.

"So tell us about yourself Nadeara. You must be from a long way off for your talent not to have been discovered until now."

"Yes Archmage," she replied formally, "My family comes from a small island called Hentill, which lies just off the north coast of Avsan, but I've spent most of my life at sea. When my trading boat docked in one of your southern ports a few phases back there happened to be a mage at the dock. She told me I have the Gift and helped me to use it for the first time. Once I was sure for certain what she had been telling me was true, I sold my cargo, said goodbye to my crew, and left my ship in the capable hands of my first mate. I then accepted her offer to return to Aramar and train my abilities here."

"Hmmm… Perhaps we should send out an expedition to Avsan if there is so obviously untapped potential there," Tolmarak mused.

"I doubt that would be welcome, Archmage," She replied.

"Although it was my choice to come here, the high council of Avsan has no great love for Jeranon or its people. If you tried to send recruiters to steal away their most talented people, they would surely take exception, maybe even to the point of retaliation."

"I see," Tolmarak replied as he unconsciously stroked his short, well-groomed white beard, "I see. You seem to know a good deal about the workings of Avsan's politics Nadeara. Having never been there myself I am curious as to how you come by this information?"

"I have a friend who is married to one of the council members," the black-haired woman replied calmly as she held the archmage's steady gaze.

"Well then, perhaps we will be able to use your contact to renew relations with their leadership at some point," Tolmarak suggested thoughtfully.

Avsan had not been at war with Jeranon for many, many years. Nevertheless, the two countries had cultivated an attitude of distrust towards each other over the centuries, not fully having had diplomatic relations since Eldrik the Black's era.

"Perhaps," Nadeara replied noncommittally, though something in her manner made him suddenly wonder if she were even telling the truth.

Tolmarak cleared his throat as he regarded the other students who were sitting patiently, though Jayden was being a little too quiet for his liking. He was still staring straight ahead at the empty wall in front of him, his hands gripping the arms of his chair hard enough to make his knuckles stand out white, although there was little of it to show on his face.

"At any rate," Tolmarak said, breaking the silence, "That's in the future. Now let us continue."

There were still two of the students who hadn't introduced themselves besides Jayden, whom he decided to leave until last. The first was a younger girl with long brown hair, still older than the age which most new magi were found. She looked to be perhaps two or three years older than Billy.

"You must be Missy then?" Tolmarak said kindly, and the girl nodded that he was correct.

"And where might you be from?" he asked to prompt the young mage, who had decided not to offer any more information.

The youngest of the three women looked around the room nervously for a minute before she answered, but when she did, it was with a clear voice and defiant tone.

"I'm from Angara," she announced proudly, a challenging look in her eyes.

Angara, Tolmarak knew, was a farming village to the extreme north of Jeranon, situated between the hulking mountains known as the Ice Ranges and the Great North Sea. It was one of the most remote places in the whole of the kingdom, and the foul weather coming in off the ocean or down from the mountains constantly beset the hardy folk who lived in the coastal town. In addition, there were far more tangible threats to the area from the wild beasts and other exotic creatures which dwelt upon the jagged slopes. In truth, Tolmarak had never seen the virtue of living in such a place. The region held no special benefits, economic or otherwise, unless you counted its very isolation from the rest of the kingdom as one he supposed. Where the people of Jeranon made their home was of course none of his concern, but if there was one thing that made Tolmarak irritable, it was not understanding a thing. Why anyone would choose to live in such an inhospitable place when there was so much arable and unoccupied land just on the Sammorand Plains alone was beyond his comprehension.

"That's quite a way from here," he said to the girl, "Nevertheless, you are more than welcome within these walls."

"Now," Tolmarak said as he turned his attention to the beautiful young woman who had Jayden so on edge without ever having said a word, "You must be Lady Firerose."

"That's correct, Archmage," the young noblewoman replied as she nodded her head, sending her long, flame-red hair cascading over her shoulder.

"Perhaps you would be so good as to share your first name with us?" Tolmarak asked with just the faintest hint of a smile on his weathered features.

"Of course, Archmage. My birth name is Clarion, given by my father the Earl of Pereset and his wife Theresa on the day I was born. Is there anything more you would know, Archmage?" she replied perfectly politely.

Tolmarak studied the girl for a second before responding. If the young noble were going to use her court manners as a shield it wouldn't make it any easier for him to stitch these five apprentices into the tight-knit group they needed to be. Better that he put a stop to the problem here and now, although the girl wouldn't be happy to hear what he was about to say.

"Clarion, and all of you as well, there is one thing which is important you understand today. That thing is that your past life is no longer relevant."

He held up his hands for quiet when Nadeara began to speak, and continued.

"Of course your relationships with those outside the college can continue and so forth, but what you must come to terms with is that as of today, you are magi, at least to the outside world. What you did before now, what you were before now, whether a trader or a farmer or a noble makes no difference whatsoever. That being said, you all still have a long way to go before the college recognises your ability and skill to be at a level where you can take the formal 'Mage's' test. But it is a sad fact that from now on when you leave these college walls, most of the population, and in all likelihood some of your own friends and families, will no longer see you at first for a person. Rather, they will look at the mage's mantle which is the uniform of our order, and see it above all else."

He looked at each of the five students in turn, and only Billy seemed pleased at that idea, although as always Tolmarak had trouble reading Jayden's blank expression.

"Take heart though, it's not as bad as I may make it seem. You will find new family and friends here who will stand by you against whatever odds life may throw at you. However, you will also come to realise that when out in the world, the actions of other magi will affect the ungifted's perception of you as much as your actions will reflect on them. That is why it is so important for each of us to act for the good of Jeranon, and sometimes, just as importantly, also to be seen to be acting in the kingdom's, and its peoples, best interests."

"That's why becoming an Archmage requires more than power alone," Nadeara offered shrewdly.

With an approving nod, Tolmarak smiled.

"Exactly right Nadeara. Part of the reason for the line between the rank of Mage and Archmage is so the general populace can know with confidence that only those who have served Jeranon and risked their lives for that cause on no less than three separate occasions are promoted to our highest rank. There are some here in the college who have the power to attain the rank, but have shown they are duplicitous in their dealings, or have delved into other darker areas of study which the citizens would never approve of. There are even one or two who lack the courage to step forward and take what could be theirs if they would but show they had the mettle to stand against a foe, any foe, in defence of their homeland."

Nadeara nodded in understanding while both Firerose and Missy seemed surprised. Billy was hanging on his every word as though it was all some kind of terrific adventure. Jayden was still giving no sign he was even listening.

"Unfortunately for you Lady Firerose, Clarion... Your burden is multiplied by the college's need to remain politically neutral as we serve the king and Jeranon itself. Like a few others among our number, you must come to grips with the fact that when inducted into our order, all past ties to nobility and future title are legally severed."

At this Firerose seemed to deflate a little, though she had obviously already been given this information long ago.

"Thank you for the reminder, Archmage," She said politely, but with steel in her eyes.

Tolmarak sighed quietly, but found he couldn't put off Jayden's introduction any longer.

"Jayden, it's your turn," Tolmarak said loudly enough to get the boy's attention, whilst trying not to make it obvious what he was doing.

The brown-haired young man took a deep breath without shifting his gaze, gripping the seat arms a little harder before he slowly turned to face the others. For a moment Tolmarak thought it would be all right, but then Jayden caught sight of Lady Firerose again, and from the way his intent gaze locked on her pale features Tolmarak knew there was going to be a problem.

Lady Clarion Firerose returned Jayden's unblinking stare with a level one of her own, though she seemed less than pleased about being the object of such intense scrutiny.

"Jayden," Tolmarak said again, and it was enough to make the young man break his gaze, closing his eyes and tilting his head away for a moment before looking back at the others, who were all now watching him closely.

"My name is Jayden," he said eventually, his voice hoarse, low and level, "I come from Grandell," he added haltingly a moment later.

"My father is a trader and runs a small fleet of fishing and trading vessels and my mother takes care of the family vineyards and estates. I first met Archmage Tolmarak as my ship was leaving the dock here at Aramar, although I didn't know his name at the time."

Tolmarak suddenly had the feeling Jayden wasn't going to stop at a simple introduction.

"If you don't want to go on, you don't have to," he interjected softly, but Jayden continued to speak without even breaking his rhythm.

"I came here to try to convince Count Dael, our local, noble..." At that Jayden grimaced as if even the word had a foul taste to it. "That he had beaten me, and that I would no longer oppose his arranging a barely legal marriage between himself and Rhianna, my love, who wanted none of his attentions and had not agreed to the marriage. When I returned to Grandell, it was to find he had moved up the wedding to that day, and that Rhianna had killed two of the guards holding her prisoner. I found her on a ledge above the cliffs, fighting with the count and two of his guards. Dael ordered me killed on sight and after we had fought, he stabbed me in the chest and the gut, mortally wounding me. He then forced Rhianna to leap to her death rather than return to the town and become his bride that very same day. I would have died too if the archmage had arrived a single minute later."

Jayden forced himself to look at Firerose then, though Tolmarak could see he was struggling for control.

"You, look... exactly like her," he said to the young noble in a half-strangled tone as Firerose's hand moved to cover her mouth at the raw emotion in Jayden's voice.

"Except for your hair. Rhianna's was more the colour of fresh straw," he finished sadly as he turned away.

Tolmarak had never actually seen the girl Jayden had been grieving for over these last few phases, and he had cursed himself a hundred times since then for not arriving at the cliff-top ledge a handful of moments earlier. If he had, all of this could have been avoided. Still, there was nothing for it now but to move forward and try to teach Jayden the necessary arts despite the fact that Tolmarak knew he would never have the boy's undivided attention so long as Count Dael lived.

"I am, so sorry for your loss, Jayden," Firerose told him sincerely, the cold look she had given him a moment before completely absent from her expressive face. As she hesitantly reached out a comforting hand though, Jayden pulled his own back, avoiding her touch.

"But you have to understand," She finished, moving her hand slowly back to her own chair, "I am not her."

"I know," Jayden replied slowly, "How I know."

Then he once again surprised Tolmarak by adding, "I just need some time to get used to it. Excuse me," he said, and then stood and walked out the door without another word.

Tolmarak let him go this time. The boy had made progress today whether he knew it or not, but he clearly needed to sort through all the things he had just said and still felt. Unfortunately, time was one of the few things even an archmage couldn't manipulate, and they were fast running short of what little they had left.

"Will he be all right?" Firerose asked, concern clear in her voice and all hint of her imperious manner suddenly gone.

With a glance at the empty doorway Tolmarak sighed.

"I hope so," he said in earnest, while also mentally thanking the young mage for so effortlessly breaking through the noblewoman's haughty defences.

Tolmarak went to the door to see if Jayden was still there in the corridor, but there was no sign of the young man. With a thoughtful nod, he returned and took his seat, facing the others as he began to teach them the absolute basics of using the arcane arts.

The last bloom of summer's late run into dawn of autumn was all but over now, and outside the college building the first leaves were changing colour and getting ready to fall. If he was supremely lucky it would be a long hard winter with heavy snowfalls, and he would get an extra few weeks to train his students before the dawn of spring melt arrived. Whether they were ready or not, the king's army would surely march against Heramiir's forces at that time and try to win back the lands the traitorous archmage had taken by strength of arms over the last few phases.

Tolmarak couldn't help but shudder at the destruction

Heramiir's uprising was going to instigate, not to mention the damage it had already caused the college's reputation since the rebellion had been declared. The declaration Tolmarak had been forced to formally write to the king first thing this morning, distancing the two arms of the college, Miralthrall and Aramar, from each other could cause as many problems in future as it solved. Especially if they managed to somehow restore order in Jeranon without having to resort to an all-out civil war. But like too many things these days, that concern had to remain one for another time.

One he fervently hoped they would all live to see.

'We are taught from childhood that our imaginations are enough to empower us to change the world. Even now, I cannot conceive that my focused intent was not sufficient to bring about the victory I so clearly imagined.'
Excerpt from the trial of Eldrik the Black.

CHAPTER 14

THE GIFT

Meet in the stables at first tolling.

It had been Archmage Tolmarak's final command of the previous day.

The class had been studying the foundational theories behind the use of the Gift from dawn until sunset for two weeks now, but from the old man's comments last night, the time for theory was finally at an end.

Today the archmage intended them to go out into the forest and practice with the Gift for real, and Jayden found himself a little apprehensive, even though he had used four of its five different aspects already. The first had been on board Crest when Tolmarak had called to him with his manipulation of air. The archmage had explained on the trip to Aramar that in Dael's chambers he had counteracted Tolmarak's binding spell with both air and spirit. Tolmarak had since helped him break through and use the elements of both earth and water, though fire eluded him despite months of practice.

The last two weeks had been arduous, and not just

because of the protracted days spent studying the introductory theories of magic. The young noblewoman, Clarion Firerose, was a source of constant unease during the hours Tolmarak's classroom forced them together. Not that it was her fault, but the uncanny resemblance she held to Rhianna made it extremely difficult to even look at her without falling into memories he would just as soon stay buried, thinly as they were.

Jayden opened Strider's stall and patted his equine nose affectionately as the horse snorted a greeting. A minute later, a scuffing noise at the stable door drew his attention away from tightening the saddle girth. As he walked the few steps to the gate to investigate, he caught a glimpse of long red hair disappearing into a stall further down the row.

He sighed. After speaking to her that first day he had avoided Firerose whenever possible, but he couldn't keep that up forever, especially with Tolmarak and the class riding out alone today.

"Wait here," he reluctantly told the horse as he gave Strider an uneasy pat, then left the stall. There was no one else around as he made his way to the other end of the stables, and even most of the equine inhabitants were still fast asleep.

First tolling, as it was colloquially known, was in fact nothing more than the sounding of the bells at six in the morning, and signified the start of the working day for many industries.

A few minutes from now the giant bells at the centre of Aramar were due to ring out the new day, and the stable hands would be appearing for work at any moment.

Struggling against his own hesitation, Jayden made his

way around the corner of the stall which held Lady Firerose's mount and came to a halt just inside. He waited while she turned from saddling the fine black mare she had already owned before coming to the college.

"Hello Jayden," she said quietly.

There was an awkward silence as Jayden tried to think of something to say. All the while, a little voice in the back of his mind was shouting at him to remember this wasn't really Rhianna, even if the two of them did look almost identical.

"I'm sorry, for the way I've treated you... over the last few weeks," he eventually got out.

"I understand," she returned, "After that first day, Archmage Tolmarak pulled me aside and told me the rest... your attempt to take revenge. Even about the guard who tried to help you despite his oath of service to the count."

Firerose looked down at the straw covered stall for a moment before returning her gaze to him.

"I am sorry if I remind you of what you've lost Jayden, but if even half the things Tolmarak has told us are approaching are true, we need to find some way to work together without this thing interfering with our studies."

The sound of approaching footsteps ended their brief conversation.

Billy and Missy entered the stables together, the two had formed a fast friendship over the last few weeks, and they were joined a moment later by Nadeara. The youngsters continued past the stall without noticing Jayden and Firerose, lost in some conversation of their own. Nadeara saw them however and turned her head to acknowledge them with a surprised, though cheerful nod before continuing down the long row of stalls.

From somewhere in the distance a deep resonant ringing began as first tolling was struck, marking the start of the new day. From out the back, Jayden could hear stablemen entering from the quarters behind the college stables.

"I'd better finish getting Strider ready," Jayden blurted out as he left Firerose to her tasks and walked back to his own mount's stall.

A few minutes later a flustered Tolmarak strode into the stables. Without a word his grey warhorse came trotting out of its stall of its own accord, allowing the head groom, who had appeared a moment before, to burden it with saddle and tack.

"Mount up!" Tolmarak called as soon as his steed was ready, and Jayden and the other students complied, although Billy had to be helped onto his horse by one of the grooms. The boy was still ill at ease on the fine chestnut roan which Tolmarak, and most likely the college itself, had gifted him with since he hadn't owned one on his arrival.

Billy was an orphan from Silvertown in the south, and after spending the last few weeks together Jayden felt a little guilty when he realised that one fact was still all he knew about the boy. Other than that he was apparently too small even to mount his own horse.

Jayden moved Strider over to where the other students were assembled on their various mounts and Tolmarak began to address them.

"All right, I apologise for the delay, but I was unavoidably detained. Now that we're all here, let me tell you why I asked you to come."

The archmage paused a moment to catch his breath and then dove back into his speech at a rush.

"Today we ride out northwest to a place known as the range. This is where you will begin your real instruction in the Gift's uses. Whilst on the range you will exercise the utmost caution. Accidents have happened before to those who pushed themselves too hard, and tragically those accidents have on occasion been fatal. With the proper attentiveness however, these risks can and will be minimised. But heed this well. New students are normally instructed in theory for a year or more before we allow them within spitting distance of the range. You have been here for two weeks. No matter how confident you feel, no matter how ready you might think you are to put your powers to the test, I am telling you right now, you are not."

"Then why are we going out there?" Nadeara asked as soon as Tolmarak fell quiet.

The archmage sighed.

"Because as I told you that first day, we have no time," he answered, the frustration clear in his voice.

"For a fresh apprentice to become an archmage, it takes on average somewhere between twenty-five to thirty years."

There was a startled look from Billy, whose entire life to this point hadn't lasted half that long in total.

"I have to try to get you ready to fight and be victorious over those with decades more knowledge and experience than all of you put together, in less than a year. So, for your own sakes I implore you to do your absolute best in achieving control of your powers whilst I am available to teach you."

Tolmarak looked at each of them in turn until he was satisfied his words had finally sunk in.

"All right. The day is waiting," he announced, then cantered his grey warhorse out through the barn door and into the vast stone-paved courtyard.

There was very little talk as they rode their mounts out through the not yet busy yard and then through the ring of dragon and flame carved pillars which surrounded the college buildings.

Soon they came to the city proper and began making their way through the early morning crowds which filled the streets heading to their places of work, or the great markets which stood outside the ancient walls.

The city streets were busy for this time of morning Jayden thought. Thankfully, their white-lined apprentice magi's cloaks, and more importantly Tolmarak's silver-lined one guaranteed most people moved aside so they could move more freely through the crowd. After all, who knew what mysterious and important business an archmage might be about, especially one as well-known and respected by the commoners as the king's adviser.

As the day began to warm, the six of them made their way through Aramar's streets until at last they came to the place where the new wall was being constructed. By the look of it, the trench for the foundations had all been dug away now, thanks in large part to the magi's efforts. The next phase of work had begun, and the deep gouge which now wound its way around Jeranon's capital was beginning to be filled in places with the stonework that would serve as the foundations for the massive construction.

An unfamiliar sensation caught Jayden's attention, as though a slight rippling in the air had washed over him, though there was no breeze to speak of. When he turned to see what had caused the momentary chill he stopped, startled at what he saw. Over to his left Jayden's eyes locked on a tall Mage in the blue-lined cloak of that rank. The man was using the Gift to lift a massive stone block off a cart led by an eight-ox team, the beasts all looking exhausted despite their numbers. He watched the Mage concentrate as he waved the block over to where a squad of soldiers were setting mortar under the direction of a master mason, then set it down gently and precisely in the correct location. As soon as the block was down the chill passed and Jayden shook his head to clear it of the strange sensation, even as Tolmarak rode up beside him. For a moment Jayden hadn't realised he'd stopped until the archmage looked over at where his gaze lay and said, "You felt him use the Gift?"

"I think so," Jayden replied with a slight frown, "It was like... a disturbance, in the air itself."

Tolmarak nodded and clapped him on the shoulder.

"Well done Jayden, as you grow into your skills you will be able to detect more and more subtle uses of the Gift, and from farther away. It is a skill to cultivate, one you will find most valuable on the battlefield," the wrinkled archmage imparted as he turned to continue riding.

"Jayden! Archmage!" a familiar voice shouted at them from down in the trench.

* * *

Tolmarak turned at the shout, along with Jayden.

A soldier already filthy despite the early hour of the morning was making his way up the steep side of the trench to meet them.

"Wyll!" the young man beside him called back with a grin when he finally recognised the mud-covered figure coming towards them, "It's good to see you again."

"And you," Wyll returned as they clasped hands in greeting, "I must admit I was more than a little surprised when I looked up a moment ago and saw you both riding by."

"Hello Wyll," Tolmarak said to the young guardsman. "You're looking awfully dirty for this early hour of the morning."

"Ahh… yes Archmage. I managed to slip on the side of the trench on my way in this morning. No excuses, Sir."

Tolmarak couldn't help but laugh at the earnest response. Wyll was covered from head to toe in dark brown mud scattered with lumps of half dried clay, giving him a wild aspect that would have better suited a swamp troll than a soldier of the king's army.

"Hold still," Tolmarak told him with another short chuckle before using a flicker of the Gift to disperse the comical amount of mud and clay from the guardsman's form. After a moment the simple task was complete and Wyll once again stood before them, recognisable as the young man who had travelled with them from the Anchorhead Promontory.

"Time's up Wyll," a voice called down from inside the trench, and Tolmarak looked down at the source of the shout in surprise.

"Karthael, is that you down there?" he shouted to the Arborii ranger.

"Indeed it is Archmage," Karthael answered as he nimbly climbed out of the deep trench to join them.

"Karthael, my old friend, it's been too long," Tolmarak

greeted the Arborii as he reached the place where the group was standing.

"Fifteen years," Karthael returned as he inclined his head to the archmage.

"Tarrent told me he had placed this youngster under your instruction," Tolmarak remarked, "You seem to be keeping him busy."

"Yes Archmage, there is much to be done and little time to accomplish the tasks we've been set," Karthael said with an emphatic swish of his light grey tail.

Tolmarak looked over at Jayden and Wyll, who had continued their relaxed conversation while their superiors greeted one another, and Tolmarak abruptly realised that Jayden considered Wyll, at least, to be a friend. The boy had made a lot of progress in the last few weeks, rarely falling into his darkest moods anymore, although it was clear he was still uncomfortable with Clarion's appearance. Nevertheless, Jayden had shown considerable improvement in his state of mind since he'd had the Gift training to focus on, and Tolmarak would do all he could to aid that recovery.

"I need you to do me a favour," he said quietly as he took the veteran ranger aside.

Karthael nodded his agreement without hesitation and the archmage continued.

"Believe me when I say that no one is more aware of our current time constraints than I. Even so, I need you to give Wyll and his squad permission to leave the barracks at dusk on sixth day so my class and your squad can meet somewhere and spend some off duty time together."

"Is that truly necessary old friend?" Karthael protested. "You know how little time we've been given for the training of these men, and to complete the wall as well…"

"Believe me, I know," Tolmarak replied.

"Allow me to be forthright. Jayden has had many crimes committed against him by a member of the nobility, including the murder of a loved one. His training, not to mention his mental and emotional recovery from those events is currently at a crucial stage. When it comes right down to it, he is powerful enough, though he doesn't yet know the extent of it himself, that having his mind on the training and his loyalty firmly with the king and college is worth disrupting the routines of a hundred squads."

As Tolmarak spoke he watched the frown grow steadily deeper on Karthael's face, until when he was finished the Arborii ranger whispered pointedly, "Just how much of a threat does he pose?"

Tolmarak gave a quiet harrumph, "None. If we gain his loyalty. Let me say instead that even with my own extensive experience, I would be hard pressed to defeat him if it came to that, even with his current lack of knowledge. It is my hope that should it be required, he will be the one who will make a final stand against Heramiir, for none of our other brethren here in Aramar are potent enough by half. Not even myself," he finished in a whisper.

Tolmarak had known Karthael on and off for almost fifty years, and he knew the effect his admission would have on the stoic Arborii.

"I will do as you ask," Karthael agreed after a moment, "And please my old friend, send word if you require anything of either myself or my men. I have no love of war, but if it comes next spring as we all believe it will, I would rather be fighting by your side than with any other commander."

"We've worked together well in the past, don't be surprised if I take you up on that offer before too much longer," Tolmarak answered without hesitation.

Karthael nodded in acknowledgement, then turned to the others.

"Come on Wyll, you can catch up with your friends on sixth day at the Man at Arms," the instructor said brusquely.

"With your leave Archmage?"

Tolmarak nodded, and the two soldiers went back down into the trench to re-join the rest of their comrades while Jayden and Tolmarak rode over to where the other students were waiting a few paces away.

"I've organised some time off for you this coming sixth day," Tolmarak told his students once he and Jayden re-joined the others. "However, I want you to do something specific with it."

There were curious looks all around except from Jayden, who was showing a small, but rare smile.

"Let's get moving," Tolmarak said as he guided his grey warhorse, Wind, forward once again. "I want you all to go to a tavern called the Man at Arms and meet up with a squad of soldiers, one of whom Jayden and I are already acquainted with."

"To what end, Archmage?" Nadeara asked, her blue eyes curious.

Tolmarak studied the olive-skinned woman for a moment before deciding he didn't yet want to reveal his plans for the group, so he gave her an excuse.

"As you advance through your training, it will become necessary for you be familiar with at least a few members of the king's army. Besides, some new magi fall into the trap of thinking themselves better than the average citizen, who must use their hands and minds instead of the Gift. While it is true we have many advantages, we are still just men and woman, and loyal servants of the king, just as they are. To this end I want you to get to know some of the soldiers you will be fighting beside on the field of battle, as you all will if you progress far enough through the training. Without proper guidance it is far too easy for a commander to begin thinking of the goal of battle as victory and their men as the way to achieve it. I promise you, when that time comes, even a victory on the field will taste like ashes unless you can walk away honestly knowing as many of your troops survived as possible."

Having satisfied Nadeara's curiosity, Tolmarak looked around at the others and then set a good pace up the shallow incline. The road turned northwest as it left the city and past several miles of farmland until finally, hours later, he led them up a dirt track which led off to the west and away from the road and farms.

After another hour of riding, he guided them out of the thick trees which encompassed the path over the last few hundred spans and into a large clearing devoid of any form of vegetation. As he cast his gaze around the clearing to make sure it was empty, all he could see was devastation. Blackened rocks ground into not much more than pebbles littered the entire area, and what appeared to be small hills were actually just the parts of the range which hadn't been blown into deep crevices by destructive magics. The barren, pockmarked land was surrounded by a startling contrast of tall thick oaks and ash trees along with a layer of tangled, thorn riddled undergrowth which kept the range closed to all but the most intrusive trespassers.

All was as it should be.

Not that anyone in their right mind is likely to try trespassing on an area where they know we come to practice the elements of the Gift too dangerous to use on college grounds.

"Welcome to the range," he announced dramatically as he dismounted with a flourish.

The others followed his lead, and without asking questions led their horses over to a side of the clearing which Tolmarak indicated.

Just beyond the tree line was another small clearing, this one filled with verdant green grass and an idyllic bubbling spring. The five students followed him into the glade, and with puzzled looks at each other left the horses there unattended at his instruction before following the archmage back to the range.

"Shouldn't we tie them up or something?" Billy asked with a frown. He still wasn't comfortable with the large animal, and Tolmarak knew the small boy considered it to be an unpredictable beast at best.

"Unnecessary," he replied as he walked over to a thin tree stump with a large but unremarkable piece of quartz stone lodged at its peak. With a casual motion he waved his wrinkled hand above the quartz and placed his thumb and two fingers in shallow depressions on the stone.

Within moments a thick dome of grey fog had formed around the small clearing where the horses were standing, blocking them from view.

"There are many types of magic in this world," Tolmarak said to the surprise of his students.

"We magi primarily use the Gift, though there are other more... arcane arts out there."

He hesitated for a moment, deciding how much of the truth it would help to reveal to them right now.

"Within the boundaries of the Gift however there are two fundamental ways of utilising your natural power. First, direct spell casting, which involves the process we have been discussing for the last several weeks; imagination, focus and execution. The other method for utilising the Gift is through the creation and use of arcana such as this device," he told them, pointing to the now dimly glowing quartz crystal.

"These arcane devices are divided into two types. The first type, like this one, can be designed to cast a single specific spell, though they hold no power of their own. By constructing such devices, a less experienced mage can actuate a difficult spell on multiple occasions with much less effort or risk. They can achieve this by directing their own innate strength to trigger the device, usually through a simple spirit spell which I will show you as soon as you are capable of learning it. The second type however, are arcane items which hold power of their own, and can be used without accessing the Gift itself. Some of these are semi-permanent such as cold boxes or streetlights, which can run for several years or even decades before being recharged by a competent mage. There is also a sub-branch of these self-powered devices capable of casting a single powerful spell without accessing the Gift. They are rare however, and strictly controlled because anyone, even one of the Giftless, can activate these items should they come into possession of such an artefact. For that reason the head of the college, who of course is currently myself, must give written permission before each one can be produced, and we must account for them at all times."

He stopped then to take a breath before continuing.

"I'm sure you can all see the obvious problems if a child were to stumble across one of these artefacts, or a criminal for that matter."

He looked around at the students to make sure they were all paying attention, then continued.

"The spell this quartz device produces is complex, though not too difficult for any well trained mage. Since the range is used so frequently by less experienced magi however, we decided it would make matters easier just to install one at the site and be done with it. Its function," he said, motioning towards the concealing fog, "Is to create a screen around the clearing where the horses are kept. This barrier muffles both sight and sound as well as being a minor physical barrier so the spell casting of their magi will not upset the horses. Neither will it allow them to wander out onto the range where they might come to harm."

"Ahhh," said Billy, finally understanding why it hadn't been necessary to picket their mounts.

"Could we get through it?" Nadeara asked as she studied the ethereal barrier.

"With the Gift, easily, but the horses have no such magic," he replied with an amused grin.

"But enough theory for now, let's get down to what we came here for," he said, before walking out on to the scorched surface of the range with the others close behind.

Once they reached the centre of the clearing, Tolmarak turned and sat facing them on the coarse, pebbly ground and motioned the others to do the same. When they were all seated in a rough semi-circle before him, subconsciously choosing the same places they occupied in his classroom, Tolmarak decided it was time for a little test. With a thought he lit a small flame between himself and the students and kept it burning about a foot off the ground. Billy sat back quickly, startled as the flame leapt into being, while Nadeara nodded to herself at some private thought.

"Here is what I want you to do," he told them matter-of-factly, trying not to let them know this was anything out of the ordinary. He would be very surprised, and very pleased however, if even one of his students could accomplish the task he was about to set.

"This flame is being generated by the Gift rather than any physical fuel. Aside from that one detail however it is in every way a normal flame. Strong wind, earth or water will put it out and if I feed it with fuel, or more fire magic, it will burn hotter and eventually consume the tinder as any other flame would."

He looked around at their faces to make sure they were all paying attention before continuing.

"All I want you to do is affect the flame any way you can by using one of the four elemental magics we have discussed over the last few weeks," he told them. Then sat back to wait for the inevitable questions which were sure to follow.

For a moment there was silence as the students regarded both him and each other in consternation as they looked at the flame, until finally Nadeara muttered, "Imagination, focus, execution," and began staring intently into the flame. The others caught on after that and began applying their wills to the task.

Tolmarak knew if any of them began to succeed it would make it harder for those trying to use different or opposing elements, like two children pulling at an object from both ends. He was curious to find out if this idea would occur to any of them. He had high hopes Nadeara would be the one to figure it out. The olive-skinned trader from Avsan seemed to have a highly inquisitive mind, and Tolmarak knew well that students who desired knowledge for its own sake were usually the first to grasp any unfamiliar concept.

For almost half an hour there was virtual silence as the five of them tried manipulating the small flame without any visible result. Billy finally began fidgeting, frustrated by his lack of success at what he must have thought seemed such a simple task.

Tolmarak sighed. He shouldn't have expected so much. After all, manipulating a flame was a lot harder than simply bringing one to life in the first place, since it required not just the use of an element, but the translation from one element to another. Not to mention that the activation of any spell without the need of incantations or hand gestures, but with the will alone, was primarily in the skill realm of either thoroughly experienced magi, or sometimes even new archmagi themselves. Just one more thing he had been hoping to skip with this exceptionally powerful group of students.

He was about to stop the exercise when a fey chill rippled through the air, emanating not from Jayden as he had expected, but rather from the young noblewoman, Lady Firerose. Tolmarak's eyes widened as the flame turned clear and then melted away into the ground as it transformed into a bubbling liquid which was still hot to the touch as a drop splashed up and landed on his hand.

"Excellent, Clarion. Truly excellent," he exclaimed, "I was starting to wonder whether I had jumped too far ahead of you all with this exercise, but now I can see my confidence was well placed."

Firerose couldn't help but smile a little at his enthusiasm, and Jayden even managed a join in as the other students congratulated her on being the first to complete the task and use the Gift in an intentional, if not entirely controlled manner.

"All right," Tolmarak interrupted after a moment, "Now that we all know you're up to the task, let's try again shall we?"

Nadeara nodded a moment ahead of Jayden, and even Missy and Billy both seemed willing to put aside their weariness to have another go, now that they'd seen one of their classmates succeed.

A moment later a second tongue of flame was dancing before the students and Tolmarak told them to begin.

"Not you Clarion," he said as she went to join the others.

"You seem to have quite a strength in water, next time I want you to try augmenting the flame with even more fire," he told her quietly so as not to break the other students' concentration. "But for now, rest. The weariness will take you in a moment."

Firerose agreed without complaint, already beginning to feel the effects of using an element of the Gift for the first time. It was nothing compared to the sickness which accompanied the awakening of any new mage. Still, it was less than pleasant, and Firerose quietly moved off a few feet to rest while the others continued working on the flame. For long moments, silence once again reigned until Nadeara looked up at Tolmarak with a puzzled expression.

"It feels different this time," she said, "More malleable, though I still can't transform it."

Tolmarak motioned at her to go on, and after another

moment of concentration she looked over to where Lady Firerose was attempting to stay awake as she watched her classmates proceed.

"Who is using which elements?" Nadeara interrupted, shaking the others from their focus, and prompting a small but pleased smile from Tolmarak.

"Water," Jayden responded, "Why do you ask?"

Nadeara looked at the two youngsters. Billy answered wind while Missy said she was trying earth.

"Were you all using the same elements before?" she asked with a thoughtful frown.

It was right on the edge of her mind now Tolmarak knew, hoping Nadeara would make the final connection on her own.

The others confirmed they had been using the same elements as before and Nadeara smiled as she understood.

"Two using water," she muttered with a frown, "And one each in earth, wind and fire," which she herself had been trying. "Only now Firerose is gone and Jayden is the only one using water."

"That's it! We're working against each other," she announced, forcing the others to sit up and pay attention.

"Why?" Tolmarak asked, though from his expression Nadeara would know she was on the right track.

After a long moment of thought she spoke, even while still studying the flame.

"I think our wills are counteracting each other. I'm using flame to try to burn the flame hotter, Jayden is trying to douse the same flame. Billy and Missy are both fuelling and attempting to disperse the flame with earth and air. It's like what you were saying the other day about counter spells working better if you knew how to use the opposite of whatever the target spell is composed of to attack its magical fabric."

She looked up at him to see his reaction to her theory, and he gave her a pleased nod.

"Correct, you have a quick mind Nadeara. So what then should you do to increase your chances of success?" he put to the group as a whole.

"Use the same element?" Billy asked.

"Close," Tolmarak returned warmly, "but not quite."

"Of course!" Nadeara shouted, before blushing slightly at her outburst.

"You were saying?" Tolmarak prodded after a moment's silence. She was close to the truth now, he was sure of it, and he didn't want her to stop the train of thought until she had realised the last step of the puzzle.

"Not the same element, but the same intent," she said quietly as the light of understanding sparked in her excited blue eyes.

"Does that mean then we can join our wills to focus the casting of a spell, or increase its power?"

"Yes and no," Tolmarak answered.

"The mental picture required to not only see reality but alter it in a certain way will never be identical in two unique minds. If I were to say to you 'put this fire out', would you conjure in your mind it simply disappearing, or would you douse it with water, or earth, and from where would that come? Or would you have the wind disperse it? And how strong a gust would that take? And from which direction? No, to affect a stable object or spell such as the flame, two or more magi can only manipulate it loosely in the same way to bring about a certain effect either more powerfully or more quickly. What if I commanded, 'douse this flame'? You might all use water at once, adding to each other's spells to successfully put it out without counteracting each other. In no way does that mean your spells were joined though, as your imagination is still not in alignment. For instance, how cold would the water be? How much would be needed? What would its source be? You would still be casting your own spells, but they would have a cumulative effect if rendered correctly with similar enough intent, putting out the fire faster. This is a vital skill as two or more magi can sometimes create effects above their own level of power if aligned closely enough in intent. Conversely, when you are talking about casting a spell initially, then the answer is almost always no. This is due to the split second timing and identical imagining of the situation which would be required to join the spells, rather than just casting two of the same, instants or millimetres apart, or with slightly different results."

"If we could link our minds or powers somehow, we could do it," Nadeara proclaimed. "I know you told us the first day that would be impossible, that a mind can be used to access, but can't be accessed itself," she paused for a moment.

"What makes you think it's not just a skill the college hasn't learned to master yet?" the olive-skinned islander asked thoughtfully.

For a moment Tolmarak just stared at the young woman in front of him, then laughed.

"The College of the Arts has existed since before the cataclysm brought our people to these shores three thousand years ago. But if you think we've missed something then you are welcome to try to get the king to give you permission to research it," he told her with a chuckle.

Nadeara nodded, taking the suggestion seriously.

"Very well," he said when there were no further questions, "Once again."

"Try using flame," Jayden added for the rest of the group's benefit.

Nadeara shrugged and the two youngsters nodded their heads in agreement.

For long moments nothing happened as the students concentrated, then Tolmarak felt something akin to a faint breeze on his face, though the surrounding air was still. The tell-tale waves of the Gift in use washed over him, although the flame still hadn't been affected.

An instant later the breeze became a full-blown gale and Tolmarak instinctively threw a Gift-wrought shield around the flame as it blossomed into a fiery ball which pulsed against the edges of the hastily erected barricade. Missy jumped in fright and both Billy and Nadeara threw up their hands to cover their faces as the heat blistered them and they scrambled away from the small inferno trapped inside its shining blue prison. Jayden alone remained where he sat, calmly in his place and staring at the flames as though in some form of trance. Tolmarak threw up a second layer of shielding to protect Jayden from the conflagration he had called up, which was still raging inside its small prison.

"So that is how it is done," Jayden said matter-of-factly, and with a casual wave of his hand both flame and shields vanished without a trace.

The others watched Jayden in wary silence as he lay slowly back on the blackened stones of the range, exhausted from touching the final element of the Gift.

Tolmarak released a breath he hadn't quite realised he'd

been holding, and painfully wiped the sweat off his scorched brow as he regarded the boy from Grandell with a mixture of awe and fear, trying hard to let none of it show on his face. The barrier he had hastily thrown up to keep them safe from the searing heat had barely held out against Jayden's mystical flame. With an inward shudder Tolmarak realised that Jayden had scarcely exerted himself as he broke through whatever mental barrier had stopped him from making use of fire magic before now.

"All right, that's enough for today," Tolmarak said, trying not to let his voice shake as he got up and helped Jayden to his feet. Firerose had definitely not used a water spell before either he thought, since she looked every bit as exhausted as Jayden now did.

Under normal circumstances, the amount of mental vigour expended during the kinds of spell they were just using was only very small. However, breaking into a new area of the Gift always drained the new mage to a dangerous level of fatigue, and the two students who had succeeded were now feeling the full effects of mental muscles not only used, but over-exerted for the very first time.

He would heal them all before re-entering Aramar, but for now the burns they had all taken were little worse than a bad day in the sun, and would serve as the day's final sobering lesson. They drifted back over to the second clearing in silence, small stones crunching under their feet. Tolmarak released the spell which penned in the horses and each of them remained lost in their own thoughts as they waited for the fog to dissipate. He gave the order to mount up as soon as the spell cleared. After securing Jayden and Firerose to their saddles with a minor spell of air, the small group made their arduous way back into the city, tired but hopefully with a new-found caution towards the Gift. He would have liked to keep the exercise going while they had the momentum, but blocking Jayden's spell had rattled his focus more than he wanted to admit. If another accident occurred, he wasn't confident of being able to contain whatever might happen in time.

With his students' safety in mind, he led them back along the track towards the road leading to Aramar. As they rode, he spent his time deliberating what to do when the time came, somewhere in the very near future, when his power was no longer sufficient to control his most gifted, and troubled young student.

'Let the drums announce our presence, let them be a revelation to our enemies that our new realm stands united, and that we fear them not!'

Surviving excerpt from a speech by Howeth DiBear, leader of the Teraliv forces prior to the first Jeranonian offensive of the Wars of Founding.

CHAPTER 15

THE MAN AT ARMS

"This must be the place," Billy announced as they arrived at a rickety building in one of the furthest outlying streets of Aramar's western quarter.

Jayden looked up and saw the ill-maintained tavern boasted a decrepit, faded sign depicting a well-muscled arm holding a sword over a worn green background. It seemed to be the mark they'd been told to watch for, and the five of them stopped in front of the closed doors.

The sign hung at a strange angle to the tavern, making an eerie creaking noise as it swung on one rusted chain. Dawn of autumn was fading, and high autumn would soon bring its tempestuous winds and falling leaves, but for now only a strong breeze stirred, causing the sign to occasionally clank as it collided with the tavern's wooden exterior. From the looks of the paint scraped from the wall beside it, the sign had been broken for some time.

An hour had passed since sunset, and on either side of the tavern's entry stood a flaming torch held securely in the grasp of a heavy iron bracket. Instead of purveying warmth and welcome however, the flickering light contrived with the creaking of the sign to give the Man at Arms a sinister aspect, more so than was probably warranted by the well-known watering hole.

Nadeara gave an encouraging nod at Billy's youthful enthusiasm, and after a doubtful look at the state of the building, pushed open the solid wooden door.

As the door swung back, it released a thick waft of smoke issuing from a partially blocked chimney above the bluestone hearth, and they were immediately assaulted by the raucous sound of musicians plying their trade in a far corner of the room. With a dubious glance back at the others Nadeara stepped inside, followed closely by Billy and then Missy, who both looked excited at the prospect of going into the smoky tavern.

Jayden hesitated outside the door, alone with Firerose, and couldn't help uttering an anxious sigh.

"Are you sure you're ready for this?" the slender girl asked gently.

Jayden looked at her for a moment before replying, still not entirely sure how to relate to the young noblewoman. He'd made an effort to begin conversing with her this last week. The results had been mixed. Things between them were anything but relaxed, but at least he could look at her now without her striking resemblance to Rhianna causing the vivid flashbacks it had those first few days in Tolmarak's classroom.

"I think so," he answered, as he forced himself to look at her face while he spoke.

"Come on then," she said, nodding toward the door with a reassuring smile.

Jayden tried to return that smile, even managing a small amount of success. It was still all he could muster while looking into his murdered love's mirrored features. As soon as she looked away he let it drop, then followed the young noble, ex-noble, he had to keep reminding himself, inside the crowded tavern.

His first impression of The Man at Arms was one of clutter. On a low set stage in a far corner of the room, the musicians played a boisterous tune which had more than a few of the tavern's many customers tapping their feet. Tired serving girls threaded their way between tables to deliver the Man at Arms' wares. The furniture, along with the building itself, was all fashioned from the same dark wood which had been polished some unknown length of time ago. Far from refined though, it had uniformly lost its sheen from the constant use and exposure to the acrid smoke hanging throughout the room like a grey mist as it eddied around both patrons and staff alike.

"Over here!" a familiar voice called above the noise of the music and nearby conversations.

Jayden looked across the room, trying to identify where the call had come from, and soon spotted Wyll standing at an oversized round table. It was occupied by several other men in the green and brown uniforms of the king's army, some of whom were also motioning them over.

After a moment's hesitation, Jayden wended his way through the crowded tavern, eventually arriving at the large table where Wyll and his companions were already seated. The Man at Arms was known to be a nexus for off-duty soldiers on liberty, and avoided by most of the local civilians. The residents around these parts knew there were other watering holes close by where they were not as likely to be caught up in the middle of a soldiers' brawl.

As a result, the vast majority of the tavern's customers were men, and both Nadeara and Lady Firerose found themselves receiving an undue amount of attention as they threaded their way through the crowd. The black, white-lined cloaks each woman wore assured that none of the tavern's patrons got too out of line as they crossed between the narrowly spaced tables. Most of the soldiers seemed content to watch as the two women passed, although there was a loud whistle from one of the more unruly customers, which the women blatantly ignored.

When they eventually managed to make their way across the crowded room, Jayden smiled and nodded a greeting to Wyll. The guardsman proffered the seat next to him which he had kept vacant, while the others spaced themselves out among the soldiers wherever there was room.

*   *   *

Wyll was suddenly speechless as he looked across the table. For just a moment, in the dim light, he'd been sure Rhianna was sitting down with them. But no, although this woman looked similar enough to be her twin, there were subtle differences not only in her appearance, but also the way she held herself. Probably court bred, he assumed, and then abruptly wondered how Jayden could stand to be so near her.

Glancing over to his friend they shared an unintended look, and Wyll saw the mage's thoughts were running along the same line as his own. He decided not to bring up the topic unless Jayden did so first.

They made a strange collection Wyll thought, especially the two youngsters, both of whom looked happy to be there, but out of place among the table full of grown-ups.

"It's good to see you again Jayden," Wyll said, trying to smooth over the awkward moment as the five magi found their places, "It would appear the mage's life agrees with you for you to smile so readily."

"As does your new station Wyll," Jayden returned, "You look as fit as an ox. They must work you hard at the training camp."

"It's true it's tiring," Wyll answered with a sardonic grin, "But I think I've learned more in the last phase than I did in the whole time I was in the guard back home."

He hesitated for a moment, unsure whether he had said too much, but Jayden's only response was to take a deep breath and then slowly nod.

"Anyway, I suppose some introductions are in order," Wyll said to break the uncomfortable moment of silence before it could really take hold.

"For those of you who don't already know, I'm Wyll," he said to the other magi.

"The short fellow to my right here is Bosric."

The shortest of the guardsmen stood, surprising them all by executing a perfect courtly bow to both Firerose and Nadeara before regaining his seat.

"They're called manners," he said jovially to the dark-skinned Marad, who was staring at the red-headed knife man with an incredulous look on his face.

Next in line were the brothers, Sarran and Charran, who introduced themselves while they kept an interested eye on a minor altercation a couple of tables across from their own. Somehow a spirited wrestling match between two heavyset soldiers had begun, both combatants looking as if they knew what they were about. After a moment, the smaller of the combatants changed his grip and his opponent seized the advantage, twisting slightly and sending the smaller man crashing into the neighbouring table. If it had been occupied Wyll thought a full-scale brawl might have erupted right then and there, but as luck would have it, its occupants had left shortly after the match began. The winner helped his opponent up from the floor, and both men stretched their arms and backs. The loser shook his head in disgust before handing over a silver coin, both of them returning to their places at the table where the rest of their squad had been cheering them on.

Sarran and his brother exchanged a glance, and the younger brother excused himself, leaving the table as the introductions continued. Sarran handed him a silver coin as he left, and Charran nodded in silent agreement before threading his way across to the other table.

The introductions went on for another minute or so, although neither Seth, Nadeara nor Marad seemed interested in sharing much more than their name with what each of them saw as the newcomers.

Marad, the dark-skinned giant of a man, had been a little quieter than usual over the last few days since he had made his intention to try for command of the squad known to the rest of them. Until then Wyll hadn't given the issue much thought, assuming Karthael would take command once their training was complete. However, he'd asked the instructor about the situation the following morning, and Karthael had bluntly responded that he had other assignments to complete.

That probably meant the position was up for grabs, if

one of them showed the required skills to impress the instructor.

Wyll wasn't really sure which of his squad mate's he wanted for the role. It was likely to be Brendan or Marad he supposed. Cale seemed to have a sharp wit and was very close to the best swordsman in the group, but his lack of speech would likely rule him out of contention, as would Bosric's unpredictable personality and the brothers' simple nature. Neither Tauman nor Kienan boasted the necessary experience or skill for the job, and that only left Seth or himself. Wyll counted himself out of the running as he had no desire to even apply for the position. He knew there were others in the squad more capable of leading men into battle than himself, and truthfully, he didn't want the responsibility of ordering men onto the field when it likely meant some of them wouldn't return.

Seth, on the other hand, was an entirely different kettle of fish. Wyll had sparred with him only twice during the time they had been training together, and the strange man with the raven black topknot of hair had comprehensively thrashed him on both occasions. Wyll knew himself to be no seasoned veteran, but he had always been counted as being ahead of his peers in learning the blade. The ease with which Seth had disarmed him within moments of starting the drill, not once, but on both occasions, left Wyll wondering just where exactly his opponent had learned his skills.

The most frustrating thing about it was that Wyll knew a standard sword wasn't even Seth's first choice of weapon.

After seeing his skill with the blade, Karthael had told Seth to fetch whatever gear he chose from the smithy so the instructor could drill with him personally. Instead, the top-knotted warrior's response had been to re-enter the barracks and emerge with a pair of three-foot-long curved scimitars. They were strange blades, serrated on both sides and enamelled with black resin that shone a deep red as the sun reflected off them. Just above the hilt on either side of each sword sat a small device which looked like a pipe attached to a miniature crossbow string. A strange device since a bow of that size would have trouble sending a bolt much past the end of the blade.

Karthael had seemed offended when Seth appeared with the weapons, and Wyll had caught the Arborii giving him sideways glances ever since. The instructor had never really trusted the man who exuded such an aura of menace, even though Seth had done nothing to reinforce the nagging sensation the others felt when in his presence. After that day though, he had also treated Seth with respect.

"It's starting," Bosric said, nudging Wyll's arm to get his attention.

Wyll gave him a confused look and shrug.

The short man gestured across the room with his head and grinned his ever-present grin.

"Should be interesting," he said as Wyll and the rest of them turned to watch.

While the others were introducing themselves, Charran had made his way over to where the other men had been wrestling a minute before and convinced the larger of the two previous combatants, the winner, to agree to a match. A match probably based on the coin which Sarran had given him as he left.

For Sarran to offer the stake so willingly, he must have great confidence in his younger brother's ability, and Wyll paid more attention to the two men who were now facing off and ready to begin.

One of the soldiers at the other table called the start of the match, and for a moment Charran and his opponent continued to stand where they were, both men motionless, though ready to spring as they took each other's measure.

The pair were of a height, as well as similar builds, and Wyll found himself unsure who would be able to gain the advantage. It would either come down to speed or technique Wyll decided as the soldier from the other squad made a lunge and then stepped back out of reach before Charran could take a proper hold.

A short serving girl with shoulder-length blonde hair and big green eyes finally visited their table and ales were ordered all around, except for Billy and Missy, whom Nadeara told the serving girl to ignore on account of their age. Instead she changed their orders to unfermented apple cider and stared them both down when they protested. Firerose also abstained after a glance at another table's fare and decided against ingesting anything either stored or prepared from the Man at Arms' kitchens.

Once she had the orders, the girl disappeared from the common room and reappeared only a minute later with a large tray filled with mugs, prompting more than one favourable comment about the service. She moved off to her next task, and they busied themselves with their drinks.

After a moment Wyll noticed from the corner of his eye that Bosric had made no move to claim his ale, and a glance at his squad mate showed that his instincts were correct. With the slightest of grins, he saw Bosric staring speculatively in the direction the serving girl was heading, but for once he wasn't grinning and a tiny frown of concentration was etched on his forehead. Wyll turned to face the usually cheerful man and ask him if anything was amiss, but even as he did so Bosric's usual grin suddenly returned in full force. Wyll's eyes couldn't help but follow his gaze, just in time to catch the last instant of a shy smile thrown back over the pale girl's shoulder as she rushed off to disappear from the smoky room on her next errand.

A loud cheer went up from the patrons across the room as the musicians finished up a lively tune, and the singer called loudly for the crowd's forbearance while they took a quick break, and a cold drink to go with it. A moment later Kienan got up from the table and excused himself before venturing off across the room, giving Charran and his wrestling opponent a wide berth as he passed by the still struggling pair.

"So why are we here?" Marad asked in his usual blunt manner as he looked around the table at the gathered soldiers and magi.

There were blank looks all around and Wyll tried to motion the sizeable man to stop the line of conversation, but Marad either didn't see or was disinclined to cooperate with Wyll's subtle gesturing.

"I mean, we all know it's so you two can catch up," the giant of a man continued in his booming voice. "But surely the instructor and an archmage, the king's advisor no less if what I hear is true, wouldn't interrupt our duties just for that?" he concluded dramatically, as if it were a thought none of them might ever have had if it weren't for his own deep voicing of it.

"So, any ideas?" Marad asked as he leaned his dark-skinned arms on the stained wooden table, which was only just lighter than his flesh.

There were thoughtful looks from some of the soldiers and magi. Billy and Sarran both seemed much more interested in the ongoing wrestling match a few tables over though as the two men each continued trying for enough leverage for a throw.

After a minute of virtual silence Cale slid his writing pad into the middle of the table for all of them to inspect. On it only a single word was written, one which Wyll had not considered. In his own mind, meeting his friend was enough justification for coming here today. Though now that he thought about it, for once Marad actually did have a valid point.

Some of the others nodded as they saw the writing on the pad, and both Nadeara and Seth voiced their agreement of the idea.

'Mageguard.'

Wyll had heard the word bandied about in the camp several times since he'd arrived in Aramar. From his time spent on the road with Captain Ravenburg, he knew the elite group known as the mageguard were soldiers handpicked by the various magi and entrusted with their physical safety when the spellcasters were out in the field. Reputedly, these men answered only to their mage and the college as a whole. He knew that Captain Ravenburg was their leader here in Aramar, but the captain had not been very forthcoming when Wyll questioned him about the subject shortly into their journey. Most of what he knew for sure came purely from his own observations of the small group escorting Archmage Tolmarak during their long march here.

As a soldier there were much greater rewards to be found as a member of the mageguard as opposed to a rank-and-file trooper, both in pay and adventure. By the same token, the hazards of the post were said to be both numerous and unforgiving.

The more he thought about it, the more Cale's suggestion made sense though. After all, how could you hand pick people you hadn't met? Although from his admittedly limited understanding of such matters, no one in this group of magi should be needing a retinue for the next several years at least.

Then a thought struck him.

Their training regime must be as rushed as ours is.

Probably more so, he realised a moment later, since the mage's arts took far longer to master than simple swordplay. Although like swordplay, he supposed you could master the basics quickly while the art and finesse of it was what took up the years which followed.

There was a loud grunt from across the way and Wyll looked over just in time to see Charran go down on one knee, hoisting his opponent off balance as the other soldier moved in to press his apparent advantage. With a hoarse cry the soldier realised his mistake as Charran made his move, using the soldier's momentum to stand and pitch him over forward, leaving his opponent lying stunned, several feet from where he'd been a moment before.

"Yeah! That's got 'im!" Sarran cheered, thumping the table with his fist and drawing the rest of the group's attention to the end of the match.

Charran straightened and rolled his shoulders stiffly, but gave his squad a wave and a grin as he helped the other man to his feet. There was a general grumbling at the other table as the two combatants returned. Even so, the soldiers of the losing man's squad handed over several coppers each to Charran, along with the two silver pieces his opponent had staked for the match.

With some final words Wyll couldn't make out, Charran returned to their own table and resumed his seat, spreading his winnings out on the table for all of them to see. With a grin he handed back the silver his brother had staked on the fight as well as several coppers as if on a whim. He then called the same girl over who served them before to order another round of drinks for those who were interested.

"And a round of ales for my friends at the table over there," he motioned with a smile.

The serving girl seemed surprised by Charran's sudden largesse, but shrugged as he handed over most of the remaining coppers from his winnings.

"Is that enough?" he asked, a simple question.

"More than enough Sir," the girl replied, shooting a quick glance in Bosric's direction before casting her eyes back to Charran. She blushed slightly as she saw the red-haired man already watching her with an approving smile, which Wyll was only just able to see in the dim, smoky light.

"Well, good. Keep the rest for yourself then," Charran said with a wink, completely missing the exchange.

"Thank you, Sir," she replied, blinking in surprise before she left for the kitchen, ignoring the shouts for service from several other tables.

Charran must have known the tip was overly generous, but the ale was cold and the service was good. Besides, he was clearly in a fine mood from besting the bigger soldier, the more so since he had won the equivalent of nearly two-and-a-half silvers from the men at the other table.

Soon enough the pale serving girl returned with a large tray and distributed their drinks among the soldiers and magi before brushing past Bosric's chair on her way to the other table. The red-headed soldier's grin became slightly wider as he merrily watched her go, knowing full well there was plenty of room between his chair and the one behind.

The soldiers at the other table looked surprised when she reached them with the ales Charran had ordered. Then even more so as the girl pointed to Charran, who raised his mug in salute to his opponent, who reciprocated with a nod before returning his attention back to his own table and friends.

"I think we must at least be being considered as mageguard candidates," Brendan said in his usual thoughtful manner. "And after eight years already as heavy cavalry in Silvertown, I for one would welcome the chance to be part of something other than another heavy cavalry unit."

It was no secret that Brendan looked to be a frontrunner for command of the squad, and if Seth was better than him with a blade, Brendan was a gifted tactician and a natural leader. Marad still thought of himself as the obvious choice for command though, and it was beginning to create a rift between the two men. So it was no real surprise to anyone except the magi when he snorted his contempt at his squad mate's words and refused to meet the level stare he gained in response.

Off in the hazy corner of the room opposite their own, the musicians had taken the stage once again and a slow but steady drumbeat began sounding throughout the room. Before long, the unaccompanied percussionist shifted the rhythm several times into a far more complex beating which somehow still retained the original flow, whilst being a totally different cadence.

Although he couldn't be sure through the smoke, Wyll thought this man was a different one to the musician who was playing before the break, and he wondered what had become of the original drummer.

The buzz of conversation in the room decreased notably as this new song, so unlike the ones the group had been playing before picked up its pace, until just at the right moment, when it seemed the drums could beat no faster, a large deep-toned string instrument Wyll didn't know the name of joined in. It added its low resonant notes to the tune as its master slid some device across the long strings with precision in counterpoint to the frantic beating of the unknown drummer.

Although there were no words to this nameless tune, just about every patron of the Man at Arms was listening intently now to the almost primitive overtones of the drums. The player of the deep-toned instrument nodded at one of his compatriots who was holding a fiddle, waiting for the appropriate time to join in the pulse quickening tune. As one, they launched into a furiously fast counterpoint melody which only sought to compliment the frenzied pounding of the drums, rather than override or make the percussion secondary to their own efforts.

By now most of the soldiers scattered throughout the room were tapping their feet and nodding their heads in time to the song, and even several of the serving girls stopped working briefly to behold the spectacle. For another minute or two the song endured, incredibly picking up speed again and again until the unknown drummer's hands were moving far faster than even Wyll's attentive eyes could keep up with across the hazy room.

The song wound itself up into a crescendo of noise and speed as the room watched in awe and then abruptly, at some invisible signal between the musicians, it stopped.

So sudden was the end of the tune that for a moment there was complete silence throughout the Man at Arms, as if every man and woman in the tavern were holding their breath.

A soldier at the closest table to the band roared his approval at the unusually rousing piece.

The sudden noise seemed to break some sort of trance, and the tavern filled with the shouts of patrons and staff alike crying their approval and calling out for more. The new drummer tried to beg off, but the crowd was having none of it. After a minute or more of unrelenting cheering the musician reluctantly agreed to play 'one more tune', though it was spectacularly obvious even from Wyll's far corner of the room that he greatly enjoyed the crowd's attentions.

This time however, the unknown musician didn't return to the drums, but begged the use of the other man's fiddle, which was handed over with only a moment's hesitation. The fiddler then swapped places with the original drummer, taking his now empty chair as he returned to his instruments. A moment later a lively tune was struck up which once again had the patrons of the Man at Arms tapping their feet and grinning to themselves in amazement over the mysterious fiddler's skill.

"Your friend has quite a talent," A shy voice said from

behind him as the serving girl returned to collect up their empty mugs, though he thought the comment was more addressed to Bosric than himself.

"My friend?" Bosric asked, unsure who the girl was referring to.

She blinked at him and studied his face for a moment as if to be sure he wasn't making sport of her.

"The musician, the one who was sitting at this table just before," she prompted with the beginnings of a smile.

"You didn't know it was him, did you?" the girl asked, genuine amusement creeping into her voice. But Bosric, along with the rest of their table had already turned to peer into the dim smokiness of the far corner to see if it was true.

"I don't believe it," Wyll breathed in amazement, "That's Kienan playing like that?"

"Is that his name?" the girl asked, "The one who was sitting there?" she motioned at the only empty seat at the table.

"Yep, that's him," Bosric replied in awe, "I had no idea he could play like that," and after a quick glance around the table, "I don't think any of us did."

From the expressions of amazement on his squad mate's faces Wyll knew it was true. The man had brought no instrument to the camp in his belongings, nor tried to seek one out since his arrival that Wyll had heard of. To say he'd caught them all off guard would be an understatement of epic proportions.

"My name's Bosric," the man beside him eventually said to the blonde girl who was still standing at his shoulder, absently staring at the corner where the band continued to play their almost recklessly cheerful song.

"Linda," she said with a smile which lit up her huge green eyes.

An impatient shout from across the room echoed the word.

"Linda! Back to work girl, I pay you to serve the customers, not to socialise with them!"

Linda quickly moved off with an apologetic glance and Bosric turned to see the shout had come from a portly, middle aged woman who nearly filled the kitchen door with her bulk as well as her presence. She stood for a moment, a wooden cook's spoon gripped firmly while scowling at him, hands placed on ample hips in the age-old matriarchal sign of disapproval.

Bosric couldn't resist the temptation to grin at the woman and wave, which brought a cocking of the matron's head and a huff before she whirled and stalked back into the kitchen.

Wyll couldn't help but chuckle at the scene as the musicians finished up their tune and Kienan handed the fiddle back with a respectful bow to its owner. He then made another to the crowd who were still quite audibly showing their appreciation.

Finally Kienan was able to make his way back to the table and took his seat as if he had just gone for a short walk to get some air. The only thing that ruined the image was that as soon as he saw the perspiring mug of ale still sitting untouched at his place, he took it and drained it all in one long pull.

"Of all the musicians who came to my father's estate over the years, I don't think I have ever heard anything quite like that before," Lady Firerose suddenly declared with a smile.

"Thank you, milady," Kienan replied as he placed the empty mug back on the table.

"The first piece comes from far to the south on the distant island of Avsan which I visited several years ago."

At that piece of information Nadeara gave him a look which no one else but Wyll seemed to notice.

"And you played it well," she admitted thoughtfully.

"And from where did the second song originate, master musician?" Clarion inquired.

Jayden couldn't help but stare at the young noblewoman for a moment. He knew she had been of the nobility, but she hadn't reverted to this formal style of speech whilst inside the college walls since their very first meeting. Until now he had not thought her the kind to change her manner so completely dependent upon whom she were relating to. Maybe the entitled attitude of the nobility was more entrenched in her than he'd suspected. Then again, perhaps he was only now seeing for the first time how she really was, instead of always comparing her to Rhianna, whom she so much resembled in form.

"Ah… the second piece was something I just made up," Kienan answered a little nervously.

"You mean you wrote that?" Firerose asked, clearly impressed.

"Well, not exactly milady. I just sort of, made it up as I went," he said with a self-depreciating grin.

There was a sort of hushed awe from them all at the statement. Most musicians wouldn't have been able to play the songs Kienan had just performed even with copious amounts of practice. That he was capable of improvising something like that was truly impressive.

"If we're going to be here for a while, I'd better get that

staff before the smithy closes," Charran announced as he stood and left the table, giving Kienan a companionable nod as he did so.

The man had practically been drooling over the new staff that had been displayed in a blacksmith's shop window on the way in here. His old staff was still sturdy as far as Wyll knew, but the one Charran had seen was bound up in iron for most of its six-foot length. In addition, it sported a clever but sturdy catch system which allowed a custom-made foot-and-a-half blade to be attached at either end. Wyll agreed with him that the design would have many advantages over a normal staff, and while it would be heavier, he thought the technique of the weapon would differ only a little from Charran's old weapon of choice. In truth, he was only surprised the staffman had waited this long after winning himself enough silver to cover the cost.

"Do you ever sing to accompany your playing, Kienan?" Firerose asked after Charran's departure.

"No milady," he answered with a grin. "I'm afraid that while I've never met an instrument I couldn't play well, I am doomed forever to sing like a half-squashed frog."

Clarion smiled in genuine amusement and Bosric snorted a short bark of laughter, making Missy laugh in turn.

Across the room the original musicians launched into another lively tune, and whilst it lacked the wild edge Kienan's playing had brought to the tavern, the crowd seemed to approve nonetheless.

Conversation around the table turned to the more mundane aspects of the everyday life of the conscripted. Most of the soldiers found the mage's stories fascinating, but Billy couldn't get enough of the squad's' recounting of the sword drills and horse charges they were constantly being put through in the mad rush to be prepared by next spring.

Eventually Charran returned with his new weapon, which he leant against the table next to his chair, unwilling even to take his eyes off it long enough to rest it against the wall behind him as he re-joined the group. More drinks were ordered and the soldiers and magi talked long into the night about the coming war, although other, less pressing matters were often diverted toward when they came up in conversation.

To Wyll's surprise and relief, even the usually quiet Jayden began to take part in the discussion later on in the evening. For these few hours at least, it appeared the young mage would find his way back from the brink of despair after all.

But eventually, when nearly all the other customers had left and the musicians had long since packed up and gone home, it was time to head back to the college and camp five accordingly. There were parting farewells all around as the groups took their leave of each other and left the smoky tavern.

Bosric looked around one last time to see if Linda were still there, but the girl had disappeared without a trace soon after the cook had reprimanded her earlier in the evening. With a sigh and a shrug, he followed the others out into the cold, windy street and headed around the back of the tavern. A stable boy was sleepily waiting for the last few mounts to be taken off his hands for the night and Wyll flipped him a copper in thanks.

The squad quickly saddled their horses and mounted up, and had soon left the stable on their way down the starlit road which led back toward the Emerald Sea, and eventually, their bunks.

They would all regret losing sleep tomorrow, but to a man they had relished this free time and were in high spirits as they cantered past the outlying districts of the capital.

To Wyll the night had been doubly beneficial. Not only had the first few free hours they'd received in weeks seemed a blessing from the Maker himself, but his thoughts were now a lot more at ease over his friend's state of mind.

He had thought his companion on the trip from Grandell was slipping further and further into darkness and despair, but clearly college life was doing Jayden a world of good. With that in mind he nudged Socks to a swift gallop for no other reason than to feel the wind in his hair. He grinned at the simplicity of the feeling, and wondered abruptly if the changes he acknowledged within himself since coming to Aramar were as drastic or apparent to his squad mates as the ones he could now see in Jayden.

When between a rock and a hard place, one must either become infinitely malleable, or infinitely harder. To remain in one's present state is to be crushed.
Teraliv Proverb.

CHAPTER 16

THE VILLAGE OF NESTARN

"Let's get this over with," Hassan told Jarl as they surveyed the farming village of Nestarn from a nearby hill.

It was just before dawn, but the lights shining from the predominantly single-storey village windows marked their sprawling target in the foggy high autumn morning.

In the weeks since he'd been plotting with Sir Luke from Seal Cove, his men had moved northwest and taken Railain without needing to resort to violence. As it turned out, the smallest of the three villages Nereth had ordered him to convert had been only too happy to shift their allegiance. In large part they chose to do so due to the fact that Railain was close enough to Miralthrall that an expedition of magi had traditionally been sent to the village at the changing of each season. These magi would see to the health of the people, taking care of those sicknesses which only a mage could cure, not to mention helping with their crops and whatever other needs the inhabitants might have. Keeping those boons intact had been far more important to the villagers than having the protection of the king's peace.

He supposed he couldn't blame them; war hadn't touched this part of the country in over a century. All the farmers of Railain would be used to seeing from the nobility was a tax collector, and the odd troop of bored and restless soldiers travelling between Miralthrall and the garrisons in the south.

After leaving the tiny village behind they had travelled north, back across the Mirallyn River and all the way to the coast where the border of Elota and Vaross Duchies met.

Nestarn was a different story altogether.

The largest of the three targets on his list, it would more properly be called a small town than anything else. If it came to a fight, the village might be capable of rallying just enough men to cause his troops problems. Not enough to defeat the seasoned veterans, but more than enough to make subduing the town violent, and probably bloody work.

He had sent his men to gather up the peasants in the outlying districts as he had in the other two villages, with instructions to the unit commanders to meet in the town square at dawn. In the distance, he could now see them approaching to the east and south.

With perhaps half an hour left until they reached the deadline, Hassan ordered his own column down into the village of oddly shaped houses. The majority of the dwellings were triangular structures sporting a sharply sloped wall running from ground to pinnacle, all angling away from the water to protect them from the constant squalls coming in off the Great North Ocean.

"Squad leaders, spread out and wake the locals. I want them in the square in half an hour," Jarl announced as they rode into the extreme edge of town.

"Go find whoever's in charge and bring them to me," Hassan told his second in command, then continued on as Jarl motioned to his own squad to follow as he went to perform the errand.

A few minutes later Hassan arrived at his destination with only a small group for escort. The other columns began trickling into the village square on cue, and several minutes later his men were mostly accounted for. The returning soldiers took up guard positions at the perimeter of the square, surrounding the clearly frightened townsfolk. Before they'd split up, he'd ordered his lieutenants not to answer any questions as to their reasons for being in Nestarn until he addressed them personally. That sense of uncertainty would serve him well.

Hassan waited at the top end of the square for a few minutes longer until Jarl returned with a deep scowl on his face and a portly man escorted by ten guards keeping a wary watch. Hassan watched the procession flatly. When Jarl had left for the noble's house, he'd had a dozen men at his back.

The portly man strode right up to Hassan and spat in his face.

"Traitor!" he hissed, forcing Hassan to whip the broadsword out from the scabbard on his back and strike the tall noble across the ear with the flat of the blade. The man went to his knees in shock, although his wits seemed undimmed by the blow. Hassan wiped the spittle from his face and replaced his weapon in its scabbard.

In truth he admired the man's nerve, but couldn't allow the portly noble's actions to rile up the crowd. Not if he hoped to achieve this task without having to commit murder in the process.

"On your feet Sir," He instructed the leader of Nestarn village.

He waited for a moment until the portly noble had done as ordered, then studied the heavyset man. The mayor of Nestarn was in his mid-forties, bald on top but with a thick, dark brown horseshoe of hair around the sides and back of his skull. He stood at over six feet, and his ample girth gave him an imposing aspect.

"Listen very carefully to what I am about to tell you, Mayor..." Hassan began.

"Squire Hastor Nestarn," the portly noble told him proudly, "As in a direct descendant of Geoffry Nestarn who founded this village over five hundred years ago!"

Terrific.

"Well, Mayor Hastor Nestarn, let me first say that I quite like your odd little village. It would be a shame if I had to burn it to the ground."

There was a flicker of outrage in the squire's eyes, but Hassan cut him off before he could speak.

"I have no wish to do any such thing though. Truthfully, I don't even want to be here," he added, trying to somewhat placate the incensed mayor.

"The only reason I am is because Archmage Heramiir holds me under duress. If I do not fulfil his orders, he will kill several thousand loyal citizens who were captured when he conducted his treachery in Miralthrall. These civilians include my own family, so don't make the mistake of doubting for one moment that I will carry out those orders. If that makes me a traitor then so be it, but if so then I betray a king who can survive without me. The families of those who resisted, who are now under Heramiir's control, and to whom I remain loyal, will not."

"What do you do here?" the furious mayor was eventually able to get out, his voice a mixture of anger and disgust at Hassan's words.

"Archmage Nereth has set me to converting some of the villages surrounding Miralthrall to his cause. Nestarn is one of those on my list."

"I see," the mayor replied, "And what exactly does this 'conversion' entail?" he asked with a pointedly raised eyebrow.

"At this point only that you accept Heramiir as your new ruler, bow to his authority, and that of the College of the Arts instead of the king's. Furthermore, you will not support the king's forces or agents in any regard, but will comply with any order given to you by a ranking mage. Finally, you are required to fly the college banner from the village flagpole, replacing the king's standard," Hassan recited wearily.

The man looked more and more defiant as Hassan gave him the list, and Hassan knew there would be trouble unless he could convince the mayor of the seriousness of his situation.

"You killed two of my men," he whispered, changing tack.

"Yes I did," Hastor replied, even lifting his chin a little as he confirmed it, unrepentant.

Hassan nodded as his eyes grew momentarily cold.

"Burn his house and holdings to the ground," he ordered loudly enough for the crowd to hear, "Take his horses if he has any, we could use some extra mounts."

Jarl nodded and moved to obey, gathering up some few men as he went.

The mayor watched Jarl leave, and Hassan noted the

squire's indecision as he did. When the captain was almost gone from sight Hassan said privately, "Your other option is to cede control of your village to the archmage, now. If you defy me, your holdings burn. If you incite your people to a riot, the entire village burns."

For a minute longer he watched the agonised look on Hastor's face as Jarl disappeared from sight with his small entourage before adding, "If you wish to change your mind, best to do so before your home goes up in smoke. Once it begins, no order I can give will stop the flames."

That wasn't entirely true, he could once again order Derrack to smother the blaze, but it gained him nothing to let the mayor know that.

Mayor Nestarn was looking around wildly now, and Hassan could sense him balancing the training and outfitting of Hassan's mounted soldiers in opposition to his own people, who were weaponless, but far more numerous than the archmage's forces.

"Don't even think it," Hassan told him, "Not if you care for your people at all."

"Riders coming in!" one of his soldiers shouted, prompting both Hassan and the mayor to look at the nearby hill which overlooked Nestarn to the east.

Hassan's heart skipped a beat at the sight before him. He opened his mouth to begin shouting orders, but then calmed as he realised the several thousand horsemen and infantry about to pour into the village were riding with the black banner of Miralthrall's College of the Arts at their head. That dread icon had been made known on every major battlefield in the west for close to three thousand years, he had fought under it himself, but seeing it now for some reason gave him a very bad feeling.

"Make your decision Hastor, your time is up," he absently said as they both watched the army continue to pour over the hill.

With a last defiant sneer the mayor's shoulders slumped. He was beaten, but fortunately he knew it.

"All right," he answered, "I'll accede to your demands, as will the rest of Nestarn."

Hassan studied him for another moment before deciding the man was telling the truth.

"Smythe!" he called to a nearby soldier, "Recall Jarl and the men before they carry out my orders."

With a crisp acknowledgement Smythe was off, his horse galloping up the street as soon as he was clear of the villagers, attempting to catch up with the lieutenant and his men in time.

The mayor turned back to Hassan and gave him a brief nod, though he couldn't bring himself to thank Hassan for the respite.

The crowd waited in virtual silence for the next few minutes as first Jarl and his men returned, and the army on the hill stopped their advance, waiting while a small group at the front broke off and rode down into the village.

"Quickly! Raise the college standard," Hassan called to Jarl as he suddenly realised the identity of the man at the head of the approaching party. Jarl jumped to obey, and was just finishing the task as Archmage Nereth, in his ever present black enamelled plate armour and black, silver-lined cloak, came around the corner of a sizeable house and into sight of the village square and flagpole.

"Wait here and don't speak unless you are asked a direct question," Hassan told the mayor, who looked indignant until he saw the worry written on Hassan's features. The mayor reluctantly nodded, and Hassan walked away from him to greet Nereth, where he hopefully wouldn't have to deal with them both at the same time.

After the most cursory salute to the archmage and his entourage he felt could get away with, Hassan spoke with a contempt he couldn't quite hide.

"Nestarn is yours, Archmage."

Nereth regarded him for a moment as he surveyed the scene, clearly displeased with something.

"Nestarn is Heramiir's, Hassan," he replied with a faint, mocking grin, "And so are you. Don't forget."

"You make me sick," Hassan couldn't help adding, his voice carefully pitched so only the archmage and his entourage could hear. "You are every bit as much the traitor as Heramiir, but you are also just as much a slave to his mad whims as the rest of us. You just haven't realised it yet."

There were shocked looks from some of the black-cloaked magi who stood around the armoured archmage, but Nereth only grinned.

"Well, as one of his mad whims, I have your new orders with me and I'm sure you'll be impressed by how large a part we have chosen for you to play in them."

"Wait for me in my command tent," he ordered, motioning to the hill where the small army was waiting, some of the troops in the centre erecting a large canvas pavilion which was the only structure visible.

It meant they would leave today, otherwise the entire hill would be in a flurry of activity right now setting up the camp.

With a sarcastic bow Hassan left the group of magi behind and grudgingly mounted his steed before riding out of the village and up the hill to where the command pavilion was being set. All around him the army was unusually subdued as he approached. Most of the men were infantry he noted at a glance, but there were enough horse detachments scattered about to provide support if they were attacked in the open.

Still, despite the order of the scene, there was something decidedly odd about the small army which Nereth had gathered here, though he couldn't quite place what was niggling at the back of his mind.

With a small surprise he recognised a face amongst the ranks and walked over to meet a young man who had just been assigned to his unit before Heramiir's treachery had begun.

"Where is this force heading soldier?" he asked without preamble.

The inexperienced guard looked up at him with a spark of recognition and then grimaced.

"Somewhere to the west, Sir. That's all we've been told."

Hassan nodded and ordered him to carry on before turning away. He should have known better than to ask such a low-ranking officer. With a frown he scanned the crowd for someone of higher rank and immediately his eyes fell upon Captain Fanning, an able officer with whom he had served on the western border a few years back.

"Hassan!" Fanning called in a voice more suited to a bard than a soldier as he saw his former compatriot approaching.

"Devlan!" Hassan replied heartily. It *was* a relief to see his old friend again he realised, even given the circumstances.

"I'm glad you're here. We need to talk, now," Devlan said quietly once they were standing face to face.

Hassan nodded and Devlan led him away from any soldiers who might overhear their words before looking cautiously around.

"Nereth has spies everywhere," the bearded captain began, "And I suspect Heramiir has his own eyes planted throughout the army as well. I can't vouch for this, but I think they watch Nereth's men as much as they do ours."

Hassan raised an eyebrow at that. He would have to confirm it for himself, but if proved accurate it might become possible to create a rift between the two archmagi using some well-timed disinformation in the right ears.

Something Devlan had just said made the uneasiness he was feeling lurch to the front of his mind.

"What do you mean when you say Heramiir's men watch Nereth's as much as they do 'ours?'"

The bearded captain looked at him for a moment before making a subtle gesture at the soldiers which surrounded them on all sides.

"Look around Hassan, tell me what you see?"

Hassan frowned but did as he was asked, and after a brief study of the resting men, a shiver of dread made its icy way down his spine. He knew them. Not every man of the five thousand or so assembled troops of course, but he recognised at least one in every two or three men by sight if not by name.

"Where is this army headed?" he asked as all the pieces suddenly fell into a sick kind of sense.

"We only know we head to the west and that we're to meet up with a column of ballistae and catapults at the top of the great staircase. What has me concerned is that just about every man who was captured in the initial coup, and is recovered enough to march and fight is here."

"Along with enough of Nereth's own men to make sure we don't try anything rash," Hassan conceded as he shook his head in denial.

"But what's the target," Fanning asked, "We don't have enough forces for a major assault, but this is overkill for anything less..."

"Stonekeep," Hassan whispered, "That has to be it."

With a look that combined both fury and deep fear, Fanning nodded in agreement.

"He's going to feed us to the wall," Hassan grimaced.

"Thereby saving his own men for the real assault and getting rid of an inconvenient problem, those of us still loyal to the king, at the same time."

Hassan felt sick. The only reason he was here now, doing the traitorous archmage's bidding, was to safeguard the lives of these men and their families back in Miralthrall from Heramiir's retribution. But if they were about to be wiped out in what was sure to be an abortive attack on the massive double fortress, then he could wait no longer. It was time to act.

"I want you to rally as much support among those still loyal to the king as you discretely can. I don't have a plan yet, but I tell you this, I will not allow these men to be killed for no other reason than so a bloodthirsty traitor can be rid of them!" Hassan hissed.

With a glance down the hill he saw Nereth and the other magi had now left the town square and were heading back to the camp.

"Don't attempt to contact me, just get the men ready. When the time is right, I will find you. Now go, before the archmage sees us together. It won't do to have him even more suspicious of me than he already is."

Devlan nodded grimly and walked away after giving a salute which Hassan returned, as if he had just received a report from a subordinate. With a glance down at Nereth's progress he traversed the short distance to the command pavilion without drawing attention and stepped inside.

The sight of a table full of refreshments greeted him to one side, and before doing anything else he helped himself to a cup of wine and one of the largest apples he had ever seen. He moved to a chair at the head of a long wooden table which was obviously meant for Nereth and lounged in it, indolently placing his feet up on the furniture while he waited for the archmage to return. He couldn't say why he suddenly felt like tempting the archmage's wrath, perhaps it was because he no longer had anything left to lose. If Nereth succeeded in feeding his men to Stonekeep's walls and he somehow survived, Hassan had no intention of following him any longer. The men he was protecting with his obedience would not be alive to care, and without them Nereth would no longer have any excuse to persecute their families. Even an archmage as arrogant in his power as Nereth had to know that if he started murdering woman and children in the streets of Miralthrall, the entire city would rise up against him. A good number of those soldiers he had already turned to his cause would likely be among them. A great deal of the problem, Hassan thought, was that as power hungry and tyrannical as Heramiir and Nereth were, they ran Miralthrall at least as efficiently as the old duke had done. Wandering patrols of soldiers and magi had seen crime depleted down to almost nothing since the coup, making the streets safer than they had been in years. Commerce was carried out as it always had been, except for trade with Aramar, though precious few merchants not of the nobility traded or imported goods from that far away, and Heramiir didn't care about pleasing them.

For the most part, the merchants and workers still prospered or not as they'd always done, and since most people's lives were going on as they always had, most of the populous had no direct reason to rise up against the new order. There were those directly affected by the coup of course, but the few thousand men taken captive along with their families, and others who were truly opposed to Heramiir's rule, still only made up a small percentage of Miralthrall's population. Add the fact that what remained of Miralthrall's guard was now loyal to the new order, and the power of the magi themselves, and you had a city where it was far easier just to go about your everyday life. Risking your safety by resisting a regime which had possibly even improved your quality of living since coming into power was not a priority for most of the populace. Even if that regime had accomplished their goals through bloodshed and treachery.

It wasn't long before Nereth pulled back the flap of the tent and entered. Hassan gestured the assembled magi who filed in behind to join him at the table, as though it were he and not Nereth in supreme command of this army. He wasn't at all disappointed with the look the archmage threw him in response.

"I'm glad you've availed yourself of the refreshments," Nereth stated, trying not to let his impatience show as he poured himself a glass of wine which he chilled with the Gift.

"I doubt that," Hassan returned.

One of the magi in the blue-lined cloak of his rank took

a menacing half step forward, but was stopped short by a subtle gesture from Nereth.

The archmage took the seat on the other end of the table and the other two archmagi with him seated themselves on either side. Still standing were four other magi with whom Hassan was unfamiliar, and waiting nervously with them was Derrack, the young mage who had travelled alongside him on this trip, spying on his command the entire time.

"Nereth, let me start this meeting by saying I know your plans for this force, and I have no intention of going along with them."

If anything, Nereth looked vaguely amused by his words, even raising a cynical eyebrow as he asked in a carefully neutral tone, "And which plans might those be?"

Hassan sat up straight in his chair as he slid his booted feet off the table and placed his hands flat on its surface, discarding the wineglass and fruit he had held a moment before.

"The plans," He replied coldly, "Where you think to attack Stonekeep Castle, feeding the men captured in the coup to the fortress' wall to give your own troops a better chance at storming the gate."

There was a moment of stunned silence in the room, then with a shocking suddenness Nereth's wineglass exploded in his thickly gauntleted hand, causing several of the tent's occupants to start.

Tossing the dripping wreckage of the glass aside Nereth's face lit into a feral grin.

"I was going to attack Karver, but now that you've given me the idea, I think I'll take you up on it."

It was a thin lie, and they both knew it, but Nereth was furious.

"I won't do it," Hassan told the magi quietly.

"Attacking Stonekeep with this few men and no heavy siege machinery is suicide. Apart from any consideration for the fortress' defences, Stonekeep's garrison is ten thousand strong. Surely twice the number of men you have brought here with you."

"Don't be so naïve," Nereth snapped as he stood, picking a tiny shard of glass from his cloak.

"You will be just as obedient as a dog on a leash so long as Heramiir controls the fates of your family and those of your men. What's more, you will lead the attack on Stonekeep, not I. You will have no heavy support, you will not have enough men, and for your arrogance I will not allow my magi to assist in any direct attack on the fortresses or garrison. They will be support only!" Nereth shouted, finally out of patience, or perhaps needing to save face.

"If you disobey my orders, your men will die. If you are insolent just one more time, your family will die! And if you cannot take the castle with minimal losses," his voice subsided into a sudden savage whisper, "Neither the hostages nor your men will live to see the sun go down that day."

He has a way of contacting Miralthrall at a moment's notice, Hassan realised with an unpleasant start. As far as he knew even archmagi weren't supposed to be able to do that kind of thing.

One of the other archmagi was grinning at Nereth's tirade, but with interest Hassan saw several of the younger Gift users, especially Derrack, looking decidedly uncomfortable with what Nereth was proposing.

None of them spoke out.

"You ask the impossible!" Hassan responded flatly.

"Even were I willing, how can I possibly accomplish the task with only these resources?"

A slow smile spread across Nereth's face.

"As the commander of this force you will have to work out the details for yourself, or do you still deny you will do this thing?"

Hassan grimaced.

"I'll do it," he snarled after a moment, furious for both the situation Nereth was placing him in, and because he knew the archmage was right. So long as the civilians were kept hostage in Miralthrall and Nereth could get to them before Hassan could, his hands were tied.

Just as I am now tied to Heramiir's new regime.

Once he used violence to aid the traitor's cause he would not be welcomed back by the king's forces even if he did manage to get the men and civilians away from Heramiir's grasp.

"Then get out," Nereth told him flatly, "Order the army to march."

Hassan stood and stalked out of the tent, but just as he lifted the flap Nereth called after him, "Hassan, dawn of winter will be fully on us in less than two phases. Be done before then."

With a snarl Hassan let the tent flap drop behind him. Stonekeep Castle was at the very best over a phase's march from here.

He spotted Jarl returning from the village below and ordered him to form up the men. One of his nearby soldiers was holding his mount and Hassan took the reins before vaulting up onto the horse's back.

"Prepare to move out!" he called to the assembled

soldiers, who looked confused for a moment at the change of command, but there were enough seasoned veterans among them who recognised the speaker that the order was quickly obeyed.

Within a quarter hour the small army was on its way, heading southwest towards the great staircase. Hassan stared across the cultivated farmland which dominated the horizon, and tried not to let his true thoughts show on his face as they rode towards Stonekeep. It was the most heavily defended castle on the western border, and with the exception of Miralthrall and Aramar itself, the largest military structure in all of Jeranon.

And to combat all that I have five thousand infantry, which is less than a quarter of what I would attempt this assault with if I planned it myself. A few units of cavalry in support which will be almost useless once we arrive, and some light and medium siege weapons which will not penetrate their defences, and no Gift-wrought aid.

To top it all off, when they finally arrived at the mammoth double castle they would have considerably less than a phase to accomplish Nereth's impossible task.

He sighed bleakly and booted his horse onward.

We don't have a prayer.

'The most commonly used spells on a field of battle are those related to fire, explosions, and bursts of raw power. They are therefore the most expected and most easily defended against by any opposing force with access to the Gift. The effective battlemage must therefore learn to master the element of surprise in addition to all other elements of the Gift.'
Excerpt from 'Advanced Warfare and Tactics.'

CHAPTER 17

STONEKEEP

Stonekeep, Hassan thought for the hundredth time that morning as he stared up at the fortified stone battlements. Up here in the foothills of the Dark Iron Mountains the clouds were thick and heavy, and on this cold autumn's dusk morning they coasted low enough to take hold of Stonekeep's towers, giving the impression the massive battlements had no end, continuing forever up into the ether.

It was insane. Attacking Stonekeep was suicide. Yet if he couldn't pull it off, the lives of both his own family, and his men's' families which Heramiir still held in Miralthrall would be forfeit.

They had arrived at the castle late last night, well after the sun slipped behind the tall peaks of the mountains. He had ordered his forces arrayed beyond range of Stonekeep's defences, and set up camp for the evening since there was no possibility the castle's sentries wouldn't have spotted them coming from miles out. There would be no protracted siege here, and no element of surprise either. Stonekeep's garrison would be ready.

This morning was soon enough to begin this madness.

Gathered behind him were five thousand infantry, archers, and some cavalry, along with several dozen crew's manning the catapults, ballistae and battering rams which now made up his command. How he was to take the most fortified castle along the border without trebuchets or mangonels he wasn't certain. If he'd had either those resources, or the support of the magi in Nereth's entourage, Hassan thought it might at least have given his men a slight chance of success. The whole trip here, Nereth had continually insisted they could succeed even over his explicit objections. Until finally, in a heated argument just two nights ago, the archmage had described in detail exactly what would happen to his family if he failed to carry out his duty.

My duty! As if I owe that traitor anything!

On reflection, punching the archmage hadn't been the smartest thing to do at that point, especially considering he'd broken the arrogant fool's jaw. It had been extremely satisfying however, even if it had earned him a severe beating and Nereth's continuing ire.

He massaged his bruised chest where the archmage had gripped him, nearly crushing his ribcage in a retaliatory binding of air, and sighed. Somehow he had to get out from Nereth's watchful eye long enough to plan their combined escape from Heramiir's clutches. He had long ago decided that when they made their final escape from Miralthrall, his men and their families would have to make their way east to lands still held by the king. How he would accomplish that particular miracle was still unclear, but a chance would present itself eventually. It had to. There was simply no possibility they could fight their way clear of Miralthrall.

A passing bird cried out a shrill challenge overhead, drawing his attention back to the mammoth fortress. The one advantage he could claim from this assignment was that Stonekeep's defences were primarily oriented towards the west. Stonekeep was the major obstacle keeping the western nations from passing through the mountains, and while the eastern side of the double castle was by no means weak, it was at least not quite as impregnable as the other.

He had fought here for his king on more than one occasion over the years, and he knew the colossal fortress well.

Stonekeep was divided into three major sections, the southern keep, the northern keep, and the wall and killing zone to the west, which guarded the pass through the mountains. Beyond the western wall there were three further sets of gates that protected the entrance to Jeranon. Each had its own set of defences which could slow down the enemy for hours if not days while the rest of the garrison could be made ready for a major offensive. After that, if an enemy made it all the way to the end of the pass, right as the mountains dropped away and the passage became flat ground, there was Stonekeep wall encircling the gap in the jagged terrain. This final obstacle was twenty feet thick and over sixty spans high. Yet even it was overshadowed by the giant forms of the two isolated keeps themselves as they stood watch over the primary entrance to the end of Stonekeep Pass and the Sammorand Plains beyond.

Fortunately, none of that would be a concern during the initial attack. All he had to worry about was the eastern wall and the mammoth twin keeps themselves. Still...

The magi who would normally have been stationed at the fortress had all been recalled to Miralthrall several days before the coup, Nereth had informed him at their last meeting with a slight knowing grin. Hassan hoped he was telling the truth, but had no way of confirming the information since only another mage could sense their auras, unless the enemy revealed their powers on the field of course.

As he rode towards the outer gate on his midnight black steed, Hassan sat his saddle tensely, eyes never leaving the approaching battlements. At his side rode Derrack, the young Mage. Nereth had given the boy private orders again, though Hassan was beginning to wonder from some of Derrack's comments over the last phases whether he was quite as much under the archmage's control as Nereth clearly assumed him to be.

"Halt where you are, or I will order you fired upon!" a terse voice called down to the two approaching riders.

Hassan couldn't see the speaker, but the shout came from somewhere over the forty-foot-high steel portcullis which was the only way into Stonekeep from this side of the mountains.

He motioned Derrack to comply. When they had both come to a halt, he studied the wall above the closed gate for a moment, trying to discern exactly which of the dozens of archers who had just revealed themselves on the parapet the order had come from.

"Who commands here?!" Hassan called back to whoever had given them the order.

"In the king's name, I do. Now take your traitorous army and be gone wretch!"

There was something very familiar about that tone, and with a sinking feeling in his stomach he realised it belonged to none other than Tamgen, the Duke of Keril's oldest son. The old duke must be away on some business of the king's or Hassan knew only death could have pried the white-haired old man away from his beloved mountain fortress.

Hassan's first post when the king had sent him to the west had been here at Stonekeep, and he and Tamgen had immediately become rivals in the arts of tactics and swordplay. Hassan counted him a close friend. The sobering realisation that he would now have to lead an attack on the man's home and loved ones, one he had to make succeed, tasted far worse than the bitterest ashes in his mouth.

"Tamgen, I need to speak with your father," He shouted back to the waiting archers upon the wall.

There was a long moment of silence, then a single figure stepped up between the crenulations and looked down upon the pair of riders who had so brazenly approached the locked and fortified gates.

"Hassan!" the dismayed figure exclaimed after a minute, "Please tell me it is not you in charge of this traitorous rabble my old friend."

Hassan couldn't help a defeated sigh, his guess about the mysterious commander's identity had been correct.

"I would give much to do so Tamgen, but Archmage Heramiir holds the lives of my family, as well as those of my men's, hostage against my cooperation in his schemes. I am afraid he has ordered me to take Stonekeep, as a hedge against it being a thorn in his side next spring when the king's army will surely launch a counterattack from the east."

"I see," Tamgen answered sadly, "You of all people know I cannot allow Stonekeep to fall to any foe, lest the dark nations have free rein across the mountains."

Hassan nodded silently.

"I know," he said to himself, but the words carried anyway.

After a moment he looked up at the length of the wall and the double keeps beyond, which were slowly being revealed by the retreating mist, before returning his gaze back to the garrison commander.

"I... ask, for your surrender old friend. I have no wish to waste the lives of men on either side of these lines, but this is a fight from which I cannot withdraw, no matter how much I might wish it."

"Don't do this Hassan, you know I can't let you take what you want. Even if it means slaughtering every man you send against our walls."

That was all. No offer of surrender, no backing down at all. But then, he'd known exactly how this would play out as soon as he'd realised the commanding officer's identity.

"I will grant you safe passage back to your lines now old friend," Tamgen called down to him from above the gate.

"But heed this well. My mandate is to hold this castle against all enemies of Jeranon and the king. If you attack Stonekeep Hassan," he added resignedly, "I will have no choice but to meet you as such."

Hassan nodded miserably, but in acceptance. If their positions had been reversed, he would have done no differently.

"I wish it hadn't come to this," Hassan answered, unsure for a moment whether his words had carried up to the parapet or not.

"Come on," he said heavily to Derrack, who was for whatever reason looking agitated.

He turned his horse away from the castle and walked the animal a few steps when he heard the slow shout of command from behind him.

"Present arms!" Tamgen had bellowed to his men, an order most commonly reserved for the burial detail of a fallen comrade.

Fitting, Hassan thought as he closed his eyes painfully for a moment. One way or another, it was doubtful they would both live through the day.

Hassan turned his horse slowly back towards the castle. The sight before him made him want nothing more for a split second than to charge at the gates, leaving Nereth and his cronies far behind. To demand entrance to the castle so he could fight alongside his true comrades for his king. The thought of what those actions would mean for his family though made the moment pass swiftly, leaving him hollowed out inside. His hands were tied so tightly to Heramiir's plots now that he could do only one thing.

The three or four hundred archers along the wall had shouldered their bows and stood stiffly at attention, saluting into the misty morning light as the bright sun began in earnest to eat away at the fog and cloud which still shrouded the keep.

He returned the salute of the soldiers as he stared up at Tamgen.

"Goodbye old friend," he whispered, and although

Tamgen couldn't possibly have heard the words, the distant soldier nodded in understanding.

Without another word Hassan once again turned his horse and rode back towards the camp, not even waiting for Derrack to catch up as he fell into the blackest of moods. As he reached the command tent, he pulled up hard and dismounted the puffing horse as he stalked into the pavilion with Derrack on his heels.

The young mage had improved his riding ability an impressive amount since they'd left Miralthrall nearly a season before, and he now had no trouble keeping up with even the veteran soldiers in Hassan's unit.

They entered the tent at almost the same time, Derrack a step behind and to the side of Hassan, an unintentional position of deference which Hassan thought caused the flat glance Nereth gave them as they entered.

"Well?" Nereth asked, sitting alone and at ease in his shining, black-enamelled plate armour, making the single word an order to report.

"If you want it, you'll have to take it," Hassan told him insolently, no longer caring what the archmage threatened him with. After all, his only choice now lay between the lives of his three thousand men or so and their families back in Miralthrall, and the ten thousand loyal soldiers assigned to Stonekeep Castle.

Nereth worked his jaw for a moment. He'd had Archmage Larola heal it, but it made Hassan smile to see Nereth's mind insisting the recent injury should still hurt.

"What did you sense?" Nereth asked, turning his attention to Derrack.

With the slightest apologetic glance at Hassan, Derrack showed finally where his true loyalties lay.

"There are three magi in there," he answered, revealing his private orders.

Hassan's lips thinned, he hoped Nereth took it as a response to Derrack's information. By keeping these private orders from him, Derrack had unwittingly shown he couldn't be trusted enough to be brought into the conspiracy to undermine Heramiir's power base. Hassan had been considering bringing him in on the secret, even though he was a mage and supposedly loyal to the college. The boy had strong views on several things Hassan agreed with, and he had been hoping the mage could prove to be a precious ally. Suppressing a snort, he realised that was probably why Nereth had assigned him such an inexperienced and idealistic Mage in the first place. The traitor was certainly sly enough to try a ploy like that without the boy's knowledge, just in case Hassan let something slip.

Hardening his resolve, he tuned back into the conversation.

"One is much the same level of power as I am, another is slightly weaker, but the third is most likely an archmage from the aura I felt as we approached. That one is a definite threat," Derrack reported with a calm beyond his years.

"Must be a visitor from Aramar," Nereth mused, "All of our most powerful magi are accounted for."

He looked at Hassan's glowering countenance for a second before asking, "Are the men ready?"

"They are," Hassan replied stiffly.

Nereth gave him a guarded look and began a slow turn around the tent.

"Despite what you think Hassan, I want this position taken. I wouldn't be going on the offensive if I didn't think we could win," he said in the lecturing tone a stern father might take with a recalcitrant child.

"Due to the fact there are still several Gift users inside despite my order to leave, I will allow you support from the magi and archmagi who are with me. I will still not allow them to directly attack the keep's themselves. Other than that they are at your disposal for the duration of the battle."

"And what will you be doing while my men are dying?"

"I will be waiting for their archmage to reveal themselves during the battle. At that point I will neutralise the threat to your men," Nereth told him as he began pacing the tent in his soundless black armour, no trace of a brag in his voice.

Hassan felt a slight shiver run down his spine. Either Nereth was the most arrogant and stupid man he had ever met to so casually dismiss a fully trained archmage, which he knew from personal experience was far from the case, or else Hassan had seriously underestimated the archmage's abilities.

"Follow me," Nereth ordered, and led them back outside the tent to where the rest of the magi were waiting.

"For the duration of this battle you will obey Hassan's orders as if they were my own. The only exception being that under no circumstances will you directly attack the keeps," Nereth told them without preamble, "It is a test of his command."

"Is that wise Archmage?" a young man in a blue-lined cloak with dark brown hair and the same coloured eyes asked without deference.

Although there was no hint of challenge in his tone, the young mage's stony stare gave away nothing of his feelings on the matter. Hassan noted him as one to keep a sharp eye on. There was something not right, something alien about the hollow look in the man's eyes which disturbed him deeply.

With a shudder Hassan broke eye contact and gave the magi their orders, which they took with no further questions to the archmage.

Hassan knew Nereth was one of, if not the single best strategist in Jeranon, but he still couldn't help feeling a deep disgust with himself when the traitorous archmage nodded approvingly of his plans.

*   *   *

"Begin!" Hassan shouted as he stood at the head of the small army.

The morning mist had all but burned away now, leaving the sky blue and cloudless around a scorching sun, which at this point was still thankfully at their backs. It had also revealed the full scope of the mountain fortress which lay before them as the rams and ballistae began to roll ponderously forward, escorted by their crews and a small guard of men.

Hassan looked to his left where the magi were spread out from each other along the battle line, and gave a curt nod as he saw them following his plan. He turned his attention back to the scene in front of him. Within a few seconds the air freshened as the magi worked their skills upon the very fabric of the world, calling up the wild storm he'd directed them to create. If it worked as intended, the manufactured storm would minimise the damage the enemy archers could inflict on his men from the safety of the fortress wall.

490

At first it was nothing more than a stirring of wind as the rams continued their inexorable march towards the huge steel portcullis that barred entry into Stonekeep's grounds. As several clouds rapidly and chaotically appeared at the various magi's behest, heavy rain and sporadic bursts of lightning began to descend. The defenders suddenly found themselves under attack on two fronts as the unpredictable winds threatened to knock them from their perches while they waited nervously for the rams to come into range.

As the first siege engine did just that, someone on the wall called for the archers to fire. A flight of brightly flaming arrows arced out from the stone wall, causing the men rolling the machine to duck under its sheltered roof as the projectiles came hissing towards them. Most of the arrows were doused by the still hardening rain, or else sent off course by the now blowing gale before reaching their target. And yet, enough struck the lead ram's roof that its crew faltered for a moment before continuing, though no bodies were left behind in the volley's wake.

Hassan breathed a silent sigh of relief.

So far so good.

There were only five rams in his command, and as they made their way to the gate, the enemy archers released volley after volley of tarred and flaming arrows against them. He had considered holding one or two of the machines back as a precaution, but decided against it as he didn't have enough men for a second assault. There would be no siege, no wearing down their opponent, no opportunity to have sappers dig under the walls or any of a dozen other options that all required the one thing Nereth had forbidden him, more time. Winter was fast approaching, and they had no choice but to assault Stonekeep at its full strength. In some small way Hassan was glad. Today would see an end to this disgrace, one way or another.

The wind picked up its swirling intensity as the magi concentrated their efforts now on pooling their existing spells to synchronise them into a single, somewhat combined front, rather than the overlapping tempests which were currently working against each other. Within moments the roaring of the storm was all Hassan could hear even though its full fury was centred on the walls of the keep. The rain was also centred across the field on the mammoth fortress, although the wild winds were carrying enough of the water as far as Hassan's lines for it to be an irritation.

He wiped the rain from his face and continued to observe. The defenders up on the wall were clearly growing frustrated with the lack of success they were having on the advancing rams.

As the first of the enormous machines ran headlong into the portcullis, a vat of boiling pitch was tipped over the side of the wall to splash hissing on its target below. The wooden roof of the ram took most of the boiling sticky liquid, but enough of it splashed past to send several of the soldiers manning it to the ground. Hassan could see it clearly, but their agonised screams were muted by the fury of the storm Nereth's magi were continuing to build. The wind around Stonekeep was racing so fast now that most of the fired arrows simply changed direction within a couple of spans and flew off into what was quickly becoming a manufactured hurricane.

By luck, or maybe skill, one of the flaming arrows eventually struck the lead ram. The wood ignited the liquefied pitch and sent the rest of the soldiers still manning it scampering away from the doomed machine as the burning liquid began to quickly consume their only cover.

Hassan could see the squad commander giving quick orders which his men obeyed even in the midst of the storm and arrow fire; he noted the man's performance in the back of his mind.

Down near the gate, those of the reduced squad still able to fight moved to help the crew of the second ram, while the moderately injured men were set to helping their more seriously harmed companions back to their own lines.

The second ram crashed against the gate next to the first and rebounded as the men regained their grips to pull it back for another try, but the giant portcullis seemed all but unaffected. They pulled the ram back about twenty spans before the men began to roll it ponderously forward once again.

A commotion above the gate drew Hassan's eye as the massive machine ambled forward.

He couldn't quite make out what was happening, but the defenders seemed to be having some sort of problem as smoke and little sparks of flame rose from behind the parapet.

It took a moment, but Hassan finally realised one of the errant arrows streaming around the wall must have ignited a pot of pitch being readied above the gate. Flecks of the burning liquid were now being picked up by that same wind and tossed about the area, causing no substantial damage, but certain pain and distraction to whoever they touched.

With an abruptness that shocked even the Stonekeep

defenders, the second ram simply exploded with a crack audible even over the raging storm, throwing kindling and body parts in all directions. Hassan couldn't tell how badly the men had been hurt, but he grimly noted that of even the least injured looking troops, none of them picked themselves up straight away.

To his right Nereth closed his eyes and seemed to focus on something only he could see before glaring at a section of wall over to the extreme right of the keep. The archmage took a deep breath and with no more indication than that, the section of wall he had been focusing on exploded into incandescent flame. For a few seconds the tableau held, then Nereth threw up his arm in a reflex action that saved both their lives as the enemy mage he'd been targeting returned the archmage's fiery assault with one of his own.

As his vision cleared from the blinding light, Hassan realised he had only enjoyed the protection of the mystical shield because he happened to be standing close to the archmage at the right moment. All around him, other men not so fortunate were lying dead or stunned on the long grass of the plains, and at this distance the storm did nothing to cover the cries of the injured.

Down at the wall, the third ram crashed against the gate and this time it at last appeared to have some effect, although only a slight one.

If we can hold out long enough, we should be able to gain entry to the grounds at least, he thought grimly.

"Wait here until I deal with this archmage," Nereth told him bluntly, before walking forward in a straight line directly towards where the deadly blast of flame had originated.

494

Hassan's ballistae were in position now, and taking shots at the huge vats of pitch being readied above the gate to be used on any attackers who made it that far. Although the gale still affected the ballistae accuracy, the heavy six-foot, steel tipped shafts strayed from their courses a lot less than the far lighter arrows.

Another blinding flash of flame struck Nereth's shield, but the armoured archmage continued his steady stride towards the wall without interruption.

The third ram had wheeled back now and joined the fourth as they both rushed at the gate simultaneously, and with a crash that was audible even against the howling wind, the giant portcullis began to give.

*   *   *

Whoever the unknown archmage on the wall was, they were simply a bug to be squashed. Nereth couldn't afford to think about them in any other way. But even some bugs could bite if you let your guard down. With that in mind Nereth approached the eastern wall of Stonekeep warily. He had no doubt this was the one whom Derrack had said would be a definite threat, and Nereth agreed. The unknown mage did not possess his level of power in the Gift, but neither were they far enough below as to be insignificant.

Unfortunately that meant the enemy mage already knew where he was, seconds before Nereth could detect his opponent's aura, and his location. It was something he was well used to since few magi were his equal in sheer strength. He would just have to be cautious, as always.

He continued to walk until he could finally sense his

hidden attacker. His own first strike had simply been at where the enemy's attack had come from, and no sane mage would stay in the same place after they had revealed their position to an enemy Gift user. Not unless they were sure they had the upper hand at any rate.

Now that he could clearly feel the other mage's aura for himself, Nereth knew his opponent did not.

There was a subtle change in the air and Nereth reinforced his shield as another blast, this time formed of razor fine shards of ice flew at him from the wall. With a thought, Nereth added to his defence by flash heating the air in front of his shield to help diminish the impacts. The instant the opposing archmage's spell faltered, he retaliated with the strongest blast of earth and fire he could muster. In one fell moment he demolished the section of wall his opponent was hiding behind, the concussive blast of stone and residual power shredding the weaker archmagi's defences and sending him ducking for cover behind the next crenulation. Nereth followed up with a bar of flame before the man could escape, which should have turned him to a cinder where he stood, only it didn't.

So… That is their strategy.

The archmage was using all his strength for his offensive abilities, while his weaker compatriots stayed out of range and worked in concert to maintain a defence around him, keeping him safe.

It was a time-honoured strategy among small groups of magi when one of them was significantly stronger in the Gift than the others, and against most spellcasters it would be quite effective. Nereth knew himself to be one of the most powerful archmagi in Jeranon, and possibly the entire world. This tactic would avail them little against him.

Reaching out to the air in front of him he concentrated on the wall, made a fist, and then pulled his gauntleted arm abruptly back to his side.

In the distance one of the enormous stone blocks that made up the crenulations along the wall came crashing down at his behest, and Nereth smiled.

Behind the now missing block the surprised mage was finally revealed to his sight. Nereth wasted no time imagining up a torrent of earth and ice to blast the enemy combatant with, and allowing the Gift to flow through him, used that power to alter reality to match his vision. A vision which in the space of one long second shredded both shield and archmage alike.

He let the spell fade and saw the ruined body of his opponent's body slump down and off the front of Stonekeep's wall even as he felt the archmage's aura dissipate into nothing.

Taking a deep breath, Nereth reinforced his shield once more as he looked over the battlefield.

The rams had made progress buckling the gates. Unfortunately, while the spiralling storms his magi were still employing as a defensive measure were keeping much harm from coming to his own troops, the artificial hurricane was also doing little to actually damage the enemy position.

With an intense effort Nereth reached out with all his considerable focus and managed to slowly, one by one, with the aid of the other magi, bring the chaotic winds being generated by his various spellcasters into order. He envisioned them spiralling tighter and faster and with more cohesion than they ever would have done at nature's bidding, or the other magi's for that matter. It took every scrap of power at his disposal, and several minutes of mind-numbing concentration to bend the vast array of spells to his will, but it was not beyond him. When he was finally satisfied he had full control of the various storms, and the hurricane was spinning as rapidly, and with as much deadly force as he could fashion it into, he threw his whole strength of will at it.

In response, he could sense the other magi cede complete control of their own portions of the newly focused hurricane as the resistance from their spells dropped away. With an amount of effort Nereth dared not allow to show, he abruptly sent it hurtling along the fortress's outer wall. It lurched down the length of the ramparts as quickly as he could visualise it travelling, his strength and clarity of focus dwindling at an alarming rate.

The hurricane staggered along the fortification far more swiftly than a man could run, clearing the structure of shrieking defenders as it violently hurled helpless men to their deaths by the score.

In its wake, a few stragglers remained who had held fast to their surroundings, but hardly any of them were left in fighting condition.

Nereth knew he had done his job well as the enemy arrow fire all but stopped in an instant.

When the hurricane had finally covered the length of the wall, he let go of the spell immediately, allowing the storm to return to its former chaotic state as the other magi took up control of individual portions again. Nereth found himself breathing heavily from the exertion, his hands shaking slightly, every muscle taut as he dispassionately regarded the piles of mangled bodies now littering the ground for a hundred spans around the castle's outer wall. There would be just as many inside and out of sight. Some were still moving painfully he noted, but not many.

The task had been almost beyond him, and he now felt too drained to do anything more than walk slowly back to his own lines where a deep silence now ruled the ranks. As he passed Hassan he simply said, "Continue," before retiring to his command tent.

*   *   *

Hassan could only stare at Nereth in bewildered silence as the armoured archmage made his way calmly back to his tent, stepping inside without a backward glance. The traitor had just killed at least a thousand defenders. A thousand men, and yet he strode past Hassan and the rest of the force as if it were nothing to him at all.

Suddenly, all of Hassan's plans for leading a civil insurrection when the king's army arrived fell into dust. No one could compete with that kind of raw power. He had fought beside enough magi over the years against the western nations to know what Nereth had just done should not have been possible. No mage could focus and control a storm which had taken eight other powerful magi and archmagi working in as close to concert as possible to bring it to the ferocity it had already attained.

Down at the gate, the sound of the rams continuing their inexorable work brought him back to the present. The machines were beginning to make an impression on the colossal steel frame, but Hassan forced himself to take the time to think. He had fought on the same field as Nereth

499

twice before against the west, and both times he had seen how powerful the archmage was in the Gift. One of the most powerful in Jeranon from what he was told. But never had he seen Nereth perform a spell which was so far out of the realms of most magi's ability. Not even during a desperate struggle, years back when his unit, including Nereth himself, had been sorely pressed by a regiment of Imbic mutations who had made it as far as the eastern foothills of the Dark Iron Mountains.

From deep in the great outer wall of Stonekeep a sudden clinking noise came, and Hassan called out for his men to be ready.

Either Nereth had been holding back a major portion of his talent from everyone, even in that life or death struggle, or else the archmage had suddenly come into a fresh source of power unavailable to the other magi. He was sure the other Gift users wouldn't appreciate that if they knew. It was something to keep in mind, and maybe a chance to create another small division.

There was the grinding noise of metal on stone followed by the sudden opening of a small concealed sally port to the right side of the main gate. A score of heavy cavalry issued from the port, some bearing small earthenware pots and others flaming torches in addition to their usual weapons and equipment.

Finally.

This was what he'd been waiting for. The ram's had never been a good bet at breaching the primary gate, but he'd served at this castle and knew its defences intimately. Tamgen had made a mistake in forgetting that, and the next few minutes would decide whether his mad attack plan had a chance at succeeding or not.

"Fuse that gate open!" Hassan shouted to Derrack over the noise of the squall.

The young mage had been waiting in reserve for this very order. He nodded and began to quickly mouth an incantation, focusing his attention on the small opening in the wall from which the last of the riders were now emerging.

"Keep the storm going until we're all inside, and at all costs make sure that port stays open!" Hassan yelled across the field to the black and silver clad archmage three over in the line. The man gave him a frown at the tone of the order, but also a single nod of acceptance as he returned concentration to his task, leaving Hassan to his own.

"You two, wait one minute and then follow as quickly as you can!" he shouted to Derrack and the next mage in line. He took a deep breath as he surveyed the castle in its entirety one last time.

"Forward!" he roared to the waiting troops, who immediately gave voice to a wordless cry as they began the short run toward the high walls of Stonekeep.

While he'd issued his orders, some of the soldiers guarding the rams had moved away from their machines a little to meet the cavalry before they could get to the lumbering siege engines. The defenders of Stonekeep were adamant in their task though, and with Hassan's army baring down on them, rode around the waiting soldiers before they realised they wouldn't be engaged.

Behind him Hassan could feel the thundering of the ground as close on five thousand men charged after him.

The ram crews were able to make one more shuddering impact on the gate before the cavalry reached them.

The first rank of horsemen smashed the pots they

carried against the side of the siege machines, the broken jars oozing a thick black liquid which could only have been pitch across the engines. Once done, the riders drew their swords in an attempt to hold off the defenders long enough for the second rank to put torches to the thick liquid.

Within moments the three remaining machines were engulfed in flames and the small unit of cavalry were retreating in haste back towards the sally port.

As the last of the riders disappeared back inside the walls, Hassan could see a few defenders had have regained the walls, or perhaps they were new companies, but the charge had begun and nothing could be allowed to stop it.

The rams were fully ablaze now and his ballista had once again begun shooting at targets along the wall as Hassan's small army charged towards the gates of the massive fortress. As soon as they were in range, a hail of projectiles leapt from the arrow slits of the twin keeps, cresting the walls and landing amongst his men. Due to the continued ferocity of the storm cells only a few hit their marks, doing so more out of blind luck than any skill of the bowman, and the charge continued.

As he bore down on the massive portcullis Hassan could see a rank of bloodied archers inside, probably those who had survived the fall from the keep's wall earlier during Nereth's little display of power. They had reformed into a small company and were waiting to put a shaft into the first set of men who approached the gate.

"Ware the gate!" he called urgently to the men streaming down the hill behind him.

As he veered off towards the narrow sally port, he glimpsed some of his men following closely behind as he pulled his old broadsword from the scabbard on his back.

In the back of his mind Hassan knew that if they were to take the twin castles today, he would have to kill nearly as many loyal soldiers as the amount of civilians he was trying to save. He darted through the opening and threw himself sideways as low to the ground as he could get to avoid the waiting hail of arrows which by all rights should have ended his life. One glanced off the side of his breastplate, and then other men were through the gate, charging ahead and taking the archers' attention off him long enough for him to rise. In that moment, everything became simple.

Loyal they might be, he thought as he followed the few men who had run past him during the moment he was on the ground into the fray, but at least these men had chosen this life. His family, and those of his men, had not.

As he charged at the waiting archers, the defenders fired purposefully at the attackers. Their sergeant had the presence of mind to make his remaining men fire in small groups, reducing the chance of several men aiming at the same target.

Hassan's men continued to pour through the gate behind him and when the attackers were only a few seconds away the commander ordered swords drawn as he moved to the front and met Hassan's charge head on. The man ducked low at the last instant, attempting to cut Hassan's legs out from under him. He barely avoided the unexpected stroke by jumping wildly over the man's low arc and parrying the thrust of another soldier in mid-air as he crashed into the man. The impact sent them both down behind the line of wounded archers now acting as swordsmen. As he smashed at the man's nose with the hilt of his broadsword, which thankfully he'd kept his grip on,

Hassan could hear the sound of steel on steel behind him as his own men engaged with the troops from the garrison. Another quick strike to the temple and the man he was wrestling with fell unconscious. Hassan immediately rolled forward and away from the fight while he regained both his feet and his bearings.

The former archers were being overwhelmed by the flood of men barrelling in the sally port and for a moment Hassan could stand and survey the scene. What he saw wasn't promising. Both keeps had opened their gates and defenders were flooding out en masse to meet the attackers who had so easily breached the walls of the mountain stronghold. Hassan knew his men would be overwhelmed in moments unless that tide was stemmed.

As if in answer to his thoughts Derrack came running up beside him along with another young mage Hassan didn't know.

"Seal those gates and keep them closed no matter what!" he shouted over the storm. The driving rain was a nuisance as it worked down between armour and skin. The wild winds it brought with it though were most welcome as they continued to keep most of the arrows still being fired from the slits in the two mammoth keeps from accurately hitting their targets.

The two magi nodded wetly, and both began mouthing different incantations as they each focused on sealing one of the apertures from which defenders continued to pour.

He glanced around. There were about five hundred of his men within the courtyard now, and about four times that number of defenders on the walls and in the yard with more exiting the keeps during every passing second.

"Defensive circle! Hold the gate!" Hassan roared. He didn't think his voice had travelled far enough over the howling wind, but he soon saw other men passing on the order. Within seconds the men were forming a semi-circle shield wall around the gate so their reinforcements could make their way through the narrow opening and into the courtyard unassailed.

"Strengthen the wall!" Hassan shouted to the men who were only just coming into the fray. As they did so the first elements from the southern keep crashed into the attackers, breaking through by sheer weight of numbers as they ploughed into the rough line of men defending the only entrance to the keep. For a moment chaos reigned until Hassan diverted the steady stream of reinforcements into the breach, creating a second line of defence which by default put the defenders back on the outside of the circle.

There was a grinding noise as the entrance of the northern keep folded in on itself, simply narrowing until it sealed seamlessly as though there had never been a door there in the first place.

Seconds later a thick wall of fire blocked the entrance to the southern keep, and several men who had been using the exit at the time were set alight as the Gift-wrought flames suddenly appeared out of nowhere.

Hassan looked at the two magi and nodded his thanks before returning his attention to the battle. With the flow of defenders halted for now, and his own troops continuing to pour into the keep, it was only a matter of time until the scales turned and his own men had the advantage of numbers, if they could hold out that long.

From on top of the wall, an enormous pot of pitch was suddenly toppled over the side into the courtyard. Men screamed and fell silent as it splattered its boiling contents across a section of Hassan's formation. A moment later the actual pot, a huge thing of iron and steel came crashing down behind the scolding liquid, doing significant damage of its own as it smashed down among the troops and bounced. The sound of it hitting the paved yard was like the ringing of the huge bells at the centre of Miralthrall and Aramar. The now dented construction rolled a short way and came to a grinding halt, fetching up against the base of the fortified wall.

A moment later the sudden assault was followed up by a flight of flaming arrows which managed even through the driving rain and wind to strike the pitch and light up a section of the defenders' circle in glowing tongues of flame.

"Put that out!" Hassan roared to the two magi who were already beginning their spells as he spoke. The sudden noise and light behind their lines had caused several of his men to hesitate for an instant, and Hassan suddenly found the circle shrinking as the keep's defenders gained a slight advantage.

"Hold the circle!" he bellowed as he cut down a soldier who had rushed through the gap where the flames were now almost doused. A quick look around showed him there was now nearly as many of his own men inside the wall as there were defenders; the next few minutes would tell the tale. He grabbed a nearby soldier by the arm and shouted at the man.

"Get to the sally port, direct the men coming through to reinforce the breach!"

He let go of the soldier's arm and ran towards the area where the flames and iron pot had damaged his lines enough that the keep's defenders were creating a beachhead between the wall and his circle. The situation was not improved by the sight of several dozen heavy cavalry kept at the garrison for the express purpose of clearing the courtyard, galloping towards them.

"Find the magi, tell them to attack the cavalry!" he bellowed to Jarl, whom he spotted still trying to fight on the line though clearly wounded. His oldest companion nodded once as he stepped backward quickly, disengaging from the fighting and limping off as quickly as he could to find one of the black-cloaked men while Hassan traded places with him.

The remaining defenders who had not yet engaged his men were running as fast as they could towards the breach, trying to flank the line and widen the gap in the attackers' defences before Hassan could reinforce it again. He locked swords with a defender and quickly kicked the man hard in the knee, knocking him off balance before finishing him with a quick thrust to the neck. As quickly as he was down another stepped into his place and thrust clumsily at him with an overhand stroke which he easily countered. The clumsy thrust was just a feint though, and his opponent held an off-hand dagger which he used to good effect as he dropped to his knees and thrust upwards with more speed than Hassan had expected. Hassan twisted in time to stop himself being skewered, but still the thin knife took him in the right side, punching through his armour and sliding several agonising inches into his flesh, causing him to fall back to the ground and into a puddle of spent pitch mixed with blood, and out of the line. He immediately felt a set of hands pull him out of harm's way while another soldier took his place on the line, engaging his former opponent.

"Are you all right?!" Derrack shouted over the sounds of battle and storm.

"Just stupid," Hassan answered painfully, his vision clearing after a particularly bright strike of lightning. The knife had cut him deeply he knew, but he wasn't having any undue trouble breathing, so he thought it must have missed his lung.

"Help me up," he added after a moment.

Derrack looked at him incredulously, but complied without further comment.

The other mage had also arrived and was wreaking havoc among the charging cavalry, having dispatched nearly half of the unit by himself. The line seemed to be holding well in every area except where those on the wall had broken it moments before, and his men now outnumbered the defenders two to one as they continued to flood through the tiny sally port. If they could end the threat from the cavalry, the courtyard would be theirs.

"We have to break their charge," he told Derrack, trying not to breathe too hard as he spoke because of the stabbing pain his wound now gave him every time his chest expanded with air.

The young mage looked at the riders who were nearly upon them and nodded.

"Can you stand on your own?" he asked.

Hassan nodded and Derrack let him go, taking a step forwards as he did and beginning a quiet chant while making intricate gestures with his hands. When the horses were less than fifty spans off, Derrack shouted and pointed, and the ground ahead of him trembled, causing both men and horses to halt as they lost their footing.

"Charge them!" Hassan shouted to a score of men who

had just arrived inside the courtyard and weren't yet engaged in the fight.

The sergeant in charge of the men took one look at who had given the order and gave a hoarse cry as he led his men out of the relative safety of the circle and into the midst of the cavalry. The horses were spooked by the still shifting ground, and couldn't seem to regain their balance. With their charge irrevocably broken Hassan's men ran to engage them.

Whether because they had two legs instead of four Hassan couldn't tell, but the men fared much better on the trembling ground than the animals. Within moments the cavalrymen were either pulled down from their mounts and dispatched or else had jumped to the ground of their own accord and were attempting to fight on foot. Their heavy armour was more than an inconvenience without their mounts' speed and reach to balance it out, and in less than a minute Hassan's troops had overwhelmed the two-dozen cavalrymen who had made it that far. His men were returning to their lines when a blinding bolt reached down from the southern keep and struck one of the young magi full in the chest. His body blackened as it cracked, eventually shattering as it toppled and hit the slowly deepening pool of rainwater now covering the courtyard, although Hassan was quite sure the mage had been dead well before it came to that.

*   *   *

In shock, Derrack stared up through the rain at the castle window where the bolt which had felled his companion originated from, and without realising what he was doing simply reached out to the aperture, causing the entire room to explode in a great gout of flame. The debris showered the courtyard at the base of the keep with fragments of stone and furnishings, leaving a jagged, four-span hole in the keep's wall.

The mage's aura in the tower faded as soon as he struck, and Derrack knew he had killed his target. With a glance at his fallen companion he realised that he didn't even know the man's name, and with a sinking feeling realised he should have been paying more attention to where the enemy magi were.

It's my fault he's dead, Derrack berated himself. There was still one mage left in the northern keep, and for a moment it surprised Derrack to find it was the lesser of the two magi he had dispatched a moment before. Judging from the enemy mage's aura there was no way a Gift user of such limited power would have been able to defeat either Derrack or his companion in a fair fight. Even caught off guard as they had been, the assailant must have used every bit of strength he possessed in the Gift to work a spell like the one he just had.

He would have to be far more careful in future Derrack suddenly realised, but for right now he could only feel relief that it wasn't his own broken body lying discarded on the stones of the courtyard.

*　　*　　*

The fighting was nearly over in the yard now, with the few defenders who remained alive and fit fleeing for the safety of the keeps. Hassan's men began to follow, but he called them back from the chase with a little help from Derrack who was able to amplify his voice so the men could hear his orders over the continuing storm.

"You're hurt!" Captain Fanning exclaimed as Hassan's old comrade-in-arms came over, limping slightly but otherwise unharmed.

"I'll be all right," Hassan assured the big man, whose wide chin contained far more wiry red hair than his scalp, "Take two companies and clear the wall Devlan. Accept any surrender offered. In fact, offer it to them unless you're directly threatened. We might be enemies today, but they are still loyal servants of the king and I want no more bloodshed than is absolutely necessary."

Devlan nodded gravely, "That's the Makers own truth."

"I'll get it done, colonel" he said, then saluted and turned to take command of some of the fresh troops still pouring into the courtyard.

Turning to a sergeant whose name he didn't know, Hassan told the man to take his company and act as stretcher bearers for the wounded, with a strict admonition to see to men on both sides of the fight.

"What now?" Derrack asked him as he began a brief inspection of Hassan's wound. The boy was no expert in Gift healing, nor was he a master of the Herbalists and Apothecaries Guild, but his training, like that of all magi who had passed the first tests would have included battlefield triage. Namely, how to use the Gift to stem the flow of blood and stop infection taking hold of a wound.

Using a wisp of spirit magic Derrack surveyed the point where the soldiers' knife had penetrated the armour and found the cut was clean.

"You'll heal given time or a mage more skilled than I," Derrack told him, while Hassan endured the inspection, trying not to breathe too deeply.

"What can you do now? I need to be functional for the next several hours at least."

Derrack thought for a moment before answering.

"I can slow the bleeding and deaden some of the pain but that's about all. Sorry, I'm only qualified in the most basic healing practices so far."

Hassan nodded in mute acceptance as he continued to watch his sodden men make their way through the restrictive gate.

"It will have to do."

He judged that nearly the entire army was in the courtyard now, and as soon as the walls were cleared, and the men rested for a minute they would have to move on one of the keeps. Which one he hadn't quite decided yet. He thought Tamgen was likely in the northern keep since that was where the command post for the entire garrison was located, but it was likely better defended than the southern keep for just that reason. There was also the mage who was still loose somewhere inside the northern castle to contend with.

Derrack mouthed a complex incantation and Hassan felt the pain immediately lessen as the spell took effect, then watched as the bleeding slowed to a mere trickle as Derrack completed his work.

"The pain is not gone, merely masked," Derrack warned, "And if you inflame the injury, the blood flow will return to normal within moments."

"I know the drill," Hassan told the young mage with a half grin, half grimace, while he waited for Devlan to return with news that the outer walls had finally been cleared.

By the time Captain Fanning came back down the stone

stairs and reported the task was complete, the rest of Hassan's men had caught their breath or were seeing to the wounded who might be saved.

Unfortunately, the dead would have to wait.

"Prisoners?" Hassan asked, but Devlan only shook his head.

"I don't think they believed me," he said with a frown.

"Make them!" Hassan growled as he turned away from his old friend.

Still undecided as to which castle to attack first, the roaring crack of an explosion interrupted his thoughts as the blocked in entrance to the northern keep was flung outward across the yard from inside.

"Charge!" Hassan roared, and his men reacted immediately, running at full speed towards the new opening in the northern castle, their boots displacing small splashes with every pounding step. Hassan tried to keep up, but before any of them could approach, the defenders were rushing out of the gaping entrance to meet the attackers head on. It appeared they were attempting to use the same strategy Hassan had employed a moment before in creating a bridgehead so more of their troops could enter the fray and push their opponents back.

Foolishness. Even if the entire castle turns out into the yard, they will still be outnumbered two to one.

The strategy had only worked for him because he could continuously replace his losses with fresh troops. But they must know that, a little voice suggested in his head.

Grabbing a passing soldier and jolting his own wound in the process, Hassan grimaced.

"Get back to the magi on the line and bring half of them down here now! Tell the others to follow three minutes later!" he shouted, then continued to run haltingly towards the battle, his right arm now a little stiff and slow of movement as he went.

As soon as the magi started moving, their spells would be interrupted unless they were especially strong in the Gift or of a particularly focused mind. Hassan knew he had less than five minutes to get his men inside one of the castles before the defenders could use their bows to devastating effect.

A thought occurred to him and he stopped four soldiers from joining the fray.

"Get to the corners of the castle, and report immediately if you see enemy troops approaching from the western wall!" he shouted over the continued howling of the storm.

His men were pushing the defenders back towards the castle entrance now, having more success at it than the Stonekeep garrison had. It wasn't luck or even skill, simply that the defenders had not had enough time to strengthen their line before being attacked and overwhelmed.

"Keep going! We need to get inside!" Hassan shouted to his men after their momentum slowed to a crawl. The pain in his side was slowly returning now. He must have jolted the wound worse than he'd thought when he'd grabbed that passing soldier.

After a minute or more of the holding action the defenders began backing off slowly as it became clear they could not hold the hasty position they had thrown up outside the door. Hassan's men pressed the attack, forcing them slowly back inside the main keep itself, through a long entry hall and finally into the huge chamber which lay beyond.

There were several doors leading away from the

chamber on the other three sides of the room and Hassan knew well what would happen as soon his men entered.

Someone called his name and Hassan was relieved to see the three magi standing just behind him had arrived in a timely fashion.

"Block off the exits on those two sides of the room," he told them without hesitation, pointing at several openings to his right and along the far wall. His men continued to stream into the antechamber and a moment later there was a shout from somewhere in the keep as defenders began to pour out of every entry in a planned ambush. Hassan nodded. It was as he'd expected, and probably would have been quite effective save for the four magi he now had at his side. Within moments four of the room's twelve doorways were sealed and then four more along the far wall, leaving the defenders who had rushed out of them cut off and behind Hassan's lines.

"There is still a mage in here somewhere," Hassan cautioned them before moving into the centre of the room. He had perhaps two thousand of his troops in the chamber now. A good many of them were busy keeping the defenders still exiting the passageways to their left busy, but there were enough unoccupied that the hundred and fifty or so defenders cut off when their exits closed were no longer a threat.

"Surrender!" Hassan shouted at the cornered men, "You can't win and you can't escape. Don't die here for nothing," he called over the echoes of steel and stone.

"Why should we believe you?" a grey bearded old captain shouted nervously from behind the line.

"I know why you fight so hard," Hassan told the man, "I served here, and I know what's up those stairs."

He knew he had the man as a subtle look of fear crossed the officer's features for an instant, he must have family among the civilians who would be sheltered in one of the top floors of the giant castle.

Although Stonekeep was a military installation, it was also a small town in its own right, and maintained a host of civilian workers who kept the garrison running smoothly, from cooks to tailors and merchants to engineers. Not a few families lived there full time as well, either because of commerce or because they had husbands or fathers amongst the garrison's officers.

"Amplify my voice," he told Derrack calmly, and the young mage complied.

"Orders!" Hassan barked over the noise of battle, and all but those in the front lines of the fighting stopped for a moment to listen.

"There are civilians upstairs. They are not to be harmed in any way unless they offer deadly threat. Every surrender by either civilian or military personnel is to be accepted and honoured. There will be no more bloodshed today than is absolutely necessary to carry out Nereth's orders."

He nodded to Derrack, who let the spell dissipate as the veteran captain looked Hassan up and down, studying him as if his life depended on his coming to the right conclusion. And Hassan supposed that from his perspective, it did.

Looking around at the room the captain knew there was no escape to be found, they were surrounded by an overwhelming number of Hassan's troops. Being a tall man, he could make out over the crowd that his comrades across the way were being pushed back further into the corridors with each passing moment. No rescue would come from there. Hassan could see him measuring it up. The fight continued, but the first battle for the northern keep was over.

Privately Hassan acknowledged that it would have been a profoundly different outcome had the dozen archmagi who were normally stationed in each keep still been present.

Hassan's men were firmly ensconced in the antechamber now and he grimaced as he did a quick estimation. There were only about three to four thousand of his command remaining if he judged correctly, and that number would be reduced again while the men finished sweeping the castle, room by room. Then they would have to deal with the southern keep and even the walls and towers which lined the canyon to the west. Suddenly Hassan realised that despite the almost miraculous ease with which they had breached the walls and taken the yard, he still didn't have enough men to see this through without it turning into a bloodbath. If they were to be victorious here, he needed a quick resolution to this fight. He had to find Tamgen, and that meant fighting his way up the stairs to the command post six levels above their current position before his old friend realised the same thing he had.

"Your choice, Captain?" he asked the veteran. He could afford to waste no more time here, a fact which must not have been lost on the old soldier as the grey bearded veteran cursed.

"Put 'em down boys. This corner of the room is not worth our lives," he snarled, then sheathed his sword and removed the scabbard from his belt, laying the old but functional weapon on the floor stones.

Hassan gave the man a brief nod, then sectioned off a detachment of his own men to collect the weapons from the defenders, while another, led by a somewhat recovered Jarl, stood guard.

"Put them with the civilians as soon as is convenient," he told the captain, who saluted as Hassan turned away.

The fighting had moved out into the corridors now and Hassan could see the stairway leading upwards was clear of troops for the moment.

"You. Bring your men and follow," he said to a passing captain and motioned Derrack to follow, along with one of the archmagi. The soldiers formed up around their injured commander and the two Gift users, and the hundred or so strong party climbed the broad set of stairs watchfully, expecting an attack at any moment.

They made it to the third storey on the switch-backing stairs with only minor skirmishes, after that the way was blocked by defending troops intent on allowing them no further. Hassan was forced to order the two magi to clear their path as his men began to be driven back, and eventually the survivors were able to ascend to the sixth floor, though not without a disturbing amount of bloodshed.

As they rounded the entrance to the seventh floor where the command post was located, the thirty or so men who had survived the frenzied fighting were charged by a group of defenders. These men were desperate, intent on keeping the command room safe from the invading forces running almost unchecked through the rest of the keep.

There was hard fighting for a minute or two, and although he tried to stay clear of the actual combat,

Hassan's side felt as though it were on fire each time he was forced to lift his heavy broadsword for a strike. Just as abruptly as the defenders had attacked, the few remaining survivors withdrew from the entrance of the stairway and fled down a long corridor with his men in close pursuit.

The first of Hassan's men to make it around the corner at the end of the corridor were greeted with a hail of bow fire which felled half a dozen of the soldiers before the rest could halt their headlong chase.

"Ambush!" someone called needlessly, and for a moment all was silence except for the heavy breathing of the tired men and the groans and screams of the wounded.

The command post for the entire garrison was just beyond this next intersection, and Hassan kicked himself mentally for not anticipating the defenders' tactic. The pain in his side had grown bad enough to distract him, and he could see blood once again seeping from the wound.

Taking a deep breath, he turned to the two magi beside him.

"Can you stun the men in the next room long enough for us to charge them?" he inquired.

The two Gift users in their black cloaks conferred for a moment and then the archmage nodded.

"Close your eyes and cover your ears," she ordered, and Hassan gestured for his men to follow suit.

For a moment nothing happened, then a light, blinding in its intensity even through his tightly shut eyelids appeared all around them, a crack like thunder peeling right there in the corridor followed, shocking in its abruptness. After a second, no more, the light faded as suddenly as it had appeared, and Hassan called for the charge.

"Take as many prisoners as you can. The garrison commander is not to be harmed!" he shouted as the men ran round the intersection to knock down the half dozen archers who laid in wait, but were now standing or flailing about as they tried vainly to see the approaching attackers.

With a minimum of fuss the archers were disarmed or knocked unconscious and Hassan's last twenty men continued on.

"Destroy that door please," Hassan painfully asked the archmage as they came on a formidable iron bound portal which was no doubt locked and barred on the other side.

The archmage nodded, and the door exploded inward, knocking aside men and furniture as it made contact. His remaining men wasted no time charging into a sizeable room sporting a huge westward facing balcony which overlooked Stonekeep Pass.

The men in this room were not quite as incapacitated as the ambushing archers had been, but neither were they in any condition to mount a coordinated defence. The exploding door had caused significant damage inside the room and Hassan's men took advantage of the situation, knocking soldiers down and disarming them before they could fully recover. Within a minute they had subdued the nobles and officers of Stonekeep along with their personal guards, those still of a mind to fight being knocked senseless by the magi before they could rally.

Hassan surveyed the command room and found not much had changed since he'd served here all those years ago under Tamgen's father. With a sudden surge of shame he bellowed at his men to clear the area and take the captives with them.

"I think I'll go look for our wayward mage," The archmage declared before leaving as well.

"Derrack, you stay," he ordered as he went over to where Tamgen was still sitting stunned against a wall, where he had fallen during the brief struggle. Tamgen's face was mottled purple and red, and his eyes were swollen shut from where debris from the door had battered the top half of his head. With the young mage's aid, he helped his wounded friend gently to his feet and then back to the chair behind his desk in the centre of the room. Not that Tamgen was likely to consider him a friend anymore.

When the command room was finally empty of all but the three of them, Hassan sighed.

"How did it come to this?" Tamgen asked dispiritedly.

"I don't know," Hassan replied, leaning heavily against the wooden desk for support, favouring his injured right side, "But I do know that unless we stop this madness, several thousand more men will not live to see the end of this day."

"What are your intentions?" Tamgen asked bleakly as he searched blindly around the room for the source of his old friend's voice.

"I've already ordered all surrenders to be accepted, and no civilian is to be harmed except as a last act of defence."

Tamgen nodded slightly, "At least you still have that much honour,"

"Will his sight return?" Hassan asked with concern.

Derrack nodded.

"I think so," the young mage replied, "The main impact seems to be above the eyes themselves, but I can't guarantee anything until they have been properly examined.

Tamgen nodded minutely at the news, but apart from that gave very little reaction.

"It's time for you to surrender," Hassan said as gently as he could. He knew Tamgen was a proud man, and Hassan loathed the need to bring his old friend to his knees, but this madness could not be allowed to continue any longer.

"You know as well as I do that without the compliment of magi Stonekeep usually boasts, combined with the number of magi Nereth commands now on my side I have sufficient forces to overrun Stonekeep's remaining forces if you make me. We both know I can't win decisively with this many troops, but neither can I withdraw without forfeiting the lives of my soldiers' families back in Miralthrall."

"What do you propose?" Tamgen asked through clenched teeth. The man was prideful, but never stupid. "You know I cannot let Stonekeep fall lest the western nations have free reign across the mountains. You may have weakened us too far already."

Hassan sighed. "I know, but I cannot stop. Surrender Stonekeep to me and stand down your forces. Do that and we avoid a bloodbath which I would eventually win anyway. In return, I give you my word I will cease all hostilities against your men as soon as you comply, and have my magi help with healing your wounded. It's the fortifications Heramiir wants control of Tamgen, not you or your men. He wants to ensure that Stonekeep is not used as a base to sortie against him next spring, and he needs to be certain its defences are not decreased while he's busy with the king's army by doing so."

"And what are my soldiers to do once you have this control?"

"Some will have to stay here and help defend the castle from the western nations, others will join my command. The same goes for the soldiers I brought here with me, but they will be relieved by fresh troops from Miralthrall within the next two weeks I'm told. Life will continue much as it always has. The magi will return to help defend Stonekeep, but I will have to leave someone else in charge, at least temporarily. You understand you won't exactly be trusted quickly or easily because of all, this..."

"You're someone to talk about trust?" Tamgen returned, his voice sullen and resentful.

Hassan gasped as a stab of pain worked its way through his chest and he leaned even more heavily against the polished wood of Tamgen's desk.

"This is a hard thing for all of us Tamgen. But I know you. You would have made the exact same choices I have had it been your family and those of your men against the wall instead of mine."

For a moment the blinded man seemed about to object, but then his shoulders sagged, and he whispered, "Would I? I suppose I would have at that."

He stood slowly, even gracefully for a man who'd taken a head wound bad enough that he couldn't see.

"I have your personal word you'll keep the civilians safe and have my men healed?"

"You do," Hassan solemnly promised.

Tamgen folded his hands behind his back as he grimaced, a single tear falling from his sightless eyes as he said words which had never been uttered in the nearly three thousand years since the castle had first been constructed.

"Then on those agreed terms, Stonekeep is yours. I yield."

*   *   *

"Riders coming in!" a distant lookout shouted.

Hassan looked up tiredly to see the two soldiers heading out of the morning mist and into the camp. He watched for a moment as the men conferred with the lookout and saw the man point in the direction of the command tent near where he was standing.

It had been nearly two days now since Tamgen had surrendered, and Hassan's wound had been seen to by one of the magi. It would probably be stiff for another few days while it finished healing on its own. Hassan knew the mage could have done a better job had he wished, but with this many wounded they were conserving their strength by doing only the minimal amount necessary to ensure life. It was common field practice, and ensured they could see to as many of the casualties as possible with what strength remained to them after the battle, at least until they'd dealt with all the critical cases.

Seeing the riders were definitely headed for the tent he began walking down the gentle slope of the camp to intercept them. If Nereth heard there news first there was no guarantee he ever would.

The two men saluted as they approached, and Hassan returned the gesture quickly before asking, "What news?"

The two soldiers looked askance at each other for a moment and then the senior one reported.

"We were sent to Clearbrook to scout the village Sir," he began with a frown.

"When we arrived at the site, nothing was left. No houses, people, fields, not even a chicken remained," the man reported in clear agitation.

"It was completely destroyed?" Hassan demanded. Clearbrook was not a city, but neither was it a small rural village either.

"No, Sir, not destroyed. It was gone. There is nothing left, the path to the village simply ends in the grass. At first we thought we had taken a wrong turn somehow, but after backtracking a way we realised we'd gotten it right the first time. Clearbrook no longer exists, Sir. I'm a tracker, have been for twenty-odd years, it's as if the village never was, even the grass looks undisturbed. I just don't understand it Sir," the veteran scout finished in a rush, clearly rattled by what he had seen.

"And you can confirm this?" Hassan demanded of the second scout.

"Yes Sir. I don't have a clue what to make of it, but yes, I saw it with my own eyes as well."

"Very well," Hassan replied, suddenly deep in thought, "Take your news to Archmage Nereth, he's in the pavilion," he pointed to the command tent at the crest of the hill.

"Then get yourselves something to eat," he told the men, who saluted again and rode off.

There was something very wrong about the account the soldiers had just given him, but he couldn't quite credit that the men would lie when it would be such a simple matter for him to check the information. Nor did they look drunk as might be supposed from their report.

He was still deep in thought minutes later when Derrack came thundering past him on a horse at full gallop. A moment later Nereth exited the pavilion and called down to him.

"Section off a hundred men, Colonel. We leave for Clearbrook immediately."

WINTER

She is the one thing all races hold in common. She is our doom.
One of the few known fragments of Oo'vi Lore.

CHAPTER 18

THE BLACK LADY

"Today you will leave the camp for a weeklong practice patrol," Karthael announced from the doorway, causing the men of squad four twenty-two to spring from their beds at his early morning arrival.

By now they were well used to the Arborii instructor appearing at random times before each dawn. 'To get you accustomed to waking and being alert when the unexpected occurs,' as he had once explained to them.

Today clouds dominated the sky, and an icy wind blew through the open doorway making everyone shiver, everyone except Seth at least, who even in his small-clothes stood calm and in control as always.

"With winter about to begin?" Tauman commented without thinking.

Wyll wrapped his arms around himself for warmth as Karthael came inside. By the look of the sky through the open doorway the sun wouldn't be showing itself above the tree line for at least another hour.

Kienan yawned, apologising before the instructor made comment.

"Military operations run in every season," Karthael remarked sternly, drawing a grimace from Bosric.

"Easy for you to say, Sir. You have fur," the short red-headed man said with a laugh.

Karthael blinked eyes far larger than a human's as he regarded the shortest member of the squad, though his expression as ever was difficult to read.

"Your patrol route," the instructor began again as if Bosric had never spoken. "Will be as follows."

"Take North Road to the Camar River. Head east along the path running adjacent to its southern bank until you exit the eastern border of the Emerald Sea. Once there, travel south along the forest border until you reach the third watch tower. Head west for a day, directly through the Emerald Sea until you arrive at the Arborii town of Emereth's Glade. From there a guide will meet you with further instructions. Questions?"

There was a moment of silence which Marad broke abruptly, "Are you not coming with us, Instructor?"

Karthael shook his head in an almost human gesture.

"I have orders which will keep me occupied for the next several days at least," he replied, looking them over one by one.

"In my absence I am leaving Brendan temporarily in charge of the squad."

No one was truly surprised at the choice, but Marad seemed on the point of objecting before Karthael nailed him with a hard look.

"You will all obey his orders for the duration of the mission," he said, their gazes locked until eventually the dark-skinned giant of a man looked away.

"Rest assured, you will all have a chance to prove yourself in a leadership capacity before your training is through.

That seemed to mollify Marad's pride somewhat, and the big man eventually gave the Arborii instructor a half nod of acceptance.

"Now, unless any of you have the desire to question my orders further?" Karthael looked around at them again, prompting a chorus of negative answers, although Wyll could have sworn Bosric had said 'no, fur' in a response well timed enough to be drowned out by the others.

"Ready yourselves for the patrol and leave the courtyard in twenty minutes, I've already sent for your horses and supplies."

"Yes Sir," Brendan replied smartly, even though Karthael had already turned and was halfway out the door by the time he spoke.

For a few moments no one said anything else, then Cale turned towards his bunk and started pulling out the rough wooden chest which held his belongings.

"You heard the man," Brendan said as Cale flipped open the lid and started rummaging through the contents.

"Gather your gear and see to your ablutions. We ride in twenty."

There were nods and grins all around. Marad even grunted his acknowledgement as the men began hastily dressing, more from the cold than any sense of modesty which remained after living in such close quarters for so many phases. First their uniforms went on, and then the heavy leather armour including the thick gauntlets and face guards which they were required to operate in while completing their training tasks. Once they were done and had visited the privy, the men returned and set about gathering their weapons, saddles, extra cloaks, and anything else they might need for the extended patrol.

Bosric began humming a wordless tune as he finished with his things and shoved the chest back under Tauman's bunk, which lay beneath his own.

"You're happy?" Tauman remarked to the shorter man as he also finished, closing the wooden lid of his chest and pushing it back in next to Bosric's.

"Are you kidding?" the short man replied, "A full week away from here, and all we have to do is ride. That means no drills from sunup to sundown for the next few days for a start. Besides, I've travelled across most of Jeranon at one time or another, but one thing I've never seen is a genuine Arborii town."

Tauman nodded in considered agreement before returning Bosric's ever present grin. The red-haired knife man reacted by giving his taller companion a good-natured slap on the shoulder before the pair of them headed out the door and into the massive courtyard of camp five.

By the time Wyll finished gathering his things and strapping on his sword, he looked up to see only Seth was still in the room, and already on his way to the door. He shoved the chest under his bunk and followed the top-knotted man, who after these last phases together, Wyll now thought of as the most dangerous of his companions by far. Surprisingly, Seth held the door open long enough for Wyll to step through with his things before the warrior himself exited the barracks. There was little doubt left in Wyll's mind these days that a warrior was exactly what the man had been even well before the conscriptions had forced him into the army.

"Thanks," he said.

Of all the men in the squad, Seth was the only one who still kept to himself after these last few phases of training.

Some of the men considered him standoffish, and others gave wary glances when they thought he wasn't looking, though Wyll was sure he knew they did it. There was just something about the way he moved, the way he looked at you that made you uneasy. A kind of deadly quietness which always made you think he was on the point of violence. Not that he had ever acted on it that Wyll had seen, and he was sure he would have heard if any of the others had.

He tried to study his squad mate unobtrusively, but Seth's face was as calm, and as cold as ever.

As he came out into the predawn dimness, Wyll's breath froze on the wind, and he was glad for the extra cloak he'd packed in his bags as he walked out into dawn of winter's first real freeze.

All around him snow was lightly falling, though he was grateful the howling wind from last night had died down substantially.

"So where are you from?" Wyll asked, as much for something to break the silence as to find out the answer. Seth was notoriously tight lipped about his life before being conscripted, another thing which set the others on edge. They all knew they would be marching to war as soon as the snows melted, and no one wanted to do it with a man they knew nothing about guarding their backs.

"If I told you," he said with a rare grin, one which set Wyll's teeth on edge, "I would then have to kill you. Better you don't know, yes?"

Wyll missed a step before continuing, less than half sure Seth had been joking. It sounded like a joke. Surely it had to be. But if it was, then it was the first he had made since coming to the camp.

The two of them walked the rest of the way to where the others were waiting in silence. When they arrived, Wyll saw that all the horses except his own had been brought out, including a dappled packhorse laden with sacks of what must have been provisions.

"Where's Socks?" Wyll asked the others.

There were shrugs and shaking of heads all around, and when it became obvious no one knew, Brendan told him to go to the stables and find out what the hold up was. Wyll slung his saddlebag and saddle across the packhorse's back and began jogging off toward the huge structure on the other side of the camp, hoping he would warm up as he did.

A few minutes later he arrived, and just as he was about to go inside, a young boy met him leading Socks out by the reins.

"He wouldn't let any of the other grooms near him," the boy said, passing the thin strip of leather over to Wyll's hands as Socks gave him a friendly nudge with his head.

"Thanks, Andrew," Wyll said, remembering the boy's name, "The way you are with him and the other horses, I'm sure you'll be head groom here in no time."

The boy gave him a broad grin as Wyll vaulted up onto Socks' back. Without wasting time he turned the horse to ride bareback over to where the others were trying to keep their hands warm, and the light snow away from their faces, as they waited in the cold twilight of predawn for his return.

When he dismounted to reclaim and attach his saddle and bags Brendan raised an eyebrow in question.

"Socks took exception to being led by the grooms," Wyll

told him as he worked, thick leather gauntlets and his cold fingers conspiring to make the simple task a little more tricky than usual. Soon enough though, his bags were tied firmly behind the saddle. With a hardly needed step up in the stirrups Wyll leapt up onto Socks' back and Brendan ordered them to move out.

When they reached the north gate a few moments later Brendan motioned for them to stop. The gate guard, who looked alert and professional despite the falling snow and last hour of his watch, stepped out in front of them and issued a standard challenge.

"Squad four twenty-two departing on assigned patrol," Brendan answered crisply.

The sentry glanced at the list he was holding for a moment and then nodded.

"Everything's in order soldier, good luck out there," he responded while throwing them a quick salute which Brendan returned as the guard moved aside to let the riders pass.

"All right then," Brendan said to himself as he got his brown stallion moving with only a cursory look to check the others were following his lead.

For half an hour they rode up North Road through the gently falling snow. Soon enough the sky lightened around them with the first glow of dawn, which today was marked only by a lightening of the clouds above. Birds sang in the trees, although Wyll was hard pressed to put names to more than one or two of them as they called out the new day. Eventually the path divided, the left fork heading further north to Aramar as it crossed the Camar River. The men knew it well as they had been using it to go to and from The Man at Arms on sixth-day's for several phases now.

Without so much as slowing though, Brendan turned his war trained mount down the other path, the one leading east. It paralleled the south bank of the Camar for some time before exiting the Emerald Sea for several miles as they passed Aramar. Its spiderweb of docks boasted dozens of moored ships ranging from small canoes to three-masted behemoths like the one Jayden's family owned. Beyond them, the view of the city on its slight upward slope from the river's opposite shore was spectacular. Both the palace and the College of the Arts' buildings were visible, and from here even the new wall they had been digging the foundations for could be seen running in a ring around the city. For more than an hour he took in the sight of Jeranon's capital as they rode, but eventually the path reached a fork of the river and it forced them into a more southerly direction.

As the icy morning dragged by there was little talk amongst the men. For once Wyll was grateful for the normally irritating leather face guard and gauntlets which were part of his temporary armour until the weapon smiths back at the camp had finished with the squad's plate mail. That was what they would ride to battle in, along with fifteen-foot steel tipped lances Karthael assured them would take down even an Imbic if they struck home competently.

Sometime around mid-morning, the forest border abruptly cut east and engulfed the path. From one step to the next, the men found themselves riding under the canopy of giant trees which had lost none of their leaves to dawn of winter's new hold. Soon enough the sound of rushing water filtered through the forest and the men began looking ahead with a little more interest. A mile or so later they crested a rise in the forest path to reveal a swiftly moving tributary, its wide, clear flow rushing along in haste to join the south fork of the Camar somewhere to the east.

Brendan pulled up his horse, the animal's breath still freezing on the wind even at this hour, and gave the river a hard stare, his lips thinning to nothing in irritation.

"Where's the bridge?" Sarran asked unnecessarily.

They had all stopped now, and even Seth was looking around with a puzzled expression at the path which ended a few paces from the riverbank.

It stopped abruptly beside one of the biggest trees Wyll had ever seen, even in the Emerald Sea, though if a bridge had ever connected it to the other bank, there was no sign of it now.

With a deeply perturbed expression Brendan got down off his horse and crossed the few steps to where Tauman was taking his turn leading the packhorse. The tattooed veteran rummaged through one of the bags for a minute before locating the package he must have known the instructor would place within, and dragged out a small oiled leather folder. Carefully unfolding the contents, which Wyll saw was a map with their patrol route marked in pencil, along with where they should be by the end of each day's ride. For several moments Brendan studied the map before shaking his head and handing it off to Cale, who also looked it over before shrugging and passing it back.

"All right," Brendan spoke up for them all to hear, "We're in the correct spot, but as you can all see, there's no bridge," he told them irritably.

"Spread out, see if you can find some other way across,

meet back here in half an hour regardless of your results."

And just like that the men moved off.

Karthael had made a good choice putting Brendan in charge of the mission Wyll thought, and wondered if the others would have been as ready to obey those same orders if it had been him chosen instead.

After scouting the river to the east for some time he headed back to where most of the others were already waiting. A few extra minutes saw them all once again gathered at the end of the path where the bridge should have been.

"Anything?" Brendan asked Seth, who had been the last to return, and presumably gone the farthest.

The top-knotted warrior only shook his head in the negative though, and for a moment Brendan seemed on the verge of losing his normally even temper.

"I can't believe the instructor would send us out here on a wild goose chase," he declared at last, "There must be some way of getting to the other side. Ideas, anyone?" he asked eventually.

"Is there another crossing?" Sarran inquired.

Brendan nodded.

"Yes, but it's a good two-day ride south into the Emerald Sea. Even if we took that path and cut cross country to where we need to be, we couldn't hope to complete the patrol in under ten days, and we're due back in seven."

"I don't suppose we could build a raft?" Kienan suggested, even as Brendan shook his head.

"With this rough water the horses would never see the other side," Tauman said before Brendan could speak.

"You don't cut wood in an Arborii forest," Seth abruptly

announced, giving Wyll a start. The warrior with the black topknot of hair almost never volunteered information without being asked. The fact he had chosen to do so now seemed to lend more weight to his words than his calm voice would otherwise have warranted.

"You're both right," Brendan said with a nod, "Come on people, there must be something we're missing."

Socks began to frisk a bit in the chilly air of the forest, and Wyll let him have his rein since they were not going anywhere for the moment. A few steps later Wyll found himself beside the giant tree which straddled the end of the path. As he looked across the Camar to the far bank, he couldn't help but notice the path on that side also ended at the base of another giant bole very much like the one he was now sitting next to.

The trees along this part of the river were vast, stretching a quarter mile off the ground and spreading their enormous branches far out across the river. Some of the largest ones even blocked off the sky in places as they intersected with counterparts which had grown out from the opposite bank. A thought struck him, and as Wyll looked up, he couldn't help but grin as his hunch was borne out. The immense tree he was perched under was one of those whose branches were large enough to reach out and entangle with those from the other side. He followed the entwined branch with his eyes, and as he was suddenly sure it would be, he saw that the tree joined to his from the other side was the very one growing at the resumption of the path.

"Good boy," he breathed, giving Socks a pat on the neck. The white stallion gave him a look Wyll could only describe as smug before rubbing his head against a small patch of discoloured bark which Wyll had taken for moss at first glance. Socks then gave him another meaningful look and took a step forward so Wyll could reach the small, slightly redder patch of bark himself.

What have I got to lose?

Wyll shrugged as he placed his hand on the coloured patch, vaguely disturbed that he was taking directions from a horse, even if Socks had been proven to be no common mount.

There was a sudden loud rustling noise from far above, causing the men to stop their ongoing discussion and stare up into the foliage. A moment later what looked like a huge latticework of branches came into view rapidly enough that several of the men grabbed at their reins in an attempt to get out of its path, before realising the foliage was moving too slowly. The others looked at him as he took his hand off the tree, prompting the latticework to halt in mid-air, suspended by some kind of vines from above.

With a grin Wyll replaced his hand on the patch, and the platform once again continued its downward journey, until a minute later it was resting on the forest floor beside him.

"All aboard," he said with a grin that rivalled Bosric's, while the red-headed knife man laughed out loud.

Brendan gave him an approving nod and stepped up onto the thick platform to inspect it more closely. After a few moments he turned back to Wyll and said, "Send me up. I want to see what's up there before we try to move the horses."

Wyll nodded, and hoping it would work both ways he put his hand back on the patch of colour, immediately sending their temporary commander up into the treetops and out of the squad's sight. A few anxious minutes passed as the men waited for a signal until finally Brendan shouted for Wyll to let him down.

When he was once again safe on the forest floor, Brendan looked at the horses for a moment in thought.

"We've found the bridge," he announced with satisfaction, "And we should be able to lead the horses across if we can get them up there without them panicking."

"Blindfold them," Tauman said.

"As long as they can't see how high off the ground they are, they shouldn't get too out of control. We just need to keep them calm while that, thing, is in motion."

After considering for a moment Brendan decided to take Tauman at his word. Although the unremarkable looking man claimed to be a modest grain merchant from Damerette, it had become clear very early in the training that he knew more about horses than all the rest of them put together. Wyll didn't know what the man's actual story was, but he was convinced Tauman had been something far more, or at least far different, than what he claimed before being conscripted into the king's army.

"Do it," Brendan ordered, "And lead them all the way. This isn't the time for mistakes. I don't want to lose anyone today because their horse decides to bolt. Clear?"

There was a chorus of 'yes sir's,' and a nod from Marad as the men set about digging shirts or whatever else they could find in their packs to wrap around the horses' eyes. Some of the mounts tried to resist being blindfolded, but soon all but Socks were readied and calmed by their riders. Socks of course chose to be wilful, simply walking himself onto the platform over Wyll's objections, even as he was trying unsuccessfully to dig a shirt out from his bags. The stallion then stood calmly, waiting for him to follow.

"Man, I swear there's something not right about that horse of yours," Marad said as he watched Socks' performance. Wyll grimaced and nodded ruefully as he went to stand beside the half rahara steed.

"All right, we'll have to do this in two groups. Wyll, Cale, Sarran, Marad and Kienan, you'll head up first. Call when you're clear of the… platform, and we'll bring it back down and follow you up."

He went to stand beside the patch of coloured bark and looked at them to make sure they were set.

"Ready," Wyll told him, and with that Brendan placed his hand on the patch and sent them smoothly up into the trees.

"It seemed faster before," Sarran commented after a moment.

"Probably the weight," Kienan replied just as casually as it lifted them into the treetops, though his eyes betrayed the fact he was anything but calm.

At last the living platform came to rest without so much as a visible join, next to a vast flat-topped branch ten spans across.

Wyll led Socks out forward and waited for the others to make their way off the platform and onto more solid footing, ensuring they were well away from the edge before calling down that they were clear. A second later the platform abruptly began to move, and Wyll took an involuntary step back as he found himself looking off into a quarter mile of empty space below.

"I'll cross and find the control for the other side," Marad announced as he began leading his dun stallion across the bridge's expanse. Surrounding the huge interlocking branches was a wall of foliage thick enough that the horses couldn't have seen through even if they'd wanted to. Where the roof of the living corridor should have been was another matter however, and open to the sky. Sporadic drifts of snow were still falling from the clouds, covering green and brown foliage with white where they landed.

"Bring us up!" Wyll heard a faint shout from below, and he hurried to where another coloured patch adorned the still thick trunk of the giant tree.

A minute or so saw the rest of the squad safely up and off the platform, and they quickly but carefully crossed over the bridge in single file, despite there being plenty of room to either side. No one wanted to get too close to the edge, especially not leading the blindfolded horses, which were still mostly calm, but beginning to frisk a little at walking while they couldn't see.

Soon enough the squad crossed to the other side of the bridge. The distant sound of rushing water far below the treetop walkway keeping their minds firmly on the task.

"Same order as before," Brendan announced when they'd all caught up to where Marad had located the control for the platform on this side of the river.

In minutes it was done and almost anticlimactically both groups of men and horses were safely back on the ground on the eastern bank of the tributary without incident.

"If that's their idea of a bridge, I can't wait to see what that village, what did the instructor call it, Emereth's Glade, looks like?" Kienan said half to himself, though loud enough for them all to hear.

"Speaking of which, we've lost some time here and we

need to be at the edge of the forest by nightfall according to the map," Brendan reminded them as he stuffed the folded parchment back into the packhorse's bundle.

Bosric gave Wyll a shrug as their eyes met, along with his perpetual grin.

"So why are we still sitting here?" he asked flippantly of the men.

Brendan gave him a look halfway between disapproval and amusement before shaking his head with a laugh.

"Let's go," the tattooed commander ordered. He booted his brown stallion to a gallop and rode off down the southeast path towards their destination, never seeing the hidden figure watching their progress from a well concealed hide just a few spans into the forest.

*   *   *

By nightfall the squad had emerged from the eastern edge of the Emerald Sea and located a suitable campsite for the evening. They had arrived an hour later than Brendan had been hoping, but eventually the time lost looking for the way over the river had been mostly made up. In the distance, farms could be seen in a nearby valley, but this close to the forest, the flat, grassy ground was bare of habitation by either human or Arborii. Thankfully, enough dead wood for a fire lay strewn about from a recent storm to get them through. The night was clear and cold, but the snow had stopped earlier in the day. The men were all grateful it hadn't yet rained since leaving the camp.

The next morning Brendan ordered them to carry their own rations and place the spare firewood on the packhorse. It wasn't much, but he knew they would all be glad of a little extra warmth tonight should it snow again during the day.

A few minutes ride to the south saw them crest a steep hill, revealing the first of the watchtowers Karthael had told them about. It was a hundred spans high and made of a shiny black stone crisscrossed with creeping vines and mosses. It reminded Wyll of the lighthouse in Grandell, but unlike that well-maintained structure, the watchtower had an air of something ancient and decaying about it.

The only real surprise of the day came as they were riding past the base of the ancient structure and a captain in the uniform of Aramar's garrison stepped out of a concealed doorway and waved them down.

"Squad four twenty-two?" the bearded man asked in a gruff voice, getting a 'yes sir' from Brendan.

"Which camp are you from?"

"Camp five," he returned smoothly, as if the tattooed man had been expecting this all along.

The bearded man nodded and then called up to the sky. "Stand down."

Wyll looked up just in time to see a half dozen heavy crossbows disappear back over the top of the tower's railing. He swallowed hard.

"You're right on time," the captain told them with approval in his voice, "See you keep it that way recruits. Dismissed."

Brendan returned the man's salute and the bearded captain went back into the tower, the door closing behind him so even the vines looked undisturbed against the door's worn surface.

"Hmmf," Marad snorted as Brendan kicked his horse to

a trot without a word, getting the squad moving once again.

By nightfall they reached the second tower and the captain in command came out to challenge them just as the first had. A thin man with a balding head, he offered them a place to spend the night out of the rain which had just begun to fall, and Brendan gratefully accepted the offer. The horses were tied up on the ground floor while the men were billeted in some of the empty bunks the under-manned tower had spare.

They left at daybreak, thanking the officer for his hospitality before riding all day through chill conditions until an hour before sunset, the third tower finally came into sight.

Again they were challenged and sent on their way, although the officer cautioned them that if they wanted to have a fire tonight, they had best collect the wood before heading into the Emerald Sea.

The man went back inside his tower and Brendan ordered the others to collect what wood they could find as a freshening wind abruptly came in from the east.

Seth was sent ahead to scout for a campsite inside the Emerald Sea while the rest of them searched for whatever firewood they could recover. A half hour later they met back at the entrance to the forest path. There wasn't much wood Wyll noted, but it was better than nothing on a night as cold as this. Snow had begun to fall in earnest now, and Brendan ordered them in amongst the trees as they waited for Seth to return with the position of their campsite. Outside the forest's protection the sky had greyed and the short grass beyond the forest's edge was covered with a ghostly white as the dim sun sank below cover of the Emerald Sea. Dawn of winter was finally upon them, and with the first real snows, everything that had happened to him over the last few phases solidified in Wyll's mind.

When these snows stop, we march to war.

Wyll pulled his cloak closer about himself and turned at the sound of a horse. A moment later Seth appeared at the limits of their snow obscured vision, cocking his head and meaning for the squad to follow.

A few minutes of careful riding through the snow-covered undergrowth brought them to the mouth of a deep cave which looked to work its way into the side of a rock embankment crowned with an ancient, towering bole.

Without a word Seth got down off his horse and led them inside to where the fissure opened into a cavern easily wide enough to hold the men and horses.

Wyll couldn't help but look around in the dim light. The striations in the rock made it strangely beautiful, and a myriad of tangled roots had worked their way down through the stone at the back of the cavern to rest in a pool of gathered water. A fire was quickly built under a thin fissure which led out to clear air above, and they fed the horses from their dwindling supplies. Wyll was privately hoping they would be restocked in Emereth's Glade as they clearly didn't have enough food on the packhorse to last out the week. Still, the night passed uneventfully, and the small fire gave off just enough heat so that no one woke more than slightly chilled in the morning.

Breakfast rations were handed out and the men quickly readied themselves for yet another day in the saddle. As dawn rose, they left the sheltered warmth of the cave and returned to the path which would lead them ever deeper into the Emerald Sea, and the Arborii town which was their mandated waypoint.

They continued riding until well after midday, again eating flatbread and cheese as they rode, until they rounded a corner in the path which opened out to a clearing two hundred spans across.

Wyll reined Socks to a halt as he stared at the scene before him. Curiously though, none of the others so much as slowed their pace as they headed for an opening in the forest wall on the other side of the village.

Emereth's Glade, it must be. But why aren't the others stopping?

All around the clearing Arborii were standing motionless, watching, although they otherwise appeared to be going about their everyday lives. A grey-furred fletcher was plying his craft on a nearby stool, holding the arrow he was working on with his tail so that he could use both hands. A young Arborii, perhaps even by human standards, carried a basket of laundry on her tan head, her too large eyes watching the riders in utter fascination. Elsewhere Arborii children had been playing a game with sticks and a large gourd, and every one of them was silent, watching, waiting for the humans to pass.

What is going on? Wyll thought as he moved out into the clearing, following his oblivious squad mates.

Wyll had some slight knowledge of the Gift from Jayden, and he belatedly realised there was something not entirely natural occurring in Emereth's Glade. It wasn't until an Arborii child in the path of the horses tiptoed gracefully out of their way though, being very careful not to make even the slightest of noises, he realised the others truly couldn't see it. What's more the Arborii seemed to know the humans were blinded to their presence, there was no other reason for them to be remaining as quiet as they were. They must have some kind of mystical ward in place which shielded their village from prying eyes, but from their actions Wyll thought it a good bet the warding didn't stop sound getting through as well.

He had heard vague rumours in the camp that the Arborii villages within the Emerald Sea were well hidden, for protection and privacy supposedly, though he'd heard nothing about the Gift being used to achieve it. Why he should be able to see the village despite their ward when the others clearly couldn't Wyll did not understand. This had to be what the rumours were getting at though, or at least Wyll very much hoped so, otherwise he was about to look really, really stupid.

"There's no need to hide," he called, prompting the rest of the squad to stop and look back at him as if he'd lost his mind. "We're not here to harm you. Is this Emereth's Glade?"

"Wyll, who are you talking to?" Brendan asked in consternation.

Wyll just looked at him for a long moment with a grimace before waving his hand around the clearing, knowing how his next statement would sound.

"At this village full of Arborii," he answered with a nervous grin, "You really can't see them at all, can you?"

Brendan, and most of the others as well, looked around the clearing again as if wondering whether Wyll was having them on.

"That's not funny Wyll," Marad declared, "We're wasting time here Brendan, let's go."

Brendan gave the big man a withering look in response.

"We go when I say, not a second before. Is that clear, Marad?"

The ebony skinned giant of a man looked away after a moment and mumbled something incoherent, but held his place as he looked around the clearing once again.

"What can you see Wyll?" Brendan asked as he studied what to him was only a large patch of grass devoid of any major trees.

Wyll took in the surrounding scene before reporting to his temporary commander, though still feeling self-conscious of what his squad mate's must be thinking right now.

"There are several buildings, most are at least two stories high and made of, something. It doesn't look like wood, but it's not stone either. The structures are latticed into the trees somehow. There are at least a hundred Arborii around the village who I think we interrupted going about their usual daily routines, including the child standing beside your saddle who is trying very hard to be quiet."

Brendan glanced around him with a clearly sceptical eye, but reached out suddenly to where Wyll was looking, only just missing making contact as the child ducked nimbly out of his way.

"Almost," Wyll told him as he got down from Socks' saddle and walked over to where the elderly fletcher was sitting, until he was close enough to reach out and touch him.

"Is this Emereth's Glade?" he asked again as the old Arborii looked up at him, his huge brown eyes fearful, and yet curious in a way that implied he had no idea what manner of creature stood before him.

"Indeed it is," a resonant voice said from the edge of the clearing nearest Wyll, making the others all spin in their saddles as the newcomer approached, all except Seth, who showed no sign of surprise.

"I had wondered when you would reveal yourself," the top-knotted warrior casually told the ochre and tan-furred newcomer, bringing a disapproving frown from Brendan.

"You knew we were being followed and said nothing?"

"He is no threat," Seth replied, "He's been shadowing us since we crossed the Camar tributary."

The Arborii raised a surprised eyebrow but nodded in confirmation.

"I shall be more careful to conceal myself in future," he said.

"I am your guide, had you not found your way up to the bridge I would have helped you to cross."

"But that would mean we would have failed, correct?" Brendan asked thoughtfully, to which the Arborii nodded his agreement.

Karthael had surely known about the bridge when he sent them out, and other than a test there was no other reason something that important would have been left out of their instructions on what was supposedly a 'practice' patrol.

The guide then turned to Wyll.

"I do not understand how you can see them," he said, tail raised slightly in genuine confusion.

"The binding which hides and protects this village should stop any human from seeing it without using arts of the most powerful kind. Correct me if I err, but unless I miss my guess, you are no mage," he announced, his long tail swaying slightly.

"So, what are you?" he added under his breath while studying Wyll with an intensity that made the hair on the back of his neck stand up.

"What are our orders?" Brendan eventually asked when it seemed the Arborii would volunteer no additional information.

With a start, the guide left off his study of Wyll and turned to face the tattooed commander before speaking for all of them to hear.

"An hour down this trail you will find another road leading directly north back to Aramar. It would normally be a four day trip as the path tends to wind some. You must follow it north to the edge of the Emerald Sea and then head east to the bridge that leads to Aramar, returning to your camp by nightfall of the third day."

There were a few groans, but Brendan motioned them to silence as the guide continued.

"Do not stray from the road. A straight line from here to your goal might be quicker, but you will fail if you do. And there are certain… dangers, in the woods for those who do not know our ways. Finally, this part of the test is about endurance. Whatever rations you still have left will have to suffice until you return to your camp. I am permitted to tell you however that you will come across a spring in a few hours where you will be able to refill your water skins."

"Is that all?" Brendan asked when the Arborii fell silent.

"Yes, except this. You've done well so far, not one squad in fifty makes it across the tributary crossing without being helped. Keep going. The road ahead will not be easy, but the ends will justify the means if you pass this part of the test, and that is more than I should probably tell you at this point." With a friendly nod the Arborii walked back into the tree line and was immediately lost to their sight as he blended in with the surrounding foliage.

With one last look around the village, Wyll walked Socks away from the Arborii fletcher as Brendan ordered them out.

"And to think I was looking forward to 'seeing' an Arborii village," Bosric said, his ever-present grin intact despite his disappointment. With a shrug he prodded his horse to a canter, following the others as they headed back into the forest.

*   *   *

It was well after nightfall on the second full day after leaving Emereth's Glade when Brendan finally ordered them to halt for the night. They had made good time the last two-and-a-bit days since leaving the village, and if the men were all tired, cold, and hungry, at least they were on schedule. They might even be slightly ahead, and Brendan was confident they would reach the edge of the forest by mid-afternoon at the latest. If they could reach that mark, it would give them more than enough time to reach camp five by the nightfall deadline the guide had set.

Of their Arborii shadow no more had been seen, not even by Seth, or at least that was the answer he gave when Brendan had asked him a few hours before. The firewood had all been used up days ago, and the men were feeling the effects of the snow after two chilling nights.

At least no one is complaining seriously yet, Brendan thought with thanks.

They all knew the conditions would be much worse if it weren't for the sheltering presence of the enormous trees which surrounded the path and kept the worst of both wind and snow at bay. Besides, despite the freezing temperatures it still hadn't rained except for that one night since they had left camp, and for that Brendan was extremely thankful. If they got soaked in this weather, it would be impossible to dry off without lighting a fire, and that was out of the question until they left the Emerald Sea behind.

"All right, that's far enough for now. Kienan, Tauman, take care of the horses. The rest of you spread out and find us a campsite," he ordered the men, who quickly dismounted and dispersed into the nearby forest on both sides of the path without further comment.

The temperature had dropped considerably since the sun had gone below the horizon, and a freezing wind had just started to whistle its way through the trees not a few minutes before. It was a good bet there would be heavy snow tonight.

Probably in the next hour or two, he thought as he left the path himself to help the others look for a suitable place to shelter from the coming storm.

The sound of snow crunching drew his attention, and he thought he could make out what looked like Wyll's form in the almost pitch dark which sheltered under the forest canopy. The path had been well lit by the rising moon, and smooth enough that they had been able to ride the horses at a walk even after sundown, but under here it was a different matter entirely.

"Is that you Wyll?" he called; his hand ready to draw his blade if the shadowy figure was not who he thought.

"It's me, Sir," the young man called back hesitantly as he looked over in Brendan's general direction, though he clearly couldn't see exactly where the voice had come from.

Without warning there was an ear shattering crack, and the hint of something massive moving in the darkness.

*   *   *

"Brendan, look out!" Wyll shouted as mountains of snow fell to the ground in the direction the commander's voice had just come from. There was a screech of twisted wood and then another crash high above which sent even more snow tumbling to the forest floor. As Wyll's gaze snapped upwards, he realised with terror that one of the ancient trees was falling straight towards where his squad mate had just called to him from.

"Brendan! Move!" Wyll shouted again as he set off at a dead run in the incredibly dim light, praying he didn't trip on root or rock in his mad dash to be away from the falling tree. Severed branches and snow rained all around him as he covered his head with his arms and continued to run. For a moment there was silence, then the very ground shook as the ancient bole came thundering to the forest floor. It bounced once and then rolled to a stop as it fetched up against another of the great trees, its closest branches not more than thirty spans from where Wyll now stood, panting and looking at the size of the fallen trunk in disbelief.

Taking a hold of himself he couldn't help but give an abrupt bark of laughter at still being alive, even as his hands shook uncontrollably with nervous energy. After the colossal impact the forest had become intensely quiet, as if every living thing were catching its breath, and suddenly Wyll froze.

"Brendan?" he shouted into the darkness. There was no response.

"Brendan!" he tried again as he began running back to where he thought he'd heard the tattooed man's voice only moments before. He was nearly there when he saw a figure move in the darkness. He breathed a sigh of relief. It lasted all of half a second until the figure turned, revealed in a thin shaft of moonlight allowed to grace the forest floor by the gap the fallen tree had left in the canopy above.

Whoever that is, it isn't Brendan, he thought as he began running again to where the shadowy form was standing over something pinned under a branch thick enough to be a tree trunk in its own right.

"Brendan," he gasped as he came close enough to see what the figure was looking at, and now reaching down to touch.

"Get away from him!" Wyll yelled at the willowy stranger even as he drew his sword awkwardly from its sheath as he ran.

The figure, dressed all in black flowing robes he could now make out, continued to reach out its pale hand as it concentrated on Brendan's broken form.

"I said get away!" Wyll screamed as he jumped a fallen branch and came into the moonlight himself.

The woman suddenly straightened with a jerk and looked at him, spinning so fast that the hood of her cloak fell back to reveal the most beautiful face he had ever seen. One which had haunted his dreams since he had been old enough to walk.

"I know you," he whispered in shock as he skidded to a halt, his sword seeming to fall of its own accord from fingers suddenly numb.

The woman's hair was black as her garments, offsetting her pale skin and ruby red lips in the dim light. He couldn't tell whether she was more shocked or frightened by his presence, but she wasn't moving a muscle as she studied him with eyes that spoke of both deep terror and excitement.

"You can see me?" she finally asked, her voice thin with emotion.

Wyll nodded slowly.

Suddenly there was the sound of crunching snow from behind him and he looked over his shoulder to see what was approaching.

"Over here!" he called when he saw the silhouettes, which from their disparate heights must have been Bosric and Marad running towards him.

Only an instant had passed, but when he looked back to where the woman was standing it was as if she'd vanished into thin air.

"What?"

He knew he was tired, but no one could move that quickly or quietly, of that he was sure as he looked around in the dim light, trying to see where she had gone.

"What happened?" Marad asked as Bosric knelt beside Brendan's badly wounded form.

Wyll just looked at him for a moment before pointing at the fallen tree, not bothering to answer. Bosric looked up and shook his head.

"He's still breathing, but it will be nothing short of the Maker's intervention if he lasts the hour," the short man told them matter-of-factly.

"Rig up a sling and get him out of here," Wyll said without thinking as he retrieved his sword, "We have to try for Aramar, a mage is his only hope now. If he makes it that far," Wyll added as he got his first good look at the gaping wounds in Brendan's right leg and torso, where stray branches had punctured straight through the big man's flesh at several points.

"Where are you going?" Marad demanded as Wyll strode off into the forest.

"When I reached him there was a woman standing over him, but she disappeared when you two came close. I only turned away for a moment.

"A mage?" Bosric asked hopefully.

"If she was," he answered nervously, "She wasn't one of ours. Still, she might know something that can help. See to Brendan, I'll catch up with you on the road," he told them as he began searching the surrounding snow for footprints.

'Death is, unfortunately, a finality. While the Gift can be used to reanimate a body, the soul which once inhabited it cannot be recalled. Therefore, the temptation to use the vile art of necromancy must be avoided at all costs, as the recalled soul is never that of the host, and in all likelihood, not human.'
Excerpt from 'The Gift'

CHAPTER 19

WHAT MUST BE

"Sarran, ride ahead and bring back one of the magi. By the time you return we should be nearly at the gates," Seth ordered in a no-nonsense tone. "I'm not sure how Brendan's made it this far, but I would very much dislike for him to die within sight of the greatest healers in the known world."

An unrelieved grey dawn, broken only by mist and sleet had settled over the countryside as the squad emerged from the Emerald Sea, still on the northbound road to Aramar. The litter they had strung up between the packhorse and Brendan's mount to carry the critically wounded man had slowed their progress considerably, but had held out well over the last day and a half. Still, after thirty-six hours in the saddle without a real break the men were exhausted, not to mention half frozen from the now constant snowfall.

It's a good thing we weren't sent a week later, Wyll reflected. Otherwise, getting the litter out of the Emerald

Sea might well have proved impossible as the ever-thickening flurries gradually coated the ground, turning everything a dull white as the Arborii forest was finally adorned in its winter garment.

As it was, they had been forced to waste precious time finding another way around a deep valley a few miles back. The road to the opposite side ascended steeply enough that there it was little more than a goat path; one the litter horses had no chance of negotiating.

They should have been able to cover the distance in half the time, but with the inclement weather and Brendan's severe injuries, they had wasted the entire morning finding another way back to the road. The men were all painfully aware of how long the trip had taken as they finally, finally came within sight of Aramar's looming presence, all thoughts of making their scheduled check in at camp five long since forgotten.

At first, no one had expected the tattooed soldier to last an hour after taking such horrific wounds back in the forest. As time had dragged on and the number of used and bloodied bandages had mounted and then run out, replaced by strips of cloth taken from the men's spare clothes, some of the squad were becoming nervous. None of them claimed to be either healer or mage, but it was clear to them all that their tattooed compatriot should have died long since, if only through the sheer amount of blood he had lost. Yet even now, breath after shallow breath still moved his chest up and down, and his heart continued to pump weakly despite the gaping wounds across his torso and right leg.

Wyll watched tiredly as Sarran rode off towards the city gates at a reckless pace, silently wishing him luck as the scarred staffman disappeared into the low-hanging mist.

It seemed like hours later, after crossing the North Road Bridge, that the mist finally parted to reveal the construction works on Aramar's new outer wall. The slightly brighter spot on the clouds where the sun should have been suggested that in truth only a fraction of that time had passed. A few minutes more and they were into the city proper where lamps were glowing faintly on either side of the broad streets. People made ghostly shapes in the mist as they went about their business in heavy winter cloaks, most with hoods pulled up over their heads, giving them a furtive look as they hunched against the icy cold.

There was no trouble getting the litter through the streets today since most people seemed to be staying indoors. Wyll was grateful they weren't further delayed as they made their way laboriously towards the College of the Arts, attempting to get Brendan there as smoothly and quickly as possible.

At the main city gates their uniforms and the wounded soldier on the litter were enough to get them through the checkpoint with only a few seconds' delay. They hurried on.

Sarran should have found one of the magi by now, surely.

Wyll thought again about the woman he'd seen bending over Brendan's injured form back in the forest. He knew himself to be a fair tracker, but after searching for any sign of her passing, he had come up empty. He didn't understand.

Even an untaught child should have been able to track her across snowy ground, he thought again in frustration. After an hour of fruitless searching though, he had given up and re-joined the others on the road, the experience leaving him deeply troubled. The way he saw it, the woman had to have been a mage, though a friendly mage should have at least attempted to heal the tattooed soldier. The guide back in Emereth's Glade had been explicit about not leaving the road. At the time they'd all thought the Arborii had meant not cutting cross country to reach camp five faster. Perhaps he had meant it literally. There was a slim chance she was some fey creature native to the Emerald Sea which could impersonate a human's form. Either of those options still left the question of what she had been about to do to Brendan when Wyll had interrupted her. What they couldn't explain, and what he had been trying to ignore until now, was why he had dreamed about her on and off, in every crystalline detail since he had been old enough to walk. It was her. He was sure of it. More than sure in fact. He knew it in some way he didn't quite understand, and no matter how hard he tried, he still couldn't shake the feeling that something had begun back in the forest that would have far larger repercussions than just Brendan's injuries.

After what seemed like ages, they finished traversing the city streets through the thickly falling snow. After stopping briefly to talk their way past the guarded gates to the College of the Arts, they resumed their plodding march, continuing on shivering horses until they were inside the very ring of columns which circled the college's major buildings. The flame and dragon sigil carved into each of the stone pillars was barely visible as the columns disappeared up into the thick fog still clinging to life, despite the cloud obscured sun having been up for several hours.

There was an audible sigh of relief from someone as a

pair of horses finally came into sight, one bearing Sarran, the other a snowy-haired old man in an archmage's cloak.

Wyll saw Sarran motion towards them and the two men changed course to intercept the small group of half frozen riders. Wyll told the rest of the squad to stop as soon as Sarran had seen them, and proceeded to loosen the straps which held Brendan's litter between the two horses. By the time Sarran and the archmage reached them, the men were lowering Brendan to the ground so the old mage could inspect the wounds more freely.

"Archmage Tolmarak," Wyll said respectfully, and couldn't help a slight grin as he noticed the grimace on Sarran's face from the corner of his eye. His squad mate obviously hadn't known the archmage he'd convinced to accompany him was the king's own advisor. Come to think of it, none of the others had met the distinguished old mage either. Not unless by chance they'd glanced up that one time Jayden and Tolmarak had run into them while working the trench for Aramar's new outer wall some phases back.

"Wyll," Tolmarak returned with only a slight frown, as though unsurprised to see him.

"I should almost have expected you to be here," the archmage greeted him as he dismounted, seeming to float down from his tall grey warhorse.

Wyll passed over the remark, though not because he wasn't curious as to what Tolmarak had meant.

"We need your aid Archmage," he said without further delay, "Brendan was pinned by a falling tree inside the Emerald Sea. He should not have lived as far as I can tell, but he breathes still, and his pulse is weak, but there."

"Remove the covers," Tolmarak ordered without

hesitation, and then gasped when Marad and Cale did exactly that.

"How long?" he asked as he knelt stiffly in the snow beside the fallen soldier. He examined the gaping tear which ran a hands-width across Brendan's torso from right shoulder to left hip, and the smaller one along his right leg through which bone and torn muscle could clearly be seen.

"Thirty-six hours Archmage," Kienan replied in a strained tone.

"That's not possible," Tolmarak whispered as he continued his examination.

"If nothing else, he would have bled out within hours of this happening."

Wyll shared a look with Cale. The mute lancer had written much the same on his Gift-wrought pad when he'd first examined Brendan's wounds back in the forest.

"I can heal the wounds he has," Tolmarak said after a moment, loudly enough so they could all hear. "But as weak as he now is, the chances are very high that his body might not be up to taking the stresses of the healing. He may well die despite my skills. Then again, if he has survived this long, perhaps he will recover without my intervention?" Jeranon's foremost Archmage added in a slightly confused tone which made the possibility seem a very long stretch indeed.

"There is substantial risk either way. Does he have any family in Aramar?" Tolmarak asked, "If he does, the choice should be theirs."

Wyll looked around at the others for a moment but none of them seemed as though they were about to speak up, so he answered for them all.

"He is from Silvertown in the south, Archmage. If he

has any relations in the capital, he never spoke of them to us."

He looked around again but there were only a few confirming nods, and when no one said otherwise Tolmarak nodded.

"Very well, then the choice must be yours. Healing will probably kill him at this point, but leaving him as he is... The simple truth is I do not understand why he still breathes at all."

Wyll looked at the others again, but with the exception of Seth, who gave the slightest of nods and Tauman, who shrugged in a noncommittal way, Marad and the rest seemed unwilling to meet his questioning gaze. Why he should have to make this decision he had no idea. He had no more authority than any of the others, but it was clear none of them wanted to commit to a choice that might lead to Brendan's death, at least not while someone else might do it for them.

Taking a long hard look at Brendan's broken form, Wyll tried to find some spark of hope in himself that his squad mate might recover on his own from the horrendous wounds he'd taken. But after looking over the torn and missing flesh and multiple broken bones again, he eventually had to admit that such a spark did not exist. The wounds were just too severe to heal on their own, no matter that Brendan had somehow clung to life thus far without a mage's healing.

Wyll didn't really think about what he was saying as he heard the words leave his mouth, but in his heart he knew it was the only chance his squad mate had.

"Please try, Archmage," he said quietly, and immediately heard several breaths being released behind him from some of the men, though if anyone had favoured a different decision they didn't speak out.

The king's advisor nodded, gently placing his hands over the gaping cavity in Brendan's chest which exposed nearly all of his ribs at one point or another, and began doing something with the Gift.

To the others it appeared as though Tolmarak simply knelt there with his eyes closed and his hands suspended over the wound, or part of it anyway. As the white-haired old archmage began inching his hands up along Brendan's torso though, he left whole flesh and skin where only a ruined wreck had existed moments before.

A minute passed, two, as Tolmarak employed his powers and the men watched in stunned silence, even Cale, who claimed to have seen a mage's healing years before joining up with the army.

By the time Tolmarak took his hands away and wiped them clean of Brendan's blood on the snow beside him, he was wheezing from the effort, or maybe the cold, and Wyll moved quickly to help the old man to his feet. Below them Brendan's chest was moving up and down faintly, and Tolmarak nodded to himself in confusion.

"I was sure..." he muttered, and then, "The wound on his leg must be treated by more mundane means until he regains some strength. As it is, I do not understand how he still breathes, but for the moment, we can be thankful at least that he does," he said with a satisfied smile.

"Thank you Archmage," Wyll told the old man sincerely. The comment fervently echoed by the others, even Marad sounding as though he meant it while Cale simply nodded with eyes that said as much as any of the others had out loud.

"Bring him out of the cold," Tolmarak ordered as he tiredly moved clear of Wyll, having caught his breath at last.

Six of the others picked up the corners and middle of Brendan's litter and followed Tolmarak and Wyll as they set off for a flat-roofed building adjacent to the college, hidden from the vantage point of the entrance. Tauman and Bosric also remounted and gathered up the horses before following the slow procession across the courtyard.

A few minutes saw them inside the complex where Aramar's elite mageguard soldiers were garrisoned, and Tolmarak immediately sent a runner off to prepare a room where Brendan could be properly cared for.

As they walked down several long but blessedly warm corridors, Wyll looked around at the torn banners and ancient weapons adorning custom made niches every few feet along both sides of the stone walls. Several times along the way a soldier in a black uniform adorned with the flame and dragon symbol of Aramar's College of the Arts over their heart would give Tolmarak a respectful bow. They would also give the squad of conscripts a measuring stare as if to assess any threat they might pose, then just as quickly dismiss them as they passed.

Wyll had of course heard stories of the almost legendary mageguard as a child, and then in more detail when he had joined the army back in Grandell. Even so, he couldn't help wonder what kind of man, what kind of swordsman, could calculatedly look at someone like Seth and dismiss him as not being a threat. If it had just been the one, Wyll thought he could have chalked it up to sheer arrogance, but each time they passed one of the mageguard in the corridors they got the same measuring look. The soldier would then continue on, unconcerned, as if even by themselves they could deal with any trouble the nine members of the squad might cause.

"Dangerous men," Bosric muttered as a soldier, not much larger than the red-headed knife man, passed by while looking at them as he might have a piece of furniture, rather than a squad of armed and capable soldiers.

By the time the small procession arrived at the room where Brendan was to be cared for, Wyll was certain every off-duty soldier in the complex had 'casually' passed them by, but Tolmarak said nothing, so neither did he.

The archmage ordered a master from the Herbalists and Apothecaries Guild brought to tend Brendan's leg. The wizened old woman and her assistant arrived quickly, and the thin, severe woman immediately hustled them all out of the room so she could work without interruption.

Once the door was closed Tolmarak showed them to the bathhouse where he directed them to change into clean uniforms and meet him in the mess to break fast. Near exhaustion, half frozen and hungry, the men were all too happy to comply. To a man they were soaked through, and most had at least a little of Brendan's blood on their clothes from changing his dressings as they rode.

The men went inside and found a strange apparatus that a servant who was cleaning the rooms showed them how to operate. Apparently, the huge arcane object had been designed by a mage hundreds of years ago, and had no other purpose than to heat water for the baths.

"I could get used to this," Marad declared as he activated the thing and nearly scolded his half-frozen hand on the steaming flow which immediately issued from the large brass pipe.

A short time later as the men soaked away the bone numbing cold in their respective baths, a group of servants appeared with a pile of towels and their saddlebags. Before the last man left, he informed them he would be waiting outside to show them to the mess hall when they were ready, his tone implying that should be as soon as possible.

With a sigh, Wyll realised Tolmarak would already be waiting for them, and grudgingly left the wood rimmed iron tub of steaming water to dry himself and put on a fresh, if crumpled uniform.

At least this one is not covered in blood, he thought tiredly as he dressed.

Apparently the others had received the message too, and within a handful of minutes they were all out in the corridor with saddlebags slung over shoulders or carried in their hands. As soon as Kienan appeared, the serving man turned and led them down several corridors until they entered a huge room lined with tables, which could only be the mess. At a table near the serving area, Tolmarak was sitting with his back turned to them, and when they approached he looked up from his morning meal. It comprised a steaming, but now nearly empty bowl of porridge and a small piece of fruit cut in half which had greenish flesh and a brown furry skin which Wyll didn't recognise.

A look towards the kitchen and a slight nod from the archmage was enough to prompt the kitchen staff to bring the same for Wyll and the others. The food was joined by a large pitcher of freshly squeezed orange juice and another of water for the group as well as various pots of butter, honey, and spices for the meal. Despite their ordeal, the men couldn't help but grin at each other as the food was served, although Seth seemed more surprised than happy as his portion was set in front of him.

"Do the mageguard always eat so well?" Tauman asked as he poured a generous amount of honey onto his porridge.

Tolmarak nodded slowly as he swallowed a bite of the strange fruit.

"When they are here, yes. Much is demanded of the guard during their training, even more once they are in the field. Less than one man in a hundred is chosen from the regular army to train with us, and less than half of those make it through the training. By the time they reach retirement age, only about one in five who finish the training will still be alive to collect their pensions. But every man who makes it into the guard will see things he never envisioned as a child, never believed in when he heard the stories in his youth, and never imagined in his most adventurous dreams."

There was silence all around since most of the men had stopped eating, spoons forgotten halfway to their mouths as they listened to the old archmage's words.

"Any man here would sacrifice himself for his comrades or his mage at an instant, and kill as quickly to protect them. But every one of the protectors, that is what the mageguard call themselves, is bound by a strict code of honour they would not deviate from even if it required their life. That is the dedication a man must have if he wishes to serve in the mageguard, for once accepted, there is no going back to the time when you thought of the world as a place ruled by men."

Tolmarak took a last bite from the fruit and then stood.

"One of you can stay to watch over Brendan if you so

wish. The rest of you men will return to camp five and report to Karthael once you have finished your breakfast.

Wyll volunteered without hesitation, and the archmage nodded as if he had expected no less. Without another word Tolmarak walked slowly to the door before turning back to say.

"By the way, you made the right choice coming straight here instead of going back to the camp. I think your friend will live, now."

Wyll gave him a relieved nod as the archmage left, then went back to his food, barely noticing the thoughtful glance Seth gave him before returning to his own plate.

"At least we shouldn't get chewed out by the instructor for going off mission," Marad said around a mouthful of his rapidly shrinking supply of porridge, "Not with what that archmage just told us."

"I think I'm going apply for a transfer to the mageguard when we finish our training," Kienan announced as he finished the porridge and gave the furry skinned fruit a dubious stare. Shrugging, he peeled the skin back and took a cautious bite out of the thing before making an approving sound and finishing the rest off in short order.

Tauman just stared at the black-haired musician for a moment before saying, "Are you serious? You heard what the archmage just said. Only one in a hundred gets to train and half of those don't even succeed. That means you've got a one in two hundred chance of just getting in, and even if you manage to do that, he said only one in five lives long enough to retire. That means you have a one in a thousand chance of living through it!"

"You can be a rather cheerful fellow sometimes Tauman," Bosric interrupted with a sardonic grin, "But I'm with Kienan. What better way to see the world than to travel with a mage?"

As he finished eating, it occurred to Wyll that neither of them would get the chance to find out. When they concluded their training, it wouldn't be because they had learned all their instructor could teach them, it would be because they had run out of time and were marching to war.

Suddenly Wyll didn't feel like eating the strange fruit and put it into his saddlebag as he stood.

"I'm going to see if the healer is finished with Brendan's leg. I'll see the rest of you back at the camp tomorrow I guess."

There were waves and a few comments, though some of the men were still busy with their food.

Wyll left the mess hall deep in thought and set off into the maze of corridors which made up the mageguard barracks, walking in what he hoped was the right direction.

*   *   *

Just like that it was done. He had planted the idea of adventure in their minds and now he just had to sit back and watch it grow.

Tolmarak gave the slightest grin as he listened to the squad's conversation with the Gift. Already two of them had said they intended to try out for the mageguard, and unless he missed his guess, none of the others would be too hard to convince with a little effort. None of them really mattered to his plans, at least no more than any other potential recruit. It was Wyll he had a vested interest in, and the junior soldier's friendship with Jayden, who would eventually need someone level-headed to lead his guard. It was true that there were any number of officers with more experience than Wyll, but none of them knew how to deal with the boy's intransigent nature better than the young man from his home town.

Besides, his instincts were telling him that Wyll had his own part to play in the coming war. He had only had this sensation twice before in his life, but both times listening to it had averted a major catastrophe, and he wasn't about to start ignoring it now. Apart from all that though, he was just running into the young man far too often for it to be pure happenstance. First in Grandell where Jayden stumbled across what was probably the only guardsman in the entire castle sympathetic to his cause, without even intentionally looking no less. Then when his class had ridden out to the range, and it just happened to be Wyll's squad they rode past when there were thirty-five or forty thousand men working the new wall each day; and he had just happened to look up at the right moment to see them pass. Now a great tree fell in the Emerald Sea, which happened about as often as a solar eclipse, and managed to hit an Aramarian soldier where quite possibly no human foot had ever trod. It didn't touch Wyll, rather mortally wounding his commander who should have died within minutes from his wounds. Only the man didn't die. He kept on breathing, his heart beating even now, despite everything Tolmarak knew to be true about the human body and the injuries it could and could not take before failing completely. That it had been Wyll who had decided to bring the fallen man back to Aramar was no great surprise, Tolmarak had always seen the leadership potential in the boy, even if Wyll himself could not. It was the icing on the cake that the soldier who had been sent ahead, a man he had never met and who also didn't know who he was, had straight away found him out of all the magi in Aramar. Not only making it past all the college's checkpoints, but convincing him to travel out to reduce the travel time of his squad, which also happened to be Wyll's.

It was possible it was all coincidence, each time. But Tolmarak had never been a big believer in accidents, and coupled with the strange feeling that Wyll was somehow significant, he couldn't credit it at all. He decided it would be best for them all to keep Wyll close until he could determine what part the boy had to play in the coming conflict. Jeranon had to be protected at all costs, and until he was sure whether the boy would become a force for good or ill, he had no intention of letting him roam freely. There were more than enough wildcards in play already. This one at least he could keep some measure of control over for now, and even more so once he got the boy and his squad into the mageguard.

Tolmarak listened until he heard Wyll's footsteps fade, the boy walking back up the corridor towards Brendan's room. Once Wyll had left, he set off toward the college's main building himself, and the ten thousand other things which still needed to be taken care of before the snows began to melt.

*   *   *

It was hours later when Wyll woke.

He had finally been allowed into Brendan's room when the healer, apparently a noted member of the Herbalists and Apothecaries Guild, had finished whatever it was they did and sown up the wound. A servant had been sent for the seat in which he now slumped as he struggled to wake after what felt like only a few minutes rest.

A slight rustling caught his attention, snapping him alert as he realised he was no longer the only other person in the room.

Shooting to his feet, Wyll needed only a glance at the smooth pale skin and lush figure of the stranger to know she was the same woman he had found leaning over Brendan back in the Emerald Sea.

"Who are you?" he asked deliberately, causing the black clad woman to spin, startled as if she hadn't known he was there all along.

For an endless moment she was silent as she composed herself, regarding him with an intent stare which made the hair on the back of his neck stand on end.

"Why ask questions when you already know the answers, Wyll?" she replied in little more than a whisper.

Wyll stood stock still for a moment, except for his left hand which moved unconsciously towards his sword hilt, or at least where it would have been had he not removed it to try to get some sleep. Now it lay on the chair behind him, out of reach and probably as useless as a means of defence from this woman as a jug full of milk might have been.

"How do you know my name?" he asked as he backed up a step.

Instead of answering though, she just smiled slowly before tapping her chin with a long, black enamelled fingernail.

"What should I do with you, Wyll?" she said in a weighing sort of way, "You can see me, and you might therefore in time be able to harm me. My work is far too important for that to be allowed, so by all rights I should take you now, even though it is not yet your time."

Wyll backed away another step and bumped into the chair behind him.

He couldn't help but swallow nervously.

"What do you want?" he tried again as he compared the image from his dreams to the strange woman before him. They were one and the same, he was certain of it.

"You know that as well, Wyll. It is his time. Past time, now," she said with the smallest motioning of a slender finger towards the unconscious form of Brendan lying still and asleep on the bed behind her.

Wyll wanted to back away even further as he began to grasp what she was implying, but found the wall had gotten in his way.

"You are not the Black Lady," he told her, willing it to be true. Even he could hear the uncertainty creeping into his voice though as she took a graceful step towards him, reaching out a finger. An unknowable expression flickered across her face and she hesitated, her ankle length raven black hair swaying gently as she moved.

She sighed faintly as she studied him at length.

"It has been so long since I have had someone to talk to. Twenty thousand turnings of this world around our sun. No, I think I will keep you alive for now. Just remember that should you ever cross me, I can take your soul at a touch and nothing in this world could stop me or even slow me down."

Wyll forced himself to take a slight step forward away from the wall and speak. As powerful as this woman might be, there was just no way she could be what she seemed to be implying. Then a thought occurred to him.

"You never had need of threats in the dreams, Sa'rayna," he managed to get out after a moment.

There was a shocked flicker of recognition in her eyes at that, and it hit Wyll like a hammer.

All his life people had ridiculed him when he told them about the dreams. Well, all except Jayden anyway, but this woman he had envisioned all those years in perfect clarity knew that name. A name he had never once in his life heard spoken on another's lips, and the one part of the dream he had never shared with anyone. It was too much coincidence to push aside.

"How do you know that name?" she asked with a quiet intensity that made Wyll suddenly feel as if he had just mounted his own gallows block.

Instead of answering her though, he just forced himself to smile slowly as she had done a moment before.

"Kill me, Sa'rayna, and you will never find out," he told her eventually, while a little voice in his head screamed at him not to be a fool.

My sword might be on the chair beside me, he thought grimly back at it, but a battle can be fought with weapons other than steel. Besides, if she truly was who she made herself out to be, steel would be useless in any event.

"You interest me Wyll. Most men would run screaming the moment they knew my name. But you stay, even now."

For a long moment Wyll studied the woman he knew as Sa'rayna and wondered how much he could reveal without compromising his own safety. Maybe he was being a fool, but there was something about this woman that made him trust her. He still wasn't convinced about her being the dreaded 'Black Lady' who knew the moment of your death wherever you were and came to take your spirit to the next world. How he could not believe that part, and yet still trust this woman made no sense to him as he continued to study her, but he did.

He was about to speak when she looked away, and he realised he'd been staring.

"I'm sorry, I meant no offence," he blurted truthfully. After all, only an idiot or a madman would want to offend death herself. And yet, Sa'rayna, whoever she really was, might very well be the most beautiful woman he had ever seen.

"I... am not offended," she replied at length.

Wyll silently breathed a sigh of relief, which he hoped Sa'rayna didn't notice, one which caught in his throat as she turned back to Brendan's still form and took a graceful step towards the fallen soldier.

"What are you doing?" he asked as she closed the rest of the distance between herself and the sickbed.

"What must be done," she answered slowly as she reached out a hand towards Brendan's chest.

With a sinking feeling Wyll suddenly realised what she intended, and Black Lady or no, he was not about to stand by while this woman ended his comrade's life.

Before he could overthink things, Wyll took three quick steps and gently but firmly took hold of the pale wrist Sa'rayna was extending toward the tattooed man. As his fingers closed on her exposed skin there was no resistance at all, and his hand continued to make a fist, passing right through both bone and flesh with no visible result.

Once again the hair on the back of Wyll's neck thrilled up straight as he snatched his hand away and stared wide eyed at Sa'rayna, who was giving him a shocked look of her own.

"You dare much, Wyll of Grandell," She said after a moment of apparent indecision. "Fortunately for you my touch only conveys the spirit onwards when I wish it so. Do not do that again though. After twenty thousand years of death, my patience is somewhat… lacking."

Strangely enough though, her expression softened once she had said her piece. She looked at Brendan again before turning back to Wyll, who took the moment to study his hand, which was apparently none the worse for passing through this apparition, or whatever she was.

She can't really be the Black Lady, she just can't.

Even as he thought it, Wyll realised he had subconsciously backed up to put himself between her and where Brendan lay, still unconscious, as he had been since the tree had fallen on him back in the forest.

"It is his time," she said gently as she moved to go around Wyll and reach the tattooed veteran.

Wyll moved with her, trying to block her access to the bed behind him.

"I am sorry you have to see this Wyll, truly I am."

Again that sense of trust flowed through Wyll at her words, but trust or no, he was not about to let her get to his squad mate and do… whatever it was she wanted.

"Please," he said quietly, "He is my friend."

What else could he do? He couldn't restrain her, and he was no mage to use arcane arts to stop her from having her way.

"I know," she acknowledged, almost as though she were trying to soothe a fretting child, "But it is his time. It is what must be."

Again she reached out a hand and Wyll moved to block her with his own mass. Rather than pull back again, Sa'rayna simply slid her ethereal arm through his chest and out the other side to brush Brendan lightly on the cheek, and then across the forehead once.

With a disheartened flinch, Wyll finally moved aside to see what she'd done to his squad mate, and sucked in a deep breath at what lay before him.

Brendan's chest no longer heaved slowly up and down, and a quick moment of pressure at the tattooed man's wrist showed his heart was silent as well.

"You killed him!" Wyll accused as he turned back to where Sa'rayna was standing. She was a span away and had her head bowed and her hands folded in front of her as if to give him that moment of privacy while he confirmed his friend's demise, but met his eyes when he spoke.

"He should never have made it this far Wyll," she told him softly. "His time was back in the Emerald Sea, but when you called to me, I was so stunned you could actually see me that I fled before I could finish my task."

"You murdered him, Sa'rayna," Wyll accused.

"If a man falls off a cliff, or an animal attacks him, is it my fault?" she demanded with a frown.

"What if a soldier lops off his enemy's head in the heat of battle, is that also my fault when his flesh can no longer continue?"

"But his flesh had been healed! There was no need for this."

"I do not take life," she finished, almost pleading, "I simply convey the spirit onward on its journey when its time in this world is over. For every living thing that time eventually comes, and his was two days ago. If I had let him live, his future actions would disturb the entire fabric of the world, and that must not be allowed to occur."

Wyll looked at her in consternation for a moment, not because he didn't understand what she was saying, but because he thought perhaps he did. Her words seemed to match those of one of the peasants back in Grandell, an old drunk who was eventually run out of town for his worshipful attitude towards the Black Lady, towards death.

She stood there after that, neither of them speaking for a long time as they studied each other intently.

It was one of the hardest things Wyll had ever done in his life as he looked again at his squad mate's lifeless form, but eventually he forced himself to speak.

"I... believe you. Sa'rayna," he told her, and was immediately rewarded by a certain tightness lifting from her face, one he hadn't known had been there until it was gone, making her even more beautiful, if that were possible.

"I must go now Wyll, there are others whose time draws near, but we will meet again," she said with a sad smile, one which left Wyll cold.

It must have showed on his face because she suddenly laughed, smiling for real.

"Not like that. But soon."

In the blink of an eye she was gone.

Wyll just stood there for a long time thinking about all he had seen, and then about Brendan's body already beginning to cool on the bed behind him. Suddenly the small sickroom felt oppressive as he studied his friend's corpse, and he had to turn away.

Listlessly gathering his sword belt and donning the cloak which lay across the back of the chair, he opened the door, nearly running into the healer who had already reached out to do the same from the other side.

For an instant the two of them just looked at each other before Wyll said, "You're too late. He's gone."

The healer held his gaze for an instant, before hurrying past into the room to see if there was anything she could do despite the private's assertion.

Wyll only continued down the corridor without another word, wrapped far tighter in his own thoughts than he was in his thick winter cloak as he tried to pull some kind of sense out of the experiences of the last two days, and the dreams of the last twenty years.

'For a mage, the difference between truth and lies is a razor thin path. For that is what the Gift is, the ability to change reality from one state to another via the visualisation of an untruth.'
Excerpt from 'The Gift'.

CHAPTER 20

QUESTIONS

Wyll pulled his cloak close as the dawn of winter wind whistled its way through the dimly lit cobblestone streets. The slow drizzle had started about half an hour ago and was bitingly cold, the combination quickly leaching all sensation from his ears and nose as he wandered aimlessly through the capital.

He could not explain the events of the last two days.

Brendan was gone, and Wyll was struggling with a state of shock after what he had witnessed at the man's deathbed. He had seen her many times in his dreams, this apparition who answered to the name of Sa'rayna and claimed to be the fabled 'Black Lady'. He knew that when he returned to camp five, the others would demand to know why Brendan had died against the prognosis of both archmage and master healer. They would also want answers as to why their temporary commander had survived so long in the first place, despite his horrific wounds. If he told the rest of his squad what he'd seen they would never believe him. He might as well tell them he'd been visited by the Maker himself. And yet, in his heart,

Wyll knew he now held the answers they would demand, and that his squad mates deserved them. Thinking on how that information would be received though was enough to make him wonder if he shouldn't just keep his mouth shut.

As the chilling rain intensified, he pulled his cloak even tighter before coming to a decision.

If for no other reason than his own sanity, he had to tell someone about the things he had seen. They might try to throw him in the dungeon, taking him for a lunatic. Perhaps they were right. The only other possibilities were ones which didn't bear thinking about; that the beautiful woman who had stolen away Brendan's life at a touch had been telling the truth. That he had been talking with the Black Lady, with death herself. That he had dreamed of her, correct in every detail, since he had been old enough to walk.

The other alternative was worse. That she was no more than an extremely powerful mage, one he had just let kill his friend.

Either way, there was only one person he knew of and trusted who might have some clue as to the truth of the matter, whilst also not thinking he had gone completely off the deep end.

He had to talk to Jayden.

It wasn't that he didn't trust the other magi, but at least he had already told Jayden about his dreams on the way from Grandell to the capital. Even though they hadn't known each other as well back then, the young mage hadn't laughed or made light of what he'd had to say.

The decision made, he turned the next corner and headed back through the city towards the college as the freezing rain picked up its pace and the wind stirred itself into a squall. All signs pointed to this winter being a short one, though nature seemed to be doing its best to make up for that with intensity. The lamps which dotted the streets were already being left on during the day due to the fog and sleet, and it wasn't even high winter yet.

He'd been wandering for many hours since leaving the college barracks, but his aimless course seemed to have taken him in something of a circle through the city. It only took a few minutes of brisk walking through the icy night to return to the college grounds, where the guards recognised and admitted him through the gate.

He couldn't see the top of the structure as he approached due of the fog, but he had seen it before. Being from a coastal town he couldn't help but compare the magi's seat of power to a vast conical seashell rising out of the courtyard.

As he crossed the yard, he thought he heard the plaintive bawling of a goat from somewhere nearby, but dismissed it as his imagination when he couldn't locate the source.

He stepped under the cover of the portico at the main entrance, pulling the hood of his cloak down and studying the dimly glowing doorway for a moment. He frowned as he realised that in all likelihood it was warded to keep intruders out. There was no gate to speak of, and anyone could just waltz in otherwise, though who would be stupid enough to try sneaking in the front door of the College of the Arts he wasn't sure.

"Stand before me Wyll of Grandell," a voice like musical chimes called to him as the doorway pulsed brighter.

Wyll gave a start, caught off guard by the bodiless voice.

"Who are you?" he replied, looking around for the speaker's source, "Where are you?"

"I have had many names," the voice countered, and this time Wyll was incredulously able to trace the tinkling sound to the glowing doorway itself, "For now I am Tammy."

"Tammy?" Wyll replied curiously over the noise of the rain outside the entrance.

"What... are you? If it's not a rude question," he amended.

"It is not, but it would take too long to explain my nature to you Wyll, and I am not allowed to do so in any event. Suffice it to say I have the power to act as an oracle at this time."

"Now stand before me Wyll of Grandell, and allow me to speak this message which I have waited untold years to pass on."

For a moment Wyll just stared at the doorway.

"How could there be a message for me from untold years ago?" he asked cynically, "I'm only twenty-two summers old."

"In time you will find the answers to all of your questions. I can only tell you the message is true, and given to me by the one who gave me the power of clear sight nearly five thousand years ago."

"And who was that?" Wyll inquired.

He couldn't quite credit what the strange doorway was saying, but the distraction was welcome. Besides, he was curious as to what name it would come up with for the prescient who had foreseen his birth five millennia before its occurrence.

"That also I may not reveal, for fear of changing the flow of what must be."

What must be, he thought bitterly, *that again*.

"I have to go inside. There's a mage named Jayden I need to see," Wyll abruptly told it, no longer interested in this line of conversation as his reason for being here crashed to the forefront of his mind.

"Listen and hear me well, Wyll of Grandell," the oracle told him in a much more commanding voice.

"When chaos reigns, you must retrieve the gem from the King of the Dead and return it to the Well of Tears. Help the two become one, help the one to become. Find the three or fail, and fear not the door nor the trail. Do this, or all you hold dear will fall into the destroyer's grasp."

For a long moment Wyll looked at the oracle in consternation before barking out a sarcastic laugh.

"I don't even know what that means," he told it in exasperation.

His friend was dead, he was soaked through by the freezing rain despite his thick, oilskin cloak, and he'd had more than enough of this strange creature's meaningless posturing.

"Are you going to let me enter or not?"

The doorway pulsed bright for a long second and then the chiming voice sounded, quiet and discordant as though a harpist had struck a wrong chord in the middle of a song.

"Remember," it whispered.

Wyll clutched at his head for a long moment as the oracle's words etched themselves in his mind, and then almost without pause, the pain was gone.

"What did you do to me?!" he demanded as he came to stand right at the threshold of the glowing doorway.

There was no response.

"Are you going to stop me from going inside?" he tried again.

If it didn't respond this time, he decided he would chance tripping a ward. The so called 'oracle' seemed to want him alive to do something he didn't understand, so he was fairly certain he wouldn't be injured even if he did trip some arcane defence.

There was a moment of silence, and just as he was about to step through the voice returned.

"I never intended to stop you, Wyll. I did only what was necessary."

"I don't understand," Wyll told it in annoyance, "What good is the message if I don't know what it means?"

Again, that moment of silence, as if the oracle were considering how much to say.

"You will discover the meaning in time. My job was simply to make you recognise the signs when you saw them, not to change what must occur."

"What must occur? If I'm so important then why can't you be more specific?" He asked, his brows drawing down in confusion.

"I could, but then things would change. You will discover the meaning in time, now go. I have already said far more than I should."

Wyll stared at the oracle for a long minute in confusion, but the doorway had returned to the same dim pulsing as when he'd first arrived.

Wyll was a soldier, and knew when he was being dismissed, so he took the chance to step through the door into the main entry chamber of the college building before it might speak again.

He took a long glance around the large circular room and wondered where to start. There was nobody else in sight, although he could hear the sounds of servants working from somewhere nearby. There was a wide, elaborately carved staircase running the perimeter of the room, the underside of which was always visible as the conical walls ascended into the heights of the college building.

The sound of footsteps reached his ears and a moment later a young serving girl, no more than sixteen or seventeen he guessed, came out of a door a quarter way around the circle to his right.

"Excuse me," he called out, startling the girl so badly she nearly dropped the broom she was carrying and stared at him as if he'd grown horns.

"Can you help me? I'm here to see Jayden, he's an apprentice here."

"Who are you?" the red-headed girl asked in a tight voice, as though forcing herself to speak to him.

"My name is Wyll," he told her calmly.

There was something not right here. He'd had a lot of different reactions from girls he'd just met over the years, but if he didn't know better, he would have said the pretty girl in front of him was terrified. Not that he'd done anything which would warrant such a response.

Maybe they just don't get many visitors here, he thought with a shrug.

With another quick look around, Wyll realised it would take him hours to search the place by himself, but the girl was just standing there so he decided to change tack.

"I have an urgent message for Jayden of Grandell. He will not be pleased if I do not deliver it in a timely fashion."

Not exactly true he supposed, but it seemed to do the job as the girl shook her head and muttered something he didn't quite catch.

"Follow me," she said, before leading the way up the stairs, broom clutched like a weapon as she tried to keep an eye on him even though he was behind her.

"What's your name?" he asked as they began rounding the ascending staircase for the fifth time. There was no response from his guide as they entered a doorway leading off towards another part of the enormous building, following a long corridor lined with closed doors on either side.

So far he had not seen another person, neither mage nor servant during the trip, and he was becoming a little uneasy. There must be hundreds of magi, and many times that number of servants in a building as large as this.

"I don't mean you any harm," he said as the girl glanced nervously backwards at him yet again.

She missed a step and nearly fell, blushing as she regained her footing just in time, then stopped at a door as unremarkable as all the rest. She knocked softly.

"Yes?" a muffled voice called from inside, and Wyll was relieved to recognise it as that of his friend.

The door opened a moment later and Jayden just blinked at the sight in front of him before offering his hand in greeting.

"You're welcome of course, Wyll. But how did you get in here?" he asked after a moment, "The wards are supposed to still be intact. You should have just rebounded off them as if you had walked into a wall."

"I thought you might have something like that in place," Wyll replied with a wry grin, "But Tammy said she wouldn't try to stop me from entering."

"She spoke to you?!"

Wyll abruptly became aware the serving girl was still

standing there, and making calf eyes at Jayden no less he noticed with a slight grin.

"We need to talk," Wyll said with a subtle gesture at the girl.

Jayden nodded in understanding.

"Simone, please ask Archmage Tolmarak to come to my room at his earliest convenience, and then get the kitchen to send up something hot to drink for three."

The girl gave him a smile and a 'yes Jayden' as she made a graceful curtsy which was ruined by her trying to hide the broom from the apprentice magi's eyes.

"You must be freezing," Jayden said with a grin, "Hold still a moment."

Wyll did as he'd been bidden while Jayden raised a hand towards him and concentrated. He felt a strange, hot sensation run over him and realised that he was now completely dry, as though he hadn't been out in the storm less than a quarter hour past.

"Thanks." He shook his head ruefully as Jayden motioned for him to come into the compact room, which was clearly meant for one. There was only a single chair which Jayden gestured for Wyll to take, the apprentice mage taking a seat on the edge of his bed, the only other suitable piece of furniture in the room.

"I don't know where to begin," Wyll said as he sat, looking out the small window bolted closed against the storm, or at least at the reflection which gleamed off its surface in the room's yellow lamplight.

"At the beginning is always best." Tolmarak told him in a vexed tone as the old archmage swept into the room.

Jayden and Wyll stood as he entered, and Tolmarak took in their identical expressions at a glance.

"I was already on my way to see you," he remarked in explanation of his oddly quick arrival as he took the chair Wyll had been occupying before telling the others to sit. Jayden motioned Wyll to take his former place on the end of the bed before closing his eyes for a moment and sitting on what appeared to be some form of invisible seat which he had pulled out of thin air.

Tolmarak raised a white eyebrow and chuckled.

"That's hardly an approved spell," he said in an exasperated tone as he studied Jayden's work.

"Make sure you dismiss it when you're done or someone is likely to trip over and break something," he chided, though a slight smile softened his words.

Jayden returned the archmage's grin as if the old man had complimented him, which Wyll supposed he had in a roundabout way, before they both turned their attention on him.

"How did you get in here?" the archmage asked pointedly, once again staring at Wyll in consternation.

"Apparently Tammy let him in," Jayden replied with a raised eyebrow before Wyll could work up an answer.

"What?!" Tolmarak exclaimed, his head swivelling from Wyll to Jayden.

"Tell me exactly what happened boy, and leave nothing out," the white-haired old archmage ordered in a rush.

So that was what Wyll did, as matter-of-factly as he could. He started with rushing to Brendan's aid when the massive tree had felled him in the Emerald Sea, then continued on to finding Sa'rayna standing over Brendan's body and all that entailed, and their long march back to Aramar. From there he dully related how his squad mate had finally met his end, and for good measure finished the recounting with his strange conversation with the self-proclaimed oracle just minutes before.

By the time he finished, the two magi were both staring at him with stunned, incredulous stares, and Wyll could well understand why. Had it not been he himself involved in the events of the last two days, Wyll was certain he never would have believed the tale either.

For long moments there was silence from the other two men, and Wyll was not sure if they expected something else from him, or whether they were just chewing over what he had already given them in their own minds.

There had been one point though, when he told them what Tammy had said to him, that the two magi looked at each other with a startled glance that seemed to hold more than mere surprise at the message.

"You've heard what Tammy said before, haven't you?" he asked, taking a guess at what that look had meant.

Tolmarak looked up at him with a bewildered expression and shook his head.

"Never," the archmage replied, "Though some parts of what you say Tammy spoke to you are similar in nature to what she told Jayden when he first arrived at the college last summer.

Wyll stared at the young mage, who returned the look levelly and recited what the oracle had told him.

"For many long centuries I have awaited this day Jayden, so hear me well. The very world itself stands at a crossroads the like of which has not been seen since the time of the builders' demise, and you will be the wedge on which the scales turn. Heed the prophecy when you find it, listen well to your dreams even though they are only a fragment of the whole, and find the meaning of the symbols. Together these three will see you through the dark time ahead. They will see us all through."

Wyll shifted uncomfortably as Jayden finished.

"It's strange," The young mage said with a slight frown, "I remember her words as if they had just been spoken, but the rest of that day seems no fresher than memory could account for."

"Hmmf," Tolmarak muttered, "It seems our esteemed oracle has a few more secrets than any of us knew about," he mused, as if his mind were on something else entirely.

"Tell me Wyll," the old archmage asked, "If I bring you an artist, do you think you can talk them through drawing up a portrait of this woman, this... Sa'rayna?"

"Yes Archmage," Wyll answered without thought. One thing he was absolutely sure of, was that he would never forget the beautiful face he had dreamed of for most of his life, the face he had now seen in the flesh.

Or in person at least.

"You are welcome to remain at the college for the remainder of the night." Tolmarak offered as he stood.

"There is a room prepared for your use in the mageguard complex, but come dawn you will return to camp five and report to Karthael to continue your training. Time is growing short I fear, and there is too much still to be done."

"Yes Archmage. Thank you," Wyll responded, then cleared his throat nervously when Tolmarak made to leave.

The archmage turned to face him and raised a snow coloured eyebrow while Wyll stood and clasped his hands behind his back.

"Ah, Archmage, what of Brendan's body?" he hesitantly inquired.

"I will examine it myself to be sure there was no foul play involved, and then he will be laid to rest in the soldiers' field with due honours either tomorrow or the next day depending upon my findings. I will send a rider to your camp with orders for your squad to attend. And Wyll, when you've finished burying your friend, come and speak with me again."

"Thank you again, Archmage," Wyll replied, this time with a respectful nod of the head, "I'm sure the men will appreciate the opportunity to pay their respects, as I will."

Tolmarak returned the gesture, then opened the door with a bony hand and left the room just as Simone reached for the other side. The girl was forced to move lively so the three mugs of steaming liquid she carried on a silver-worked tray didn't spill all over both the archmage and herself.

Tolmarak took a moment to frown at the girl before she dropped a curtsy and went red in the face, but the archmage barely noticed as he continued out the door.

A moment later she came in and quickly put the tray on the chest of drawers before turning to leave without so much as a word.

"Before you go Simone," Jayden said in a neutral tone which stopped the girl short.

"Yes, Jayden?" she asked shyly, turning back to face him with still red cheeks.

"You're lucky the archmage was too preoccupied to notice the two shadows your feet made under the door while you were listening. It would be, unfortunate for you I think if he had, yes?"

Wyll didn't know who to look at first. Jayden, who was doing a very good impression of a father who had just caught his young child with her hand in the cookie jar, despite the fact there couldn't have been more than four or five years between them, or at Simone herself, who had gone at least twice as red as she had for the archmage's disapproving frown.

"You're lucky we had finished discussing anything of importance, or I would have told the archmage as soon as I saw you there. Don't let me catch you eavesdropping again. Understood?"

"Yes Jayden," she whispered, mortified. She dropped into a deep curtsy which was far more elaborate than the one she had made for Tolmarak before practically running out the door in her haste to leave the room. The silver tray she left sitting on the drawers, forgetting it entirely.

For a moment there was only silence, then Wyll got up and took two of the steaming mugs and preferred one to Jayden.

"That was... a little harsh, don't you think?" he asked conversationally as he sat on the chair which the archmage had vacated.

"Perhaps," Jayden replied in exasperation after taking a swallow of the hot liquid, "But maybe that will finally get her off my back."

"The girl's been following me around for nearly two phases now and she absolutely refuses to take any kind of hint. I even told her flat out that I wasn't interested and it didn't slow her down for a minute. I am sick of 'accidentally' running into her five, even ten times a day when I'm in the college building. So yes, it was a bit harsh. It was also well deserved."

By the time Jayden ran down, Wyll was having trouble not laughing out loud as he took another drink to try to cover his mirth.

"Yes well, that's neither here nor there," Jayden added, taking a drink himself, obviously realising how he'd just sounded.

"Besides, she really shouldn't be listening at doorways," he added as an afterthought.

"Of course not," Wyll agreed in his most diplomatic tone, whilst trying to hide his amused grin behind his cup.

For a few moments they both sat in silence, lost in their own thoughts and taking the occasional drink of the hot spicy cider Simone had brought up from the kitchens.

For a while talk turned to the coming war, the winter which by all signs would peak within the phase, and the thaw which would follow a few weeks later. There was no longer any real doubt among the men, Wyll told him, that there would indeed be war. Jayden agreed the magi also thought a confrontation to be inevitable since they had received news just yesterday of the king's envoy slain in cold blood by Heramiir's men.

A timid knock at the door some time later announced the arrival of the artist Tolmarak must have summoned, and once sufficient light was brought to bear by Jayden's arts, Wyll got to work guiding the woman's sketching with his descriptions.

*   *   *

Jayden didn't know what to think about Wyll's tale. That Wyll believed it wholeheartedly was obvious, and Tolmarak had not rejected the possibility out of hand either. The Maker knew, Jayden had seen enough strange things in the last few phases, which even one year previously he would have never believed existed, to casually dismiss the idea himself.

And yet, the face which was eventually revealed by the artist's skill was... stunning, if in an unusual kind of way. Not at all what he would have expected from the being who supposedly took your soul into the next world when you died.

Eventually the young soldier beside him sighed, "That's her," he said quietly, "That's Sa'rayna."

"Do you think you will see her again?" Jayden asked after a moment as the artist began putting her materials away.

Wyll just turned to face him without a word.

"If she truly is who she claims to be, it is inevitable, sooner or later," he added hollowly, "But with war coming, I fear it may be there will not be much of a choice."

Jayden didn't know what to say to that, or even entirely what Wyll meant about the last part as the woman left with the drawing. He drained the remains of the now cold cider from his mug, barely pushing down a flash of sudden fury and pain as he wondered whether that face had been any comfort at all to Rhianna as the sea had swallowed her whole.

'There are many mysteries in the world, chief among them are these; who built Miralthrall, and what so compelled the western nations never to utilise that massive vacant city with its towering fortifications prior to, or even during the Wars of Founding? Had they done so, our forces might never have won that war, and Jeranon itself might never have existed.'
Excerpt from 'Jeranon, an historical summary.'

CHAPTER 21

THE PROPHECY OF JOINING

Heramiir woke to a darkness so profound that for just a moment he was not entirely sure whether his eyes were even open.

After long moments he groggily felt at the ground around him, he was lying on something cold and unyielding.

Stone, he thought as he stiffly rose to his knees. *Still in the cavern then, but not the main chamber.*

The deep blue stone of that floor had generated a tangible heat which he had been able to feel even through his thick walking boots, a heat which was now nowhere to be found.

Bringing a small light into existence with a thought, Heramiir surveyed his surroundings. As he stood, he wondered who else was down here, or whether the master had access to enough power even from inside his prison to move him into this cave. A cave which had no visible exit or entrance he saw as he completed a quick turn around the confining space. The room was little more than ten feet on a side, with solid rock forming every surface.

Pulling the earth closed to cover the exit is easy, Heramiir reminded himself as he studied his surroundings. He himself could do it with ease. That knowledge didn't help him discern which direction the main cavern lay in however, or if he was even anywhere near where he had started. It might be just as easy to head up towards ground level and then back down to the master's chamber from Miralthrall's basement. Besides, if he headed off blindly and picked the wrong direction there was every chance he might run out of air before he found another cavern.

"A quick search shouldn't hurt though," he muttered to himself as he reached out with the Gift and opened a narrow passage in a random spot on the wall. He was careful to close the chamber behind him enough to keep the air pressure at a roughly normal level.

As he took his first step, Heramiir's vision failed as if his Gift-wrought light had gone out. He felt a flash of panic at being suddenly blinded, the more so as he felt the minor spell still floating ahead of him. He couldn't help but gasp as a scene of alien grandeur floated abruptly into view. Heramiir found himself standing at the precipice of a cliff, looking over its edge. Below him a great city was being constructed around a lake with four points, and thousands of workers were scurrying over what looked like a massive dam which would create the fifth side of the waterway.

"Miralthrall," he breathed. He was witnessing the

construction of the master's city. Far from being built over the course of generations as would have happened had men constructed the massive stoneworks, the entire city seemed to be under construction all at once. It was as if there was a grand design the city had been planned to by a single builder. Heramiir shook his head in awe. This level of engineering was beyond even the wildest dreams of Jeranon's architects.

There was a moment of darkness and the scene was replaced by another.

He could see through the eyes of a man as he walked through a glowing green ring of, something, and went from night to day in the space of a heartbeat. He stepped out onto a tropical island, the twin suns high overhead making even winter on Erenmire seem like the peak of high summer back home.

Circling the small island, the Empress' fleet of warships had converged, and as soon as they spotted him fired a barrage in his direction. With a thought he erected a shield and waited the few seconds before the volley of ammunition exploded all around him, burning trees to ash and tearing great furrows in the ground. He smiled as the air cleared, his shield fully intact. The Empress should know by now that the weapons of this world were not powerful enough to harm him, yet she persisted in her foolish defiance. In that one thing, he almost respected her.

Reaching out a hand he concentrated on the lead ship, a vast construction of metal gliding effortlessly along the water. It was enough to take his interest for a moment, wondering how the inhabitants of this world had dreamed up a way to make metal to float without the use of magic.

He would have to save one for study when he was done here.

Closing his outstretched hand into a fist he watched, grinning as the immense vessel crumpled in the distance as easily as a sheet of paper would have in his hand. There was a violent explosion from somewhere inside, and when the flames finally cleared, all that was left of the once mighty vessel was a collection of shattered remnants which quickly submerged beneath the choppy surface of the waves.

The rest of the fleet fired another volley, which he ignored as he turned his attention to the next ship in line. This wouldn't take long.

Once again there was a moment of blackness and Heramiir wondered what he was seeing.

"They're here. Hold the doors at all costs," he heard himself order the few men who had made it to this chamber alive. They'd been driven back to the capital, or at least so their enemy thought, committing their entire force to what they assumed to be a last assault on his collapsing lines of defence. He had laid this trap well, the spell the council were about to complete would destroy the city and everything within a dozen miles. If he had timed it just right, the enemy would have broken through their final defensive lines and entered the capital fully to loot and destroy whatever was left. It was a desperate tactic that would kill every man still standing including himself. 'A truly steep price for victory,' he reflected, but a generation of bloody warfare against the foreign intruders had left him with no other choice if his people were to survive.

There was an ear shattering crash, and when he looked

up a gigantic creature with two heads and a dozen snakelike arms holding a variety of vicious weapons stood in the doorway.

Turning his back on the creature he nodded to the high caster. "Now."

There was a flash of brilliant light.

Blackness.

Quicker and quicker the images came, of ages long past and worlds so alien he could barely comprehend what he was seeing. Always there was magic in use though, either being employed by whoever's eyes he was watching through, or else by someone nearby, until finally the cascade of images was simply gone.

Heramiir stood gasping for breath, his pale blue Gift-wrought light still hovering before him as he found himself back in the cave, where he must have been all along he supposed.

Heramiir had never considered himself one to frighten easily, but even he was forced to admit the ease with which the master could manipulate his mind was disconcerting. Suddenly he wondered how long he'd been in here. There was no way to tell.

Come, the master's voice whispered in his mind.

Heramiir looked around the sealed cave for a moment before realising he could now feel the power emanating from the master, or perhaps his prison, off to the east. How he knew it was east he had no idea, but something had changed inside him while he'd been watching those alien scenes run through his mind's eye. He felt inexplicably good now that they were finished, a sense of rightness flowing through him which he had never experienced before. It was as if some goal he had been working towards for as long as he could recall had unexpectedly come to fruition.

With a start he realised he could remember each of the scenes as precisely as if he had been there in the flesh. A slow grin spread across his face as he recognised that in each of the visions an entirely unknown magic was being wrought, and that he understood how those spells had been performed.

With a tingle of excitement, Heramiir moulded the stone back in the direction the master's prison lay and walked towards him.

Within a dozen paces the wall ahead opened out to reveal the main chamber, and Heramiir snorted in amusement.

"So you did survive," the master chuckled as Heramiir crossed the cavernous chamber and came back inside the ring of glowing crystal spires, "I had hoped you would be powerful enough to withstand the sending."

Heramiir eyed the prison warily.

"What did you do to me?"

"What you wanted," the master replied, its voice sounding amused.

Amused... It could have killed me, and it sounds amused.

He had to admit though, whatever the master had done, he felt good, powerful he realised after a moment's thought.

"That's how you will teach me?" he asked curiously.

"There is something I wish you to see," the master told him, flatly ignoring Heramiir's question.

Heramiir ground his teeth, but answered, "And that is?"

"Follow the light," the master replied.

Heramiir ground his teeth as a dim glow appeared. He looked over his shoulder to see the hated cold blue flame which had led him relentlessly for days to bring him here floating a span off the polished marble floor, its flickering blue light cast between two of the glowing columns.

With an irritated sigh Heramiir did as the master bade him, and as he neared the glowing sphere it moved away, just as he'd expected it would

Eventually he neared the outer edge of the cavern, just about opposite to the doorway with the strange runes which held so much power, and yet seemed to do nothing at all.

The sphere moved off to the left a short way and then stopped, casting its steady blue light on words written into the wall with what looked like the Gift, in a hand not much different from his own.

For a long moment he stood there, repeatedly reading the words, studying what he was sure was an ancient prophecy which had lain buried here for untold years while the oblivious world carried on above.

"*You are correct,*" the master confirmed into his mind, and Heramiir nodded to himself as he spoke the words out loud, memorising them as he went.

A TIME SHALL COME. EMPIRES SHALL RISE.
A TIME SHALL COME. WAR SHALL RISE.
A TIME SHALL COME. DARKNESS SHALL DESCEND.
A FEW SHALL BE BORN. THEY SHALL RISE IN THEIR TIME.

A MAGE OF DARK ASPECT WHO SHALL NEVER BE DEFEATED.
A BOY WHOSE PAIN SHALL TEAR HIS SOUL

ASUNDER.

A BUILDER WHO SHALL DESTROY ALL THAT WHICH STANDS.

THEY SHALL DRAW OTHERS TO THEM, AND BATTLE SHALL BE JOINED.

A WARRIOR LIKE HAS NOT BEEN SEEN SINCE THE WORLD'S FOUNDATION.

A GENERAL WHOSE EVERY THOUGHT SHALL BE OF BETRAYAL.

A POWER FROM TIME IMMEMORIAL, UNMATCHED BUT FOR ONE.

ON THESE SHALL THE WORLD'S FATE BE DECIDED.

IN THOSE DAYS, THE EARTH SHALL BE RENT.

IN THOSE DAYS, THE SEA SHALL BE MADE ALIVE.

IN THOSE DAYS, THE WIND SHALL BE GIVEN FORM.

IN THOSE DAYS, THE FUTURE SHALL BEGIN.

AND TWO SHALL BECOME ONE, AND CHAOS SHALL REIGN.

AND TWO SHALL BECOME ONE, AND HOPE SHALL BE LOST.

AND TWO SHALL BECOME ONE, AND THE PAST SHALL BE DONE.

AND ALL THAT HAS GONE BEFORE SHALL BE FORGOTTEN.

Would you understand what it means? the master whispered teasingly into his mind.

"I would know what you think it means," Heramiir replied shrewdly.

As powerful as the creature calling itself the master was, he was getting fed up with the half answers it gave, even on the rare occasions when it did choose to answer his questions.

Heramiir expected the creature to be angry, but instead it laughed into his mind.

"Did I say something amusing?" Heramiir asked it flatly.

I have given you a bare taste of power and a little knowledge and you are like a kitten that has just discovered it has claws. But you are still just a kitten to me Heramiir, and just as easily disposed of should I wish it.

For a moment Heramiir considered a retort, but then crossed his arms and waited, ignoring the master's comment as he read over the ancient writing once again.

I am the power from time immemorial, the master announced into his mind with a touch of irritation once Heramiir had finished inspecting the words.

Heramiir felt a flash of pettiness at the subtle triumph, but said nothing as he turned to make the long walk back towards the prison once he was sure he had memorised the ancient script.

"And what would that make me, the 'mage of dark aspect?'" he asked sceptically.

He had done some unsavoury things to ensure his rise to power, but enough to be referred to as 'of dark aspect' in an ancient prophecy? He wasn't so sure of that, yet none of the other descriptions seemed to fit.

"Perhaps," the master mused aloud once Heramiir had reached the circle.

"And the one who matches you, they were of your race, the builders? They were the one who imprisoned you weren't they."

"Yes!" The master hissed.

"I was betrayed by the one closest to me and left here to rot for aeons while the world turned above, forgetting its true masters, forgetting my name! My name... what is my name? I had one once, but it's been so long since anyone used it that it seems to have disappeared. But I remember her name, or at least I did. You will find her for me Heramiir. You will be my hand and my eyes while I am locked in here and in return you will have all the power you could wish for and when I am released, you will be at my right hand, my agent; my avatar."

Heramiir's eyes narrowed at the master's erratic recital. *This creature is not stable.* The most powerful being in the world, and it was quite possibly insane. Could he really release it out into the world? Could he afford not to? It was unlikely his larger plans could come to fruition without its aid. After a moment he dismissed the many questions rampaging through his mind. Whether the creature before him was sane or not, it alone could give him what he needed. He had no choice but to continue dealing with it.

At least for now.

"Where would you have me begin the search, builder?" he asked in what he hoped sounded like a compliant tone.

"She always liked to surround herself with the people of this world. She had a strange fascination for them I never understood," the master whispered, its voice changing from fond to utter fury in the space of a heartbeat, enough so to make Heramiir take a wary half step back.

"Find her!"

"You must be more specific," Heramiir told it carefully,

"I do not have the resources to search every town and city in the entire world."

For a long drawn out moment there was only silence from the glowing prison, and Heramiir was beginning to wonder whether the master had even heard him.

"In the centre of the biggest city you will find her. Use your mind witch to coordinate the search. That was always a rare talent, one you should make far better use of," it added, suddenly calm.

My mind witch? Heramiir wondered, and then it clicked.

"You mean Deshara," he replied, and the glowing shaft of light pulsed brighter in response.

"If this builder has your power, as the prophecy suggests, how am I to deal with her?" Heramiir asked without relish. He was no coward, but neither was he one to go on a suicide mission at the master's whim, or anyone else's for that matter.

"You will not have to. Once I am free, I will deal with her myself. She was able to imprison me only because she betrayed my trust, but I was always the stronger, and that will not be allowed to happen again! Now give your mind witch her orders. After twenty thousand years my patience is at an end, let the search begin and do not fail me in this Heramiir, or you will spend the rest of your unnaturally long life screaming."

Heramiir's eyes narrowed at the threat, but he gave a low bow anyway.

"As you command, Master," he replied formally, something in the creature's tone making him absolutely sure that if he baulked at this order, the master would carry out his threat with little thought for the consequences, if any.

"What should I tell Deshara to look for?"

Again, there was a long moment of silence, as though the creature imprisoned before him was lost in its own dark thoughts.

Learn, it whispered into his mind.

Once again a cascade of strange images flowed across Heramiir's vision, and this time he knew he was looking through the master's own eyes, in the distant past before his imprisonment below Miralthrall's basements had begun.

In the vision before him stood a woman of exquisite beauty, her fiery red tresses setting off the bluest eyes Heramiir had ever seen, her full figure and lips speaking of a sensuous creature. He also remembered a voice which sounded like music when she laughed. Yet there was something… not quite human about her, and it stood the hair on the back of Heramiir's neck up straight.

Then just like that the vision was gone, though a crystal-clear memory remained.

For a moment Heramiir was silent until a half-remembered thought made him delve back into the memories the master had shown him a few minutes before. He recalled a time when he had been a king, or at least he had been looking through the eyes of a being who had been king. One who had a mind witch amongst his servants. According to the memory, there was a certain way you could focus your thoughts, one that a mind witch could pick up from anywhere in the world if they were talented enough.

Deshara, he called out with his mind. *Deshara, Attend!*

For a long minute there was no response and Heramiir began to grow angry. He knew from the ancient memory he was doing it right, but still there was no answer, until finally a hesitant, *Archmage?* floated weakly into his mind.

I have a task for your spies, Heramiir told her in silence. *There is a woman I need found. I have reason to believe she resides near the centre of Aramar.*

I see, Deshara returned a little more confidently, her communication a little stronger this time. *How will I know when I have the right woman?*

Learn, Heramiir ordered as he sent the image he had gleaned from the master's mind through the strange connection he had initiated with his mind witch.

There was a long silence after that, then a thought which might have sounded like she was out of breath had they been using words to speak.

What do you wish done when I find her?

Watch and report back to me her whereabouts.

Perhaps he had made that last sending a bit too strong.

It shall be as you command Archmage, Deshara replied, and without waiting for anything further, Heramiir severed the connection and returned his attention to the master's prison.

"It is done."

"Did you think I had not noticed?" the creature within acerbically replied.

To that Heramiir had no immediate answer, but if the master could pick up his communications with Deshara, her talent became a lot less useful than he had suddenly hoped it might be.

A mage of dark aspect, he mused. Was it too high a price to pay for his goals? Perhaps, but if the first part of the ancient script were true, then so was the other, 'who would never be defeated.'

With the slightest of smiles Heramiir realised he didn't care. If there was truth in the prophecy, then so be it. If not, nothing had changed.

"Teach me," he said as he turned back to the master's prison, and for once the master acceded without a word.

A wound inflicted by an enemy scars the body. A wound inflicted by a friend scars the soul.
Common saying of the Teraliv race.

CHAPTER 22

THE OATH

A merciless wind howled around a pair of men as they stood, facing each other across a wet stone plateau which overlooked the sea for a hundred leagues in any direction. Under a sky blanketed with pitch black clouds they moved, circling as the driving rain hammered them while they took each other's measure. In his right hand Jayden held his serpentine Oo'vi blade, but in the dim light of the storm it seemed lighter than it should, somehow diminished.

As he looked across the plateau at his adversary, Dael raised an impossibly long and sharp rapier and took a lazy swing in his direction. Jayden moved to block it, but as the two swords connected, his ancient Oo'vi weapon evaporated into mist which the thundering rain instantly carried away. Dael smiled knowingly, and Jayden just stared, horrified at his now empty hand as his one-time friend slashed his rapier through the air as though it were a whip.

The needle thin blade writhed towards Jayden like a snake as he frantically dived away from its point.

He landed hard, and when he looked back at Dael an

instant later, the count's sword had disappeared, and a knife, its tip missing, had inexplicably taken its place in his hand.

'You never were my match with the blade,' Dael's scornful expression seemed to taunt him through the downpour.

For a long moment all except the storm was still as Jayden climbed to his feet. With a single swift motion Dael's arm uncoiled, loosing the broken blade from his grasp and hurling it upward into the cloud riven sky.

Up and up the blade flew, impossibly high as it was lost in the writhing clouds. In an almost blinding flash of lightning Jayden caught sight of it just in time, streaking out of the sky, his heart its only target.

He leapt backwards desperately, trying to get out of its way. As quick as he was though, the knife still cut his chest deeply as it fell from the clouds and bounced off the rocks at his feet with a clang audible above even the crashing of the storm.

It should have stopped there, but instead of bouncing to a halt the broken knife launched itself out over the ocean again as if of its own will, not falling, but staying level with the plateau. Jayden squinted his eyes against the rain, desperately trying to see where the animated blade had gone. Once again, lightning illuminated the scene just in time to catch a glint of shining metal hurtling towards him from the darkness. Again he desperately leapt away, but the pain from the slash across his chest slowed him enough for the blade to bite viciously into his right arm as it passed, continuing out over the treetops next to the plateau.

With a rising sense of panic Jayden turned and saw

Dael standing, arms crossed as the driving rain fell around him. The sadistic grin on his face saying no quarter would be given, or considered this night.

The split second of distraction was costly for Jayden as he was shoved forward onto his knees, a white-hot pain in his side where the quivering knife now lay embedded in one of his ribs.

"I tire of this," Dael said, speaking at last as he reached out a hand and summoned the broken blade to his grasp. The pain of knife tearing away from his flesh caused Jayden to fall to the hard stone of the plateau.

In what seemed like no time at all Dael was kneeling over him. To Jayden's utter horror he found he could not move so much as an eyelid, his body frozen as Dael held the bloody knife above him for the final stroke.

With a last burst of defiance Jayden strained to move his frozen muscles, but to no avail. It was as if Tolmarak had him in that spell of air all over again, just as he had the first time they'd met.

Dael grinned as rain poured down off his silhouetted form and brought the knife down hard, sinking it into Jayden's heart.

With a sudden lurch of movement Jayden woke sweating in his own bed in Aramar's College of the Arts, his sheets a tangled knot on the floor and his hair matted into an unruly mess from the night's exertions.

With an infuriated sigh, Jayden lay back on the mattress and stared at the smooth ceiling dejectedly as his pounding heart slowly returned to a more normal pace. Without thought he ran his left hand over the spot where Dael had stuck the knife into his chest in real life in what had become an unconscious habit. He couldn't help but shudder at the uninterrupted skin where Tolmarak had used the Gift to heal the mortal wound.

It was a new nightmare he'd had these past few nights. As bad as it was, it was still a thousand times better than having to watch Rhianna leap to her death in crystal clear detail each and every evening when he could no longer keep fatigue at bay.

Many phases had passed since that night, and he no longer believed it should have been him instead of Rhianna who had died on the plateau, though even now he would have traded their fates if he could. Dael was the one at fault, the only one, and it was Dael who would ultimately pay the price for those crimes.

Over the course of the last phases, Tolmarak had taught him all he had learned so far about using the Gift, as well as freely sharing the wisdom of his many years as an archmage. But more than that, the old Gift user was also working to show him how to focus his energy into more constructive pursuits than dwelling on revenge; though that would eventually come Jayden promised himself yet again. He had resisted Tolmarak's attempts at first. The old man had his own agenda. Even so, he was forced to admit that he was yet to catch Tolmarak in a lie, or acting against the best interests of his charges.

With a slight flicker of interest Jayden realised he was coming to respect the old man as a person, as opposed to him just being an archmage, and the leader of the college, and the king's advisor.

I must be getting cynical if that's what it takes to impress me now, he acknowledged with a sigh, before swinging his legs off the bed to sit up slowly.

With no more warning than a soft footstep in the

corridor outside, his door softly opened. The movement caused Jayden to start as Headmistress Anora, the matronly old woman in charge of the serving staff who worked the college grounds, popped her head around the corner and scanned the room at a glance. Seeing he was already awake she opened the door the rest of the way and came into the room, crossing the small space without a word to open the pale green curtains which covered his only window. The bright morning sunlight streamed in as a pair of heavily muscled porters entered, carrying a large copper washtub between them before filing back out of the room with only a nod for greeting.

"So, today is the big day I'm told," Mistress Anora said as she stepped away from the small window and turned to face him, glancing at the tangled wreckage of his bed sheets as she did.

"So I'm told," Jayden replied noncommittally.

With the slightest raising of an eyebrow, Mistress Anora reached down into the copper tub and retrieved a canvas wrapped package, which she then held out for Jayden to take.

"From Archmage Tolmarak."

He took the package and placed it on the bed beside him. The lack of any overt reaction caused the old woman's eyebrows to draw together slightly in disapproval.

"We both know what's in it," Jayden remarked, forestalling the obvious comment he could see the head servant about to make.

"Hmm, well, be that as it may, it wouldn't kill you to show a little enthusiasm."

Jayden looked up and gave the matronly woman the slightest of smiles, which he doubted made it as far as his eyes. It was about all he could manage after so recently waking from this latest dream.

"The nightmares again?" she asked sympathetically.

"I don't want to talk about it."

He could feel himself going red from embarrassment as he realised every servant in the palace must have heard the gossip by now of how he'd been found a few nights ago. The first time he'd had this new dream, he'd apparently been thrashing in his sleep and calling out Rhianna's name loud enough to wake half the floor. To make matters worse it had been Simone, the serving girl who had a crush on him, who'd been the one to have to wake him from the violent nightmare.

"Then don't," Mistress Anora replied, "And I've made sure no one else will either," she said, causing him to go even redder still at the confirmation the episode was indeed common knowledge.

"Anyway, Archmage Tolmarak will be waiting for you at the entrance to the courtyard at second tolling, about half an hour from now."

A serving girl he didn't know entered with a tray holding an opaque pitcher of some chilled liquid and a bowl full of porridge complete with servings of honey and butter. She placed them on his desk before leaving as privately as she'd entered.

"Thank you."

"You're welcome Jayden," she told him in her motherly tone, "Just try to remember, it's not the items in the archmage's package which are important, it's what they represent that holds the true meaning."

Jayden looked at her for a moment as he considered her words, then offered the universally short nod of a person who has deliberated and conceded a point not necessarily to their liking.

Mistress Anora smiled again as she saw his reaction, then pulled the door closed behind herself as she left Jayden to eat and bathe before Tolmarak required his presence downstairs.

With everyone out of his room Jayden sat down on his only seat to eat the hot meal. When he was done, he used a spell he had recently learned with very little difficulty to transmute the air in the copper tub into water, which he then heated with a small spell of fire. He even managed all of it without having to resort to gestures or incantations to achieve the desired effect, an effort not even Tolmarak could have faulted.

When he was finished bathing, he dressed in the customary black garb of the magi and added his white-lined apprentice's cloak. With a thought he changed the water back to air so the servants could remove the copper tub without the extra weight, and turned to face the bed.

The package Mistress Anora had delivered was still lying there, its canvas covering wrapped and tied off with a leather cord waiting to be cut. With a tiny fire spell Jayden severed the cord and unfolded the canvas with his hands to reveal a new cloak identical to the one he now wore, save a single detail. This one had a blue lining, which represented the rank of Mage. Picking the precisely folded cloak up from the bed he slung it over his left arm as Tolmarak had instructed him the night before. He opened the door, hesitated a moment, then left the tiny room which had been his home since arriving in Aramar for the final time. When he returned to the college this afternoon, his things would already have been transferred by the servants to his new quarters, which he was told were a significant improvement over the ones he currently occupied.

The walk down the spiral staircase was usually a quick one for Jayden, but today he was held up time and again by magi, and even a few of the servants, all of whom wanted to congratulate him or say 'good luck' for what was about to come.

When he finally reached the ground floor of Aramar's College of the Arts, it was to find Tolmarak waiting patiently by the main door.

"If you're ready we'll leave now," was the old archmage's only comment as Jayden joined him on the floor of the structure several minutes ahead of schedule.

"I am," he replied just as briefly, and with a nod the two men left the building to find their respective mounts waiting for them, each held by a groom sporting the dragon and flame symbol on their tabards.

With a nod to the groom, Jayden handed him the blue-lined cloak and mounted Strider before taking back the cloak as well as the reins which the groom preferred. A moment later Tolmarak was also ready, and the pair set off towards the heart of Aramar.

Within a few minutes they had passed the tethered goat and the boundaries of the college grounds, entering the city proper to make their way slowly through the early morning crowd of people.

Usually the streets in this part of Aramar were not too cramped, but right at the moment the throng was busy trying to get to their places of work before second tolling was sounded across the city, unlike in the summer phases. The traditional start of the workday had shifted now that winter had fully arrived, and the hours of usable daylight were far shorter and colder. For most the snow blanketed journey was hard going, but the horses, and the distinctive cloaks the two magi wore meant most people gave them a little extra room. They continued along their silent way to the king's great fortress, which overlooked the very heart of Aramar, for some time until Jayden spoke up.

"Ah, Archmage. There's something I've been meaning to ask you for a while now. Why is that goat tethered in the middle of the college grounds?"

Tolmarak just gave him a slightly amused sideways glance, but no answer was forthcoming, and Jayden sighed in mild irritation.

"Do you remember the ceremony?" Tolmarak finally asked as they crossed into the palace grounds, the guards allowing them to pass freely through the bailey and into the inner stable yard which was reserved for nobles and visiting dignitaries.

And magi too apparently, Jayden thought as he nodded an affirmative response to Tolmarak's question.

When a groom hurried up to take the horses the two men dismounted, and again without speaking they walked through the wide wooden doorway which lay before them and up a shallow staircase which led into the palace itself.

Around him, Jayden couldn't help but stare at the ornate tapestries and precious ornaments which lined every wall and niche. He had thought the college building was grand, and had been correct; but the palace's unabashed display of wealth and culture far outweighed it in every respect.

At the end of the corridor lay an arched doorway, and beyond it stood a vast room at least fifty spans high. The distant ceiling was held in place by great columns sheathed in black marble and inlaid with what appeared to be designs wrought in gold leaf which ran throughout. Jayden realised he had no earthly idea what this room was used for.

Tolmarak continued to lead Jayden through the palace's grand halls until they came to a vast wooden doorway, polished till it shined and inlaid with the king's royal emblem of a white rearing horse wearing a crown on a red background. A pair of men armoured in full plate, enamelled in the reverse colours of the royal emblem guarded the door. The king's personal guard.

As the two magi stopped a dozen feet from the door, the guards in front of them crossed their halberds in perfect unison, blocking the way forward.

"Who wishes to come before His Majesty, King Erian the Third of the House of Savani?" One of the men asked, although it was impossible to tell which of them had spoken beneath their all-encompassing white enamelled helmets.

"One who wishes to serve," Tolmarak intoned in a voice both calm and yet powerful at the same time.

"And who is this you bring before his Majesty?" the guard asked. Again, Jayden could not tell which of them spoke.

"One who is prepared to serve as I have, with honour and loyalty to His Majesty the King," Tolmarak spoke the ritual's formula, just as he had instructed Jayden the night before.

"Young servant, know it is death to enter the king's presence with a false heart," the guard once again intoned.

"I come with no thought but to serve," Jayden said precisely, and with as little emotion as possible. It was not entirely true of course. There were things he wanted far more than to serve, but as Tolmarak had told him the night before, 'The formalities had to be observed.'

"Then come," the guard told them, and as perfectly as before the two guardsmen raised their halberds out of the way, each pulling the wooden door behind him ajar to permit the magi to enter.

Once the massive wooden frame had swung out of the way, a red carpet lined with gold trim was revealed. At its distant end stood a three step marble dais on which the royal throne of Jeranon's kings and queens was raised, as well as two flags, one to either side of the throne. To the left stood the same design of the crowned horse, and to the right flew the flag of Jeranon itself. Unchanged since their people had first come to these shores, it was a deep blue field on which a brown silhouette of a three-masted ship sailed on a stylised green laurel branch instead of a water line. The ship's figurehead held a silver sword out straight to point the way.

There could be no mistaking whose authority was supreme here, and all who gathered at the royal court could see the king's decisions handed out from the elevated position of the massive, carved wooden throne which dominated the stand.

Jayden and Tolmarak walked in unison towards the dais, and as he'd been instructed the night before, he kept his eyes firmly on the lowest step of the three. He tried his best to ignore the assembled throng of nobles whom he could see to either side of the hall from the corner of his eye.

When he was three paces short of the dais Jayden stopped and knelt, allowing the cloak which still lay across his arm to pool on the carpet beside him. Tolmarak proceeded an extra step before also making his obeisance.

"Whom do you bring before me Archmage Tolmarak?" an ageing voice asked from just out of Jayden's line of sight, where the monarch presumably sat his throne. Jayden couldn't help but admire the casually complete confidence in his voice as he addressed the most influential mage in all of Jeranon.

"I bring Jayden, my king, son of David and Lyssa Torell, your loyal subjects and merchants of Grandell."

For a second Jayden thought he heard a snort of derision from somewhere in the crowd, but didn't dare break the ceremony just to try and see who it had been. There were far too many of Jeranon's upper level nobility focusing their scrutiny on him right at this moment for his liking as it was.

"To what end do you come before me Jayden of Grandell?" the king asked solemnly.

"That I might serve you for the greater good of this kingdom," Jayden returned according to the ritual.

"And how would you seek to do such a thing?" the king intoned.

"I would request most humbly that I be granted the rank of Mage, along with the totality of responsibilities which ensue from such rank."

"Do you, Tolmarak, Leader of the College of the Arts, vouch for this man, that his heart is pure, that his words and his intent are true?" King Erian replied.

"I do so swear," Tolmarak answered without so much as a backward glance.

"Then rise Mage, and serve this kingdom with your life, and if needs be, your death."

At that, Jayden rose and waited as Tolmarak turned to face him, and as the final part of the ritual dictated, loosened the drawstring of his white-lined apprentice's cloak, allowing it to fall limply to the floor. Tolmarak took the blue-lined cloak that was the insignia of a full Mage's rank from Jayden's outstretched arm where it still waited. With a practised hand, he arranged it over Jayden's shoulders, tying the drawstring closed to finish his portion of the ceremony.

"Let all witness this is Jayden of Grandell, Mage and defender of my realm. So says your king."

"Long live the king!" Jayden and Tolmarak returned in unison as the other nobles in the room echoed the final line of the ceremony. Jayden gave as courtly a bow as he was capable of while there was a short smattering of polite but bored applause from the onlooking nobles. He rose and stepped backwards three paces, again in time with Tolmarak before turning to leave, but not before he caught sight of a familiar face, one that instantly made conscious thought impossible as Jayden's heart hammered in his own ears.

"Murderer!" Jayden roared as he took a sudden step forward. The word echoing throughout the throne room as every pair of eyes swivelled towards where Jayden was furiously advancing on a smirking Count Dael.

*   *   *

As soon as the new Mage had moved, the king's personal bodyguards had placed their giant shields, and themselves, between him and the king. Their white enamelled armour broken only by the red form of the king's insignia, the colours in reverse to show that although they were the monarch's most trusted guard, they themselves were not part of the royal household.

"Come, Jayden," Tolmarak said in his most authoritative voice as he grasped the boy's upper arm, attempting to bring some semblance of reality, and more importantly, consequence back to the young man's anguished mind.

With a sharp tug Jayden broke free of his grasp and continued advancing on Dael without so much as a backwards glance. The young count still had a smug, knowing grin on his haughty face as he watched the newly elevated Jayden raise his hand to cast a spell.

"Jayden! No!" Tolmarak yelled as he sensed the young mage draw from his powers and wrap a band of air and fire hard enough around the count's torso that an audible crack echoed throughout the room. It was followed immediately by a no longer smug cry of pain as Jayden's spell burned deeply into Dael's flesh, choking the life from the man whom he hated more than anything else in existence.

"I said no!" Tolmarak roared as the doors to the throne room slammed open and the pair of household guards who had begun the ceremony came storming into the room. The lead soldier drew his scimitar while running at Jayden faster than should be possible had his heavy steel armour not been augmented via the Gift. The other stopped a step inside the doorway and drew his bow, knocking one of the arcane arrows the royal guard all carried as he took perfect aim at Jayden's heart.

What happened next was a blur.

Tolmarak threw the strongest spell of air he could at

Jayden, sending the boy sprawling halfway across the huge room. The younger mage rammed into a crowd of nobles, all of whom were suddenly trying to be anywhere else as the royal archer released an arrow not even Tolmarak's considerable ability with the Gift could have stopped. He should know, after all, he had wrought them himself. With Jayden's concentration abruptly broken, Dael dropped limply to the floor, barely conscious but still alive as Jayden tumbled to a halt.

Now that the young mage was no longer there, the arrow intended for his heart fortunately managed to also miss the nobles who had not yet fled, embedding itself in the far wall of the room. The stone it impacted turned promptly to dust and fell from its place in the structure.

The archer looked at Tolmarak hesitantly but drew another arrow as he once again took aim at Jayden. The second guard changed direction without pause, once again hurling himself at Jayden, who was already beginning to rise.

"Halt!" Tolmarak shouted desperately as he used a simple parlour trick spell which amplified the sound of his voice a dozen times over, giving the impression of him being something vast.

The few nobles who hadn't yet scattered hastily covered their ears at his sudden roar, slinking as far back as they could into the shadows of the great hall, forced to watch the unfolding of events which they were helpless to affect.

"I command you to hold!" Tolmarak shouted again as the archer drew string to cheek and fired.

As the archer loosed his arrow, Tolmarak drew the floor up with a thought to shield Jayden from the projectile, which stuck into the warped marble and burned the stone with an unnatural green flame.

This was one of the things which made the king's archers so deadly. Each of their arrows had a unique spell placed upon it to create a different effect, making an effective defence near impossible since you never knew which of the projectiles was coming at you until it was already in the air.

Seeing Tolmarak's move, Jayden repeated the spell, taking only a moment longer to get it to work than the old archmage had. Tolmarak found the display vaguely frightening as he was certain this was the first time the boy had ever seen that particular incantation worked. But Jayden didn't stop at a simple shield. Within instants, both the archer and the swordsman had been completely surrounded and roofed in by the raised marble floor of the king's hall.

*   *   *

By the time it was clear the royal guards had been incapacitated, the king's bodyguards were already moving him out of the room. They were careful to keep the giant shields they carried completely between Jayden and the monarch, who was looking justifiably furious at having to retreat from his own throne room.

It was a fact not lost on Jayden as he regained his feet. For the first time since seeing Dael grinning insolently at him a moment before, he realised just exactly what he was doing, and where he was trying to do it.

"Your Majesty," he called out passionately, "I beg you, forgive my outburst. I bear you no ill will. But this... man, is a murderer," he continued furiously as he pointed at Dael's injured form, "And I will see him dead for his crimes."

It took a painfully stretched moment, but the king eventually ordered his bodyguards to halt their retreat, an order which they obeyed, though clearly not by choice.

"You will not," King Erian intoned as he motioned his bodyguards to stand apart a little, which they did with only a slight enough hesitation to imply they thought it a very bad idea.

"Though the sheer recklessness with which you conduct yourself in my presence suggests you are either a suicidal fool, or believe there to be some unshakable proof to your claim which might mitigate your current transgression. I do not think I believe you to be a fool," He added thoughtfully after a moment.

"Then allow me to administer the justice which is his due... Please," Jayden entreated the king, his voice hoarse with emotion as he stared the nation's ruler directly in the eye.

"No," Erian replied coldly after only the barest of moments, "There will be no, 'justice,' of that kind meted out here today."

In an instant Jayden felt his heart sink within his chest. To disobey the king's orders was treason, but avenging Rhianna's death was not something he was going to be denied, no matter what the personal consequences might be.

Without responding to the king, he once again turned his full attention back to the man who had taken everything from him. The man who had stood, dressed in his finery as Jayden had been raised to the rank of Mage of Jeranon. The man who now cowered away from him as he approached the doomed, 'noble'.

"Then I deem you unworthy to serve," Jayden replied quietly, though he knew not whether the others had heard.

"Don't do this Jayden," a quiet voice whispered in his ear.

It should have made him jump, but for some reason he seemed to have expected it. The last time he'd heard a voice projected like this, he had been sailing away from Aramar while Tolmarak spoke to him from the city docks.

"If you go through with this now, the king will have no choice but to declare you renegade and order your execution. It is the law, and with so many witnesses," he referred to the few nobles who had been cut off from the doorway by the brief fight. "It will not matter how valuable you are to the coming war effort; he will have to uphold the law. More, as the ranking mage in Aramar I will be the one to have to carry out that sentence, and although I have no desire to do so, I will obey our king's commands."

For an instant Jayden paused as he copied Tolmarak's spell so the two of them could talk privately.

"You couldn't stop me if you tried," he said confidently, though still a little winded from being hurled across the room just moments before. "I'm more powerful than you are, I know that now."

Tolmarak sighed.

"Yes," he returned eventually, "You are very powerful in the Gift. If only your sense of self control and self-determination were as strong, then you would be a force to be reckoned with."

"What's that supposed to mean?" Jayden demanded. There was only one thing on his mind right at this moment, and conversation wasn't it.

For a long moment Tolmarak didn't answer, but when he saw Jayden was too focused on Dael to think of anything else he relented.

"Do you think he came here today by coincidence? He knows sooner or later you will come for him Jayden, and that if it happens in Grandell, he will not survive. He knows he can't compete with your power. On the other hand, by forcing your confrontation here he can deal with you without ever having to lift a finger. He was no doubt hoping that while you were distracted with him the king's guards would do their job and eliminate a threat in the throne room. Had I not directly intervened and stopped them, he would have been correct."

"And he looks like the injured party and gets to go back to Grandell with a clean slate," Jayden icily completed the thought as he eyed the count with more scorn than a den full of harpies could have mustered.

"I won't insult you by telling you not to kill this man Jayden. I know you wouldn't listen anyway. But this is not the time. If you end this now, neither of you will leave this room alive. Your only course of action is to do something much harder. Stop playing into his hands and let him live, for now. Agree to finish this another day and I give you my word that when the time comes, I will intercede with the king on your behalf."

For a long moment Jayden looked around the throne room, at the king, who was growing angry at being ignored, and only holding his peace because Tolmarak had managed to stop Jayden's advance. He looked over at the cowering nobles, terrified for their lives, and finally back at Dael.

"Please understand Jayden. What you have already done would condemn most men to prison or death, but Jeranon itself will need you in the next few phases. I believe that will give us sufficient leverage with the king to ensure this whole incident is dealt with in a very different way. But only if you stop, now!" Tolmarak finished in no uncertain terms.

Again Jayden looked balefully at Dael's prone form, and then with a growing sense of unease glanced around the throne room at the cowering noble's and furious monarch. He wanted the thing in front of him dead as much as he ever had. As he looked around though, his heart unexpectedly began to return to a more normal pace, and his head cleared somewhat of the blinding rage which had taken him at seeing Dael so unexpectedly. Somewhere in the last few moments he was amazed to find he had lost the urge to sacrifice himself for that cause. Too much had already been lost because of Dael's lust for control, and Jayden suddenly felt no desire to add his own life to the tally. He would not kill himself in order to deal out justice to Dael, or die in any other way because of this murderer's schemes.

"Very well," he answered bluntly, without taking his eyes from the count's pained form.

Tolmarak uttered an audible sigh of relief but said one last thing in the quietly projected voice.

"It would make matters much easier for me if you were the one who released the royal guards."

Jayden gave a short nod and released the voice spell. Taking two quick steps he knelt down and pulled Dael up from the floor by his shirt, bending his head close to the man's ear while Tolmarak moved to the king's side and began to whisper in hushed tones with the monarch. Everyone else in the room was still eyeing Jayden as though he were a poisonous snake on the living room floor. Unsurprisingly, some of the nobles left trapped in the cavernous chamber took this as their queue to once again retreat towards the room's expansive doors.

"I will not kill you today Dael," Jayden whispered to his childhood friend, forcing as much of his barely restrained fury into the one short word as he could while still pitching his voice for only Dael to hear. "But I will kill you. For what you did to Rhianna, and to me. So until that day, count, know that nothing has been forgotten, or forgiven. Your day of reckoning draws near."

"If you intend to come for me, why tell me now and give me time to prepare?" Dael sneered through the pain.

Suddenly for some obscure reason, Jayden couldn't help but smile for the first time in what seemed like ages, not a fake smile, or one for show, but an actual smile as he locked eyes with Rhianna's murderer.

"I tell you now because when it happens you will know nothing at all, and I would have you know the end is near, helpless to stop it, watching it approach without room to flee or any possibility of living through my vengeance."

"You will never get near me. I have the castle and an entire garrison to stop you!" Dael replied, trying for arrogant bravado and failing.

With a snarl Jayden looked dangerously upon his foe and whispered into his ear.

"If the king's own cannot stop me, who are you to feel safe?" With a rough shove he pushed the pathetic excuse for a man back to the floor and stood.

A few paces took Jayden to the front of the royal dais where the elderly king now stood waiting, his expression neutral and his stance one suited for handing down judgement. His eyes though, said the boy's next words would decide his own fate, and so Jayden chose them carefully.

"King Erian, I apologise most humbly for my outburst," he said with forced humility.

"I realise now my actions were inappropriate for the setting, and more so against the laws of Jeranon, which I had just sworn to uphold. I offer no excuse for these actions, other than to say again this man is a murderer. This fact I have witnessed with my own eyes, and would have been one of his victims myself had not Archmage Tolmarak arrived just barely in time to save my life."

"Can you confirm this?" the king asked the old archmage when Jayden paused to catch his breath.

"To my considerable regret, I cannot," Tolmarak replied slowly.

"As Jayden has asserted, I arrived on the plateau where their engagement took place after the fight was already concluded. I found the Count of Grandell kneeling over Jayden's mortally injured form, making no attempt to aid him. If anything, it appeared he were watching his dying breaths as you or I might watch a fly spinning in its death throes; with mild curiosity."

"I see," the king replied with a deeply furrowed frown, "I see. So, what you are saying is the only evidence of what really happened is the word of each of these men, which will doubtlessly conflict."

"Yes sire, that would seem to be true, and yet, after travelling with and teaching Jayden for the better part of a year now, I have no doubt whatsoever he believes his account to be truth."

Jayden had to work hard to not interrupt at that point.

He believes his account to be truth? It is the truth.

"I take it then this is your recommendation in the matter?"

"It is," Tolmarak replied gravely.

"Very well, then I am left with this. Am I to take the side of a noble of my kingdom, one who is accused of murder, though by your own admission there is no hard proof? Or do I side with a boy who has just tried to commit murder in my presence, no matter how wronged he might feel, but who has the support of the leader of the College of the Arts, my personal advisor?"

There was a long silence in the throne room as the monarch's statement carried to the few occupants left in the chamber, and the king began to pace slowly across the dais, his guards never taking their eyes from Jayden.

"In matters of this nature, with no outstanding evidence to point in either direction it was common in past days for a duel to be fought if both parties agreed."

"If I may, sire?" Tolmarak interrupted, and the king nodded his assent.

"A duel would be as good as an execution in this instance for Jayden would undoubtedly use the Gift to defeat his opponent. On the other hand, if magic were disallowed then Dael from all reports would easily triumph, being far superior with a blade."

"I see," Erian sighed. "Then what is it you suggest Tolmarak? Should I lock them both away with no proof? Or would you have me decide in favour of your new protégé simply because you support him?"

"Neither my king," Tolmarak answered immediately, "I urge you to put today's matter aside until a later date. We both know what is coming in the next few phases, and for right now at least, Dael still has a county to run. Jayden also has far more to learn than he has time to do so if he is to be useful to the spring campaign. Besides, as you pointed out, there is no evidence to directly confirm or deny the events on the plateau prior to my arrival, so those events must be discounted. Having said that, if, as I believe, Jayden is telling the truth, then apart from his inexcusable timing today he was simply carrying out the natural punishment for murder according to the law. As magi are legally authorised and occasionally required to do so by the oath he had just spoken. Therefore I would submit these admittedly poorly conceived and timed actions also be discounted, rendering any sentence to either of the participants at this point unjust."

For a long moment the king scowled openly at Tolmarak before shaking his head.

"That is less than helpful old friend."

With a glare he turned back to Jayden.

"Release my guards," he ordered crisply.

With a wave of his hand Jayden sent the twin columns of marble seamlessly back into the floor. As soon as they had parted enough to reveal the men still struggling to free themselves, the king called out for them to halt.

"Take that man to a healer, then send him back to his county," he ordered, pointing at Dael, who had lain quietly where Jayden had left him, trying not to draw attention. Though whether it was from the pain of his injuries or some ploy to try making himself look meek only he knew.

Without hesitation both of the guards bowed deeply and re-slung their weapons before crossing the room to pick Dael up, supporting him under the arms and causing him to cry out in pain as they carried him from the throne room.

"As for you," the king said darkly as he descended the steps from the dais and stood before Jayden. "If you ever behave in such a manner again, I will be nowhere near as lenient. As it is, the coming war is the only thing keeping you out of chains right now."

By the time the king had finished, Tolmarak had come over to join the pair, and the monarch gave him a very significant look.

"Listen carefully to what I am about to tell you Jayden, your life depends on it," the monarch said quietly.

"Jeranon is a kingdom built on laws. Since the time of Eldrik the Black, who almost destroyed this nation in his insanity, it has been our law that if a mage leaves the path and goes renegade, he or she is hunted down like a rabid dog, and executed for the greater good."

"It's true Jayden," Tolmarak confirmed, "And as the ranking mage in the college of your training it will be my duty to carry out such a sentence. Though I have no desire at all to see either of us travel that path."

"So I can never leave the college, is that what you are saying?" Jayden replied indignantly.

"No," Tolmarak clarified. "You may retire during any time of peace after your training is complete, so long as you live by the laws of the land and refrain from using the Gift from that time on. Very few magi ever choose to take that option however, or else come back to us soon after if they do. What we are talking about is a very different thing. There have only been seven magi formally declared renegade over the last century, though the things they did to gain that status would keep you awake at night just to hear them."

"They all had different reasons and goals," the king continued seamlessly, taking up the lecture where the archmage left off, "But they did have one thing in common.

They lost control of themselves, not their power, and in the end some of them were little better than animals, some worse. I saw the look in your eyes when you first noticed Dael here today Jayden. Do not allow yourself to become one of them, do not allow yourself to lose control. It will not be tolerated."

For a long time Jayden was silent, knowing the old monarch was right, but stubbornly not wanting to admit it.

"I understand," he eventually managed to respond.

After studying Jayden for a long moment the king sighed.

"You may leave," he said slowly, as if only now making the decision, before turning his back on the pair as he began to consult quietly with one of his personal guards.

Tolmarak made a quick bow to the king's back and motioned for Jayden to do the same before leading the new Mage quickly out of the throne room. They walked silently through the palace corridors until they made it back to the courtyard from which they entered the palace and waited while their horses were brought around.

"How could you be so stupid!" Tolmarak hissed as soon as they were alone, "Do you have any idea how lucky you were to walk out of that room in one piece?!"

"I..." Jayden managed to get out before Tolmarak angrily interrupted.

"I don't want to hear it Jayden! Not another word until we get back to my study," he whispered in a manner which promised there would be plenty of words spoken once they did arrive back at the archmage's offices.

Yet despite the admonition, for right now all Jayden could bring himself to do was brood in deep self-loathing as they began the long ride through the snow and sleet which would take them back the way they had come. Vengeance for Rhianna's murder, not to mention the other wrongs done by his one-time friend had been his for the taking. Yet even with all that in the balance, at the final moment he had blinked, consciously placing a higher priority on his own safety than achieving justice for Rhianna, and the opportunity had once again slipped through his fingers.

He knew that any other choice would have been madness, would have put his own neck in the hangman's noose. Yet seeing Dael's arrogant smirk again in his mind's eye, Jayden hardened his heart to the prospect that whatever consequences might come of his actions, the next time the two of them met, it would be the last.

'Despite millennia of civilisation, constant warfare with the west has resulted in a plateauing of the Jeranonian population. As a result, large tracts of wilderness remain in the north and west as well as the islands in the Great North Ocean. These pockets of wild land still harbour many strange, savage, and exotic creatures, to say nothing of the grandest of all natural mysteries. Where do the dragons keep their roosts?'

Excerpt from the forward of 'An encyclopaedic investigation into the novel megafauna of Jeranon.'

CHAPTER 23

PROMOTIONS

"On your feet!" Karthael yelled as he shoved the barracks door open hard enough to ricochet back off Bosric and Tauman's bunks.

With little more than a groan from Kienan, the men of squad four twenty-two scrambled to their feet. Seth, as always, had moved from his bunk as fluidly as a viper, even though Wyll would have sworn the man was sound asleep not more than five seconds before.

Light was slanting in the door, and from the angle of the sun Wyll estimated it must be at least an hour after sunrise.

Karthael liked to keep them off guard as to what time he would come bursting through the door on any given morning, but he never let them sleep more than a few minutes past sunup. Wyll wasn't sure why today was any different, but he had a sudden hunch the instructor's next words would prove interesting.

As they stood at attention, they were all still uncomfortably aware of the empty space in their ranks where Brendan used to stand. It had been nearly a phase since the accident in the Emerald Sea which had claimed their squad mate's life. After long deliberation he had told them everything he had seen in the forest and at Brendan's deathbed. His tale had not been received well. He understood. If he hadn't seen her himself, he might well have laughed at the idea too. In truth only Marad had laughed openly, but he didn't think the others had believed, and it amounted to much the same thing, if a little more polite.

"New orders have reached me in regard to your training," Karthael told them without preamble.

"The first order of business is one that deserves congratulations. Since arriving here you have been assessed by certain officers of whose task you were unaware. That task was to locate, using specific guidelines, which squads could most appropriately be trained for more specialised duties. Only one out of each hundred squads here and at the other camps is to be granted this opportunity, and you have proven over the last phases that you are one of those few. Well done men. As of this moment you have been transferred out of your regular posts and into special services. More specifically in your case, squad four twenty-two, you are now officially part of the mageguard."

For a long moment silence reigned within the confines of the small barracks room the men had called home for the last five phases as each of them tried to digest what the

Arborii instructor had just said. Although they were all silent, their reactions were quite different.

Bosric started grinning like the madman he seemed to be trying so hard to convince them all he was, and did a little caper next to his bunk which made Kienan laugh, breaking the silence. Sarran and Charran looked at each other, dumbfounded, though seemingly excited at the prospect while both Seth and Tauman were frowning at something only they could see. Cale leaned back against his bunk, looking extremely satisfied with the change while Marad just smirked as if he'd expected the announcement all along.

For Wyll's part, he wasn't sure what to think. When he'd joined the guard in Grandell, he had only ever intended to serve for a few years, save some money and buy a bit of land for himself. He had never seriously considered becoming a career soldier... and yet, the mageguard was as much like the regular army, or at least so the old saying went, as a scorpion was to a bear. Which he supposed meant both could kill you, but where the bear would use its strength and size, the scorpion had to rely on other tactics to achieve the same result.

Karthael gave them another moment to digest the news, then continued.

"The second order of business is also worthy of comment," he said as the men once more focused on the instructor.

"Despite the fact that we are still in high winter, all signs lean towards the snows being ready to melt in only a fortnight, therefore it is time to appoint a sergeant for this squad. Over the last phases I have watched you all progress in your training. What you may or may not be aware of is that part of my assignment was to choose who that sergeant will be."

Once again the men were quiet, focused on the instructor's words. They had all come a long way since arriving in camp five, both physically and mentally, but who would be chosen to lead them was still up for debate.

"I don't think it will come as any surprise to you that had he lived, Brendan's experience and skill would have made him a natural choice. Regretfully that was not to be."

Wyll couldn't help but take a quick look at his comrades as Karthael continued.

Across the room Bosric looked amused by the whole situation. Wyll counted him out of the running due to his natural predilection for mayhem and practical jokes. Jared Tauman he also dismissed as the man had no training other than what he'd received here, coupled with a somewhat murky background as a grain merchant of 'modest means' as he kept telling the others. Even after all this time Wyll was still not convinced it was true. Kienan, the black-haired musician also had no previous training, and Wyll thought his willingness to play to an audience would rule him out as Karthael's choice.

Sarran and Charran, while being exceptionally strong and quite good with their chosen weapons, were simply not as bright as some of the others, and Wyll found himself hoping it wouldn't be one of them. Not that he had anything against the brothers, but it was hard to imagine either of them giving sound tactical orders in the heat of battle.

Marad was standing at ease across the room with a slight smile on his face, as if he knew a secret no one else did. No doubt he considered himself the front-runner for the command now that Brendan was no longer in the picture.

Wyll wouldn't be surprised if his own arrogance would count him out of Karthael's deliberations however.

That just left Seth and Cale. Each was intelligent, highly skilled with their chosen weapons and had experience in the field. Cale however could not speak, and although he had begun teaching them a form of wordless communication he called 'signing', it would count heavily against him. On the other hand, Seth had all the interpersonal skills of a goat. Once you got past that however, he was easily the best swordsman in the group and had a keen eye for detail, the others would perhaps follow him despite his problems integrating with the rest of the squad. Either way Wyll thought it a fifty-fifty bet between the two as he returned his attention to the instructor.

"I have therefore been left with a difficult choice." Karthael continued. "Some of you men have field experience, others have highly trained skill sets. But a leader must be more than just a warrior, he must be smart, able to make correct decisions not only for himself, but for all of you, even in the heat of battle. He must be a strategist and a thinker as well as a man of action. He must be someone capable of recognising and exploiting the various talents you all possess for the benefit of the overall mission, whilst also having the courage to lead from the front once battle is joined."

Wyll looked around at his squad mates one more time. None of them looked certain anymore, even Marad's supremely confident façade had slipped during Karthael's last speech.

"So as of today," he continued, "Your new sergeant will be Wyll."

There was a profound silence in the barracks for several long seconds at the announcement. The more so from Wyll himself who was at first sure he had heard wrong, then equally sure the instructor had made a mistake. But as the seconds drew inexorably by and Karthael made no move to recant, it became clear that he had heard correctly, and there was no mistake about it.

Wyll didn't know what to say. Instead he just looked around at the others with what he was sure was an expression of bewilderment plastered on his face until Marad broke the oppressive silence with a disgusted comment. "I guess it really is who you know…" he breathed.

In an instant Karthael was standing over the sizeable man and berating him sharply.

"I suppose you think you would be a better choice for sergeant?" he growled, and Marad, although having the sense not to say so, still gave away his answer with the direct look he gave the instructor.

"Very well. Listen up, men. Marad thinks he should be in charge of the squad. This is untrue for two reasons. One, he is arrogant to a fault, and in battle that gets good men killed."

His gaze once again locked on Marad's burly form as he continued. "Two, he is simply not gifted in strategic planning, a skill vital to any suitable leader."

Marad seemed on the verge of an outburst, even though he had to know any interruption now would earn him even more of a disciplinary action than this public dressing down.

Karthael held up a hand to forestall Marad's comment and looked around the room.

"He is, however, an excellent fighter, both on foot and mounted, a credit to himself and a definite asset to the squad. I have no doubt when the time comes, he will be right there beside you, giving his best. As will you all."

Marad seemed vaguely appeased by the sudden praise, and Wyll was relieved. Without it, Marad most likely would have become a thorn in his side, undermining him at every opportunity as he had attempted to do with Brendan before the tattooed man's unfortunate demise.

As Karthael turned to look at the rest of the room again, he gave Wyll a slight glance which seemed to say, 'it's up to you now', before continuing.

"I know some of you are probably surprised at my choice. Believe me when I say, I have been training recruits for longer than some of you have been alive, and my decision is not only final, but correct."

Wyll couldn't imagine what he'd done to earn this unexpected promotion. To be honest, he wasn't entirely sure he was ready for it. Nevertheless, he thought as he looked around the small barracks room, these men had just been placed under his command and he would have to ensure he was worthy of their trust by doing the job as well as he possibly could.

When Karthael said no more, Wyll looked around for an instant before realising belatedly it was now his job to speak for the squad when addressing an officer, and so asked, "Orders, Sir?"

Karthael nodded minutely to indicate he had done the right thing and then continued, "As of now you are officially decommissioned as recruit squad number four twenty-two. You are hereby reassigned to the College of the Arts where you will serve as members of the mageguard and receive duties and salaries commensurate with your new service.

There were grins and satisfied nods all around at that as the instructor continued.

"Wyll, take your men and report to Lieutenant Bandell at the college, give him this," he said, handing over a finely written parchment.

"I'm sure you remember him from your ride here, yes? He will have the details of your new assignment and lodgings."

"Yes Sir," Wyll returned crisply once the instructor fell silent.

There was a momentary pause as Karthael looked the men over one last time.

"You've all done well these last phases, and despite what you may or may not think, the mageguard takes no man who is not up to the standards they set. Believe me when I say those standards are high. I do not know whether I shall see any of you in the coming conflict, for now my own duties will have me on the western border for some phases. Know however that you have my respect for achieving what you have in so limited an amount of time. I would not have thought it possible when first we met," he finished with a wry grin, looking Bosric right in the eyes.

"You did pretty well yourself," the red-haired man returned with his usual, insanely happy grin.

Karthael snorted in a very human-like response and shook his head with a grin.

"Whatever fate holds in store for each of you, I know you will meet it well," he said at last, locking eyes with each of them as he did, before finally turning to Wyll.

"The men are under your command, but you are the one who must serve them," he finished for Wyll's benefit alone.

With a flick of his tail the Arborii turned and exited the barracks without another word into the early morning sunshine.

"Congratulations Wyll," Sarran said with a slap on the shoulder and a genuine smile as soon as the instructor was gone, a sentiment followed wholeheartedly from his brother and several others in the squad.

When the commotion finally died down, he looked around the small barracks room at his squad mates.

At my men, he corrected himself before saying with a grin he couldn't quite get rid of.

"All right, you heard the Arborii. Stow your gear, say any goodbyes you feel necessary and then meet at the stables in an hour. Let's get out of here," he finished only half-jokingly, "The college's kitchen awaits!"

*   *   *

"Dismount," Wyll called as the squad pulled up in front of Lieutenant Bandell, who Wyll recognised as the mageguard officer in charge of the cavalry on the long trek across the Anchorhead Promontory and south to camp five.

Having followed his own order, Wyll approached the lieutenant on foot, who nodded in recognition as the new sergeant handed over the parchment Karthael had given him.

"This all seems in order," Bandell mused to himself, "Wyll, isn't it?" he asked a moment later as he motioned for the squad to follow him towards the college stables.

"Yes Sir," he replied, a little surprised the veteran soldier still remembered.

"I see you made sergeant, congratulations," Bandell commented as they walked the half mile or so across the college grounds to where the horses were to be stabled.

"Just remember, it's a responsibility, not a privilege."

"That's pretty much what Karthael told me as well Sir," Wyll returned.

"You were under Karthael's tuition at the camp?"

"All of us were, Sir," Wyll replied.

"Hmmph," Bandell snorted, "Then you might just live long enough to finish your training," he joked with a grin.

"He's a smart one that Arborii. You would do well to pay attention to any advice he gave you. Vigilantly."

In a relatively short time they reached the huge college stables, and as they entered the open entryway, grooms appeared as if from nowhere to take their mounts. The next few seconds were a flurry of activity as the men removed their saddle packs and weapons from the animals' backs, one by one allowing the waiting grooms to walk their horses further into the labyrinthine maze of stalls and passageways.

"This way," Bandell announced when they were all done, but even as he turned to exit the cavernous building he was interrupted as a man dressed in the all black uniform of the mageguard came stumbling into the barn. The morning sunlight streaming in from outside made him just a silhouette at first. As they drew closer to the soldier Bandell abruptly rushed over to help the man, whom Wyll could now make out was covered in his own blood.

"What happened man, speak!" Bandell ordered the wounded soldier, who instead collapsed on the straw dusted floor.

"West gate," the man croaked, disoriented from a nasty head wound.

"Attack, get help... sent," he whispered, even as his eyes became unfocused and he slumped to the ground.

"Weapons out!" Bandell ordered grimly. "Get help for this man and send reinforcements to the west gate!" he shouted at a nearby stable boy, who dashed out of the barn without hesitation towards the college building itself.

By the time the groom cleared the door the men had divested themselves of their belongings and freed their weapons, though there was no time to don armour.

"With me," Bandell ordered as he drew his own sword from the sheath on his back and set off at a dead run towards the forested path which led from the west gate of the college grounds.

As the sprinting men approached the entrance, they could see signs a serious attack was under way.

Just outside the gate lay two sprawled bodies, while a third severely injured man seemed intent on dragging himself away from the fighting with the single arm he still possessed. From further up the path came the sounds of metal on metal. Without stopping Bandell sprinted past the fallen men and Wyll followed hard on his heels around the first bend in the path, straight into a scene from some lunatic's demented nightmare.

Only one member of the mageguard squad still stood fighting with the creature, his compatriots lying either dead or wounded around the immediate area. With a shout, Bandell swung his sword hard at the creature's back, the blade whistling through the air in a broad overhand stroke to impact with the distinctive clank of metal striking metal. His heavy sword rebounded without leaving a mark.

"You can't hurt it like that!" the sole remaining soldier yelled as the rest of Wyll's squad caught up. Following his lead, they surrounded what he could only describe as a vaguely crab-shaped creature of about eight foot in length, which seemed made entirely from some form of shining metal, or possibly stone. Either way, it was so smooth that when the sun reflected off it at the right angle, the light was almost blinding.

"Does it have a weakness?" Bandell called to the other guard while dancing back out of range of the creature, which had now turned to face him.

"Yeah, magic," the man responded, "Fredrick was doing some damage to it with fire spells before it got him, but not enough to stop it. Our steel weapons are useless against it, Sir!"

With blinding speed the creature took a grab at Bandell, who only avoided the giant claw by desperately diving away, leaving himself exposed for a long moment.

The momentary distraction gave Bosric the chance to strike at it from behind. The short man nimbly kicked one of the thing's damaged legs out from under it, buying a moment for the lieutenant to roll out of harm's way as the creature once again readjusted its attention, this time on the short red-headed man.

"We need to hold it here until some of the magi arrive to deal with this thing," Bandell called to the men.

"Defence only since we can't damage it!" he called again, taking a disgusted glance at a large nick in the steel of his weapon.

The thing grabbed at Bosric, but instead of jumping away the grinning maniac stepped forward, deflecting the claw-like appendage with his sword and then taking a quick step and vaulting up onto the thing's back.

"Get off there you idiot!" Bandell shouted as the creature went into a frenzy, trying to shake the little man off any way it could. Without warning it broke into a run, knocking Bandell a dozen paces back with a stray claw and forcing Seth to leap aside as it broke through the circle. Intent on ridding itself of Bosric's presence any way possible, the creature rammed itself into the nearest tree hard enough to split the trunk and send the foot-wide oak tumbling down towards it.

"Bosric. Move!" Wyll shouted, and Maker be praised the man actually listened for once, diving down and rolling away from both tree and creature before the first branches crashed down around them.

With the circle scattered the creature thrashed for a minute under the weight of the fallen trunk, allowing the men to catch their breath and for Cale to check on Bandell, who had remained motionless since being struck. The tongueless soldier gave a thumbs up as he saw the officer was still breathing.

"Get him to a safe distance!" Wyll bellowed as the creature began to use its claws to cut the entangling branches away, rapidly freeing itself from the fallen tree.

"Re-establish the circle," Wyll ordered abruptly. "Sarran, find out where those reinforcements are."

He said it all in a loud but level voice, and for a wonder even Marad complied while the large staffman dashed off towards the gate. The rest of the squad and the remaining mageguard soldier encircled the creature again, who by now was almost free, and suddenly it was all so simple.

Just do what needs to be done, Wyll told himself, and then began issuing orders.

"Hold it here, don't provoke it unless you have to, but it doesn't leave this circle. Understood!"

"Yes Sir!" came two by now instinctual responses to an officer's command, which seemed to surprise everyone, including those who had spoken. Even Seth gave a subtle nod of approval, the tiniest hint of a smile tugging at the corner of his usually expressionless mouth. The gesture seemed more suited to seeing a boy coming of age than the respect due an officer though.

Probably not too far from the truth, Wyll thought, even as the metallic thing gained enough purchase on the trunk to give a great heave and shove what was left of it off and stand, once again unhindered before them.

For a moment it turned around, surveying them all until at last it found its target.

Bosric, of course, grinned back at the creature, though the look in his eyes now was anything but humorous.

The creature slowly began walking towards him, its claws extended and raised for the strike.

"Back away slowly Bosric," Wyll ordered, "Everyone else, stay with him and hold the circle."

Wyll held his breath as the short knifeman backed away one step, then another as the creature followed, ready to strike at any opportunity. With a quick motion Bosric reached the edge of the path and darted two steps to the side, putting a fair-sized tree between himself and the advancing monster. The creature was forced to circle around the other side to get at him. Of course as soon as it tried, Bosric just shifted further around, keeping the thick trunk between them as much as possible.

Footsteps sounded behind them and Wyll risked a quick look over his shoulder to see Sarran running back towards them with Captain Ravenburg and Archmage Tolmarak riding up behind.

"Just a few more moment's boys," Wyll called to the men, though upon reflection it seemed a little strange as most of those men were in fact older than he was.

Sarran ran up and joined the circle of wary soldiers as Captain Ravenburg dismounted an instant before his smoke grey warhorse came to a halt, striding without hesitation over to where Wyll was standing, blade held at the ready.

The archmage rode up at a more sedate pace and called out in a loud voice, "End session!"

The creature immediately halted its pursuit of Bosric and folded its claws back upon itself, within seconds becoming absolutely still.

Wyll looked from the archmage to the creature and back again in consternation.

"It's a test, Wyll," Ravenburg said in his competently authoritative voice as he casually re-sheathed his sword.

"A test..." Wyll repeated dumbly, not understanding.

"But..." he said, waving a horrified hand in the general direction of the severed and bloodied bodies which the creature had savaged before their arrival.

"Yes, a test," the archmage repeated as he slowly dismounted his own steed, "One designed to teach you three things. First, things are rarely what they seem at first glance."

The old archmage waved an arm for effect and the

broken bodies which littered the pathway drifted away into the morning breeze like so much steam on a windy day.

"Illusion only," he assured them as the others dropped their defensive postures reluctantly, one by one coming to stand before the captain and archmage, though many of them unconsciously refused to turn their back on the shiny crablike thing.

"No one was killed here, though it is not uncommon for a fresh recruit or two to suffer a few broken bones in this exercise. It speaks well of you and your men that that was not the case here today. Still, there are safeguards in place to make sure no one is killed by old shiny here," he said with a slight grin.

"Old shiny?" Wyll asked dubiously, "What is it? If you don't mind my asking, Sir."

The archmage gave him a measuring gaze for a long moment before answering.

"It is a tool used for a job, much like your sword. Not to be shown off or used in anger, but for a steady purpose when all other options have been exhausted."

"The Second," Bandell said from behind them after picking himself up, "Is although the mageguard is technically a part of the king's army, it has very little to do with soldiering in the traditional sense. More often than not you will be dealing with wild beasts such as manticore and chimera, or else Gift-wrought creatures such as old shiny or elementals. On truly rare occasions you may even encounter the products of the necromantic arts. Failing all that, there are always the forces of the western nations to contend with."

"Third and finally," Tolmarak told them once the

lieutenant had finished speaking, "When fighting in concert with your mage you will almost always be outnumbered either in numbers or in strength, and often both. Occasionally you will even face an enemy your steel will have no effect on at all. The good news however is the college has yet to discover a creature which has an immunity to both steel and the Gift. So if you find yourselves in a position where you cannot harm your opponent, you must find another solution or perform a holding action, protecting your mage to give them time to deal with the threat via the Gift."

"But why all this?" Marad interrupted as soon as the Archmage fell quiet. "Why not just tell us these things?"

"A fair question," Ravenburg allowed.

"Wyll?" the captain prompted.

Wyll thought about his answer for a moment, with his new superiors and the king's advisor himself watching, he didn't want to make a mistake.

"Because with all you just described, you needed to know we are mentally ready to adapt to whatever circumstances we find ourselves in, even if on completely unfamiliar ground."

"Excellent answer. I see Karthael chose you well," Tolmarak responded approvingly.

"That's all for now," Ravenburg dismissed them. "Follow Fredrick back to the mageguard building, he will show you to your new lodgings. By now your gear has already been taken there and your uniforms will be along shortly. Get yourselves stowed away and report to the kitchen in an hour. Your first real drills will begin after lunch."

For a moment Wyll almost asked what a 'real' drill was

if this didn't count, but then decided he didn't want to know. At least not until after he'd eaten.

"Oh, and one last thing," Captain Ravenburg called as they began filing off towards the college's well-appointed barracks.

"Welcome to the mageguard."

CHAPTER 24

THE MISSING VILLAGE

"The scouts should be in sight of Clearbrook by now," Nereth said as he watched the hill-strewn horizon for any sign of their return.

Winter had taken hold on the Sammorand Plains, and the horses made their way through the lightly falling snow which hadn't yet bent and covered the long grass in most places. Winter was always short and mild out here on the plains, with snow only falling for a week or two each year. Thankfully, the all-encompassing grass which stood as high as a man on horseback throughout the plains sheltered them from the worst of the wind, leaving only the occasional patch of ice on the path to hinder their progress.

Hassan continued to look straight ahead at the landscape and ignored Nereth's comment. The hundred men in his command were columned by two's on the hard packed dirt road behind them, except for the scouts and flankers of course, but even those men wouldn't be able to see anything more than ten feet around them.

Hassan still wasn't entirely convinced about the accuracy of the scout's explanation back at Stonekeep. With an entire village reported missing though, he was taking no chances of being ambushed by enemy forces while the foothills of the Dark Iron Mountain Range stood less than ten miles to the west.

Under normal circumstances they should have been safe enough even as far as those eastern foothills, but with the strange report being taken seriously, he wanted to be sure.

Stonekeep.

The thought of what he had wrought there still made him cringe, and he suspected it would until the day he died. He had betrayed his king and his nation by leading that attack, and yet he knew if Nereth ordered him to, he would do so again to keep his family, and those of his men, safe.

As much as he had struggled against it, he was now as tightly tied to Nereth, and therefore Heramiir, as if he'd joined the traitorous magi at the outset. To make matters worse, he had yet to make any significant impact against their plans.

With a grimace he hoped old Sir Luke was doing better at keeping the king informed on current events than he was, closely watched as Nereth had him. Tactically, Seal Cove was in the middle of nowhere, and yet that might just give the retired knight the room he would need to escape notice until the king's army arrived, in all likelihood sometime during spring's dusk.

"Scout returning!"

The call from up ahead broke him out of his thoughts and Hassan booted his midnight black charger to a canter an instant before Nereth. The two of them rode to the crest of the next hill and stopped as the long range scout he had sent out an hour before reined in next to them.

"Sir, Archmage," the man said respectfully.

"Report, Masik," Hassan snapped. He had fought in many, many battles over the years, but never before had he felt... dirty, afterwards. Nereth gave him a bland look as if to say that he would give the orders, and Hassan studiously ignored the archmage as he focused on the soldier in front of him.

"Sir, the village is gone. The path to what should be the town square just ends in high grass as if the road makers had simply left off what they were doing and gone home. I checked the immediate vicinity, but any tracks have long since been washed away by the rain and snow."

Hassan couldn't help but steal a glance at Nereth now, and to his dismay saw a small tightening around the powerful archmage's eyes which spoke of worry. This close to the mountains there was only one force who could have accomplished this without raising alarm all the way from Stonekeep to Aramar.

The dark nations are taking a hand at last.

It had seemed inevitable to Hassan that they would, just as soon as they found out Jeranon was no longer united against them. But for them to strike this quickly they must have been preparing for some time before the rebellion had begun. A possibility occurred to him then which left the seasoned campaigner cold. If the western nations followed their usual tactics, it meant a full-scale invasion would soon follow. It had been over a decade since the last one, led by

Northmen with support from the Imbic Nation and the Augrahl Imperium, but Hassan knew his history. Whenever the western nations gave a lull in the fighting, whether for one year or ten, they always kept preparing, always working towards the eventual downfall of Jeranon and the reclaiming of lands they had not occupied in over three thousand years. That they had held themselves back this last decade only meant they would come again, and with more strength than usual.

Add to that the king's army, which was sure to come against them in the coming spring, and Hassan wanted to groan. Magi or no, they would be crushed between those two forces like wheat in a mill.

"Was there any sign of enemy activity?" Nereth asked.

"No Archmage, not so much as a broken plant," the scout replied with an involuntary eye twitch, which from Masik was as good as another man balling his hands into white-knuckled fists.

"Anything else?" Nereth asked when the man stayed put.

"Yes Archmage, we spotted Mage Derrack at the site of the village."

That got Nereth's attention. "What was he doing? Is he injured?"

"Not that I could tell, Archmage. We approached close enough to confirm his identity, but he was kneeling on the ground, praying. He refused to speak to us or leave the site, so with no apparent danger at hand we left to make our report."

"I don't understand," Nereth replied as Hassan closed his eyes briefly and shook his head as he half remembered a conversation he'd had with the boy phases ago, not long after they'd first met.

"I do," Hassan answered wearily. "This is where he's from. Derrack grew up in Clearbrook. His entire family, everyone he loved is… was, here."

Nereth's eyes narrowed slightly, and he nodded. "Then he'll be doubly motivated to seek out and destroy whoever did this."

Hassan's eyebrows climbed in disbelief. "You heartless piece of scud. The boy's been taken from his parents, sheltered in a tower for most of his life and when he finally gets promoted to Mage, the first thing he's assigned to do is kill his own countrymen by the score. Orders which he is so indoctrinated by you he obeys. Then, just as he is coming to terms with that disgrace he finds out his entire family is almost certainly dead, and your only response is to note that it will increase his efficiency?!"

Nereth's saddle creaked, though his black enamelled plate armour remained silent as he shifted to address the scout directly.

"Circle the area around the village as far as you can and meet us back at Clearbrook before nightfall."

"Yes Archmage," Masic replied with a hasty salute, before shooting a concerned glance at Hassan and turning his horse back the way he had come, setting off at a canter.

Once they were relatively alone Nereth turned to Hassan with barely controlled fury.

"You have no knowledge of what you speak. I care deeply for all my charges. I spend years teaching them, building bonds with them, and no matter what I do, many of them will die in the next span of phases. These are the only children I will ever have. Believe me when I say that if I could spare him this pain by murdering you where you stand, I would not hesitate to hack you limb from limb.

Sadly, some few things are beyond even my control."

Hassan felt his jaw hanging open. It wasn't the threat, that, he had expected. Nereth must have been affected far more deeply by Hassan's revelation than he'd assumed. It was not in the archmage's character to let his guard down in such a fashion otherwise.

When Nereth refused to look away Hassan eventually gave way. This was not the right time to rile the archmage any more than he already had.

"All right, fan out!" Hassan bellowed to his men as the column caught them up. "Ten span spacing, if there is so much as a brick left of this village I want it located before nightfall."

The men he had picked for this foray were all seasoned campaigners and had served with him before, each of them worth a dozen younger men for their experience and skill. He was confident that if there was anything at all left to find of Clearbrook, they would locate it in short order.

He rode in silence beside Nereth for the next quarter hour, though as far away from the traitorous archmage as he could without leaving the hard-packed dirt of the path. The strained silence hung over them until they crested a shallow hill and came abruptly upon the end of the road.

It was, unsurprisingly, just as Masik had described. The age worn path ended in a wall of long grass which looked for all the world as though it had been growing there undisturbed by human hands since the time the Maker formed the very ground itself.

A slight chill ran down Hassan's back as he looked across to Nereth, who was putting a small map back in his coat pocket and scanning the horizon with his eyes.

"This really is the correct spot," he said so only Hassan could hear.

"Come with me," Nereth ordered as he dismounted. He used the Gift to push the all-encompassing grass out of their way, the broken stalks giving off a crisp, pungent smell.

It only took them a minute to find the spot Derrack had chosen, Nereth using the Mage's aura to take them straight to him. When they arrived, the young man was still on his knees and had obviously been crying. He didn't look back at the sound of their arrival, he didn't have to.

"I'm sorry for your losses, Derrack," Nereth said honestly, allowing the silence to return.

Hassan was about to speak as well when Nereth shook his head. Hassan hesitated, then resentfully nodded his agreement. What else could he say that Nereth hadn't already expressed so simply and sincerely? The man might be a traitor of the highest order, but he was far from a brute. It was imperative Hassan never let himself forget that.

It was minutes coming, and the young mage never moved, but eventually he spoke.

"Welcome to my home gentlemen. Please won't you come inside?"

Nereth looked at the ground for a moment, wetting his lips with his tongue and taking a deep steadying breath.

"You have my word this will not go unanswered Derrack. For right now though, in this moment, I need you to put aside your despair, and focus. Reach out with the Gift and tell me what you feel."

Derrack turned his head just enough to see them from the corner of his eye, and the bitter look he gave Nereth was less than impressed.

"You know I take no course without reason. Focus."

The boy's shoulders slumped, but he did as he was charged.

"Do you feel that?" the archmage asked.

Derrack was silent a long moment, but then his head tilted slightly, some unseen force catching his attention.

"If you mean the strange tingling in my fingertips and toes, then yes, Archmage," he replied uncertainly.

"Good," Nereth said, "That is a key sign of Augrahl magic. If it were being cast while you were near, or if the spell were still active but dormant, like an untripped ward, the sensation would run nearly to your wrists and ankles. Remember it well. It is a subtle warning, but being aware of what it means has saved more than one mage from walking into a trap."

"I don't care, Archmage," Derrack responded, his tone lifeless and flat.

"Whatever spells were cast here were powerful," Nereth continued, ignoring the comment. "But it was done several days ago, perhaps even as long as a week. There must have been at least three Augrahl shaman here, and possibly a few additional weaker ones, apprentices perhaps," Nereth conjectured.

"Why are you telling me this Nereth?" the red-headed man asked, beginning to become annoyed. "I'm a little preoccupied right now with the death of my entire family!"

"You see how the residue feels stronger to the east, but also tugs to the south when you turn away from it?" Nereth continued, as merciless as an avalanche. Derrack shook his head and threw his hands up in the air as he stood, but when he saw Nereth had no intention of backing down, he closed his eyes under protest. He turned first one way and then slowly towards the south before giving a curt nod.

"There is one towards the west as well," he scathingly told his armoured mentor as he opened eyes very different from the ones Hassan knew. These eyes held no kindness at all.

Nereth nodded approvingly.

"Well done Derrack, that one is faintest, but I was hoping you would pick it out from the others."

The young mage gave Nereth a snarl in response.

"Now, tell me what they were doing?" the archmage ordered.

"Killing innocent civilians. Children," Derrack practically spat.

Nereth calmly raised an eyebrow. "Do you see any bodies here? I haven't."

For long moments, Derrack looked around the grassy wilderness in confusion.

"In fact so far as I have seen, there is no evidence anyone was even here when this happened," Nereth commented.

Derrack suddenly spun around, flattening the surrounding grass with a hand motion and the Gift. All the spell revealed though was Derrack's somewhat startled horse.

"So what were the enemy shaman trying to accomplish with such precise and concerted spell casting I wonder?" Nereth mused.

"A spell of regeneration," Derrack abruptly offered. "Cast at three points of a triangle to encourage nature to return within the boundary and cover whatever it was they were really doing here," he said in a rush.

Nereth gave a satisfied nod, "And regenerative spells do not kill people. Do they, Derrack?"

The young man's head snapped up as he locked suddenly hopeful eyes with the archmage. He shook his head when the words wouldn't come.

Nereth returned his look. "I make no promises other than this. If they still live, we will find them."

"Yes, Archmage, we will," Derrack replied, some shred of his former character reasserting itself.

"The question is why they would attack a town like Clearbrook," Nereth asked. "The place is certainly a viable target this close to the mountains, but it has no particular strategic value, nothing the western nations would want badly enough to risk giving away their presence."

"Unless this wasn't the only town they hit," Hassan blurted as a chill worked its way up his spine. "They might be trying to carve out a buffer zone on this side of the mountains so they can mass forces inside Jeranon without anyone stumbling across them until it's too late."

Slowly Nereth nodded as the three men looked at each other, for a moment each lost to his own dark thoughts.

"Call your men back Hassan, we ride on to Hillcrest immediately. If this is what we think, we don't have a second to lose."

On this one occasion Hassan was forced to agree completely with Nereth, though it left a sour taste in his mouth.

"Amplify my voice," Hassan said perfunctorily. Nereth raised an eyebrow but inclined his head toward Derrack, who made a small gesture, and nodded his readiness.

"Orders!" Hassan bellowed, Derrack's spell bringing the words clearly to all those in the area.

"Reform the column on the far side of the village. We ride for Hillcrest immediately!"

He nodded to Derrack, who let the spell fade.

Nereth placed a single gauntleted hand on Derrack's shoulder and looked him in the eye. "It's time to go. Wherever they are, it isn't here."

Derrack nodded, his eyes hardening as he looked around one last time. Failing to glean any new information, he turned and stalked towards his horse, while Nereth and Hassan returned to their own.

As the three of them met up with the rest of the men at the far side of where the village of Clearbrook should have been, he told off a pair of grizzled veterans to wait for Masik's return. They were to escort the scout back to the column, along with whatever information he had gathered. Masik's safe return was certainly important, but short of running directly into an enemy shaman, the thirty-year veteran of the scouting corps could well and truly take care of himself.

The pair gave him a quick salute. They were both experienced enough to know what was being asked of them, and disciplined enough to make sure Masik got through with the information no matter what it took.

Hassan returned the salute, and with a more informal nod to the men he turned his black charger towards Hillcrest, and moved forward.

*   *   *

Hassan let a lengthy sigh escape his lips as he came within sight of Hillcrest, or at least, the spot where the isolated village should have been. The slight rise he and

Nereth had just crested gave them an ample view of a road interrupted by the long grass of the plains. The road continued into the distance a hundred spans from where it left off, as if its builders had worked from either direction, never finishing their task, exactly as the road had at Clearbrook.

"Split your men up Hassan," Nereth said without taking his smouldering eyes off the place where the town of Hillcrest had once sat, "Find out how far this goes and then report back to Miralthrall directly."

Hassan nodded his agreement without thinking, and Nereth turned his mount and rode southeast off the path and directly into the long grass. He would no doubt round the Highland River's termination point and head directly from there to Heartland's Gate, the largest city on the plains, to raise the alarm and begin organising their response.

With a grimace, Hassan realised he had just taken one of Nereth's orders as a matter of course, and couldn't help but grind his teeth over the situation.

They are the right orders, but still.

"Squad leaders!" Hassan called to the column of soldiers behind him as he motioned them towards him with a wave.

"We're going to split up," he announced when his handpicked veterans, and Derrack, who had become like a second shadow since Clearbrook, were assembled around him.

"With two towns already attacked by what is presumably an advance force sent by the western nations, time is of the essence."

With a deft motion Hassan unstrapped a pouch on the

side of his saddle and pulled out a map of the Sammorand Plains which he had brought with him from Stonekeep.

"Each of you will scout one of these towns and see whether it has been attacked or not. If it is still standing, return to Heartland's Gate and report to me at the garrison there. If you find it… removed, continue in the same general direction until you come to a town still standing and then report to Heartland's Gate. Any questions?"

"Rules of engagement, Colonel?" a balding major with several scars crisscrossing his face asked immediately.

"Do what you can," Hassan told them all without having to think about it, "But if you come across hard proof of a western presence still within our borders, the information must reach me safely, no matter what. Understood?"

There were nods all around and Hassan began giving each of the veteran officers their squad assignments.

"One final thing," Hassan said as the last man returned to his horse. "If for any reason we do not meet up at Heartland's Gate you are to send half your men back to Miralthrall to inform Archmage Nereth of your findings."

There were muttered comments from some of the men, all of whom Hassan had picked because they had been captured and injured during the coup, but Hassan held up his hand, and with a motion silenced them all.

"I know you hate what the magi have made us do, made us become during these last phases. But if the dark nations are truly beginning a new offensive, we cannot concern ourselves with our own internal difficulties right now. The western nations will not stop until every last one of us is dead and gone. When they come, they won't care whether we follow King Erian or Archmage Heramiir. Each of you is experienced enough to know they will only come against us stronger if they see us at each other's throats."

There were some discontented mutters from the men, but no one made any comprehensible comments and Hassan knew that like him, they hated the fact he was right.

"Anything else?" he asked, but none of the men spoke out, so he nodded.

"The Maker willing I'll see you all at Heartland's Gate within twelve days. If circumstances force you to take longer, we will have departed. In that case, return to Miralthrall and report directly to me. Dismissed."

The assortment of Banner Sergeants, Lieutenants and Captains gave smart salutes and returned to their men, each squad moving off as the officer gave the veteran troops their orders. Soon, only Derrack and the remainder of the squad Masik belonged to were still with him.

"Where are we heading?" Jarl asked from behind him, being the direct commanding officer of the remaining squad.

"Greentree Lake," Hassan replied as he motioned the men to begin the ride towards the looming foothills to the southwest.

"Oh, good. I was hoping you would say that," Jarl replied blandly as they began the horses moving towards the very westernmost village in Jeranon's control.

"You've been there?" Hassan asked just as neutrally as he eyed his long-time companion.

"Not personally. Just heard stories, that's all."

Hassan couldn't help a slight frown. Jarl had been his companion in arms for nigh on twenty years, and Hassan had rarely seen the man fazed by anything short of a fully trained spell caster opposing him on the field of battle.

"What stories?" he asked eventually.

"Trust me," the black-haired man replied quietly, "You do not want to know."

Hassan just looked at him for a long moment before turning away to his own thoughts again. He had seen dozens of raids by the western nations over the years, but nothing like this game of making it look as though the attacked villages had simply disappeared. It was obviously their work, and yet they had taken significant pains at both Clearbrook and Hillcrest to erase not only any sign of their own passing, but that of the two villages' as well. It made no sense. Usually, the few raiders who made it past the border patrols rode in, killed anything they could catch and then burned what they couldn't carry off before attempting to return home. This new tactic didn't fit the pattern of strike and counter strike which the western nations usually fell into when beginning a new offensive at all.

What that left him with he wasn't sure, except that whoever was leading this attack was showing both more guile and caution than was usual. It was possible the western council had a new war chief in charge of the campaign, one Jeranon was not yet familiar with. That could prove difficult. At any rate, something out of the ordinary was happening. If it was indeed the work of the dark nations, and who else could it really be, then they were trying something new, something they had never attempted before in three thousand years of near constant skirmishing and war.

That was enough to make anyone nervous.

With a flick of the reigns Hassan motioned Stormcloud

to a trot and settled in for a ride he knew would seem to take much longer than it should.

Hassan could live with that. He was a professional soldier and used to waiting.

He only wished he could shake the nagging feeling that when they did arrive at Greentree Lake, what they were going to find there would make the wait have seemed all too short.

'To understand fear, one must first understand uncertainty.'
Excerpt from 'Advanced Warfare and Tactics.'

EPILOGUE

INTERLUDE

The sparrow preened its feathers as it sat on a stone ledge in a large enclosed area. It had flown in here through a narrow opening when the sun was high, and in its mad dash to return to the open world had become thoroughly lost. For now, it seemed safe in its little corner ledge as its tiny heart continued to pump furiously after the frenzied flight through the long corridors of the palace.

Across the vast room a door opened, and the sparrow sensed its chance to escape. It darted through the air and out the opening, almost clipping an old human in the head with its little wings as it flitted past.

The human raised its hands defensively as he saw the flash of colour racing towards him, and the sparrow found itself caught in mid-air, unable to move its wings, and yet not falling as it knew should be the case.

Archmage Tolmarak took a quick look at what exactly he had stopped, then laughed thinly at the sight. He instructed a passing servant to take hold of the little bird and release it outside before letting the now panicked animal free of his spell.

He continued into the cavernous throne room, which besides himself was empty except for the royal bodyguards and the king himself. With the news he now bore, the little bird had been lucky he hadn't incinerated it on the spot.

As Tolmarak approached the table full of maps which Erian was currently pouring over, marker pencil in hand as he made plans for the coming campaign, the monarch looked up at his footsteps. With a single glance at the deeply troubled scowl on his longest serving advisor's features, the king knew why he had come.

"It is confirmed then?" Erian demanded, though not unsympathetically as he went back to studying the maps.

For a response Tolmarak just nodded.

"What are our options?" the monarch inquired.

To that, Aramar's ranking archmage shook his head in resignation and shrugged. Only after long moments of silence could he bring himself to speak.

"After the last death we set every ward we could think of on the college building, but still nothing was tripped today. Although a lack of any and all evidence to the contrary points to it having been yet another freak accident, as has been the case with each of the other deaths, it can no longer be ignored that these... accidents, are happening at intervals of no more or less than forty-two days apiece."

The king nodded without looking up and then asked, "And in your expert opinion there is absolutely no chance these deaths were in fact, accidents. However unlikely?"

"Sire, in my expert opinion, even one death happening in the manner which any of these occurred would be almost beyond belief, but four...? At regular intervals?"

Erian nodded tiredly, forced to agree with Tolmarak's assessment.

"Then you believe it to be murder?" he asked his long-time confidante.

"Worse, Sire…"

"What could be worse than murder?" the king interrupted.

With a sigh, Tolmarak looked at his king before answering grimly, "I believe Heramiir has managed to slip a highly trained, Gift-sensitive assassin into Aramar. One who has knowledge of spells far greater than our own."

Saying nothing, the king very, very slowly put down the marker he had been holding since Tolmarak's arrival and straightened stiffly to face the head of Aramar's College of the Arts.

"If that is true old friend," Jeranon's rightful king countered with grim resolve, "Then we have a very serious problem."

HERE ENDS THE DARK TEMPEST
BOOK I OF THE DESTROYER'S WRATH

COMING SOON

BOOK 2 OF
THE DESTROYER'S WRATH

THE INEVITABLE SPRING

ACKNOWLEDGEMENTS

To my wife and children of course, for putting up with my eccentric ways, for talking about people and places that exist only in my own imagination. It's a wonder they didn't have me committed.

To my good friends and alpha readers over the years. In particular, James, Jason, Ben, Mel, and Paul, along with everyone else who freely and generously gave their time to provide me feedback and advice on characters, settings and plot lines. You all know who you are, and without reservation have my appreciation and thanks for your efforts on my behalf.

To my highly talented cover designer at BRoseDesignz, for the outstanding first impression which your work provides my potential readers, both in e-format and paperback. In addition, thank you for the outstanding banners which you crafted for my website and social media accounts. I almost feel like a real professional when I see them with my name on them...

Finally, I would like to thank the myriad editors, agents and agencies who rejected my work over the years, along with the company who offered me a world rights publishing deal and then mysteriously broke off all communication... I may sound as if I'm being sarcastic, but strangely enough I'm not. If it weren't for that constant rejection, I would never have given up on writing for a career. If I hadn't done that, I could never have come back to it years later with fresh energy and resolve, committed to entirely rewriting almost every major element of the book and transforming it into what it is today. Which is quite frankly, better.

P.S. To all of you who read The Dark Tempest and made it this far, who considered it worthy of your time and energy. If it transported you away from your daily lives even for an instant, if it provoked one thought, inspired one dream, or made you smile at all, my work here is done.

Until the next time.

Regards
N. P. Cooper

ABOUT THE AUTHOR

N. P. Cooper grew up in Melbourne, Australia, and moved to Queensland early in his twenties. He has been writing for most of his life for his own pleasure, but The Dark Tempest marks his first foray into publishing his own work. When not staring at his computer screen, he enjoys spending time with his family and friends, listening to live music, and exploring the local tidal pools with his children.

For more information on N. P. Cooper's upcoming books, appearances, and release dates, visit his website at npcooper.com